Rewriting Stella

By Dan Tuttle

red

Praise for Rewriting Stella

"To read such a fine-honed and splendid tale
is to discover universal clue
where our global society does fail
simply to love and be loved is the cure.
Tightly woven and yet taking its time,
our author in turn warms and breaks our hearts
told so brightly you may forget the rhyme
I assure you shan't e'er forget the art.
How can such 500-year old verses
reach to post-modern day and deftly tell
of our brightest hopes and darkest curses
with a timeless sense of humor as well?
Reader, you would be well-advised to dare
to search within these pages with great care."

–*LA Markuson*
Ars Poetica

Red Press
Rewriting Stella
Dan Tuttle

Cover illustration: Maggie P. Chang
Interior illustrations: Zac Karis Crawford
Editor: Katherine E. Knotts
Printed in England by TJ International (Cornwall)
Typeset in Devin

Published by Red Press Ltd.
ISBN 978 1 912157 167 (Paperback)
ISBN 978 1 912157 174 (Ebook)

Red Press Registered Offices:
6 Courtenay Close, Wareham, Dorset, BH20 4ED, England

www.redpress.co.uk
@redpresspub

#RewritingStella

To you, for sitting shotgun. Buckle up.

Stella's Uni-verse

This novel is written in Shakespearean sonnets. It abides by strict rules of length, meter, and rhyme.

Rule 1: Every line has ten syllables.

Rule 2: Every line has a rhythm that sounds like *da DUM da DUM da DUM da DUM da DUM*. A single *da DUM* is called an 'iamb'. This meter is 'iambic'. With five iambs we have 'iambic pentameter'.

Rule 3: Every line must rhyme with another. Alternating lines rhyme in three groups of four, then adjacent lines rhyme to finish the sonnet. This construction of three 'quatrains' and one 'couplet' creates a fourteen-line poem with the rhyme scheme *ababcdcdefefgg*. While you will find many multi-syllable rhymes, these are not explicitly required by the form.

Traditionally, the first quatrain sets a scene. The second introduces a problem. The third adds a twist to the problem. The couplet resolves the problem and the poem.

As a sample, here is a sonnet about sonnets:

Obsessed. The pace accelerates and slows,
in gearbox shift of clockwork calculus.
From three quatrains to couplet letters flow
in meter unimpeded—value this.
To write one properly, per Shakespeare's haunt
you start abstractly at the top, then fold
a fold, and then a second fold to flaunt
your depth, in dozen lines a problem told.
You've lit a stranger's intellect afire
and cast a striking hue through window frame
and have but two lines left to build the pyre,
loose conflagration on joined thought and pane.
For sonnets make a branding iron of lead,
script's fusing novel scenes none prior had wed.

You may abhor poetry and still delight in befriending
Stella. I did.

Dan Tuttle
May 2019

Syllabic Addenda

Englishes disagree on syllable count. Accent, speed, annunciation, dialect, and general disposition affect how each of us perceives the vocal length of certain words. I have tried mightily to confine every line in the subsequent pages to ten syllables. We may disagree about whether I accomplished that.

Words like 'prior' and 'power' can stretch or compress (*pry-ur, pow-ur*). Throughout I have aimed to use the shorter count for these words on the cusp (*pryr, powr*). Mid-word extension hyphens occasionally appear to disambiguate.

Where a word could be di- or trisyllabic, I default to the disyllabic version unless it concludes a line, where for meter's sake the trisyllabic version is superior. An example would be 'family' (*fam-ly*), as contrasted in the lines:

> *...So even if your family can't afford*
> *far travel, still know life's to be explored.*

> *...let human left from torn-up family*
> *stay off the streets by serving other brood.*

Squirrel, despite its curious inclusion of an additional *r* and *e*, rhymes with *twirl*, and has the same spoken length. Worry not: I only use that rhyme once. The Mandarin name 'Xue' in this book is monosyllabic and sounds roughly like 'shoo-way' spoken quickly. May all my past Chinese instructors forgive me.

Contents

VOLUME 1

PROLOGUE

From up to down to fortunate to hexed,
from gladdening to maddening, agree
adventuring you'll find in pages next
is true as memories made can be to me.
Unchained childhood began with what you'll read,
in many ways adulthood too was born
as self-reliance started supersede
conformist expectations feared outworn.
While chiseled by untempered nature's edge
I'd get to know my dog and friend like book.
We had but one another's binding pledge
to rise till social mores were overlooked.
This tale is mine alone, of nicer youth,
shared now so followers can trace own truth.

Stella

Chapter 1

1.

A tricksy girl named Stella once did live
among acacia thorns and *ng'ombe* poop.
In Tanzanian hinterlands rains give
sweet life to every possible food group.
But in this verdant, fertile land of ferns,
inhabited by bustards, storks, gazelles,
and lions, warthogs, bees, gnats, buzzards, terns,
our dearest Stella found herself unwell.
She'd hoped to have made friends, but she was smart.
Schoolkids at her poked fun, would tattles tell.
Performance set her in a class apart
that left her classmates feeling rattled. Stel
post-class one day, and distanced from the crowd,
inspected self's felt powerlessness aloud.

2.

"I thought at four, by eight I'd be in charge...
I get the best marks, yet can't get a pal.
The life I live's the opposite of large.
I don't belong one bit in this locale!
My grouchy Grandmum's only one at home,
which leaves me solo milking both the cows.
I lose myself in dense and dated tomes
to memorize facts as my brain allows."
She watched a dragonfly glide 'gainst strong breeze,
impressed in gale it didn't end up dead,
and dreaded many yet-undone house deeds
like hauling household water on her head.
So sitting on a log depressed and blue,
our Stella simply knew not what to do.

3.
YIP YIP! A sound behind the log surprised
this sulking girl, a pleading cry for help.
"A someone needs a hero!" she surmised,
and turned to stump to find the source of yelp.
A scruffy, fluffy, matted ball of fur
was belly-up and trapped in wooded knot,
"Perhaps some karmic credit will incur
if I can rescue such a helpless tot!"
Thus Stella reached down in the hole to grab
this mangy thing mite bigger than her head,
its whimper weak, its coat a dusty drab.
She vowed to nurse it back from left-for-dead.
The serendipity of pup's outburst
would soon the course of Stella's life reverse.

4.
Chapati from her fingers, that dog ate
with fervor, as it missed its mother's milk.
Shared minor nourishments helped join their fate
as girl and girl's best friend, or of that ilk.
She set down pup and set upon the path
to home, so she could proudly show Grandmum,
in hope for love instead of standard wrath—
perhaps she'd warm to Stel's friend number one?
Stel faithfully was followed by the dog,
along the muddy path where toads hunt flies.
Familiar fence of water hole, maize, fog
no longer felt so cloisteringly devised.
With spring in step she sauntered toward her home,
effusing joy at being not alone.

5.
"*Achaaa!*" Stel's Grandmum shrieked upon the sight
of filthy mutt next to her next of kin,
"All animals are dirty and can bite,
so leave at once or I'll make moccasins
of mangy hide!" She turned her anger near,
and spanked the girl outstretched upon her knee.
In this, poor Stella'd come to daily fear
of Grandmum. Violences drove dog to flee.
With rear end sore, Stel waddled through her chores,
from sweeping porch to pruning produce plants,
while dreaming of her lost friend's future roars
and all the things she'd change to *cans* from *can't*.
She hastened through domestic work, mood low,
disliking filial servitude she owed.

6.
Such brooding (archetypal in those days)
would melt away once moonlight brought surprise.
She'd hoped lost pup might remedy malaise,
wish soon fulfilled by silhouette pint-sized.
YIP YIP!—the faint sound pierced nocturnal calm,
and set aflutter Stella's lonely heart,
its pain relieved as if with soothing balm,
by canine form's debut through curtain part.
"*Ay! Mungu mwema!*" Stella did exclaim
upon familiar sight of puppy's mug,
black-contoured puff of joy through window frame.
She scooped him up into a mighty hug.
"From this point on," she, grinning, told the pup,
"no man nor witch nor beast will break us up!"

7.
Ensuing days, adventure was the norm,
from hopping rocks in rivers to school pranks
a true dynamic duo thus was born
and every night young Stella spoke her thanks.
When sun was high they'd chase away warthogs,
or sneak pup poop into the bully's desk,
build castles out of twigs, make forts from logs,
until the evening never stop to rest.
At night they'd sneak from house to river bed
and chase bullfrogs and pounce on lit fireflies,
cocoon in red-black *shukas*, shiver, dead
to teasing judgments peers left thinly guised.
She found fresh pulse of life in her locale,
the puppy's presence propping up morale.

8.
Though fat with bread, the puppy never grew
beyond concealed-ish carry canine size,
and so it was that Grandmum never knew
her Stella hadn't two – but four! – sly eyes.
But six weeks passed before she had the thought
that little runt she carried lacked a name.
She floated several options, but none caught
the playful puppy spirit: pluck, but tame.
He'd bravely battle bunnies, birds and bats,
he'd catch most creepy crawlies (eat them too),
chase after shrews and moles, molest meerkats.
Malaika? Moto? Juma? None rang true.
The dog to her meant sky, earth, everything.
To vaunt that value, Stella named him 'BLING'!

9.
"Ooh! BLING's so right I'm nearly thrown aback,
it's bright and spunky, turning heads like gold,
but not so overused as 'Spot'. In fact,
I'm confident my BLING will break the mold!
I've kept you from Grandmum's glaucoma view,
but don't know how to keep up the charade...
Perhaps my bag could be the avenue
to hide you alongside me, a handmade
soft-padded pouch inside my backpack for
you can't be hard to sew this afternoon.
And since we've got adventuring in store,
we'll have to make a collar for you soon."
She knew the town store once had advertised
some warthog leathers tailor-made to size.

10.
Of natural artifacts store wasn't starved,
safari trophy panoply defined
by feathers bright and ivory pieces cropped,
beast heads a-mount without their beast behinds.
Bare pockets wouldn't slow her. She'd implore
its shopkeep for paid work. Next day, she asked,
"Old *Bwana* Anton, do you have in store
a collar? I've no money, but a task
could maybe suit to pay you. Dearest sir,
I'd rather work than ask for some handout.
You understand the young entrepreneur
and gotta know some way to help me out."
And so she sat, intruder in his shop
to signal she'd be stubborn, till a mop

11.
emerged in Anton's hand for Stel to take.
His other offered bucket filled with foam
"Mm. *Sawa*, little businesswoman. Make
these floors shine." "Sure! I'll get them bright as chrome."
"*Haraka*, though, I'm hosting soon." "Oh. Who?"
"My prime supplier. Scrub it so he sees
bird trophies mirrored back in crystal view.
They're rare and merit such." Stel felt unease.
With mop in hand and bucket close behind,
fit Stella took to task and wet the floor.
BLING's skills, in fact, weren't wholly misaligned:
the harder stains dissolved as dog claws tore
them. "*Mbwa wangu*, guess today's a wash.
Together, though, we'll make this place look posh!"

12.
Some minutes in, a tragedy arose:
the mop's blob head unscrewed and bent and broke.
"Oh blast!" said Stella, conscious store would close
for big-shot broker, work half-done. BLING poked
her in the hand, encouraging with snout
the maintenance of hope amid despair.
He jumped into the bucket, then jumped out,
augmenting mop with further soapy hair!
He chomped down on the end of broken stick,
splayed near to floor for better angled scour,
took over work for Stel just in the nick
of time, for they'd been at it near an hour.
Ten minutes hence, the two now unconcerned,
old Anton to a spotless floor returned.

13.
"I clearly see reflections of my shoes
upon linoleum you've fully shined.
Good work, young girl. But wait—have you abused
my mop? It's busted!" Quickly disinclined
to pay for labors offered anymore,
he then dismissed them. "Child, you cleft in two
equipment that I use to buff the floor.
Had adult done that, we'd cry 'theft'! In lieu
I'll let you go, because you cleaned. Now leave!"
"But *Bwana* Anton, you said we'd get wares
for working." "I did not. Nor'd you achieve
results! You broke things! Scoot, unless repairs
of mop are offered." Failing *quid pro quo*,
the downtrod girl and pup did sorely go.

14.
"Suppose we'll have to stay together, bud.
Forget this collar bother. Real teamwork's
togetherness. We scraped off so much mud
with nothing in return... That guy's a jerk,"
said Stella, as she loped on down the path
with BLING beside, alert to what could be
another reprimanding: Stella's math
suggested they'd be late. All absentees
from dinner at precisely eight past eight
in Grandmum's house *de facto* sacrificed
their food without the chance to bite-prorate.
"I think," her words, "we'll need to stage a heist
to fill our bellies 'fore we're homeward bound,"
and seemed to see BLING understand the sound.

15.
The forest cornucopia availed
a feast of plant and beast, of proteined grub—
to those who knew where nourishment was veiled,
sophistication less pinot, more pub.
"I'm not enticed by looking at those worms,"
said Stella, unimpressed by what BLING dug.
"I'm pretty sure they're gooey and have germs,
I'd rather taste some honey." Then she tugged
a branch that housed a yellow swarming hive,
that swayed and twisted, further every push,
until a **CRASH!** and thousands came alive
to punish their transgressors in the bush!
They sprinted toward the water hole, BLING's snout
a-leak with grubs that twisted to get out.

16.
That swarm of bees pursued them stride for stride,
and targeted biped assailant who
had roiled their home. Stel's route had them collide –
this teeming protein mass of rage-bent food –
with mantises and toads who'd quickly prey
upon the black and yellow candy brought!
A scot-free BLING would fetch ditched hive buffet
that Stella's daring sprint allowed be caught.
With bursting speed, the girl plunged in the pond
and shivered once from chill and once from fear.
She hoped she could aquatically abscond
for long enough to dodge the striped cloud's pierce.
She stayed submerged till capillaries braced
for shutdown as their oxygen displaced.

17.
For gasps of air, young Stella burst toward sky,
pond droplets flung around as cough and wheeze
erupted, as her lungs had been denied
the air patrolled by horde of angry bees.
Seen crescent moon seemed heaven-sent, the bugs
consumed or fled had clarified its view.
The predators had acted as the thugs
that Stella sought to bid the bees *adieu*.
Emerging from the stagnant lake, Stel stood
adrip and shivering in zephyr blown
between mahogany and other wood,
wet chill transmitting from her skin to bone.
Despite the cold intensified by wind,
with honey soon, she felt no trace chagrined.

18.
She bounded back past palm and soursop,
saliva massing, thoughts of sweetness soon.
"You read my mind, BLING, nabbed that 'comb. Our crop
makes missed *ugali* meal feel picayune."
His jaws held up a gooey golden prize
she took and slowly spun, rotisserie
ambrosial. "Nature's richness here supplies
all we could want." She grew dismissory
of wasted drizzle out the bottom once
its sugars raining, runny hit tastebuds.
In comfort, saccharine bliss turns hunters dunce:
staved hunger blunts waste-guilt when drops baste mud.
In moment's eating rapture Stel felt whole,
no peer approval shading own self's role.

19.
Next morning's fog deterring not a whit,
our Stella marched to school with pup in pack,
her fear the day too short to simply sit,
that boredom soon would creep in and hijack
her honest wish she'd learn a thing worthwhile
from spending hours and days and weeks in class.
Contrast this to past two months' versatile
bush skill-building adventures. Rather, mass
and density, historic dates, and facts
all failed to boost her instinct to survive.
"This memorizing," she said, "all distracts
me from the time with BLING when I'm alive."
That day two things would happen unforeseen:
she'd make one friend and start up lifetime dream.

20.
Geography commenced at ten to twelve,
the four bells rang to start the student race
to class, all knew they had short time to shelve
their books and book it to their classroom space.
"Good morning students," customarily
announced Miss Gumi, tall before the boys
and girls. They stood up and all wearily
announced, "Good morning, Teacher," standard noise
in classrooms urban, rural, country-wide
each student copied. Stel's mind was adrift,
in daydream floating through weeks' hijinks, guide
BLING made her playful, gave her heart a lift.
She couldn't concentrate on Gumi, who
showed off to class held object hid from view.

21.
"What do you think arrived to class today?"
she asked, referring to the object held.
"A textbook published after '88?"
joked one boy. "An exam?" another yelled.
She waited. "A real soccer ball for us?"
"A solar charger we can use for phones?"
"A box of candies?" "Pencils?" Soon the fuss
devolved cacophonously. Gumi groaned.
She knew she couldn't shout them back in line,
but rather wow them toward obedience.
She let the sheet drop, showing faded lime
and periwinkle. "It's old. See the tints
have faded from green land and ocean blue."
She held first globe they'd ever chanced to view.

13

22.
"Our world," she said, "is vast and stretches past
the forests, farms and fields you know as yours,
we've seen on maps that, though we're unsurpassed
in resources, there's places like Azores
which, held by Portugal but partly free,
are rich in beauty rather than in stone.
I want you to envision sights to see,
and brought this globe as reference to the Rhône,
Zambezi, Volta, Nile. It educates
you Tanzanian future pioneers
of veldt and jungle, Asia, Europe, Strait
of Hormuz, inland seas and sands, Algiers,
I care not where you end your journeys, but
implore you venture far away from hut

23.
in which your family makes its home. Your birth
was likely under roof you now repair.
Go forth! Uncover each of your own worth
discovering the world. Become aware
of who and what your neighbors are, and why
they act one way and you believe them strange.
Our cultures differ, Paris and Shanghai
could never prosper if both rearranged
their streets and people, let alone swapped out
entire populations, one for one.
There is no guiding road or central route,
you'll never know you're done, or lost, or won.
I know you're young, your vigor and your vim
should guide you." Silence fell. Her passioned hymn

24.
was given time to percolate through head.
It wasn't too far-fetched for Gumi to
give urging sermon snippets, guidance spread
to pupils, countering school's gloomy pew.
Last month nonsensically she'd decried rules
the state imposed restricting natural things,
in tirade how tribes ought to own all jewels
(ore, plant, and animal) their homelands bring.
"This globe," she said, "is but a picture's ink,
washed-out facsimile of what is real.
And finding that takes more than space to think,
it takes your presence. Rivers' vast appeal
can only be experienced afloat.
'Tween bookish grasp and body's lay wide moat."

25.
Miss Gumi then confessed, "I have some fear
of challenging you youth this way. I've led
a lucky life to here from old Zaire,
saw things when young that frightened, and I fled.
Once refugee, now citizen. My man
as you know's trained safari guide, we go
from Cameroon's reserve Campo Ma'an
to old home's Ma'iko, to Kitulo
in southwest highlands. Foreign clients take
him out to translate nature. When there's space
I come along. It's helped me to awake
to treasures sitting right here in our face.
So even if your family can't afford
far travel, still know life's to be explored."

26.

This sentiment stretched Stel's smile Cheshire-near
as if she'd heard the words she'd waited for.
Imagination leaped to far frontier
that Gumi beckoned, hooked by dreams offshore.
Stel looked through glassless window frame toward corn,
past pupil peers, toward where Earth curled away.
What wonders only loved by better born
lay past thousand horizons worlds arrayed?
When mind's eye stupefaction ceased and Stel
returned her sight to corn-fed corneas
they focused on a penciled caravel
drawn by her deskmate's hand, adorning the
lined composition notebook space reserved
for copying down spoon-fed fact preserves.

27.

Sketched daydream vessel's shipwright was Abu.
His family moved nearby sometime this year.
Line-drawn detail suggested through and through
he'd witnessed some aquatic hemisphere.
She thought he'd worn a fez, but blinked and *Poof*
mirage. Perhaps that travel bug? Why had
she missed his doodling before? Aloof
and bookish, he'd not mixed with other lads.
He looked from sketch to her as if she'd asked
the moment Stella looked across at him,
in mutuality of something masked,
some hoped duality to spark their vim.
Shared hint of interest in the world at large
empowered Stel to take up outreach charge.

28.
"Hello, my friend!" our heroine called when
the bells to end their class began to ring.
"Are you from China? Near Tiananmen?
I hear these days we've migrants from Peking."
Abu was startled thrice. The first word, 'friend'
had not been said to him since he arrived
to village from whole wide world's furthest end.
The thought of having one was joy revived.
A second startle struck when question mark
was used in Stella's interrogative.
He'd not been asked a thing since family parked
in this odd place. His kin spurned, mocked: the gift
of being youngest. Third, at core she meant
Abu appeared to come from Orient!

29.
"Not quite. You've mixed up your geography.
You're thinking of the hats that farmers wear
to plant their rice beside the great Yangtze.
Instead, I'm from a place where morning prayer
is routine, so the bells we hear at school
repeatedly remind me that I miss
the days I once embraced in Istanbul."
While listening to Abu reminisce,
young Stella squirmed at being proven wrong,
she hoped she hadn't bungled friendship's chance
by thinking Abu's heritage Hong Kong.
"Apologies! I'm sorry. Would perchance
forgiveness be in store?" the girl replied,
"Your drawing shows you've got a view worldwide."

30.
"I dream escape. Spain, Sweden, Suriname,
pick anywhere besides the here and now."
"Why?" "Why not? Dream I'll see Dar es Salaam,
or Far East that you mentioned, like Macau
is loads more interesting than lessons here.
It's like Miss Gumi says—there's worlds out there."
"And you know... how?" Stel asked, tone kind toward peer
to not appear too skeptical. "I'll share,
but not right here in class. Let's say lifelong
I've been in flux, in transit," Ab replied.
"Okay... forget it. Rather, come along
to meet a second friend I often hide
while bound in class. We're hoping you're our third!"
She showed him BLING outside, awaited word.

31.
Abu, a bit like ghost, swayed to and fro
atop his lanky legs as if the wind
could flip him either way, as it does clothes,
considering while Stella, hopeful, grinned.
This boy could have been raised where cuneiform
was not an ancient, dead, forgotten script,
and yet his look at school was uniform,
normalcy's carbon copy: backpack zipped,
a woolen sweater frayed below his neck
its navy blue to contrast khaki shorts,
on which were several daubs of muddy fleck
from football falls. Stel thought she glimpsed a quartz
or milky pendant hung beneath his maw,
a necklace carved as crescent moon and claw.

32.
"At home," Abu began, "I'm one of eight.
We once lived well in Syria, till war
broke out in Lebanon, and our estate
became a looters' target, laws ignored.
They ousted us from title to the land,
we fled to Turkey. Left in foreignness,
jobs, food, and shelter scarce, we'd not withstand
for long. So we came here. Now sore in this
is me, forgotten as my family copes
by squatting on some land and planting crops."
Stel felt familiarities evoked
in lamentation life's but farming ops.
"My parents told of past, but still remained
attached to story royalty's ingrained.

33.
It's all affected me since I was young.
My duty's to become a worldly sheikh,
regain the face we had before we'd flung
ourselves across the world." Right then, heartbreak,
as far as it could be so felt by child
enveloped Stella, who had long without
a standard parent ever reconciled,
no mother-, father-figure. Left in doubt,
she there, with Abu, jointly understood
both longed in ways to see the wider world,
both sought in ventures meaning, wondered could
both forge their self in wilder-ness? Thoughts swirled
above their heads as if they'd conjured clouds
of dreams between them. Kids' dreams lack the shrouds

34.
adults' experience and fear insert.
Intoxicating childhood fantasy
led Stel to be a smidgen bold, assert,
"Then join us. BLING and I began to free
ourselves adventuring." Her head felt light.
What if winds couldn't sway Abu as seemed?
Her simple act of being so forthright
was tinged by risk that, offer unredeemed
from girl in search of true companionship,
would crush her confidence like bully's punch.
"You know, I heard a lonesome banyan strip
is hidden – *hidden!* – in the woods. At lunch
tomorrow, let's go bushwhack." Being new,
to children 'twas enough to go pursue.

35.
By time that BLING and Stella made it home,
old Grandmum, deep asleep, was unperturbed.
She'd never made a point of trying to comb
outdoors for Stella. Picture this suburb
as village *shamba* nestled in the hills,
with stick-mud homes spaced so farms intercede,
for agriculture was what paid the bills
since jobs weren't to be found, or even leads.
On side of path began a taller wood,
which swaddled mountain midriff, where the wind
blew pines to flex like bamboo where they stood;
foreboding sentries when the sunlight thinned.
Grandmum ensconced herself in home, alone,
with breaks for Sunday church. She liked the known.

36.
Her somnolence inured to help Stel's team,
arriving *sans* the stress of discipline
atop their minds, for Grandmum was adream
and showed all signs that she would miss it when
they entered whether loud-toed or soft-heeled.
BLING dug his bed into imagined leaf,
as dogs are wont to do. Scratched earth did yield
one comfy convex sleeping nook beneath
Stel's hand. Perhaps we're opposite of dogs,
who let imagined objects contradict
their eyes and act as asked by body's logs
encoded for survival. Nature's tricked
at least one species with genetic code,
that, passed from kin to kin, will not erode.

37.
Since finding BLING, Stel often slipped to sleep
in minutes, zonked from having filled the day.
Nor usually would BLING long count the sheep,
who'd straightaway show up in dream as prey.
Yet readying for bed, an air remained
unsettling and incomplete. Both stirred
instead of nodding gently off, they strained
to shake the air that made them feel interred.
Stel felt like she'd come close to friend breakthrough,
to finding part of her reflected. Lack
of parents, normal now, still oft ached through
to amplify her fear folks would draw back.
Attachment anchors missing as a child
nagged Stel as worries friends too'd self-exile.

38.
The dog, meanwhile, stirred, pacing thrice an hour.
He traced the border of the room, patrolled
his territory for what might have soured
their vain attempts to enter Nod's stronghold.
"Hey BLING," said Stella quietly, to test
if pup was subject to unease's haunt,
"you think our Abu's different from the rest?
He doesn't feel quite human yet. A jaunt
is what we need to really verify
if he's as wedded to adventure as
the two of us! We've got to clarify
he's got the mettle that we hope he has."
BLING acted like he understood her cause:
he perked, stopped, shook, and stretched from ears to
   claws.

39.
In no time flat they found themselves before
the house and humble home of young Abu.
They snuck around from front to backside door
and sat to quickly plan what they would do.
As Stella whispered plans, she gauged response
by checking change of puppy panting pace.
And all the while they sat and heard the taunts
of distant creatures in night's carapace.
With plan in motion, Stella threw the ball
of fluff that trusted her since rescue from
the log months back. Past life she could recall
was monotone compared to this, and glum.
She got a chill and shivered. Life apart
from drudgery and teasing warmed her heart.

40.
The window through which she had one pup tossed
lacked glass to brake the earthy evening breeze.
On it draped metal netting, crissed-and-crossed
defense against mosquito-borne disease.
At quarantining, though, the screen now failed
to serve its owners. Time had torn it up:
its mismatched mishmash wire-thread gaps curtailed
no entry of a sentry missile pup.
Stel thought of the unpleasantness of flight
while launching her beloved through the gap.
She felt a rather classic fear of heights
stirred up by watching her dog's wingless flap.
The forest howls from darkness briefly met
a thrilling **YIP!** as pup turned air cadet.

41.
The silence that ensued brought single bead
of perspiration pooled to Stel's forehead.
What could be stalling BLING's courageous lead
of Abu toward adventure, from his bed?
But once the bead had multiplied by three
the pressure weighing on her shoulders left:
emerging from the hole was abductee
Abu, leftover screen to pieces cleft.
Equipped with bulging backpack, he'd the look
of mischief glinting in his moonlit eyes,
as if at night he'd chosen not to brook
the complications daytime life disguised.
BLING back in hand, they wove past fields of crops
in search of the alleged banyan copse.

42.
Their search was fire that melted air's sharp ice
that otherwise would freeze to still their frames,
the pull of undiscovered lands enticed,
like frontiers, which to frontiersmen seek claim.
This burning purpose shielded minds from fear
that lurking in the wooded black was harm,
a thousand ghouls and goblins, gathered near
in blackness so complete, that no alarm
in ear or eye detected that the space
was filled by creatures creeping. Looking out
from makeshift path to darkness showed no trace
of what stared back. But Stella still stayed stout.
The dark pressed in like tightened seams of coal,
compressed galactically as if black hole.

43.
In daylight Stel tracked trails. Her knacks were in
good landmark cues and bearings set by sun.
At night her sensed direction wore more thin,
yet she persisted when it came undone.
Stel feared admitting flaw, was not forthright
until convinced too lost to then reverse.
"That cooing sound," Abu said with a fright,
"sounds like an omen or a voodoo curse."
"I think," squawked Stella's tremulous, soft voice,
"it's lonely birdcall waiting for reply."
"But tell me, would you really make the choice
to willingly find out?" Abu then cried.
The tension made the dampened ground feel cold
and robbed from childhood hearts all feelings bold.

44.
A **CRASH!** crashed through the branches overhead
that sent the kids flat-stomached on the moss,
with fears they'd soon be doubled over, dead
from strike of pterodactyl, albatross
or stork of prehistoric size and girth,
or bat that feasts on bits of little boys
and girls. So they reflected on the worth
of life, school, family lost, and wished-for toys.
Right then amid their second-split repose
inspired by the shadow's flight above
they heard a **YIP!** and jumped back to their toes
emboldened by the sudden act of love:
for, though the smallest of the three, BLING's shout
defended from this airborne bombing bout.

45.
Their mettle metered sonically, the wings
withdrew the baleful beast they carried high
back to the canopy of lofted things
too far from ground to be known by the eye
of creatures on the earth. Two lengthy **phews**
were heard by all things lurking near and far
and turned those scanning, watchful eyes in twos
toward where the kids were cowering. "There are
a hundred score of animals sharp-toothed
that know we're here, but don't know if we're food.
Let's jet before we let them know the truth."
"Yes! Premature departure isn't rude."
Their flighty instincts complemented BLING's,
whose bear-sized bark was backed by bite-sized sting.

46.
With pinprick firefly light as useless guide,
their travels through the undergrowth were not
entirely successful. They supplied
a modicum of safety, as they sought,
but moved them unawares yet further from
the banyan stand they'd set out first to find.
Abu's thick bag lacked bread: no trail of crumb
could guide once norths and souths were misaligned.
Then Stel burst out exasperatedly,
"Abu, can you please hurry up? We're lost."
"I'm gathering," he aspirated, "these,"
in tone deterring being further bossed.
He'd fished out oil-less lantern of clear glass
and with bugs' butts found means to light amass.

47.
When Stella first regarded it, a shock
swept 'cross her face, which now was cast alight:
it seemed Abu'd collected growing flock
of glowing fireflies so to aid their sight.
The lantern flickered as a candle would,
according to the pulse and mood of those
within it. "Worry not, I know we should
return them later. But let's now impose,
because, my friend, our vision needs a boost,
and frankly I'm a little on the edge."
The light was helpful locally, reduced
the stumbling chance amid its lumen wedge.
The flicker made false ghouls of forest shapes
but fell short of revealing clear escape.

48.
Each step was taken slower than the prior,
as fear arrested progress. Neither felt
the gentle slope that inched them higher and higher
to outcrop that stood tow'ring over veldt.
"I wish," said Ab, "the moon would break through trees."
"Me too." "When I was little, I desired
to go up there and see if it was cheese."
"Ha. I grew up where cows' milk was required
for *chai* and nothing more. What's stopping you
from flying up to moon now?" Stella asked,
reminder of request he join her crew.
"Mere time." Stel was impressed by drive unmasked.
At that age she still likened competence
to confidence. "Great! That grit complements

49.
adventuring I plan with BLING. You should
enlist with us." Right then another **CRASH!**
was heard a ways away in endless wood,
renewing fear they'd end up 'tween jaws gnashed.
Stel's body rattling prompted Ab to say,
"My parents said when roads were hard they'd start
a game so to distract mind other ways.
It stole some sting from sun and tread and heart.
What do you say we try the same?" Foot speed
had slowed to snail's, still infinitely far
from stoppage. Soil aground gave way to scree.
"I wish huge glowworm'd been in lit wee jar,
enormous bug with storm torch light to share,"
he started, as example of affair.

50.
"I wish," he said, as feet continued on,
"those hungry-looking beasts were all at fast,
religiously abstemious." Stel yawned,
the lateness beating heartbeat at full blast.
An avian apparition coursed 'cross view,
gray streak that interrupted where once were
enclosing trees. Stel realized from clue
they'd left the woods. Now dying was the *chirr*
and *hiss* of sleeping forest. Stars pierced black.
"I—**AAH!**" she squealed as sole stepped into air,
arresting self on gluteus. The lack
of earth sent ventricles on pumping tear:
"I – Ab – I'm terrified. Let's rest and sit."
"We'll hunker here till brighter light is lit,

51.
adventurer. But now you gotta play.
It helps, I promise. Lean here. There you go."
"I wish," she started, "BLING's bark kept at bay
all predators. I wish he would bestow
us both with other wishes." "It's more fun
when wishing for the animals, not us.
This is a game that's much more lost and won
by humor than by need. Ditch selfward fuss."
She pulled her *shuka* tight against the breeze,
leaned on the lifeline tree, wished for asphalt,
and searched inside for long-fled sense of ease.
Ab said, "I wish giraffes could somersault.
I rather think they'd find in tumbling joy."
Stel couldn't help but laugh, while still annoyed.

52.
Though ground gave some security, word cloak
of animals-do-human-things felt thin
against Stel's dread. Ab's remedy was joke,
right? Comfort couldn't come from simple spin.
"At least the predators are back that way,"
Abu said, "now our safety's in our hands."
"How so?" "There's no chance feet slip, plunge away
if we here plant ourselves aground. Don't stand,
you're fine." Stel probed, "But did they follow us?"
"Of course not." "Yet again you're sure." "Indeed."
"And why?" "Because we're breathing. Logic, thus,
shows that no beasts pursued us as their feed."
Hard rationality still couldn't quell
the sympathetic system's fear in Stel.

53.
Her heartbeat drowned out hearing 'cept for breaths
she heard Abu draw slowly in, let out.
Her mind fixated on a dozen deaths
imagined. Meanwhile, he'd let no threat rout
his reasoned focus. "Picture flying squirrels,
a hundred, dropped from plane. Or owls a-dance."
She eased with such imagined tumbles, twirls
of fur and feathers, Hedwig's b-boy stance.
"Nah, stick to ground. It's safer." "Still your turn."
She wondered how her favorites fit this shtick,
then realized the plight of pachyderm:
"How 'bout an elephant on pogo stick?"
"Mm, *safi sana*," came reply, "be scared
of standing near a *tembo* in the air!

54.
There can't be any doubt they'd love to jump.
To take a grounded beast and set it free
would be so kind. Herd's sonic booming thumps
would make a joyous rhythm, shift *esprit*
of Serengeti toward Zaramo drums."
Young Stella's mind, now tethered to that scene
fixated on its details and outcomes
instead of on night predators unseen.
Kids' riffing slowed along with consciousness,
anxieties now dampened and downscaled.
How stories' swaddling shrouds had spawned such bliss
would stay to Stel a mystery long veiled:
not till a decade later would she find
the power of whimsy in creative mind.

55.
Their quietnesses lengthened. They played game
till words slurred and both children slacked to sleep.
Snoozed consciences let night pass unrestrained:
perceptions logged an instant dawn. The sweep-
ing view they hadn't known they'd had appeared
with day. The howling night had been replaced
by patchwork singsong birdcall warbles near
crescendo's height. The sun soon crested, faced
onlookers near the cliff, then paralyzed
with instant showered warmth and piercing light.
It bleached away the night, impaired the eyes.
Stel felt in such deliverance, delight.
The scene well showed the sum of nature's worth
and suited swell the Pioneers' soon birth.

56.
"Abu..." Stel slowly said regarding things
the sun enlightened lightly, "Abu, I
would like you to be part of this, with BLING."
"Of what?" "Of this group I imagined my
best childhood was to feature, friends in fun.
As Afroasiatic Pioneers
we'd gather power, our wills would bend to none.
We'd use it to roam freely." Undiscussed
was concretely what they would do, where, how.
"Stel, you got a bit frightened last night but
you didn't let it stop you. That is how
I'd want to Pioneer: full-bore, uncut."
His eyes, as mirrors to the rising sun
blazed gold, a fitting hue for dream begun.

57.
"I've wanted to reclaim post of emir
since our name fell from grace when we moved south."
The hint he'd fuse the trinity rung clear
despite the words slow shaping at his mouth.
"Yes. Thanks for fetching me from sleep at home,
you picked a night I also couldn't doze."
"*Ayo!* I'm thrilled!" As xylem to her phloem,
Abu'd be there when friend-ly needs arose.
"I never thought to roam much past the bounds
of our community. With strength of three
we'll move beyond the finite world's surrounds
and into more expansive territ'ry.
This precipice we've christened very place
for Afroasiatic team home base!"

58.
As proclamation bellowed out downwind,
swept from the one-tree outcrop where they'd perched,
its sound was tailed by dragonfly, wings twinned
in interplay too fast to see. Each lurch
from gust thrust fly aside, off its first path.
"Look, Stel, it's getting pushed, yet still it goes."
Its vector carved, in retrospect and math,
intent they'd not detected in the throes
of wind-fought movement. Keener eyes would see
the insect harnessing breeze happenstance
as helping it traverse points A and B.
Right focus showed design in flapping; glance
hid underlying beauty of its strain
to dance with its environment for gain.

59.
Stel mused, "Two months ago I was alone,
with Grandmum crabby, schoolbooks meaningless.
Now my self-portrait's more a duotone—"
"Uh, 'trio', no? With BLING and me in this."
"Oh, right!" Quick comfort with them made her feel
like they'd been there her whole short life, "I want
to do more out in nature. It's surreal,
the fauna here. These beasts schools ought to flaunt."
"They do," Abu replied, "safaris are
the source of money here, and power too." "True,
I know. But lauding solely superstars
impedes fact smaller creatures can wow too."
With union set, they'd need to make up quests
unless delivered some by trusted guest.

Chapter 2

60.
In one week's time BLING, Stella, and Abu
found selves again together, path to school
stretched out in front of them. They'd had but few
more windows for shenanigans. Stel's fuel
between was work on secret gifts for friends.
"You're now both Pioneers, you're in my clique.
These badges show it." Proffered dividends
had matching elephants on pogo sticks!
Bedraggled patches gifted clearly made
by Stella's novice hand were sort of art,
cartoonily. Blobs, line dot eyes portrayed
the bouncing beast, insignia apart
from any, ever. "BLING, you, me begin
our lives with this." "This is Promethean!"

61.
In one way Stella also presaged times
when badges, points, and Snapchat trash talk took
with dopamine-inducing iPhone chimes
activities then gamified with hooks.
This patch she gave was physical, no bytes.
It suited well its era and its place.
So too did badge with BLING's protective bite
deterring divebomb bird stitched on its face.
"*Kizuri sana!* It's the perfect gift
for dog and matching human Pioneers,"
said Abu, not the smallest bit seemed miffed
by craftsmanship as Stella prior had feared.
"I like BLING's merit badge, I think it's core
that we reward ourselves for doing more."

62.
"What do you mean?" "Best decorative awards
aren't ones of gold. That's stuff you buy. They're won.
You customized it so that it records
BLING's courage. Call it 'Badge of Braves'. The fun
can come from ladders of accomplishment,
from ways to recognize our newfound skills
both practical and cattywompus," glint
in mischief's eye of wondrous future thrills.
"*Kuchizi*," Stella said, appreciative
of how he'd snowballed tiny gift she'd made
into an avalanche initiative
to orient how Pioneers upgrade,
"I'd rather strive for items we define
than to adults our future goals consign."

63.
A few days on, they found themselves at school
again before Miss Gumi, who was out
of sorts. Instead of standing, on a stool
she sat, addressing them. "This is about
a crime that I've discovered. Someone stole
a piece of precious jewelry husband owns.
You need to help me show that it's a mole
inside who took it. Housegirls, it's well-known,
cannot be trusted." Her hard eyes teared up
as she wove tale she'd tell about the case.
"It happened in my house, while we two supped.
On upstairs windowsill's long narrow space
we'd placed his wedding ring along with mine...
We take them off to eat to keep their shine.

64.
I finished *maharagwe*, got mine back,
left dishes for the housegirl, went to bed.
My husband soon found his had been hijacked
from off the ledge, and *mwizi'd* long since fled!"
She rubbed her eyes clear of their hue cayenne,
and stagily turned bare hands for kids' view.
"I need a volunteer to help, spry men
preferred. Tour scene and prove to cops it's true."
The Afroasiatic Pioneers
locked eyes immediately and therefore smirked
as if they'd each embedded in the peer
the mission: to track down whoever lurked
and would so brazenly from teachers steal.
Next quest delivered: problem-solve the real!

65.
They hurtled up to ask, after the bell,
with word 'upstairs' perturbing Stella. Such
a term tripped acrophobic inner swell.
The fear, however, hadn't Abu touched.
"Miss Gumi," Stella said, "I'll volunteer."
The teacher passed her up: "Boys are in line.
Stand back a moment; don't be galling, dear,
I told you that it's men I'm here to find."
"Miss Gumi," posed Abu as next in queue,
"I'm spry and clever. Promise I can look
around your property for signs or clues
residually left by shady crook."
"You'll look and see it's clear who culprit was,"
she said, no further word 'bout truth for fuzz.

66.
Ab nodded. Gumi said, "Come *Ijumaa*."
Departing kids conferred. "Stel, we can go
this Friday after class!" "Save your hurrah.
I've half a mind to back out and not show."
"That's silly. It's a quest, and gold's at stake."
"Help decent people? Sure. But she rejects
girls' contributions. Why work for her sake?
A disqualification due to sex
is basically black-hearted, baseless both."
"It isn't conscious, Stella, simple fear
of danger – 'twas a crime scene – made her loath
to ask a girl. Boys are more cavalier."
"Thanks for the lesson, Ab. You're quite the knight
and *clearly* wouldn't lose in a fistfight."

67.
Stel brought best Iron Man glare to bear on Ab.
Absorbing mocking blow theatrically,
he rolled his eyes as apt riposting jab.
"Don't hate the messenger. See actively
what others see. Where we live you're not first."
He sped past need for her assent: "Let's bag
ourselves a criminal!" Adventure thirst
would override Stel's ire toward schoolmarm hag.
Her negativity was useful for
adopting sharp suspicion as the lens
through which to view her classmates. Looking more
for criminals produced them: mind contends
the truth is what stems from the searching act,
ignores affirming bias in found fact.

68.
It's seen in life this pattern, off and on,
in which two people swirl into a new
reality constructed whereupon
assumption and misdoubt both misconstrue
the facts. Facts are themselves up for dispute,
but better as foundations for a truth
than slippery emotions. To refute
emotion isn't possible. A sleuth
can differentiate the two, if asked
and given time and practice. That intent
gets lost beneath lies piled in leaden mass.
Such storytime turns throng toward lies' dement.
This instance, Stel and Ab would both succumb
naïvely under untruth's heavy thumb.

69.
Next three days' searched suspicions yielded zilch,
despite review of every classmate who
had motive to have broken in to filch
the golden ring from Gumi's Xanadu.
Some time near Friday hour unspecified
they zoomed across the village to inspect
the grounds on which the villain lurked outside
the evening of the crime. They rightly checked
the bushes 'round the property for tools
discarded, maybe hidden, by the thief,
for handholds on the wall or nodules
and other artificial-made relief.
"I think you'd need the wingspan of Yao Ming
to climb this," said Abu, "Hey Stel—where's BLING?"

70.
With pause on the investigation, they
refocused gaze to ground to find the beast.
Five minutes' searching made them no headway.
"He'll turn up. Let's go in," Stel said. They ceased
the hunt. "Miss Gumi, *hodi! Hodi!*" called
Abu traditionally as a knock
on door, permission to be guest. From walled
two-story rich abode clicked heavy lock.
Their teacher nudged it open, peered with thin
eyes into dying light. "I'm here to dig
into the heist." "Yes. But, you've brought a twin
and I don't think it's task that's really big
enough for two. Can you stay out?" "No, I'm
his partner and we're both here solving crime."

71.
Four seconds and an exhalation hence
the metal door swung open, kids went in.
Stel hadn't been in house near this immense.
Was it for showing off or housing kin?
She scanned the room and found that window bars
prevented any entrance undesired.
Collected wildlife relics in glass jars
stood on cloth doilies. On walls Stel admired
three megafauna's taxidermied snouts.
She wondered what price such mementos fetched:
Stel felt Miss Gumi's husband must have clout
(or cash) for having house that cloudward stretched.
"As you can clearly see, the house is sealed.
There's not a chance the crook came from afield.

72.
It's evident the culprit was inside,
which means the housegirl." "But you said there's more."
"Oh did I? Yes, of course." "You had implied
that all of this occurred on second floor."
Indeed she'd shared a second story, so
she took them up the stairs. "That's where I said
we put the rings." Bars spaced enough for crow
to perch and snatch them. "Miss Gu, you're misled:
a rogue could climb the wall outside and steal
two rings set here." "There's little there to hold!
They couldn't. It's apparent girl concealed
the ring somewhere so she could sell the gold.
Agreed? Yes? Good. Let's end our little trip,
I'll take you—**AAH!**" she screamed. Pup screeched back,
  YIP!

73.
"Don't worry Miss, it's just my pup. He snuck
his way inside and up the stairs," Stel guessed,
since looking out she saw the gate was stuck.
He'd hopped up where Miss pointed, sniffing nest
of decoration there. Miss spat at dog,
with cobra stare of predator on spree
to add to trophies. "*Nenda* or I'll flog
you, too, Stel! *Mungu!* Get this savage flea-
encrusted ball of fluff off countertop
before he breaks the – Easter – eggs I've bought!
If I catch him, I'll pay first barbershop
that's willing to give shaving him a shot."
The kids were taken back by forceful tone,
not knowing she no animals condoned.

74.
An undeterred BLING meanwhile bounced around,
in yipping pandemonium toward host
in whom he sensed hostility. "My hound
has not a flea," said Stel, then turned to ghost
as quickly as she could. She hooked Abu
and booked it down the stairs, BLING close behind.
Once clearing outside gate, triadic crew
took respite to calm down. "Why she maligned
your BLING's beyond me." "Me too." "She was crazed."
"But not at the beginning of the scene."
"Did we do something?" "Dunno. I'm amazed
she turned so quickly sour from serene."
"She must not represent our country well
while traveling with husband's clientele."

75.
The nighttime breeze blew softly, gently though
it carried not a single lightning bug
to cast a fonder light on inked tableau
of three disheartened souls in need of hugs.
The mood, thanks to their hasty exit, drooped
as low as branches overhead where dwelt
a hundred mangoes. "Ab, did you see cooped
up in those jars the claws and bones and pelts?"
"Yes, and the dozen Easter eggs she showed."
"You think those were an imitation?" "They
weren't painted. Those were nature's hues and glow.
It felt like some museum from far away."
(The real museum they'd tour was yet five years
and thousand leagues away, of dams and weirs.)

76.
On path back home Stel carried BLING. The walk
was easy but she felt possessive since
Miss Gumi's glance transmogrified to gawk
and she said words at which Stel'd took offense.
"I'm not inclined to help her after that,"
said Stella. "Let it go, Stel. She was thrown
when BLING crept up." "That's not what fell most flat.
It's that her story doesn't seem her own.
No housegirl under such oppressive rule
would dare her life to take a ring. And why
right then? She's been there years. And why at school
did Gumi bring it up? We can't rely
on her account." "But you can't prove the crime
was otherwise..." "I can! We'll learn to climb."

77.
"To climb? You're joking. You hate heights." "I do."
"You also saw there aren't handholds outside."
"If we get good enough we could find you
appraised them wrong. They're small." "Your hands
   would slide
right off of them." "So you're an expert now?
Is this your 'cavalier' side coming back?"
He grinned. He wanted fun, no matter how,
and taking Stella's bait was easy tack.
If proving Gumi wrong would vengeance make,
and on the journey yield new worlds of trees,
then Abu would this friendly challenge take
and relish in discovered canopies.
"I'm in. Let's both compete for Monkey Crest
for Pioneers who swing above the rest!"

78.
When next day broke, as sun cast sky in lime
and peach and purple, scarlet, daffodil,
and blue, with silver molding to enshrine
each puffy cloud, the kids stood, half the thrill
arising from their predawn sprints from bed
to prearranged location where they'd start
to train to loose their anchor to the tread
of feet on ground, to master callused art
of climbing. Rope in tow and harness formed
from clever threading through a pair of slacks
they'd eyeleted, then roped, then darned. Adorned
with makeshift minimum, Ab's look there lacked
much credibility. Gusto was all
they needed, Stella hoped—and not to fall.

79.
As Stella sidled up to chosen tree
they'd use to calibrate their starting strength,
Abu raked up some greens, abundantly
amassing floral bed of width and length
sufficient to remove the pain of plunge
they knew would happen more than once. Their health
required that falls be broken by this sponge
of twigs, vines, leaves, ferns, moss, all verdant wealth
so easily available in woods.
With safety checked and rope belayed from limb,
their bodyweight on tether's swing withstood,
the joy of starting new things filled to brim
their smiles and their attitudes. "We're here
to write our legacy as Pioneers!"

80.
Without belaboring each shimmied stride,
suffice to say they progressed rapidly.
Their midday record height was right beside
the midway fork of tree, where sap slid free
from knot suggesting wound from long ago.
"I think we're on the track," Abu called out,
"to make it to the top." "Well, tally ho!"
rejoined belayer's joyful skyward shout.
Enthusiasm often gets the best
of kids engrossed in playtime wonderment.
At least, it did on this day, as wee pest
like whirling ash from fire flew under, went
in swirling eddies 'round him. It transfixed
once landing where its feet touched sap betwixt

81.
the two thick spines conjoined at trunk's midpoint,
where ants reopened gash that pooled with juice.
Gray dragonfly now stuck there at the joint
flapped wings hard, futilely. Beats couldn't loose
from perch. Its past midair complexity –
fly's tacking way through cliff winds – had impressed
Abu, who stretched. "My thumb can flex it free
if I just let this handhold go." He'd wrest
trapped soul with little nudge. His outward lean
sent Stella's spine a-shiver, fearing that
a minor slip would cause his quick careen
toward earth! (And possibly foot past the mat
they'd diligently made to break a fall
but hoped on hope they'd use not once at all.)

82.
The fear became reality as bark
stripped off the limb that levered Abu's feet,
his body dropped in unexpected arc.
With all his might he pushed, prior to the cleat
dislodging from its perch, toward where the bed
was sitting twenty feet below, its edge
five feet away. He wished he'd further spread
the pad of plants before he climbed, and pledged
that if, when hitting ground, he did survive
he'd never make the same mistake again.
The **THUD!** that struck as frame to ground arrived
brought water to Stel's eyes, which saw there, then,
unmoving body strewn across the brink
of ground and bed. She found her heart then sink

83.
in dread she'd lost her other self. Regret
swept through her body, tears welled up, she choked
away expected crying, but a sweat
of fear and sorrow broke out, unprovoked.
And in the silence even BLING stayed mum,
his canine sense suggesting something flawed.
Then all at once Abu launched himself from
the ground, and spooked them both, broke through
    façade
that he'd been hurt! To Stella's clear relief,
he asked, "Bad joke?" with grin while dusting off.
"I'm bruised, but couldn't pass up giving grief.
It's just six meters, *hamna noma*," scoffed
Abu at Stel's overt concern. "And hey,
that dragonfly—I saw it fly away."

84.
They called a pause to climbing, sat to talk,
and debrief what they'd learned. "The limits of
our arms suggest we'll never glide like hawks,
but still can scurry 'tween the trees above
pedestrians." "I'm not sure that we'll feel
the strength to climb up Gumi's wall," Abu
replied, "still think that someone climbed? Grate steel
prevents a hand from entering." "That's true
downstairs, but on the second floor's enough
space to squeeze smallish arms in." "Oh? Okay.
I hate to say it's really looking tough
to prove that wall was climbable." "One day
is all we've tried, and look how we've improved."
From terra's grip they'd not yet be removed.

85.
When weekend came they found an old thing to
help keep them occupied. "Remember when
we first got spooked? That thing dive-bombed, withdrew
when BLING barked. I say let's three go again
to find the banyan strip," Abu proposed.
YIP YIP! assented BLING. Stel lingered, reached
into her satchel, actions undisclosed.
Her hand emerged palm up, the sunlight bleached
its handmade contents: newly-crafted crest
of body falling free and 'fly in flight.
"A Badge for Numbskulls?" Abu grinned and guessed.
"No, no! It's fine to know your kryptonite
is having heart too big to simply see
and not to act to fix a tragedy."

86.
"Repairing tragedy," reply began,
"is never quite the aim of what I do.
I'd rather take the path that every man
ought to, if situation struck them too.
The circumstances here showed I could save
a tiny life by stretching—anyone
with such a chance should take it. It's not brave.
It's simple rule I made there; when rerun,
it works no matter what. Clear following
a rule is easy on the brain: result's
preprogrammed. There's no space for wallowing
about what's right and wrong amid tumult.
No, Stella, what helped set bug's body free
was hardly virtue, just rule-bound duty."

87.
"Role modeling won't work if you're no one.
You first need status to get copycats."
Abu paused for a moment, point undone.
"From someone young it's heard as soppy chat.
Wait fifty, sixty years, grow wise man's beard,
then say the very same and you'll be heard."
"The message on its own can be adhered
to, doesn't matter if it's been conferred
by me or someone else." "You've missed the crux.
The messenger's a part. The two are joint.
An audience tunes to muckety-mucks."
"The point is that the point is not the point?"
"Precisely." "That's depressing." "Take the patch."
Achievement was Ab's easy itch to scratch.

88.
She handed it to him, "I now bestow
the Badge of Selflessness upon you for
your clumsy overreach three days ago
to be that dragonfly's life-guarantor."
"Thanks!" "Now on, put yourself first, have some sense."
"When relevant, I will." He winked, popped bro
fist bump, shifted attention to commence
the banyan search. Sing-song ostinato
was crooned by birds in corners left unseen
among banana fronds and pines maroon,
a forest welcome for the figurines
whose lockstep march resembled a platoon.
But neither knew that further down the way
would sinister soon meet naïveté.

89.
The gentle slope that welcomed them began
to escalate in steepness as they went
progressively into the plant Cézanne,
its murky still-life tones tinged with lament.
To match the vibrancy of lands unknown
as colored in their minds, woods' dampened hues
weren't adequate. Through flora overgrown,
the two kids slogged along. Work helped enthuse.
"Hey, wait!" exclaimed Abu to Stella's back,
"I've seen some signs of someone else along
this route. Look over there, it's been bushwhacked."
Upon inspection, Stella saw no wrong
in Abu's claim, and vigilantly moved
so that their presence could remain unproved.

90.
Soon Stella tracked the tracks to tree that took
her breath away for grandness and for girth,
Brobdignagian in beauty beyond book's
conceivably communicated worth.
Its trunks were wider than a rhino's length,
the branches dwarfed sequoia, rosewood, birch.
It emanated pulsing floral strength
as if they'd entered chartreuse planted church.
Abu ran sideways as he set eyes on
a camo figure climbing up the trees
that lay ahead. Shrill whisper of, "C'mon!"
brought Stella from the clearing. Conferees,
they ducked below the leaves inch out of sight,
to speak about what, seen, seemed not aright.

91.
Masked spindly thing crept cautiously, its climb
a calculated game of changing weight.
It snuck so silently, a judging mime
could hardly this performance underrate.
The smoothness of the bark suggested few
positions graspable for climbing, though
the largeness of the tree meant where trunks drew
together there were natural plateaus.
Each new shelf it passed up for any rest,
feet halting not for even moment's pant.
It must have trained with goal to be the best,
defying gravity like clinging ant.
It free-climbed as if Honnold up El Cap,
rehearsed yet thought by audience madcap.

92.
It powdered hands for grip from belt sack. Shrub
concealed stooped Stel and Ab. BLING laid in pouch.
The figure stopped ascent and found a nub
to stabilize its sideways shuffled crouch.
It left the central trunk to stalk a nest
it spotted left of fork in major branch.
Once there, it reached and quickly dispossessed
large aerie of its eggs! The two kids blanched
at such a blatant trespass of the law,
which stated that you couldn't hunt a beast
without a permit: buzzard, finch, macaw,
rhinoceros, or raptor. Who policed
these woods to find this criminality?
The camo figure left unanswered plea.

93.
It slinked with snakelike grace back toward the trunk,
familiarity with every move
again so fluid as to think it sunk
from conscious thought down into routine's groove.
Controlled descent down pillar's bark face showed
an expert knowledge of which route to take.
A sudden **CRASH!** that calmness overrode
as pterodactyl form made divebomb break
through sun-occluding canopy, right at
the climber. Camouflage fatigues can't hide
effectively against a chestnut matte.
The figure, though, was hardly petrified.
Its bandaged left hand threw fistful of chalk:
such poor man's chaff and flak did talons block.

94.
Near lower branches now, its fleet descent
continued to the ground once bird reversed.
The melee left kids mired in malcontent
and wondering if it had been rehearsed.
Stretched, lithesome figure fled through undergrowth.
No understanding of what they'd just seen
perplexed and discombobulated both.
"That happened fast, too fast to intervene,"
said Stella, sensing that somehow they'd failed.
"I wonder if this happens all the time,"
replied Abu, in fear that uncurtailed
appropriation here was paradigm.
With shallow breath, they scanned the layers of fern
to any clue about the thief upturn.

95.
The minutes stretched from ten to twenty, when
it seemed their bodies' energy was sapped;
the prior vein flow of pure adrenaline
dried up as hormones shut endocrine tap.
No sign of where thief went or what thief left,
not even with BLING's help to sniff the ground,
left both kids' limbs with artificial heft
and so they sat to gather and rebound.
Abu glanced nestwards, scanned environs: "We
should try patrolling out here in these woods.
We'll be the only ones, since bourgeoisie
are busy in their cities, selling goods,"
as if the swell of rectitude turned lung
into the bellows for a judging tongue.

96.
Stel threw arms up in resignation, said,
"They'd rather look at glowing screens than leaves,
and love to sit. They're mostly overfed."
she resolutely rolled her mental sleeves
and settled it: offense of stealing meant
they'd double down on training in the deep
of woods, where they, to possible extent,
would scare off those who came to wrongly reap
the fortunes of the forest. Few months passed
in which they found their skills slowly enhanced.
On forest's stage the season's only cast
were rangers on patrol through vast expanse.
More so than had they camped among bookshelves,
they tested boundaries within themselves.

97.
As stories go, they had their crackjack team:
a couple Hobbes to Stella's Calvin lead.
As Pioneers assembled, their big dream
was beanstalk-like ascent from Gumi's seed.
One look at globe she'd held put head in clouds,
expansiveness apt for imagining.
She hooked them each with that, a hope that crowds
the cautious senses out, swift action in.
Discovering injustices nearby
had galvanized their focused righteousness,
an aim to set aright what's left awry.
In youth, they overlooked that they might miss.
Now taken bait by one adult's told tale,
they crafted selves to follow so-sold trail.

Chapter 3

98.
Back then the weather still predictably
progressed alongside seasons, carbon's layer
not yet so thick to warm restrictively:
constrictor boa Boomers left on heirs.
This regularity helped folks prepare
for when the rainy season came. Thick boots
like Wellingtons could wade through disrepair
of swampy, sole-stuck, drainless roads. Commutes
would shift from morning walks downhill to vans
traversing mountain's foothills. Stella, Ab
and farmers liked it lengthening lifespans
of crops, but also disliked so much drab.
Umbrellas made caprice rains doable
(at least, until we fund renewables).

99.
That March at end would bring the growing cool
into the air, which austral countries feel,
as distance from the sun leaves kilojoules
adrift in space, Earth's annual anneal.
The winds that coursed brought kids a heightened chill,
made worse by the resurgence of the rain,
that forced recalibration 'gainst their will
from forest puttered pace to town octane.
What jarred was nearly everything: packed space,
the sharpness of materials, the smells,
the way that birds with broadcasts were replaced,
dissimilarity of cars from cells.
Excitement faded fast. The disconnect
with time grew to a metro disaffect.

100.
Kids loafed in town. They made up games. They tried
to entertain themselves among the cars.
And yet, all things left each unsatisfied
with spending days bizarre in town's bazaars.
Some days they found with fascination toys
that other kids invented, such as trucks
whose Coke can bodies bottle caps employ
to roll down muddy lanes and bother ducks.
They crafted wands with wire prongs on the tips
to chase those trucks by rolling plastic lids,
but not one joy from this could near eclipse
the wilderness that let them just be kids.
Dispirited one afternoon, they roamed
on drainage roads that through slum honeycombed.

101.
Abu kept kicking can that BLING then chased,
with Stella sauntering four paces back.
They strolled at pace a turtle could have raced,
intention and direction wholly lacked.
As youth, their stride was short, on little legs,
accentuating length of lane and day.
"I wonder what that thief did with the eggs,"
asked boy out of the blue. "It's hard to say,"
said Stella, seeking not to dwell on what
they couldn't know. She tried a subject shift,
"It's Easter soon, let's get out of this rut.
I'm sick and tired of feeling so adrift."
Earned shillings' prize from selling toys they'd made
was Mango Fanta, split. On palisade

102.
they leaned. And looked. And loitered. Traffic lurched
in stops and starts before unfocused eyes,
they gazed into the distance from their perch
by street side fencing, both emitting sighs.
From Stella's shoulder satchel BLING peeked out
with dogged innocence, and sniffed the air.
Beyond square-meter island, all about,
the people bustled, hustled daily wares.
A coupe from 1984 passed by
and spewed gray smoke from rust-brown cracked
  tailpipe.
It seemed the urban car oversupply
caused anger of the horn-assailing type.
A shiny truck spotlit by cloud-split sun
pulled up. Reflected brightness left them stunned.

103.
The truck's insignia said *Supa Loaf*,
with three square feet of paint, the rest was pure
metallic sheen. They felt as if a stove
had spewed heat in their faces to ensure
they'd make a hasty move. Such mirror meant
intensity of sun's rare earthward shine
between the rainy bouts was toward them bent.
It left the truck with dark cloud's silver line
around the edges, forced them squint their eyes.
Then BLING unleashed a **BARK!** of mammoth verve,
and then a third! A fourth! These soulful cries
shocked. Kids snapped to, jumped. BLING this
  unreserved?
Alarm's prodigious puppy power output
had yet to show them what lay underfoot.

104.
Delirium of heat and light and haze
made difficult discernment of the form
but Stella thought she saw amid the daze
some colored swirl suggesting memories warm.
But what exactly was it? Her mind combed
through missions, expeditions, labors, trips,
through undertakings, tasks, and places roamed.
Then right on brink of breakthrough, the eclipse
of technicolor spotlight disappeared.
The truck had pulled away, the air soon cooled.
But Stella felt her mind not fully cleared,
her mental faculties by vision fooled.
Abu, through discombobulation, spoke:
"Can you believe I saw those missing yolks?!"

105.
"You what?" said Stella, face contorted in
expression of incredulousness that
within a second split dissolved, the skin
between her brows unfurled, her forehead flat:
the realization that her memories, mixed,
had settled on the same conclusion made
her almost catatonic, gaze unfixed
and distant. "Are we going nuts? Persuade
me that we haven't just been tricked. I, too,
believe I saw the eggs you mentioned. But
I don't know how that's even partly true
since we were looking at a bread truck." "What?"
replied Abu expectantly, "You saw
the same?" He rose, turned 'round, and dropped his jaw.

106.
Displayed before him lay eggs like they'd seen
the robber climb and steal from woods' bird's nest.
They lay in little baskets painted green,
on sale for Easter, origins unexpressed.
When Stella rose to join her friend she knew
that this was what they'd seen the truck reflect
and wondered how she'd been so dumb as to
not string these thoughts together quite correct.
Regardless, there they found their quest returned
despite discouragement from fickle sky.
As honest citizens, they pooled cash earned
from little playthings sold so they could buy
the eggs. They walked inside. They asked the price
and learned there wasn't one. "To be precise,

107.
what do you mean there isn't one? They're here,
we're in a shop, have *hela* and you're mum."
"There isn't, *msichana*," said cashier,
"we have some VIPs who come in from
somewhere in Asia, China maybe. We
keep certain lovely lively artifacts
for them." "Like what?" "The usual. Could be
a trophy, horn, egg, rug." "Law has impacts
on all that, right?" "Of course, we're by the book.
They tightened export laws last year. Now, go.
These things are not for you." "Man, let me look!"
"Ah, *haya*. Buy them with your eyes." She'd no
thought why they ought to go to foreigners.
She quickly searched for other door in: "Sir,

108.
do you have more upstairs? They're beautiful."
"No." "Really?" "Yes." "Oh, *tafadhali?*" "Fine.
I'll take you, then you'll leave." And, dutiful,
once short-lived tour concluded Stel divined
she wasn't wanted, left. The shop soon closed.
"That shopkeep's rather terrible," Stel said,
"I don't get how some outsiders imposed
an overriding dibs." At loggerheads
with cashier's stance, she'd angered. "Stel, it's cash.
It isn't you. They pay more." "Eggs are cheap!"
"It's like you told me, messages take flash.
Our local pocketbooks don't run too deep,
But glitzy foreign travelers arrive
and want a curio? Locals contrive

109.
to get it on the market." Stel looked down,
sun since declined and left the scene to cool.
But one fluorescent-lit glow showed the town
that commerce now competed with night's ghouls.
To Stel's delight, she knew its source next door!
The dry goods store that Stella once approached
to make BLING's collar rose to rich, from poor,
and bloomed in city's rented space. "Let's broach
the thought we're here to buy, while other climbs
to second floor from back door, then can sneak
across the clothesline." "Brilliant. I think I'm
more suited to distract aground." Physique
suggested so. "Pull the heartstrings of the gent
who ran me from his shop in discontent."

110.
The opened door revealed a man confused.
He thought he recognized the lass – or lad? –
but could not place kid properly. Child oozed
an air of pity, shirts thrice patched with pad
and stitches showing poverty of purse.
Most parents in those parts would doubtless pay
for new attire for children uncoerced,
if only having means so that they may.
"I never give to beggars," explained he,
determined mug as mask. It weakened when
the visitors stayed silent, stood, no plea.
"Mere children? Ugh, take fifty shillings then.
God's blessed me hundredfold with skill imbued,
for Him I'll share small riches I've accrued."

111.
"I've come to pay my debts," the left one said,
and offered up a thousand shilling note.
"I've worried and for months been filled with dread
because I broke your mop. I did devote
a lengthy stretch of time to learning how
to build street toys and sell them, as to save
sufficient money that would then allow
me to return. Forgive, I've misbehaved."
Her outstretched monied hand was left unmet
by matching hand from Anton, thunderstruck.
"Dear girl, these minor things are to forget.
My anger was my fault. Your blunder? Luck.
You'll give me not one coin. In fact, I owe
you for clean floors. Please, browse what's here on show."

112.
He took them in and showed them the expanse
of goods he'd come to sell in larger shop.
"I'll pay in kind for what you've done, financed
with interest." "What's the price on what's atop
the mounted bustard bust in corner there?"
asked Ab, who had a hunch the pieces would
be just the thing for aerial affairs.
"Those harnesses?" asked Anton as he stood
to reach them. "Price is nothing. Now they're yours.
Be careful with the straps, make sure you close
the buckles tightly as to help ensure
against an accidental fall." "I know
precisely how that feels," Abu said, winked,
accepted, backed through front door, tour succinct.

113.
As Anton interacted with Abu
young Stella snuck out back and up the stairs
where, lacking harness, she began to rue
that she'd been tasked with climbing; Abu, wares.
But skill returned, as skill is wont to do,
when called upon in life, though unawares,
and thus her inter-building climb debut
was swift and safe and smooth and unimpaired.
She reached the window, plopped in, curtains drew,
then tripped and hit the floor, which dust had layered.
She coughed, got up, and tiptoed downstairs through
scoped store and hoped that she was solitaire.
With pilfered eggs collected, she escaped
through courtyard, sootlike dust on most parts caked.

114.
With conscience clear and karma good to boot,
the kids could hardly wait to go return
to bird her pastel nest of eggy loot.
However, rain made grip strength a concern
since they'd been grounded now for weeks and weeks.
They chose to lay low, train at home until
convinced they'd rebuilt some of prior physique.
The stealth of tiny exercises filled
the need for modicum of questing thrill.
Such practice hiding secrets, fun when young,
runs risk of long descent on steep downhill:
when too good, secrets weave the blanket clung.
For now, they trained their hands and tightened grip
on story they'd restore eggs to kinship.

115.
You should have seen the pair at sunrise when
they met to slog through bush on righteous quest
to reunite the bird with eggs again.
Each, every minor detail was addressed:
they'd layered as to insulate from cold,
they'd ropes and harnesses to access air,
they'd rubberized their shoes to better hold
tight grip to trees, foregoing falling scares.
A comic inspiration meant from belts
they'd hung machete *pangas*, tinder, light,
as if Paul Bunyan into Batman melts,
turns light survivalist from once-Dark Knight.
And even BLING was equally bedecked,
clad snout to tail in sisal for the trek.

116.
With baobabs left at lower altitude,
the genus of *Dalbergia* filled space.
Its species *melanoxylon* previewed
mahogany and blackwood interlaced,
with vines that hung with artificial weight,
themselves the hosts for parasitic moss,
the scene a floral war, and yet sedate
to viewer seeing only groves' green gloss.
The undergrowth was thicker than they'd thought,
they thanked the fates they'd left at day's first glow
so trudging through this vast botanic wat
with footstep light would let them, *quid pro quo*
escape without calamity, unlike
when nature Abu's first night out did strike.

117.
Expecting BLING most surefoot of the bunch,
the treasured eggs Stel housed upon his back
in pouch positioned past where he could munch
his fur to quell an itch or flea attack.
And good thing, too, for forty minutes hence
a hidden root protruded from the dirt
that sent poor Stella face-first in the dense
and matted mud and leaf atop the chert.
The fall would surely cause an egg to burst—
her gadgets, thankfully, were more robust.
While prostrate there, she found she was headfirst
atop a piece of jasper, colored rust.
She bagged the ground-bound token as earth's mild
memento of their sojourn in the wild.

118.
Stel's eyeballs ranged unstopping 'round the soup
of life face planted in. She lacked right words
for how close-up inspection ever-duped.
A decade out she'd name them, overheard
in lyrics from Fiasco—he said that:
*see big worlds have their little worlds that feed
on their velocity.* Stel saw how gnats
gnawed carrion, in turn fed bigger breeds
from vaster canopies. The rap went on,
said *little worlds have lesser worlds and so
on to viscosity.* Those fractal spawn
invisible to Stella's eye, earth's slow
yet macroscopic brilliance did enchant,
Vanilla Sky-like memory bright implant.

119.
The trail they traced was hardly that, made more
by measured stomping of their boot and paw.
They hadn't fully bushwhacked heretofore,
swung *pangas*, hacking clear path route through maw.
Not everything was lost with snail-like pace,
in fact, they found themselves more apt to see
the depth and breadth of life that hastes debase
as humans toward their destinations speed.
Post-fall Stel felt like she'd donned spectacles
that showed all living things in more detail,
from beetles' colored wings to specks that, dull,
reveal each tiny insect's treaded wales.
The fascinating microscopic scale
allowed the time to simply, past her, sail.

120.
Found scaled-down splendor led to equipoise
between Stel's looking up and looking down,
eyes flitting to and fro to grasp the joys.
Young Stel became the first to see the gown
of leaf and vine, of branches twisted thick
that draped itself upon the banyans there,
presiding over open bailiwick
with stoic stateliness of legionnaire.
Their goal within the reach of eye and arm,
they shuffled up to trunk with haversacks,
equipment reminiscent of *gendarmes*
at camp in preparation for attack.
Assault instead meant climbing to replace
the eggs into their mother's twig airbase.

121.
Stel's still-held shoulder chip about the wall
at Gumi's meant she'd trained the toughest grips,
so kids agreed that Stella'd do the haul
of treasure strapped to puppy strapped to hip.
The buckles buckled, clasps clasped tightly too,
then second safety check for conscience's sake,
and she was ready for the rendezvous.
She feigned a confidence she hoped would make
a difference in performance, having heard
accomplishment is rooted in the brain,
success when visualized is then transferred
to muscles, which obey as preordained.
The folds in bark were deep and would hold fast.
Stel gulped, and prayed this climb not be her last.

122.
The first few steps, her muscles moved in sync,
precisely what she'd asked them all to do,
each working automatically. To think
would override fluid instinct, cause miscue.
And think she did when realizing eight
feet from the ground she was again airborne,
with simple harness to alleviate
the fears of gravity she'd wished forsworn.
Abu, aground, astonished was aware
from furrowed brow and carriage of his friend
that laden climb to her was not nightmare
but also not a thing she'd recommend.
His skyward gaze before hers saw a shape
that aimed to divebomb her through broad leaves' gape.

123.
Said boss was albatross by wingspan, swept
through gap in canopy with wings tucked in,
an avian device to intercept
exposed and helpless Stella. Her luck, then,
she didn't see this thunderbolt *en route*
else she'd have justifiably freaked out,
and leaped from branch in hope of parachute
effect from harness. But, untested, doubts
persisted as to whether it would hold,
and both hoped not to use it at that height.
Rich in her ignorance, Stel stayed controlled
despite the pending pull into dogfight.
Her friend below on guard as air patrol
stood stunned as if the bird his breath had stole.

124.
The impact feared approached as instants passed
and yet the time felt slower than a sloth,
like Spaceman Spiff dialed death-ray gun broadcast
from liquidate to frappé back to froth.
Our stoic Abu nearly wet his slacks
when realizing beastly beak's fine curve
directly on a line toward Stella's back—
the impact, though, avoided by a swerve!
A microsecond following the twist,
its length the lag of sound behind the light,
Abu heard **YIP!** as BLING the bird dismissed,
and Stella, now aware, did expedite
her climb to place of safety, where her heart
in frightened palpitations did restart.

125.
A glance back up the tree to Stella's perch
revealed one frightened face, four jitt'ry limbs.
Sat paranoid in fear of second lurch,
she raced through expletives and synonyms
in stressed attempt to calm. Her mind, at speed
ran through the acts of Pioneers to date,
adrenaline accelerating deed
in search of memories she could emulate
to extricate herself from doomsday dread.
She thought of jasper found aground. (Sweet ground,
its stillness and consistency...) Thoughts sped
to first night with Abu: cliffs did surround,
but he'd stayed cool. Yes. How? Slowed breath to steer
like Bene Gesserit transcending fear.

126.

Why, yes, she thought, *my memory's so distinct*
and clear because back then I thought it odd
a single ritual so plain, succinct
transmuted seething soul to calm façade.
So, bird encircling for a second pass,
she closed her eyes and focused on her nose,
while hands instinctively gripped planty mass.
She breathed in, Yoda calmness tried impose.
A tension in the air was palpable –
whether from nerves or lack of pep, or tree
unused to hosting dog and gal – doubled
when juxtaposing zen and jeopardy.
Yet ounce by ounce her body gained a peace
and from her anxious prison, self released.

127.

Inside she found a certain clarity
hid deep in tempest of her stormy mind.
(In fact, such vastness of disparity
was worth review by later humankind.)
Such halo of lucidity made keen
her brains and eyes and ears and sense of touch,
the chroma like a dose of mescaline,
the confidence to slack white-knuckled clutch.
She realized her instincts served her well,
and looked down lengthy branch she sat astride
to see the nest. But no one could propel
her safely out to it, since she'd provide
an easy target for a second swoop,
and so she paused on arboreal stoop.

128.
She reached behind her back, removing BLING
and petting him with gratitude. He'd seen
the monster thing glide down on striking wings
and fiercely barked and forced it to careen.
The structure of the satchel with the eggs
was flimsy stuffing in a carton piece,
the tangled parched grass padding bled its dregs
out top, where cinch of string had been released.
A zipper they'd preferred to use, but cash
was short and ingenuity was long,
so after sifting through the neighbor's trash
they'd put a cord where zipper did belong.
The wisdom, though, was baked in by design:
she'd turn it to delivery dragline!

129.
She thanked the lucky stars she'd trained BLING well
and buckled him and double-checked his ropes:
one slack loop 'round the branch, run parallel
to give a falling safety envelope,
and one to keep in Stella's hand to pull
precisely when the goods had reached their home,
depositing exactly one bagful
of eggs alongside brethren chromosomes.
Without delay, she sent BLING down thin bough
on which he'd balance. She could not hold her
frame on it, lest the bird's swoop disendow
of shelled kin, flipping savior saboteur.
The dog trod lightly, bothered not one whit,
as if among the monkeys he could fit.

130.
Bird shadows sliced leaf-mottled sun, its drift
from left to right showed indecision, torn
between a striking dive or thermal lift,
both curious and guarding its unborn.
Maternal instincts struck and guided act,
as bird turned sharply, tucked again in bomb,
suspicious that intruder would ransack
the stout nest over which she reigned as mom.
BLING crouched down low, stuck belly to the bough,
put both ears back and steadied for a fight,
his stance as fearsome as his size allowed.
The bird approached. BLING's posture wasn't quite
sufficiently pugnacious to dissuade
the striker, who'd seen right through his charade.

131.
Split second prior to impact, sidewise jump
saved BLING a talon's gutting there a-branch.
His claws deployed in haste gouged out a lump
of wood, burst brittle barklet avalanche.
In spite of that noteworthy nimbleness,
his gear was not as unscathed as his skin.
So close was call that bird had pilfered this:
the pogo patch that Stel'd on backpack pinned.
In leap he'd shifted closer to the roost
that housed the brethren of the eggs he bore;
a single further step, then Stella loosed
the string that closed the pouch's egg backdoor.
Though eggs arrested in twig cradle, BLING
mistakenly stepped into one gold ring!

132.
In normal times, BLING yipped at shiny things
and so it seemed like karma he'd acquire
a ring in recompense for hijackings
attempted by the bird. A true ceasefire
meant *quid pro quo*, a balanced give and take.
But let's not say that BLING had pondered thus,
and sentiently chosen then to make
an equal trade. An honest error, plus
his paws were small enough to fit inside
the fat circumference of the ring of gold
but not shake off unless he then applied
opposing pressure shrewdly, sevenfold.
And so BLING stood, with bling on left forepaw,
unable to shake ring from his dewclaw.

133.
Between repeated calls to get her dog
to come back down the branch so they could go,
Stel angered. Why was BLING in such a fog?
BLING lingered on branch, flailing, while their foe
sailed out to other tree for fleeting rest.
In desperation to be heard, Stel growled,
the sonic signal that she knew accessed
the deepest canine recesses, where howls
at moons, where licks, where dampened noses, where
the universal code of pup tail wag
lived in one cipher of extraordinaire
genetic complication. Each dog tagged
norepinephrine boost to growling sound:
to snap back to, to re-become a hound.

134.
The gambit worked! The deepest rumble she
could muster from her human vocal chords
earned BLING's regard by puppy alchemy.
He wisely retrograded trunkward toward
the safety of her perch. His stride was strained
due to the oddity she saw was stuck
on his forepaw. This thing, she ascertained,
would cause his every fourth step go amok,
inhibiting his progress, wor'ying her.
So slowly passed the seconds of return
she simply wished he'd scurry hurried, per
the danger of another swoop discerned.
At last he entered radius arm reached.
She strapped him in and readied for the breach.

135.
Stel's leaden breaths came quick, she'd failed to clear
the stress of BLING's return before descent.
But now, with dog strapped to her bandolier
and chest to tree, she hadn't chance lament.
The bird, she noticed, hadn't strafed again
but rather had returned to nest and seen
that Stella, Abu, BLING were middlemen
for fate's intent to family reconvene.
In solitary gesture, they'd transformed
from blatant enemies to neutral guests,
the temperature between them mildly warmed
above the icy levels past suggests.
Into arms wide Stel fell, Ab's face aglow.
"You've earned Swahili's version of *bravo!*

136.
I watched that bird the whole of your descent,
I think it might have understood what you
both dared to do. Must feel it's heaven-sent
to have your stolen children rendezvous
back home!" he gushed, revealing underneath
a wish to have contributed some more
to mission that he'd witnessed to bequeath
the chattels. "Hope an able troubadour
can chronicle in verse what you just did.
I mean, we're bound to grow in membership
when deeds as this reach ears of other kids.
Official histories make gender quips
impossible, because they'll know a girl
with chivalry replaced bird's oyster pearl."

137.
"I think, Abu, it's just too soon to tell
the whole wide world about our handiwork.
Recall we never got shopkeep to sell,
but used our *modus operandi*." Smirk
made way to both their faces as they styled
themselves as cloak-and-dagger operatives.
"That helps. Street reputations are compiled
by word of mouth. A quest like this one gives
the status to be heard. You told me so."
The notion floated – being listened to –
uplifted Stel, (her grounding jasper stowed)
then dropped her. "Ab, misdeed admission's viewed
with admiration from our classmates, but
with punishment from teachers." "Stel, tut-tut.

138.
You hardly cared before. You hide. This could
first put us Pioneers on global map."
"If we're not jailed." "You think they really would?"
"I stole these eggs." "You tried to pay." "With scraps
compared to what the Chinese buyers spend,
according to the shopkeep. Let's avoid
a lien on Grandmum's cows. Truth's a dead end."
"A rumor 'round the school, to kids," rejoined
Ab, "think of how they'd think of us! Adults
could never prove—" "No." Abu slumped a smidge,
dissatisfied the noble quest's results
prevented build toward fame on story's bridge.
Declining gaze showed treasury surprise:
accessory pup's ankle bore as prize.

139.
Ab stooped attentively to study what
was stuck on BLING, who sniffed at it. "What have
we here?" he asked. Stel bent to check the mutt.
"This ring's so tight we might just have to halve
a paw as to dismantle BLING and band."
They chuckled nervously. Don't jokes have barbs
of truth inside? Out there in timberland
they didn't have extracting tools, though garb
felt packed to gill with gear when they'd set out.
Abu leaned in and twisted it. "Oh, my..."
"What is it?" Stella asked. "A thing I doubt
you'll want to give its owner back." "No? Why?"
"You didn't like the way she seemed to fling
housegirls under the bus. It's Gumi's ring!"

140.
"What?! How are you so sure?" she asked of him.
"For one, it clearly fits her window grate.
For two, look here." "Is that an acronym?"
"No. 'JGG's inscribed, and next word states
'beloved'." Stel inspected, saw the etched
initials that Abu pinpointed and
retracted doubt the notion was far-fetched:
those letters rested filigreed on band.
"But why," she asked, "would Gumi's ring be here?
We also got this stone from that soil bed
I fell in." "What an odd two souvenirs
to get: one band of gold, one jasper, red.
Let's figure how to divvy up *en route,*
because until we're home, the point is moot."

141.
The avian equivalent of howl
at moon erupted then from branches high
above their heads, a bellow from the fowl
whose beady eyes traced kids' egress. "Goodbye!"
Abu and Stella shouted, with a **YIP!**
from BLING, made happy by return to earth.
They three were pleased to cede their ownership
over the lives of birds approaching birth.
The trek back home demanded focused feet
and eyes to find the footing, fend off falls,
so progress made was firm, but far from fleet,
yet hopes were high for home before nightfall.
As promised, walking conversation touched
on what to do with ring and jasper clutched.

142.
The Pioneers ignored environs as
they chitted, chatted, stooped and sprung and strode
their way back to the town. Hints of pizzazz
possessing steps to finished deed were owed.
Their speech swayed left and right, from virtuous
to evilest conniving little plots
to pawn the ring then pocket value plus
keep tight-lipped on how they'd struck the jackpot.
The longer the deliberations went,
the darker and more self-enriching schemes
revealed themselves as source of discontent,
as lies could loot all value from daydreams
of being kids with cash. The treasure trove
Stel half-sought wasn't gold, but room to rove.

143.
"We've got a million shillings, let us say,"
said Stella stepping verbally through thought.
"I'm not so sure that we would disobey
our teachers, 'cause they'd think we're little snots.
I'm pretty sure we'd have to hide the loot,"
she mulled and paused. Inhaling breath anew,
"Nor is it like we've chosen lux pursuits
that need a minor fortune to pursue."
(A decade hence she'd find that she relied
on words themselves, the cheapest of all things.)
"I really think we're happier outside,
where knowledge and experience is king."
And so in back and forth it rightly dawned
she'd little wont of money wrongly pawned.

144.
"In light of this as Gumi's ring," Ab said,
"you'd get crime pardon if returned." "Unless
I don't. Then life is over. Don't retread
your line that we get status if I fess."
"But calculus has changed: if ring is found
the world brands us burglarious." "Yes, Ab.
while it's in our possession, we're nigh bound
to secrecy. So give it back, don't blab,
wipe hands clean and go back to normalcy."
"Forgo the chance to be a heroine?"
"No. Be one, but a quiet one, quarrel-free.
Anonymously. Stay straight arrow. Bin
the limelight." Still Stel watched its carats' glints,
felt gravity toward grabbed inheritance.

145.
"What if," she backtracked, thought, "I kept that safe?
Were I to fall on harder times could gold
become my parachute? Here, folks' fail-safe
is going back to family, who'll uphold
kin's duty to give food and shelter. In
return the person works the farm or chores."
Met basic needs as trade to serve the whim
of other household masters frightened. Ores
bounced cheerfully before her eyes. "Fine, Stel.
But since our escapade's the stuff of lore.
at least we ought to pen ways we've excelled
so it can someday spread beyond our shores.
Let's keep a secret sanctioned record, then
of Pioneer adventures, wheres and whens."

146.
His other self approved. Both brainstormed names
for what those hallowed records would be termed.
'The Tome'? 'The Chronicles'? 'The Hall of Fame'?
and settled on 'The Annals', which confirmed
acceptable amount of gravity
without adjoining legalese or cant.
They buried talk that risked depravity,
this *tête-à-tête* on if they can or can't
have better future pawning ring for purse.
The power to choose pleased both. Stel loved this book,
their secret guide to self-made universe.
She rather dreamed how illustrations looked:
each one reflecting her, and yet distinct
as thousand stylized selves would there be inked.

147.
Her mind grabbed onto these and flitted through
locations Gumi mentioned anchoring
initially. Nile didn't fit her view
of high adventure, Hormuz tanker string
fell short too. Better were the Paris thoughts,
with pictured self sophisticated, 'mong
the throngs at Eiffel Tower viewing spots.
The best were Shanghai's, *kung fu* to *foo yong.*
In places Stel imagined she had grown.
In places Stel imagined she looked pleased.
In places Stel imagined she was known.
In places Stel imagined she was freed.
Could such book chance to fly against winds' fate
in course that she controlled and would create?

148.
Poor BLING continued stilted striding, kept
from full extension of his paws because
ring bound like plaster on a bone. He leapt
and trotted on remaining three good paws.
"How do you think," said Stel while forging creek,
"we're going to get that thing off BLING?" "Let's face
what's silently assaulted us: BLING reeks!
We'll need to bathe him well in any case."
"You think some suds and scrubs will do it? He
is overdue for cleaning, that's for sure."
"We'll have to find some powder to keep fleas
away again." "You're sounding so mature!
I always thought that listing risks and threats
was for adults inventing things to fret."

149.
A smirking Abu countered, "Maybe most,
but don't you think we're better off without
the dog around us turning to bug host?"
She thought a moment, saw his point had clout.
"And even when you're fine, they'll badger you
about your chores or being right on time.
On birthdays once you think you just outgrew
the babying, they'll set new strict guidelines."
"But not for me," said Stella distantly,
"because I've only Grandmum, don't have 'they'.
And she can barely do consistently
the things she needs to stay alive. Onc day
I fear she might forget. For now, no chance
she'll notice me beyond a passing glance.

150.
My life's about just me and little white
lies that I tell Grandmum to smooth the seas.
With no parental guidance, my foresight
is all I have to ease anxieties
of future. Not like anyone at school
is friendly, takes the time to understand
me. Nah—they'd rather play and ridicule
the quirky things that make them wonder, and
I happen to be quite," her eyes showed tears,
"the easy target, well, 'cause I'm a girl.
Society can't handle chicks who steer
their own lives rather than pursuing pearls."
Pal duo stopped, till that point unaware
that Stella battled social disrepair.

151.
"Take Grandmum. Past the cows, you think that she
leaves any safety net? No. Mom or Dad?
Long gone. And here's this opportunity,
this savior gold to build wished-for launch pad.
You're urging me to put this out in view,
trust, ride the expectation girls be good?
That's self-defeat: they'll brand me as a shrew,
exploit the fact I stole. They'll say I should
have never self-assuredly bucked rules,
that I'm too savage for autonomy.
And let alone that Gumi thinks girls fools—
I'll melt her ring, and ought! It dawned on me
to make my own way out: my only hope
is friendlessness – 'cept you – head down, and cope."

152.
"No wonder you reacted when I said
repatriating ring's a must. Guess 'ought'
can carry risks. Dynamics flew o'erhead
without my knowing forces that you fought.
Now that you point it out I've heard these things,
the little gendered cuts that trim your size.
I got the same as foreigner. It stings
when made to feel as lesser in man's eyes."
"You don't know what it's like. We're differ-ent."
"In some ways yes, in some less than you think.
But save it. Sun's low. We need swifter stint
a-march to make it home before it sinks."
"Keep moving," Stel to self said, "life's headwinds
aren't guaranteed to slow or selves rescind..."

153.
"I'm sorry?" asked Abu. "Just muttering,"
said Stel dismissively. She set one foot
in front of next, toward that day's shuttering.
She needed body calm for mind output.
Return to normal march, remarked Abu,
felt better, as the normal's meant to sense,
inducing zero musing, no ado.
Stel shushed him quiet and said he'd acted dense.
She watched him muse on that, saw active brain
forget to task his eyes to looking 'round.
They focused at his feet. Still, she abstained
from further hounding him. They were homebound,
she felt more hidebound: nearly spelled the same,
two letters' difference flipping warmth to shame.

154.
Delightful orange light was blanketing
the scads of shades of green, surrounding scene
enlivened with its end. Sun sank, quitting
the day they'd met adventure unforeseen.
As with all objects in the universe,
when absent warmth, the hues began to pale,
lives migrated to nests. Moonlight disbursed.
Nocturnal creatures wakened 'neath the veil.
Yet nourished by success that afternoon,
kids marched without a further voiced complaint.
Their rapid walk avoided night marooned,
steps' rhythm reinforcing jaw's restraint.
A coterie of demons filled Stel's head,
uncertainty of future yielding dread.

155.
With trouble hardly matching long-past night
they'd spent out in the forest, when Abu
used bottled fireflies as a lantern light,
they found themselves near home at eight past two.
"I'm feeling kind of energized," said she,
"and not so sure I want to go to bed,"
with ring on BLING she felt like escapee
who feared discovery, and so she fled.
Abu, his system too endorphin-filled,
was eager to accept recourse from rest.
"Let's rid ourselves of unearned fortune. Skilled
maneuvers in the air, with some finesse
are all we need to put back Gumi's ring
and free our conscience." "Dog, this just might sting..."

156.
Their little world had spun from big one's speed,
unknowingly toward darker parts concealed.
As Pioneers, they'd had to intercede,
in doing so found others wrongly steal.
It's fortunate that Stella hadn't got
the ring five years from then, perspectives changed.
Her wish for cash would complicate the plot
and find her from her other half estranged.
Decision still remained: how to conclude
their perilous possession of the ring
and whether gallant act would leave them viewed
as criminals for backyard bushwhacking.
In later retrospective to be made
they'd realize that they had both been played.

Chapter 4

157.
Contraption scheming gave kids welcome break
involving lasso mastery and knot.
BLING had to undergo a minor ache,
since ring was now immobile in its spot.
At such an hour dead early in the morn,
they didn't need to worry they'd be seen,
quite helpful when they'd send BLING on airborne
brisk escapade above the mezzanine.
From bushes at the base of Guml's wall,
they threw an end of rope up toward the grate
that covered upstairs window, each shortfall
was followed by new toss until line draped
through square atop the metal casing which
would be the topmost point of their rope hitch.

158.
Each having their equipment on their back,
the precious still-packed items from the trip,
they lightened load by finishing the snacks
and checked that BLING's equipage wasn't ripped.
The length of rope they'd threaded up above
was threaded then again through three belt loops
sewed onto dog vest's spine, replica of
the safety harness from bird's branch-bound swoops.
A second cord of greatly smaller girth,
its thickness thin, akin to but a thread
was woven through the narrowest of berths:
forced channel between fur and ring where bled
a half day's worth of chafing doggy stride.
Ring ground right through the fur and into hide.

159.

The plan was thus: they'd each take one of two
ropes strung to dog, the longer one to hoist,
the second to release with derring-do
the ring with gravity, (they'd made it moist
with little bits of suds they'd mixed atop
Lux bar soap with saliva), hoping force
of weight, applied tangentially, could pop
the ring from paw, and leave it at its source
while freeing BLING to then be lowered down,
belayed by kids who'd slowly loose the rope.
They'd be ringleaders (felt a bit like clowns)
for acrobat untrained in this 'tightrope'.
They knew the jerk at apogee'd renew
sharp pain, so prior to lift they gave him food.

160.
With heave and ho, their torpid, groggy beast
was hoisted in the air by one long line,
and after two rotations BLING had pieced
together that no struggle would align
his body back to standard angles, so
he slackened, making easy their belay.
At top, they readied ring-looped rope to tow,
and hoped to with a tug cause ring to stay
and hang upon the grate, while dog nosedives
from battle lost to gravity. In print,
a diagram of force would propose lives
were not at risk if they stayed penitent.
So rush they made most sure to then avoid,
and with affair's success were overjoyed.

161.
Success came as a tranquilizing surf,
a balm to consciences disquieted,
that washed from window downward toward the turf,
upon return of ring. "This tie, it slid
straight off directly on our first strong yank!"
said Stella with incredulous esteem.
Abu's entire thin stature raised with thanks,
his back more straight and eyes like Stel's agleam.
Their day had been so tirelessly packed
with reactivity that compliments
were first to, from the schedule, subtract,
as minds reacted to the romp's events.
Through smile upon his face rose great fatigue,
all justified through praise from his colleague.

162.
"I'm tired," Stella said, "now that it's done,"
her body in a wilt that showed the hour,
and so they packed their things to go. "Wait, one
more thing is left before home, bucket shower,"
replied Abu, who quickly cut the patch
from off his rucksack's side, the elephant
on pogo stick, and left it on the latch,
explaining, "now they'll likely tell it meant
behind the ruse were some anonymous
do-gooders. Needn't know *we're* Pioneers."
"I guess that pogo sticks aren't ominous,
okay." "We'll build our brand!" "Fine, do it." Fears
they'd be found out were still inside her head;
Ab's obstinance made Stel give in instead.

163.
Since night had long since turned to dawn's sunrise
they snuck their ways back home and into bed,
pretending that was true what would surmise
a parent: that they'd slept at their homesteads.
The energy the trek to banyan grove
had taken from their bodies took recharge.
So both kids huddled near the hearth and stove
until through calm of homeliness did barge
the hunger to again breathe deeply air
that circulates so freely out of doors,
by walls and vents and windows unimpaired,
that vim and zeal to bodies oft restores.
In all, they passed three days reclusively
before they felt themselves conclusively.

164.
The break had given each some time to think,
or rather, to let percolate upstairs
the musings taking longer time to sink
from memory clouds to conscious thoroughfares.
A hundred flashes, tedium to thrill,
swept through young Stella's hibernating mind,
from wonder at the wealth of chlorophyll
to fears that ants outnumbered humankind.
The edge of thought she hadn't quite yet grasped
attempted to decrypt gist of past week,
a soapstone mystery that logic rasped
in vain attempts to find its real physique.
All conscious tries were clumsy stabs to hew
the stone to form intrinsically untrue.

165.
Hiatus long between when Stella talked
with Abu, she discovered something odd:
they'd yet to figure out how ring had walked
from Gumi's walled-in, yarded esplanade
to deep inside a forest, up a tree,
and out a branch, and into nest. "The thief!"
she cried, as if no other nominee
could possibly have caused such complex grief.
When under tree they subsequently met,
she voiced to Ab her theory, bulletproof,
that figure camo-clad hopped parapet
at Gumi's, scaled the wall to nearly roof,
then reached with evil hand through metal grille
and took the ring from off the windowsill.

166.
"You're right, I think, that there's a chance it went
exactly as described, but I'm still mixed
on why he wouldn't, after the ascent,
have jetted to a pawn shop, right then fixed
the worry of his seizure and arrest
and made his money straightaway," Abu
replied. Then Stella saw she had suppressed
(as typical when in the truth's pursuit)
the thought she might be wrong. She'd advocate
exclusively for how the facts fit her
hypothesized reality. Dictate
it wasn't, simply first try to infer
the real: until all facts aligned to prove
veracity, some healthy doubt behooved.

167.
"So what," she said, "do you propose went on
to move the ring from Gumi's to the nest?"
their dedication to the *dénouement*
like alchemists who seek their alkahest.
"Let's take the things we know and build a case,
with only all the pieces that we've sensed
ourselves," Abu proposed, "so we'll retrace
exclusively the facts that have defense."
And so they laid out facts, as were perceived
throughout the journey, from the day the globe
began the Pioneers, their preconceived
ideas on days' undertones disrobed.
Through airing only what they'd seen and when,
they cut through falsities of minds of men.

168.
Ten minutes passed, then thirty, fifty, more,
the sun crept forth two-thirds one radian,
the facts and facts alone to air outpoured
at speed eclipsing pace circadian.
With recollected records, self-contained,
they orally arranged the token bits
in clumps that left yet fewer unexplained
loose ends. From time to time they'd stand, stage skits
to dis or prove contentious points, pretend
that they were the antagonist, with props,
they laughed as shirt-stuffed leaves caused to distend
Abu's fake Anton belly, threw fake chalks
of sand to foil the bird, each spoof but guess
to make a might more sense of story's mess.

169.
"We've looked at seven stories," Stella summed,
"disproven four, and doubt another two."
They'd undeniably with gusto plumbed
all caverns of experience and clue.
"The one that's left," Abu said, "doesn't make
a lot of sense unless you think that birds
are subject to, as beasts, human heartache
and have, at least," he paused to unmince words,
"a mild ability to reason." "Why
would such a thing surprise you in the least?
It's obvious people oversupply
opinions creatures are just food for feasts,
atop rich checkered tablecloths." "Yeah, this
whole act was bird's is my hypothesis!

170.
The bird we've noticed cruising 'round the town,
I've seen it roost," Abu began, "near school.
At least, I saw a bit of colored down
that looked a fit: long, striped with minuscule
metallic flecks." With this, his listener
leaned forward, curious to hear what's next.
"It must have sat on grate, where glistened, per
Miss Gumi's recollection, ring. Perplexed,
the bird from there would see both shiny loop
and one domestic basketful, right there,
of eggs, its very own! From its own coop!
It would have been enraged, the sight unfair
of mother's eyes through ornate iron rung
there gawking at her own imprisoned young.

171.
Its talons, as you saw, were small enough
to squeeze through hollows in the lattices.
This theory isn't purely off-the-cuff,
I've thought a while," he said, on status his
quick mind was dwelling, wond'ring if he'd solved
their ever-overarching quandary,
if nature-centric narrative resolved
their riddle. Stel as statue pondering
looked like Rodin's, her *Thinker* brow furrowed
in thorny thought. Then eyes flipped up toward sky.
Retreats into her mind looked thus, her code
to onlookers to not preoccupy
themselves with her, for outwardly her freeze
belied a mind expanding boundaries.

172.
Hiatus in the conversation was
a momentary, welcomed break. Abu's
two temples damped with anxious sweat. (Because
he hoped his logic wouldn't be refused?)
The air was tranquil, windless, waveless, still,
the jostling of its million molecules
too small to cause evaporative chill
of forehead perspiration's tiny pools.
He noticed, soon, a shift in Stella's stance,
a weight rebalanced on a single hip
away from posed at-ease. She looked, perchance,
prepared to speak, with twitching upper lip.
"It's odd, and wouldn't happen everyday.
Let's spin it in the chronicles that way."

173.
The shroud of doubt that hung between them, fog
that cut them off from outer world while hung
in heated back-and-forth of dialogue,
dispersed when Stella's words rolled off her tongue.
Uncertainty, as was perceived to cease,
left ghost of an unwished-for visitor:
conclusion where before lived just caprice,
two bailiffs where once stood inquisitors.
The pulse of joy at twisting thread of truth
was sharp, and both kids felt upwelling pride.
And yet, their verve to find, unearth and sleuth
was now, without a known demand, supplied.
Just then, once truth revealed its pyrite sheen,
could they find meaning in their ends and means.

174.
Maturing, for each kid, took different form.
While Stella had Grandmum once evenings came,
Abu was back as one of eight, in swarm
of family's flock he once again was name
and nothing more, a mouth to feed, who left
for stretches at a time without account.
He felt amid his family bit bereft
of own identity, sense tantamount
to anonymity he'd felt at school.
He segregated self away from peers,
kept public actions sized to minuscule.
He hoped that life would pay him in arrears
in future gains from studying today,
between adventures showing better way.

175.
That's not to say that Abu walked as ghost,
as haunted, surveying with discontent.
He rather took his strength from his repose,
accepted rather than misrepresent
himself. No bitter edge enclosed his view,
he more began to know he much preferred
to keep his dear companions close, but few.
This shift from sinking socially as nerd
at school uplifted his relationships
with other children, who could tell the fun
they poked at him in pure predation, quips
and taunts had dropped from great effect to none.
Alongside Stella he desired to shift
toward Pioneers from school, toward life adrift.

176.
His willful separation, like a match
transmits its fire to brethren in the book,
crept into Stella, who slowly detached
as well from mates' historic dirty looks.
They stayed as separated from the crowd
as any outside observations past
or present would have seen. But now endowed
with self-reliance, they'd upgraded caste.
They went from lowest on the totem pole
to missing from the pole entirely,
absent from all the cool kids' mind control
that turned their toady classmates liars. Free,
they sought only discovery and mirth,
and had to prove to only selves their worth.

177.
"Miss Gumi never said a thing," Abu
lamented once near first-found precipice.
"That's good, though. Single mark of our debut
was pogo patch, no names. The rest of this
is nothing we want out." "Think fairytales
were ever narratives begun like this?
A man's experience on hairy trails
that spins up orally to bigger fish?"
"Nah. People turn to print now. That stuff's lost."
They watched a dragonfly buzz off the cliff,
against the breeze, in paths that crissed and crossed,
to trace it would reveal a hieroglyph
reminding Ab of home and history—
at least, the points that weren't still mystery.

178.
"I know when I was four, I thought I'd be
atop the world when finally I reached eight,"
said Stella, legs hung off extremity,
"and now I'm there. Will I now overrate
the possibilities of twelve? I don't
exactly have command of this whole town,
but maybe what I want has changed." "Mine won't,"
replied Abu with certainty. "Renown
befits a sheikh, and sheikh I'll someday be."
Not knowing what to say, she looked instead
into his face and saw a galaxy,
its far-flung stars stampeded straight ahead,
propelled by detonation since their birth,
all destined thus to distance selves from Earth.

179.
"I guess it's sensible to give you this,"
Abu said, handing Stella a small felt
bedraggled patch. *For forging the abyss,*
it read below the title. "Since you dealt
so bravely with the bird, despite your fear
of heights, I think you get the Monkey Crest.
Your climbing took you to the stratosphere,
I doubt I could be any more impressed."
So there on ledge were Abu, Stella, BLING,
with Badges, Crests, and patches to reward
themselves for their pursuit of distant things
that prior to Pioneers were unexplored.
Then Stella reached inside her bag to get
a book bound by a jasper red rosette.

180.
"I spent the time when we were s'posed to rest
manipulating what I tripped beside,
that jasper piece." Abu's hands were then blessed
by intricate design: rose petrified
into a cover clasp o'er pages bunched,
thin fonts in capitals commensurate
with their importance (though a wee bit scrunched),
and swirl to draw eye in to denser bits.
Its title read quite clearly ANNALS OF
THE AFROASIATIC PIONEERS,
an elephant on pogo stick above
the small subtitle: OUR WORLDWIDE PREMIERE.
Unlocking all the pages from their bind,
he saw their oral history enshrined.

181.
The pages glowed as manuscripts of lore,
illuminated by a cloistered brush:
paint light from sun as metal fleck phosphor,
inked nights so dark they made his heart rate rush.
The early pages showed shared scenes, hues bright
if simple. Empty rectangles aligned
to not obscure the action. "Here we write,"
she said, "words coloring the space behind."
Ab turned few pages later and saw blanks,
"You're leaving lots of room for things to come?"
"Of course!" Last pic showed BLING airborne, 'fore yank
freed ring. "Some for where to, some for where from.
You want our public brand, but second-best
is setting it ourselves, well-hid from rest."

182.
Two prospects came to Abu's racing mind.
The first: that he in perpetuity
would be biographied for humankind.
The next: that questing had congruity
with what he'd hoped his future years contained.
The beauty of the book itself was moot
unless they planned adventures unconstrained
to earn the words behind such grand tribute.
He gazed into the distance, widened smile
with every passing moment, thinking then
of Gumi's globe, its continents and isles:
not 'whether' laid before them, rather 'when'.
"Why Afro*asiatic*?" boy, perplexed,
asked. Grinning, Stella said, "Well, China's next."

Epilogue

A decade out, I'd wise up to the facts.
It seemed so clear as child back then to think
authoritative adults hadn't acts
deliberately used to kids hoodwink.
Safari guide? Nope. Ranger in cahoots
with markets black that move the plundered goods.
From ring's blood crust I'd later on impute
the bird attacked the thief before in woods.
That camouflaged man had a bandaged hand,
and seemed so used to fighting off attack
he'd clearly frequented the place as planned
in looting circuit vast. Bird set him back
at first until he found chalk weapon's use,
dry powder thunderbolt he slung as Zeus.

Yes, Anton previewed that a bust aglide
would be reflected on his shiny floor.
Yes, Gumi's made-up story justified
the disappearance of ring husband wore.
Yes, artifacts unusual bedecked
their two locations, curios for sale.
No, never had I thought to double check
if immorality lurked 'neath the veil.
No, nor did I think to discount the word
that someone dealt me in a long-con game.
Perhaps, one day I'd also see how blurred
construction of a truth could garner fame.
But, let's not speed. Let's first fire more brick clay
to better build my life's dimorphic way.

Volume Two

Prologue

In youngest children, acts set soil for seeds
of later personalities, which sprout.
One gravitated toward gold-making deeds,
one saw gold light from sun make nature stout.
As flora sprouts up, out, and ever grows
it's hard to tell where single seed begins.
Our paths would intertwine in life's next throes
as one expects from two pea-podded twins.
We'd learned from 'solving' Gumi's errant quest
dependence on ourselves, which, similar,
quelled conflicts calmly. Augment age and stress
to yield divergent psyches, him and her.
I thus present to you the second tome:
of how we grew 'neath wing of powers unknown.

Steve

Chapter 5

1.
Stel looked past *ng'ombe* udder out to hills
so normal, slight in rise and run, and cringed.
Their cultivation, rows turned by hand tills,
reflected age-old ways none dared infringe.
They'd roll, though flat by eye, then disappear
into the shimmer heat horizon held.
They'd never matter now as new frontier:
today she knew she'd be stuck where she dwelled.
Good dwelling in such harshness needed roots,
to draw out soil's nutrients and make
plant food for ruminants' herdbound commutes.
Her roots that day were chopped when didn't wake
her Grandmum, only soul with whom she shared
a lineage. The world left none who cared.

2.
Stel's Grandmum passed in sleep pacifically,
when soul found now-enfeebled shell unfit
and rose alone most honorifically
back to that place from where life must emit.
Stel'd not had family nuclear *per se*,
her father long unknown, her mother gone
before establishing more matron ways.
Stel'd caretaken Grandmum and cows at dawn,
each day of milking milking her of fate
preferred: more exploration in the woods.
Tuberculosis she'd ameliorate
with household labor, helping where she could
so Grandmum could rest self and sharp tongue. Aid's
need passed, day's milk chore felt like masquerade.

3.
Without a public-formed security,
a social welfare system formed itself.
Tradition placed a host in surety
for household servant's debts. Cook, sweep, wash delph,
farm, tend, and such. Earn roof with servitude
let human left from torn-up family
stay off the streets by serving other brood.
To stay alive on scraps as inductee
was better than pure beggardom. There, dough
was hard to get – farms made no millionaires –
so house help slept on dirt floors, earning no
room's privacy. Host homes were simple there.
Her Grandmum's death meant fate would be controlled
by others: she'd as housegirl be enrolled.

4.
This Tanzanian system kept alive –
through bonds and low-skilled household labors long –
the folks whose rotten luck had thus deprived
of chance in social structures to belong.
Stel felt it more akin to trick than treat,
knew Gumi used hers for a scapegoat's load.
And so as Stel coaxed milk from *ng'ombe* teat
she feared she'd be stuck, bent to power unowed
if she were to remain. To overthrow
the system outright couldn't be recourse
at twelve. Perhaps eighteen? Flight drove her, foe
was buy-in to the system here endorsed.
Flight would be hers, she vowed, toward life renowned.
Such heavy burdens children lost have found!

5.
"Hey, Stel!" familiar voice exclaimed from back
behind the bound-stick structure where she sat.
She smiled at joy's inflective. Brainiac
Ab was, a once and future 'ristocrat.
Past glories lost propelled his want to be
a Someone in the future, known for Things
like treasures, once again the bourgeoisie!
It seemed that when he spoke there bubbled springs
hot with ambition, tempting, powerful,
but measured so as not to geyser out
all strength propelling them. The morn hour pulled
a recollection from her mind: devouts
were off in church, at least, the Christian folks.
Again, Abu and Stella were the rogues.

6.
"No church today?" he asked, small frame leaned on
the grass-strapped poles that held few cow-wide roof,
blue sweater accent to the celadon
that healthiest acacia held as proof
short rains had come, however short they'd been.
"I'm glad to see you, but," said Stel, "surprised
you came to see me on a Sunday." "When
folks leave I turn to you. And, I surmised
that something might be wrong when in a dream
you climbed that one tall tree we practiced with
long back. Instead of me, you fell and screamed,
no prank. The sun went out. A guy with scythe
came out to take you." There he stopped mid-phrase,
relieved life counteracted dream's displays.

7.
"Ha ha," she laughed with effort faked. "Still here.
You play dead really well, I was so sad."
"And guilty, if my recollection's clear,"
replied Abu, "you hadn't raked the pad
of grasses up beneath the trunk." "I'd not
thought you'd stretch out to save a simple moth—"
"A dragonfly." "Sure. Still, it's no mascot,
compared to whimsy elephant on cloth
evokes." "We would choose differently. But that
is neither here nor there." "You really dreamed
my undertaker came?" "Yep. You fell flat
once losing grip." "You're not far, with that theme."
"I'm lost. Do you mean something's wrong?" he said.
"No, everything is. I found Grandmum dead."

8.
The moment froze, despite the heat. A haze
precipitated milkily in air,
as if there coexisted yesterdays'
false memories, seen, that tethered Grandmum there.
Expressionless Abu turned eyes toward feet
from off horizon's wishful line, drew in
his shoulders to his body, form downbeat
in recognition of the loss of kin.
"I'm sorry," Ab said, "something cardiac
arrest at night?" "Don't know. Don't care," said Stel
whose melancholy dragged her body slack
relapsing into fear she'd said farewell
to global exploration. "What I need
is some way out of here." Abu agreed.

9.
"You're fearing what I think you're fearing," he
asked quietly to roundabout confirm
the plan they'd make would make an escapee
of Stella. Then she nodded. And he squirmed.
"Can't hide," he said, "they'd find you anywhere."
"Well, everywhere we know is pretty small.
Don't you recall how we became a pair?
Your lusty look at Gumi's globe enthralled,
when thinking hard about how big this lump
of dirt beneath our feet is. Countries change.
It's surely different somewhere." She'd quick jump
at any chance to future disarrange.
They'd orient themselves on endgame view,
while anxious they'd lack way to muddle through.

10.
"Your future staying here's not great," Abu
said weightily, as if a somber thought's
high pressure zone had briskly blown into
his weathered mind, its forecast too, distraught.
Continuing, he said, "The crops are poor.
The rainfall farmers knew for all their lives
is changing now. It's hard to reassure
yourself that you'll continue to survive."
"I've overheard that too," said Stella, "grass
is growing different places for the cows,
or so said Grandmum." Truly, biomass
behaving differently did quick arouse
suspicions of pastoralists that change
in climate turned once-fertile fields' crops strange.

11.
Combustion sounds rolled by behind them, air
compressed in corridors cylindrical
along the distant road. Its disrepair
in Tanzania archetypical
of thing that happened with the heat and rain:
age-old design that cracked with weather's pound
discouraged folks from crossing 'tween domains.
"They're inbound," Abu said while tracing sound.
"The papers said two years ago no MAC
would go that way," referring to the trucks
with hauling power so to match overpacked
grains, produce, livestock, anything a buck
could trade for. "Work in inland districts should
help bring more shillings through our neighborhood."

12.
"Chinese?" asked Stella, head not turned to look
if trucks had calligraphic characters.
"Their words and alphabet's gobbledygook,
that's all I know." The thoroughfare tricked her
young mind: each year its busyness increased,
yet all its bustle bypassed their small 'hood.
The shilling boom Abu referred to greased
another place's palms, did kids no good.
"Construction, Stel. They're here to build. It might
be something we can use for your big plan."
He stopped as if he knew she'd need one night
of dreaming flight on far-off harmattan
beside her fluffy loyal balled-up BLING,
for curiosity to mend her zing.

13.
They spent the oven day at play on parched
and sun-baked ground awaiting rains' return,
though Stella's flowy attitude was starched
in stiffened future mind cocooned concern.
A pattern they'd last year was go to climb
the recollected tree. But it was far,
and they'd learned ways in town to make playtime
a bit more adult, feigning air guitar
and actions never seen when growing up
among the grubs and chlorophyll of farms.
To pass the time they'd toss sticks for the pup,
until BLING tired and fell asleep. The charms
of nature that left gleams in recent eyes
lost glisten under worry's present guise.

14.
Expectedly, the night renewed the verve
that Stella felt toward life as Pioneer.
She'd started the society to curve
away from social expectation's sphere.
Instead of taking tome straight from bookshelves
full of advice from stranger's history
she liked blank page on which they'd anchor selves,
as Abu's pen once doodled boats at sea.
To better plan their future's sketch she made
a pact with Ab, asked him to tell no soul
that Grandmum slept her final nap, afraid
the news would spiral out beyond control.
(It would be her first lesson on effect
of stories crafted so to self-protect.)

15.
At time aligned with moment sky takes tint
of predawn breaking light in monochrome,
Stel saw reflected moon on water, print
indelibly etched on brain's astrodome.
She dreamed her dreaming future somehow passed
into the realm of archaeology,
as flooding fate thrashed life's ship, broke the mast,
left her as hapless shark food, all at sea.
She witnessed artifacts two thousand years
in age get shattered, swept into deluge,
from pots to beads of prayer, sea's new veneer
was refuse history left no refuge.
Her waking came at moment when that breath
of water dreamed insinuated death.

16.
Catastrophe imagined – landslide, flood –
though elementally impressive, did
jumpstart her senses. Staying meant the suds
of servitude. Or she could drop off-grid.
At that time she believed the flood was sign
that if she stayed, became a housegirl, she'd
drown in subservience of life defined
by loss. She'd sooner choose to self-secede
from system. It would take duplicity,
rehearsed and tiny lies, and take her far.
If doubted? Shrug it off! Insistency
gives fantasists a leverage quite bizarre.
Her plan was winding down Grandmum's estate
to buy a one-way ticket out of state.

17.
Thus Stella's spirit lifted slightly by
her notice of home social system's gap:
where in America if parents die
the custody falls to another chap,
in Tanzania laws were not applied
such that a kid with means could stage escape.
In lack of oversight thus lay upside.
She happened on the only way to scrape
together means enough to go, the prize –
still theoretical, in planning phase –
was using littleness as her disguise
to bankroll cash a four-cow sale could raise.
To milk this bovine liquidation meant
inheritance made Stel the one percent.

18.
The distance you could travel on your feet
was limited, like distance crossed by car.
She knew that flight belonged to the elite,
reduced to meaningless the concept 'far'.
So flight was where her flighty sights were set,
to unlock lands dissimilar in ways
so varied in her mind mere silhouettes
did stand where human details ought to lay.
When lightest blue and lime tipped night to dawn
the path to market glowed with daybreak hue,
this slightest girl roped cows, set foot to pawn
all four and thus turn Grandmum's residue
from beef to soulful freedom. Shillings bought
a liberty that circumstance could not.

19.
Her steely-girded scaffolding of nerves
was nearly vibrating upon receipt
of stacks of cash beyond any reserves
she'd seen in life to date. In total, meat
weighed seven hundred kilos, every one
another bill that flipped from red to black.
Bereft of standard upbringing, she'd done
the final needed act to let her pack
her suitcase for planned rocket launching ride.
She knew the market's traders each were marked
as targets by pickpockets alongside,
while little kid could move through unremarked.
That's why she'd hid the plan. She'd trust Abu,
but mission best fit her and BLING, just two.

20.
In ingot-sized block, shilling volume's threat
was possible detection by the thieves.
She didn't want the packs to make *vedette*
of her on market's stage. She placed bill sheaves
in pack that she had stitched four years ago
that tightly fit on BLING's small, sturdy back,
sized rightly so no notes would overflow
and give the robbers signal to attack.
Disguising thus her fortunes as but grains,
the loyal pair made lightly-toed vamoose,
escaping market and unlocking chains
that poverty itself could not have loosed.
Enough was stashed from sale of cows that day
to free her from the housegirl sobriquet.

21.
Across the village, parallel in time,
discussions in the Abu family home
hit ever-graver tone: their paradigm
of farming their prosperity from loam
was being undermined by climate's drought.
Ten huddled in their den, debating what
small livings they could eke from soil without
improvements. Other farms to theirs abut,
to obviate expansion. When the sons
divided up fixed maize-cropped land between
themselves, their buffer'd shrink from tens to ones,
each year of rainfall risking submarine
security of food as stores recede
and hungry mouths maintain caloric greed.

22.
In all-hands conversations Abu shrank
to corner, as was customary since
his birth. In family he was lowest ranked,
forgotten often. Yet his competence
was known—he was the quiet, clever boy,
too young to care to hear opinions from.
In time he'd find some suitable employ
and bring home for the family minor sums.
He neared the age where secondary school
was imminent. The grades on next exam
would over every scorecard overrule
and thus determine where on histogram
his future academically would lay:
with luck, he'd have the rightmost dossier.

23.
The swirling talk was anxious, voiced in haste
by heads perturbed. They'd climate havoc wrought
by once-sequestered carbons now displaced.
Heat scrambled weather. Normalcy turned not.
A hundred thousand duplicates – or more –
had had, were having, or would soon have this
fraught conversation of what heretofore
was land without a mass-indebtedness.
These echoes nationwide came oft from youth,
whose prevalence had reached historic highs.
Their futures bent to hydrocarbons' truth,
and lacked recourse to fix polluted skies.
Such problems of the commons, common are.
But new was their effect felt so afar.

24.
Their talk discharged frustrations, much as boil
produces bubbles freeing water's gas
built up from heat-resisting rangetop coil,
once pushed beyond its standard liquid mass.
Such periodic venting verbal jabs
released held ire before it turned revolt.
They slept, the days progressed, the words left scabs
on walls and ceilings. Would these pressures jolt
enough to movement? Civil war? None knew.
His family's warmth was taken from it by
uncertainties from rainfall through to coup.
Still Ab hoped to his good name gentrify
once more. The fog of sorrow spread in home
turned will ablaze when breathed through anger's *ohm.*

25.
Ensuing days he studied very hard.
His chin stayed low as if desk's gravity
against the greater planet's therein sparred.
He longed to fill his mental cavity
with every ounce of knowledge teachers left
for pupillary gobbling. Next test
would be so broad and weighty in its heft
that every hour was therefore repossessed.
Adventuring with Stella took a pause
and naturally, so she could solo mourn.
He knew when things are heavy she withdraws,
these times when living feels itself outworn.
So Grandmum's secret passing stayed on 'mum'
while Abu paper genius did become.

26.
He had no photographic memory,
built recollection talents through sheer will,
abilities innate in others he
lacked genes to automatically instill.
A brain that thought in shapes, however, was
an ally to his willpower. He would
mnemonically construct what science does
suggest is good technique that often should
augment the memory: he would weave a tale
with clues from schoolbooks he would need to know.
Remembering adventuring prevailed
above rote-memorizing folios.
His study candle burned through thick of night,
in hope success would bring escape in flight.

27.
To punctuate the dryness of the sky,
and sate the shriveled souls on plains who prayed,
a single day of storm swept to supply
the creeks with flows enough to ankle-wade.
Deniers on the radio used this
and recency (a bias humans share)
to say that Man's done naught to shake earth's bliss
with CO_2—the Right's clown doctrinaires.
As rain made waterfall of cloud, Abu
attached his sensed self-worth to mastery
of syllabus his country's retinue
of ministers, professors, teachers see
as critical to education for
the youth, New Tanzania's guarantors.

28.
Curriculum they'd test spanned many parts,
its subjects ranging English, history,
mathematics, civics, science (though not arts)
and writ, of course, in language Swahili.
That language observation cracks divide
between the kids who've resources and not:
one-hundred twenty tongues used nationwide
meant expectation kids were polyglot.
For tribal language used at home was first,
and hopefully Swahili's learned at school
though learning in a second tongue reversed
some students' scores from genius-grade to fool's.
To navigate the language gauntlet took
genetic luck augmenting studied books.

29.
His fam's trek from Aleppo to lands north
where Bosporus splits Asian politic
from Europe's, meant that English was his fourth
known language, if you count writ Arabic.
Advantages were many for the mind
whose training showed that subject, object, verb
are interchangeable. Which order binds
words into meanings couldn't Ab perturb.
In Turkish, every permutation of
these parts of speech grammatically correct,
an object, verb, then subject's not above
a verb, then object, subject. Who'd suspect
agility to modify his speech
begat a cleverness that none could teach?

30.
Linguistic mastery is but one face
of all intelligences body has.
Its kinesthetic form allows for grace
and tonal place births unexpected jazz,
its numbers side perfected by savants
allows near-instantly computed sums,
its introspective side dissects your wants,
and geospatial side makes true maps' rhumbs.
As many kinds of smarts exist as lives
are postulated for a cat to hold,
yet placement test would eight of these deny
and simply ask retell what has been told.
Evaluations sadly thus exclude
assessment of a kid's full aptitude.

31.
Young Abu's brain plasticity was high
matched by his dread and drive from family's chat
about today and futures it implied.
He'd seen hand-lettered poster, dirtied matte
hung low beside headmaster's broken door
so kids could read it. There would be reward
from China's embassy for s/he who scored
the highest on the test: they'd be offshored
and sent to Middle Kingdom on exchange,
overtly building business ties between
the countries. They were wise to prearrange
such opportunity to make serene
their future interactions. Abu'd rest
not one whit till exams showed he was best.

32.
Adventuring as Pioneers once did
thus paused as heavy waves of pressure rolled
onto the Abu-Stella shore. Amid
concern about exams, the boy was holed
up in the post-class classroom. All meanwhile
with hidden treasure Stella felt compelled
to act as normal. Wealth would not restyle
her Tanzanian life. She, rather, held
tight-gripped to secret she could buy one pass
to leave the country's border. Studies took
a seat in traincar clearly lower-class:
that part of her shrank from demands schoolbooks
could make, despite their prize. She shined when floors
gave way to soil and dirt of great outdoors.

33.
The only clouds that circled fortnights hence,
semester creeping toward its apogee,
were mental cirrus strands of penitence
for Stella, partly burdened, part carefree.
And yet the winds persisted, circular
in orbit topping Abu's thund'ring brain,
hell-bent on winning prize to be chauffeur
for kinship's clan to China's pending reign.
Convinced was he of Asian futures nigh
compounded by the pressures there at home
that even if this test went all awry
he'd somehow find a way to China roam.
His vigor bellowed by willpower's blast
grew from need to match future with the past.

Chapter 6

34.
Extreme examination day arrived
posthaste to those whose cramming time felt short,
as time is wont to do to those deprived
its surfeit due deadlines of import.
The questions ranged from relevant to ir-,
with unexpectedness in every flight,
yet Abu moved through each like summiteer,
his sights exclusively on apex height.
Exhaustion followed pencil's blunt. The day
expired at twelve Swahili time, which counts
from six a.m. as zero all the way
to dozen, then resets—norms set amount
of daylight sensically as paradigm
befitting near-equator's telling time.

35.
In classroom tightly monitored nearby
young Stella took the same exam, and knew
her marks were not as low as to deny
her passing near the bottom of the crew.
Although she sought to drop from school and class,
her masquerade that all was right at home
mandated she not stand out from the mass
in ways that could have perfect cover blown.
As twelve-o'clock Swahili time soon struck
and tinny peal from nearby church bell clanged,
the pupils turned in tests then ran amok
around the football grounds: there freedom rang.
Two months they'd be a-waiting the adults
to tally, grade, and collate their results.

36.
Far-off dry season morning when the list
of school marks would be pasted publicly
was quiet, calm, and cool, as if it missed
the memo that today they'd handpick the
one lucky student who'd to Beijing go
to study on behalf of *Bongo*, 'brain'
in word, but also slang here apropos
as 'Tanzania'. They'd be preordained
to future of employment, business, sway
by knowing Chinese, English, Swahili,
a conduit to commerce they'd purvey
across the oceans. Abu saw he'd be
returned to dignity he'd hoped achieve
if given chance to this home lengthy leave.

37.
The throng of kids was riotous when soon
the principal arrived with folder thin
to differentiate the picayune
mark-getters from those bolder-bent to win.
The kids who knew their English poor stood mum
near edges of the teeming crowd, heads low
in worry that their futures would succumb
to farming and their peers would them outgrow.
Most wouldn't make next grade, the up-or-out
of school was tragic testament to place
with resources too scarce to offer route
for all up opportunity's staircase.
Joy goosebumps rose when Stella glimpsed the board:
the *bongo* of Abu had won reward!

38.
The moment that his eyes alighted on
his name atop the list of pupils, he
felt like the caterpillar trading brawn
aground for mothlike wings, cocoon cut free.
Kaleidoscopic glee cascaded 'tween
his brain and eyes and arms and legs and knees,
as if ecstatic waves on trampoline
were bouncing ever higher toward trapeze.
He snapped back into body when embrace
of friendly strength arrested reverie
and brought his feet to earth from hyperspace.
A hug from Stella there wrapped every
fantasia of his future in regret:
they'd separate adventuring duet.

39.
"You did it, Ab, you finally found your launch-
pad out into the wider world! I'm so
excited for you," Stella said, with staunch
companion's words said *ex officio.*
"Hey, thanks," Abu replied, his jelly legs
still searching for their standard steadiness,
"I don't know what I'll do without you." Egg-
returning mission felt like eddy this
quick shift in river flow of time left far
ago. "Don't worry," Stella said, "you'll find
so much to do, so much to see bizarre
you'll not be interested in what's behind."
He looked at her with eyes that disbelieved,
excited as he was, he partly grieved.

40.
He sought to change the subject, harking back
to times that ended recently before
results were posted, wedging open crack
twixt two kids' futures not felt heretofore.
"I saw you made the secondary list.
You think you'll go? There's only so long you
can hide that Grandmum doesn't quite exist."
But Stella played it cool, deferred in lieu
of keeping her surprise in pocket. "I'll
keep going there, I think. I've got some time."
She'd prayed Abu would win, planned out her pile
of cash from selling cows so she'd be primed
to sneak away from fate as housegirl. She'd
self-fund as stowaway if he were freed!

41.
That night at home Abu's new life became
the topic of their conversations. Soon
a well-dressed Chinese man arrived, proclaimed
the benefits the government festoons
upon the winners of this scholarship.
Ab's passport, visa, papers, transport, food
would be arranged with speed. Soon squalor's grip
would loose for would-be scion. Grades renewed
his tenure at the institution there
for up to several years. They wanted him
to reach full fluency. He'd be a rare
resource. He hoped the skill would future limn
in gold: some time ago he promised Stel
he'd someday self past poverty propel.

42.
The emblem of achievement: silver piece
on necklace with emblazoned seals. The first
was classic armored dragon, epic beast
that through Chinese tall tales was interspersed.
It wasn't standalone mid-cloud in flight,
but wrapped 'round second item: waxing moon,
a symbol of the darkness in the light,
the yin to yang in oriental rune.
The third was customized in Latin script:
the letters of its winner's name spelled out,
proclaiming unequivocally who gripped
this medal 'mong authorities held clout.
Recipient was backed by Chinese state
that hoped in commerce they'd remunerate.

43.
Across the village, lone in little home
sat BLING and Stella at the foot of bed,
possessions all arranged in view. The tome
marked *Annals* (where their history's retread)
was the first object in the pile marked 'take'.
She sat, unclasped its buckle, opened to
the illustration of when they did break
into the shop for eggs, took rope in through
the window. "My, how risks evolved
since fearing framing as a petty crook..."
She worried inwardly she might dissolve
if her identity as writ in book
were soaked or burned or lost or marred by ink,
as if were soul and stories chain-tight linked.

44.
There weren't too many things to choose between,
as poverty meant Grandmum owned but cows—
an asset small, but large enough for lien,
both useful for the sale and pulling plow.
The *Annals*, clothes, and satchel fit on BLING,
a couple half-used pencils, one small knife,
and necklace newly-liked were all the things
she chose to pack to start her Chinese life.
For all the while Abu was studying
sly Stel spent scheming, setting up escape.
She planned to shift her story, muddying
her real identity. Concealing cape
of words would let her con her way to fame
or, short of that, at least own life reframe.

45.
Soft "*Hodi!*" at the door caused BLING to **YIp!**
and trot to see who dared disturb their peace.
That gloam-lit silhouette had scholarship
that ought to give his life a newfound lease.
Yet somehow shoulders slouched still. "Hi, Abu!"
exclaimed the girl to her companion, "I'm
surprised you came. I thought today's breakthrough
would be so big you'd spend the whole nighttime
in family celebration." "Well, sure, but
you know I'm never in the limelight long,"
he said, while eyebrows did toward forehead jut
as if to cast resigned surprise at wrong
from kin, one more omission tragedy
from blood who doubt that he'd from rags slip free.

46.
His now-wide eyes as saucers with brows raised
bombarded brain with data girl'd gone nuts.
For taking all possessions out was crazed
unless intending to— "Stel, you've got guts."
His eyeballs swept across the objects strewn
around the room, arranged in piles. "If I
were guessing, I'd say you were off to moon."
"To you, you know I couldn't say goodbye,
let's celebrate both our departures!" Grin
met Abu still-bewildered, grew again
at hatching her grand plan from what coffin
made start as sad affair. "Ab tell me, then,
when China's planned to send us oversea."
And fast explained how she'd be attendee.

47.
It took no more than minutes fingers show
to walk through all that happened while Abu
had buried brain in books to overflow
with knowledge. Stella meanwhile had pursued
her dream to leave: she'd gathered property
and cash together to fund getaway.
She'd practiced lines in case of inquiry,
now memorized. Each story fit in gray,
not black or white. The kerosene-cast light
bathed room in hues that felt like setting sun,
like Stella's Tanzanian pending flight
had ushered local night. "If boring, none
will want to listen. Blandnesses elide.
But I'll need you." "I'm always by your side."

48.
"That's what I'm counting on, because the truth
is that I'm mere hired help from here on out."
"What do you mean?" he asked. "The only proof
that's needed is that Grandmum's gone. No doubt
about it, when a girl is left alone
she'll soon become a servant. You know how
it works." And then it clicked. He said, "You've known
this whole time that I'd win? You sold her cows
to go with me, and never come back home."
She looked him squarely in the eye. She had
instinctive flight ingrained in chromosomes,
and hoped it wouldn't scare off her comrade.
"I think," he said, conspiracy in smile,
"we're going to make the most of your exile."

49.
The conversation with his family took
an insignificant amount of words.
They said her Grandmum passed, then the rulebook
of customs by adults was soon referred
to, and the choice was made that Stella would
accompany Abu as second-class,
a housegirl paying own way where she could.
The Pioneers thus leaped past first impasse
they'd feared: permission. Getting it had freed
their tongues to talk in truer words about
their origins and intentions. To mislead
about such basic things ran risks. The grout
preferred back then was pure veracity
o'er lies' backdrop, plus pertinacity.

50.
Departure morning dust had settled, breeze
confined itself two feet above the ground.
Wafts of last scent of loved acacia trees
would leave the Pioneers with noses drowned.
The inter-village *dala dala* came
on time, because it had no time to come.
For all things fit in place where time's reclaimed
away from watch-hand by mere eyeball's sum.
Abu and Stella boarded, fortunate
to have a seat in van considered treat.
As kids in cars oft packed are orphans, sit
on laps or stand with bodies incomplete
in coming or in going, feet on floor
with torsos stretched beyond the half-closed door.

51.
Their luggage cinched upon the no-rack roof,
in plaid two-handled plastic bags well-known.
For prevalence in region was clear proof
that cheapest way to transport stuff was clone
the one-use bag, quadruple thickness, and
add zipper strong enough to hold in roots.
That morning, as was typical, the land's
tremendous produce sat in sacks, the shoots
extending past bags' twine-rope ties and zips.
The women riding prior to dawn had reaped
plants stuffed in sack to sell. Their roles eclipsed
descriptions statisticians tried to keep
of what is formal work for GDP
and what is household informality.

52.
With infants squeezed by *kangas* to their chests,
those women simultaneously ran
home's childcare work and finances, no rest
from cooking, sowing, picking, selling. Man
held stake in some small sums his wife had brought
through selling extra produce. That would change
when cash migrates to phones—they'd longtime sought
accounting privacy. On seats the range
of household heroines was fairly wide,
in patterned prints with proverbs, pleasures such
as 'savings never go bad' or the guide,
'just bit by bit will fill the measure'. Crutch
for nation was their dedication, an
adhesive force as fierce as tie to clan.

53.
So Abu, Stella, and her puppy BLING
sat butt-to-butt with all these women who
brought business to the market. Life's upswing
was driving off into emergent blue,
away from home where Gumi's mystery
was faked, where fears were overcome, where speech
was known, toward lands with faceless history.
He'd gone for studies' riches, she to reach
a place where expectations' shackles fall.
Each window peek showed advertisers' paint
in blurring colors, roadside sprawl, strip malls.
Their skipping minds danced freely, no constraint
in dollar, word, or warrant barred them from
their rags-to-riches tale: to feast, from crumb.

54.
Before they'd left, in accented decree
their light-skinned Chinese sponsor clarified
they'd be received by colleague appointee
in town. He said the air'd be rarefied
in airplane, that they'd best drink water so
they not dehydrate, that they'd sit eight hours,
and that the massive noise was apropos
of engines big enough to superpower
a hunk of metal through the sky. *How odd,*
Stel thought, not having ever seen a plane.
Its easy glide through air would leave her awed,
not knowing pressure can great lift attain.
Word blast from omnipresent stereo
engendered new concern: "Ab, where we go

55.
no one will understand us." Bass wave din
shook *dala dala. Bongo* beats matched spat
Swahinglish, lyrics powered by old men's sin.
Stel grasped accustomed tongue. "Guess our chitchat
can be a secret code, then," he replied,
"for times we need to talk so no one hears.
Outsiderness in this case coincides
with opportunity: words for our ears
are ours alone. So when we need it we'll
ongea Kiswahili, hakuna
matata. Don't you think it adds a thrill?
It's fun. We'll learn. And soon we'll attune a
quick ear to how they speak. Chinese I'm sure
is learnable." (That hope proved premature.)

56.
The throughway hustle densified each mile,
with bustling auto shops, food stands, and bars.
White-collar signs and other versatile
small *biashara* plugged to passing cars.
Dar es Salaam grew up as port of call
for traders from the Middle East and from
much further, even: China did befall
its shores before da Gama rounded thumb
of Cape Point in South Africa. Schoolbooks
forget Zheng He, the Admiral, lived in
the fifteenth century and overtook
the seas. Hc could have conquered. But fleet thinned
when next Ming emperor'd abominate
non-Chinese worlds, and closed his border gates.

57.
The architecture altered, too, as they
steered deeper into city sprawl. Stel knew
that Muslims lived near coast not faraway,
but less what they would look like. Their debut
was curvature in building tops, designs
whose intricate geometry was matched
where sousing lustrous hues bucked anodyne
whitewash of plastered concrete. Gone were thatched
plant roofs, and huts of well-planned mud caked dry.
Though Zheng He was himself a Muslim, he
was not the culture conduit implied
by his arrival first. No, Dar's *esprit*
was clearly from the Middle East. It mixed
the tongues of peoples it sprung up betwixt.

58.
Swahili as a language came about
when local Bantu language family
put sprinkled nouns from Arabic throughout
its lexicon. They fit uncannily
by making simply one new class of nouns
for ported words. It matched in syntax and
in structure what the Bantu spoke. Scale down
the breadth of words a speaker need command
to few, with fewer synonyms—*voilà!*
A language meant for trade, and quick to learn
emerged. And thus those following Allah
could come and talk and trade, go and return.
Their commerce spread the language nationwide,
and converse, threaded patchwork distant tribes.

59.
But snapping back to scene where Stella sat,
smooshed sideways, shoulders sloped, the sites she saw
were sadly sights themselves, some streets showed scat
on surface, sewage systems never drawn.
Sans sanitation, public people pooped
(as privately as possible), perceived
as practice permanent, for funding drooped
for pipes and pumps to problems there relieve.
Installing infrastructure there involved
injunctions to displace inhabitants,
insolvent individuals. Unsolved
was squatters' illegality. Build fence
between the poorest and the richest, and
the wealthy slept in peace in walled dreamland.

60.
Their forward progress slowed as van began
to stop twice each kilometer, then yield
to standstill traffic. Hawkers' walks outran
them. Slower snapshots of the streets revealed
a section of the population who
sold stacks of goods identically alike:
bananas, peanuts, crackers, gum to chew.
They'd wait to sense some eye contact, then strike
at passenger in transit van, their look
as if your purchase were to give them life
and otherwise they'd starve. At first it shook
young Stella, who'd seen less-grave urban strife.
She felt a desperation in the gaze
not seen in eyes in homeland's lands of maize.

61.
"It's tough to see, Abu." "It's more than what
we're used to, yeah." His rationality
cut in with explanations: "Better hut
in village than live here. House gals get tea,
food and a floor for sleep. *Bongo* maintains
a second personality it hides.
With one it's farms, and fates fall with the rains.
With one it's towns, and what you can provide
with self-made jobs." Described part, though not whole
of how the migratory tides deprived
folks fighting for esteemed – yet lowest – role
that commerce could provide. Yet they survived,
packed in, found labors, built communities
contrasting 'gainst witnessed disunity.

62.
There lay before her new phenomenon:
expanse of color corn silk left to dry,
its texture grainy. Stel's jaw dropped upon
the sight it bordered: waves all alkali
in litmus spectrum. Textbooks gave reprieve
from disbelief. She'd heard of oceans' girth,
in dream alone could ever have conceived
of space that large not filled with dirt and earth.
Perhaps as contrast to depravities
she'd witnessed on the journey into Dar,
this view for Stel held striking gravity.
Her lifetime she'd spent hauling water far
from public tap to home, trudged can by can.
Her muscles twitched as eyes the water scanned.

63.
Its vastness frightened, weight mayhaps as large
as anything existing ever, she
believed. That sight caused daydream to discharge,
a recollection of the nightmare sea
that flooded mind and land some months ago.
Their van stopped finally not far from the coast,
She looked away from water's dying glow.
Outside the door stood uniformed man, host,
the Chinese emissary they'd expect.
He welcomed them into the beach hotel.
He whisked them past front desk, "You are both checked
in, need not worry. Flight tomorrow." Smell
delectable passed. "That's bizarre and new,"
Stel said. Man smiled, "It's Muslim barbecue!"

64.
Their bags were put in one of many rooms,
identified by number on the door.
From catacomblike corridors entombed,
they thrilled at thought of slipping off to shore.
Their minds were full and stomachs empty, so
their noses guided them next door to beach.
With drop of sun, mere charcoal afterglow
alight in half-drum barbecues cast peach
and orange light around. Some kerosene
in torches on the tables stayed the night.
They wondered how their lives had quarantined
them from these salty, spicy odors' bite.
The saffron, cumin, cinnamon, and cloves
of rich *pilau* blew gently off the stoves.

65.
The food was wondrous in its novelty,
but vista wholly mammoth stole the show.
The twilight navy struck colossally,
its undulating waves aped strokes Van Gogh.
"I..." Stella started saying, then she stopped,
stood mesmerized by how its finish flowed
like frothing monsoon puddles, each crest topped
with hint of whiteness right when it explodes.
Abu looked out upon the ocean as
a sailor unperturbed by what's beyond.
"I wonder," she restarted, "what it has
inside." His pointing finger did respond,
directed at the smoking skewered fish.
But Stella sought an answer past their dish.

66.
All dreams that night were colored by that blue.
Abu's imagined him in flight among
the stars, past home, past Dar, past Timbuktu,
revitalized the further he was flung.
The unfamiliarity of sleep
in place that wasn't Stella's childhood home
left drops of anxiousness that must have seeped
into her cerebellum after gloam,
for while adream she had that nightmare of
an unknown but important world interred
by sidelong rushing waters, skies above
all clear of rainclouds. Faces, objects blurred
when BLING nudged Stella, sensing something sour,
and woke her. Nightmares lengthened nighttime's hours.

Chapter 7

67.
The airport portal's passport pass-checks proved
both formal and forgettable. The form
of long-hall building Stella thought improved
upon the smallish structures she'd thought norm.
Aluminum machines used magic sight
to peer into their bags and look for knives.
Abu scanned signs of what they would indict
an owner for, if found. "They're saving lives,
they say, but frankly I don't know who'd bring
a *panga* on a journey overseas."
At jetway tunnel's end he glimpsed the wing
and wondered how its metal wove through breeze
to lift behemoth tube to cloudlike height
and feign to global villages unite.

68.
To feign a federation's easy through
mere economic globalism. Trade
brought cheap-bought goods to many. Gains could glue
consumers' interest. Under that charade
were nation-states each striving for more gold,
like Stel'd seen forest plants wage ruthless fight:
each root, vine throttled neighbors so to hold
place closer to scarce showered golden light.
In that kind spirit richer countries loan
persuasively to poorer ones, enmesh
debts deep in their power structures. From such throne
they bide time till demanding pound of flesh.
It's feature much as flaw, this global theft
that never stopped when colonizers left.

69.
The Chinese toiled not only in the veldt
of Tanzania—they worked routes worldwide:
from railroads laid connecting Bible Belt
to California, Rockies' peaks swirled by
a curving vertebrae of wood and steel;
from soccer stadiums and highways for
transporting ore to port past jungle's seal.
And yet those efforts paled compared to corps
reserved for infrastructure back at home.
They'd built a dam beyond the size that eyes
on standard low-cloud day could see. Syndrome
of water shortage in the north gave rise
to project to reshape a watershed,
diverting thousand miles of river's thread.

70.
Fermenting in official files were maps,
sketched blueprints filled with figures, sums, and maths,
geology's formations, heights, and gaps
traced clearly. Bold lines laid down *pro tem* paths
where ruined roads would need to reconnect,
where rural towns would swell from villages,
where settlements they lacked time to protect
would be submerged in lakebed. Tillages
of centuries would be retired, for the
top mandate from the government was 'grow',
and full employment bought stability.
So rural ways would not such progress slow.
A farming basin, million people strong
sat in the site where megadam belonged.

71.
Potential plan was locked in secret, none
were authorized to speak about it yet.
The Party could not risk that mayhem stun
the populace with premature gazette
before the plans for relocation set.
A dressing 'round the window frame would cast
an advantageous light on mortal threat
to livelihoods: recompensation passed
the incomes that they'd earn as farmers. And
the big power-thirsty cities might be slaked
with water flow's electrons. High demand
for real estate on newly-crafted lake
would surely sell for pretty pennies. Wealth
as land use shifts could be accrued by stealth.

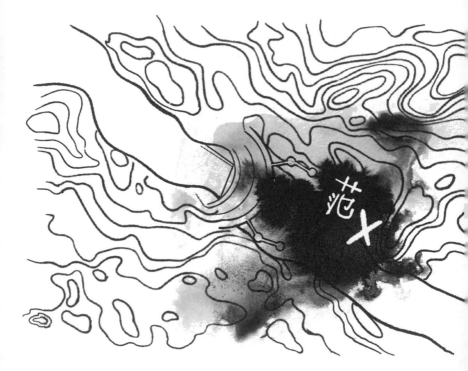

72.
But this was not yet relevant for BLING
or Stella or Abu, who had escaped
their unloved nests 'neath Tanzania's wing.
They knew not how they'd soon be shaped
by land and custom, tongue and culture, food,
and closeness to a billion comrades whose
decisions inappropriately viewed
without the local context could confuse.
As magic airplane coursed its airy track,
transporting three small bodies – one with fur –
toward hearts of Middle Kingdom, utter lack
of knowledge fate would make them saboteurs
was useful to preserve naïveté
lest Party hastily believe them prey.

73.
At lucky eight past eight their plane flown flew
through airspace of a basin's ancient town
inhabited since people first subdued
the forest's greens to farmland's fecund brown.
Egalitarian in many ways,
its households lent support past garden fence,
embodying ideals from hardship days
when Mao thought communism common sense.
Now motivated by their own fields' take,
they'd taken best Zedong and best Xiaoping,
the former lauding acts for country's sake,
the latter letting people purchase things.
This town named Fan would soon take center seat
as X on blueprint's super-secret sheet.

74.
Flown night wore on, the trio lulled to sleep
in whirring airborne chilled metallic womb—
with BLING curled patiently into a heap
beneath the seat in front where legs had room.
A noodle breakfast came with cabin's light,
set bright when stewardesses decided dawn
in local time was near enough that rite
of food to welcome day began. The yawns
took over every aisle. "Spaghetti's new
for mornings," Stel said, leaned in for a taste,
regretted it. Foreign *bienvenue*
would be improved if breakfast were replaced.
The window took her focus from the food,
the puzzle being how the sky was hued.

75.
Sky felt like purgatory, piloted.
Air's in-betweenness straddled beige and oat.
Dark rain seemed imminent, yet quiet did
persist from clouds. She'd learn that sulfur's mote
tinged skies from exurbs' growing industry.
The plane touched down. Her body full of dreams
felt blessed nigh to the point of nimbus. She
strode tightrope line between maintaining schemed
identity and ecstasy. Toes' tread
through jetway tunnel onto surer land,
earned immigration, customs go-ahead.
Arrived! Sharp brain put own fate back in hand.
Soles touching ground of foreign soil in
the Middle Kingdom loosed adrenaline.

76.
Their escort from the baggage claim was man
who held a sign with two kids' names in script
they recognized. Inscrutable deadpan
mismatched the courtesies his mouth did lip.
Adventurers made way to taxicab.
The speech exchanged between the two front seats
was fluid such that parsed-out words weren't grabbed
by Abu's brain. The words' singsong tones, beats,
were mesmerizing as pentameter.
From backseat Stella frowned, she said, "I think
they're in an argument." "I can't infer
if that's the case or, if—" their guide glanced, winked,
and smiled as if Abu's truncated guess
was truth: their high pitch hadn't meant aggress.

77.
As first impressions go, arrival at
their home was unremarkable. Jet lag
formidable had numbed their senses flat
and made once-steady vision zig and zag.
They made their way through courtesies, and learned
that hosts were wife and husband, girl and dog.
Their spaciness meant meeting soon adjourned
so they could sleep away their mental fog.
As Stella and Abu retired to bed
they split by gender, Abu on his own
and Stella toward a bunk above her head!
She'd never seen two beds stacked. Upper throne
was hers at roommate Ai's direction. Sleep
came instantly without the mildest peep.

78.
A morning passed with foreigners asleep
in Chinese household, time zones partly crossed.
A few days of adjustment and they'd keep
same time as locals. Day one, though, was lost.
They met the head of house, a Party man
named Long for 'dragon', common strong male name.
He had a job that had to do with plans,
constructing things. They found they overcame
such difficulties found when mother tongue
mismatches one another's: English brought
some useful commonality among
them. Abu hoped he'd turn to polyglot,
be first to translate nuanced thought and need.
Till then, they had one tongue from which to lead.

79.
At breakfast table bowls were full of milk,
and Stella was the first one out to try.
She smiled at Ai and sipped the warm white silk,
its sweetness and the size of spoon surprised.
"My spoon's too big!" As jester, she stretched arms
to max, as long as elephantine tusk.
Ai laughed a little, understanding. Harm's
impossible with clown-like gestures. Rusk,
plain bread, or biscuit was more common back
at home to go with morning *chai*. Stel's spoon
found different hidden treasure: egg, unpacked,
but still with hardened yolk, no innards strewn.
Defiance of experiences past
made time elongate in this breaking fast.

80.
Abu came out and altogether three
went off to school. It wasn't lengthy walk
but each sight mesmerized the escapees
from Tanzania. Sidewalk breakfasts hawked,
and scooters zipped through bike and highway lanes,
so numerous that Stella turned and said,
"These roads the last five minutes have contained
more people than I've ever met." Steam fled
from tiny restaurants with lāmiàn bowls
set out atop mold plastic furniture.
An aproned woman filling soups cajoled
them *sit and eat* she gestured; spurned, spit her
small peace upon the sidewalk. Ai waved off
concern that they'd offended: "Old man cough."

81.
Ai's English wasn't perfect, but was good
enough. Augmented with some mild charades,
it let most simple thoughts be understood.
They came upon the school, saw barricades
in front with guardhouse stopping entrants to
ensure they had credentials well in line.
Beyond security was gent sent who
had perfect ivory tower look refined.
His eighties wireframe spectacles stood front
on nose, his tweed-patch coat sought restitched hem,
his slacks fine cloth showed they'd a purpose: blunt
all doubts his institution was a gem.
"I am Headmaster Yan. Huānyíng. I've heard
we're privileged to have you here, transferred."

82.
Abu replied, "Your accent's British, sir,
and sounds like what I've heard on BBC.
I hope I'll form the same," words skittish, per
direct address from principal. "I see
your school is very nice. I'm lucky to
have such a chance. I thank your country much
for bringing me. I mean, I never flew
before. It's all so new." "We're proud of such
a program, priv'leges are ours. We here
encourage students to make foreign friends,
for whom we save slots in the mix. Sincere
commitment to a global view contends
we bring the brightest here, to China's heart
to share with their young, local counterparts."

83.
With that, the eloquent Headmaster Yan
brushed students through the double door, its arch
held fluid writing in a foreign pen
whose ink flowed thick in parts, in others parched
into thin line's suggestion. Gist unknown,
it still pleased Stella with its comely form.
Ensuing classes were discrete, but thrown
into the snowglobe memory's ongoing storm
of swirled impressions when there's far too much
to take in and describe. As newborns, each
phenomenon could drown their eyes, could clutch
and puzzle-freeze their mind. Bell's day-end screech
brought quartet to the courtyard for repose
and diagnosis of day's cons and pros.

84.
"The floors are super shiny," Stella said.
"The blackboards here are white," piped in Abu.
"The classrooms all have lights set overhead."
"The windows all have glass. I like Chengdu."
Then Ai perked up at hearing hometown's name,
and pointed circularly 'round the yard,
then looked back at the three, thumbs-up, exclaimed,
"The best!" BLING **Yɪᴘᴘᴇᴅ!** agreement. Something marred
a purely positive review, though. Stel
said, "All through lunch I caught kids pointing at
me, laughing, like they'd some mean girls' cartel."
Abu, whose eyes had scanned all day for that
mum type of ostracizing, said, "I saw
nobody making me cause for guffaw."

85.
"But seeing isn't everything, Abu.
I knew it, felt it, noticed noticing."
"You sense things, sure. I'd rather trust my view—
it's more objective." "Is it? Won't miss things
when mind's elsewhere?" "I'll try. I'll look around
tomorrow," offering some mild support.
A group of older boys passed, glanced at hound,
then Stella, Ai. Howls burst out like bloodsport
as they began to point and laugh at clique
that sat there having done naught to provoke.
Stel boiled: she'd hate the teasing and the tricks
of social standing jockeying till croaked.
Would she be victim of their senseless taunt
till placating with offerings they'd want?

86.
The instigator'd been aggrandized by
cruel act overt. Stel hoped that she could smash
that hierarchy by slicing size of guy.
She'd keep lookout for stealthy ways to trash
him. Scene mismatched high standards set in class.
This partial boarding school had English used
in half its courses, much of China's brass
sent kids there. Still, elite browbeating bruised
as had in Tanzania. Last time she
had felt it, she'd sat on a log and found
her puppy BLING, recovered her *esprit*
adventuring in forests that surround
home *shamba*. Withdrawal to her private place
might revive ego bully had debased.

87.
Ai sat as witness, yet lacked words to share
to make it better. So she stood to leave,
escort them home. The sidewalk thoroughfare
was packed, like earlier. Sad Stella breathed
in deeply, trying to move past the thought
of further teasing. Breath was her mistake:
she coughed it out, remaining overwrought,
unaided by the air's oddly opaque
gray quality. "Is rain coming tonight?"
She asked of Ai. Ai shook her head, confused.
Continued Stella, "Why's it gray, then?" Height
of clouds – or fog, or smog, or something – cruised
at just four meters overhead, the signs
across the broad-laned street held obscured lines.

88.
"It gray?" asked Ai, incomprehension sheer.
"Yes, gray, the sky here's different. Lower, thick."
Ai's look showed blankness toward the tension clear
to Stella. "Color," added Ab, who flicked
a finger toward the sky, "no good." That seemed
to turn Ai's mental cogs, loose darting eyes
in search of fitting words. Mind clearly teemed.
Mouth opened twice, formed no words in two tries.
Stel felt a pang of pity, waved point off
to Ai. Returned glance of relief showed sign
was mercifully received. Ab's ill-timed cough
kept topic live, uncomfortably. "No, fine,"
Ai finally said, "air normal good," phrase tone
as if to sprout what someone else had sown.

89.
"We've walked a longer way, I think," Abu
said after half an hour had passed. They turned
an umpteenth corner, gasped. There, Xanadu
rose up before them: four-tiered tower wormed
its way into the sky 'cross river's flow.
The corners of its shingled roofs curved up,
its arches carved as if whole studio
connived to etch the wood with verve. "My pup
would love to walk here," Stella said, in awe,
as eyes took in surrounding bamboo groves.
"The Jinjiang River," Ai explained. Flies gnawed
at limbs exposed. It didn't matter. Trove
of urban nature stood nearby! Stel knew
this park would civilize days in Chengdu.

90.
They savored for some minutes sculpted view,
and learned the park's name 'Wangjiang' meant 'view
  toward
the river', noting Ai's dad's name too used
the character for 'river', jiāng. Reward
for long day warred was dinner. Family
eponymously styled meal, shared each dish.
Its aromatic spice uncannily
oozed through all rooms. "We celebrate with fish,"
said Long, the father, mentioning that luck
was likelier to come to those who feast
on fish on Lunar New Year. He'd instruct
the kids on how their chopsticks could carve beast
that lay on platter, flesh finely preserved
through death that severed soul before 'twas served.

91.
"I've only had one fish before," said Stel,
who liked the taste but hassled with the bones,
"and that was recently." Her undersell
of pleasure with the food was pure homegrown
proclivity to mildness. Serving plates
lived in the table's center, one with rice,
one vegetable, enough to satiate
the mouths that dined. "Tomorrow will be Twice-
cooked Pork," the mother shared. The dad waxed on
about the local lore on eating meats.
The kids felt their brains overtaxed. Upon
conclusion of the meal they moved toward sheets,
to fix the snowglobe's drifting images
as memories under REM's night diligence.

92.
On way to school next day, they chatted more.
Ai shared how schedule of the day would shift,
from eight to ten they'd brave Chinese, the core
class underlying scholarship year gift.
"I like with other country people friends,"
said Ai, "school good with this. It have like you,
Nigeria, and Guinea." Dividends,
Stel later learned, were oil well IOUs,
"And Congo, Zim, and Mozambique." There, ore
and timber were *raison d'être* for loans.
"Their kids have been here longer?" "Yes." Offshored
extracted natural treasures formed the bones
of Chinese economic beast: a frame
for them, while crossbones left export states maimed.

93.
The second day of gleaming school would hurt,
its shimmer overshadowed by a stone.
For 'stone' was how their teacher's name converts
to English from the 'Shi' with rising tone.
From moment that they sat in class, no word
of English would be said. They'd need to learn
in Chinese. From her body, they inferred
some minor guidance. That class overturned
their every notion of what classrooms were:
to sit there, grilled by tutor on a book
was more intense than back home, where deferred
engagement's silence was quite widely brooked.
They'd need to think as fast as when outdoors
when faced with crises journeying outpours.

94.
"I don't know if I want to study like
you did for months for your exams," said Stel
at lunch when they took rice and rest. "A tyke
knows so much more than we do." "We're compelled,"
Abu replied, "to catch up. Now we're last."
"Of course we're last. We just arrived," she sighed,
recalling how she'd donned cloak of outcast
when Grandmum died, then switched it and shanghaied
Abu's rewarded trip. "I'm here because
it isn't home, but not because I want
to be top student. Accolades and buzz
are up to you." Then silence set détente.
Ai came and sat, arriving late. One peek
at face showed she'd need to their glee upkeep.

95.
The second night was different from the first.
Once finishing their dinner, all retired
to study in their bedrooms, none coerced
by parents. Textbooks in which they'd be mired
were long and hefty, mostly in Chinese,
its square-block prints intimidating on
the page. Their dictionary lacked the ease
of those of alphabetic tongues: now gone
were simple days of finding stuff in books.
Instead they had to look at tone and sound,
then find the section where the shapes and looks
identically matched character they'd found.
Stel first had problems finding the right 'ji'
from hundred-something possibilities.

96.
The third day came at even faster pace,
with expectations ratcheting by day.
Assignments nearly needed hyperspace
to lengthen doing time. To disobey
a deadline was to cause yet greater strife.
The fourth day passed, then fifth, then weekend loomed.
Stel felt like soldier marching to the fife,
repeat exhausting motions self subsumed.
Her solace sought in countryside, she put
keen BLING on leash and went to Wangjiang Park.
She'd left at dawn, to not be underfoot
at home and force an escort. There, hallmark
of Chinese public spaces first she viewed:
a hundred elder folks in dancing mood.

97.
The light was soft, no colors yet unveiled.
Its ambiguity made silhouettes
of hundred figures, rearmost ranks dovetailed
into the fog, as if wood statuettes.
A tonic fresh, damp, cool, mild zephyr blew
as if from where their limbs impacted air,
colliding in slow motion jiu-jitsu
in time whose silent signature was shared.
Their movements mimicked those of fluid koi,
whose golden scales brought beauty to the slow
deliberation muscles each employed
to sync in elegant adagio.
Calm humors governed how they stretched and spun
as if a hive mind moved each form as one.

98.
Demonstrably in synchronicity
with tempo of environment and trees,
the figures' acts cured all toxicity
pollution's urban reek had brought in breeze.
To watch rehearsed, premeditated moves
conducted amid silence ushered awe:
the ardent daily practice of those who've
selected dedication showed grandmas
could still produce a dance worth audience.
A sound that Stella knew instinctively
arose above what often smoggy, dense,
and pressing air did squelch: distinctively
contrasting, tweet and call and song and chirp
of birds did city audio usurp.

99.
It helped, as well, to perk up BLING, who'd been
somewhat at odds with Ai's dog Huhu, 'fox',
huge Chow whose fluff popped inches off its skin,
of disposition wholly orthodox.
Hu picked up BLING sometimes at home like log,
would fetch then drop him in the toy pile throng.
At least familiar sound of birdcalls jogged
BLING's memory back to places he belonged.
He heard them well, too, Stella thought. His ears
kept getting bigger, like old men she knew
at home whose lobes had grown throughout the years
and stretched as Masai jewelry taxed tissue.
They watched atop a round tomb, stone endowed
with script homage to poetess Xue Tao.

100.
The name struck Stel as more familiar than
majority of Chinese words she'd heard.
She couldn't place it. Pictures of sampans
(which non-historians often misword
as 'junks', inaccurate because they fly
but single sail that's striated, have oars
at aft, while junks sail three to catch the sky
as elevated sterns cut waves, perforce)
adorned the nearby decorations, scrolls
that told of times when Taoism was born,
when message moved by riverboat's pushed poles,
when Journey West, Red Chambers' Dreams tales warned
of what were acts of virtue and of vice,
through folklore's pedagogical advice.

101.
She came upon a scrap of paper left
by student of some sort, with characters
that copied poem on wall, handwriting deft,
then translated to English. There, picked were
four stanzas, short in word but long in view.
Befuddled for a sec while reading it,
Stel marveled how line's sturdy curlicue
through top-to-bottom blocked squares could transmit
a complex scene beyond what pencil'd tipped.
Dew-rinsed (it read) *their pure notes carry far.*
Windblown: as dry... (the paper there was ripped)
and fasting leaves are blown. Her own memoir
of dryness in savanna coursed through mind,
and with these mental images entwined.

102.
Chirr after chirr, as if unison.
But each (the poem continued) *perches on*
its one branch, all alone. This croon is one
that moves when million cries converge at dawn
from insects 'round the world, just here as there.
"Cicada" was its title. Stella'd not
yet come across in China tokens shared
between this culture and her life. Poem's plot
exalting nature favorably compared
to week's experience. She checked the date
and disbelieved translation. Sign declared
that Xue Tao lived right there in Sichuan state
twelve hundred years ago. Foundation for
ennobling nature dwelled in culture's core.

103.
The figures still in tai chi's trance, full sun
now muscled through the morn's obscuring clouds.
With Stel's associative mind overdone,
she walked back home through routine civic crowds.
Back at the flat she found Abu and Ai
at breakfast with sweet milk and honey soup.
Abu explained today he'd fortify
his Chinese studies so as to recoup
the time he lost to sleep this week. "Can you
tell me some more," Stel asked of Ai, "about
this Xue Tao person?" Oddball impromptu
request piqued Ai's mom's interest, who walked out
to get their dishes, then said, "I've her book
for you, some day." Stel knew not she'd get hooked.

Chapter 8

104.
Hit pause on Chengdu narrative one sec,
return to rural story of town Fan
in Sichuan's river valleys. There, redneck
provincial farmers lived, no better than
some hundred years ago—so urban lie
would lead naïve believe. Its cause was wealth.
Self-centered cities gradually untied
from rural lived reality and health.
Though living largely like they had in past,
the family Ye was hardly misinformed.
They talked about the radio, amassed
the facts on how their nation had reformed,
and shouldered on their shoulders burdens to
produce the Chinese city-dwellers' food.

105.
Clan Ye was small, though hadn't started so.
The years eroded what were once great tracts
dynastically their ancestors' chateau-
equivalent that, filled with artifacts,
was jewel-like in the valley. Over time
with each successive generation, land
was split among the sons, a paradigm
that smaller populations could withstand.
Aft' eighteenth century that system failed,
Qing emperor de-throned successive coups
for power. Meanwhile beneath the peasants ailed,
decades' upheavals endlessly renewed.
We zoom in now to Shushu, uncle who
together with Aunt Ayi tried make do.

106.
"This season's rapeseed harvest's looking good,
I think we'll make fair money from the oil,"
he said one night, "the crops have well withstood
the floods that suffocated others' soil."
Then Ayi nodded, serving him more rice.
The nod came slow, heart melancholy since
their son had left, by nearby town enticed.
She saw it not as act of dissidence,
but rather chase of opportunities
that salaried employment offered. His
departure had spurred clear disunity
among his parents, fueled the fire. "What is
important," she replied, "is that we sell
the harvest quickly, no one can foretell

107.
what's going to happen when those plans come true."
He shook his head, "You're listening too much
to village rumors' groundless ballyhoo.
You have no proof that anyone will touch
our valley. Things have changed. This twenty-first
new century has finally brought some peace
to life. We've markets, no more empty purse
to wrestle with. The famines and caprice
of government last century are gone."
He knew she spoke of gossip that town Fan
was marked alongside neighbors in plans drawn
for demolition. Party business. Man
saw little indication hearsay was
more true than speculative village buzz.

108.
But Ayi wasn't feeling passive, "I
heard we're the target from Lao Lin today.
Her son-in-law, you know, electrified
the hills in Anhui province. Underway
are plans for projects similar out west.
That no one knows the details simply means
it's normal Party politics. Protests
would break out if we knew we're smithereens."
As revolutionary long ago,
then victim of vicissitudes of ill-
informed, dogmatic government, Shu's foe
was instability. The Party filled
strife-quelling role now. He'd faith it would act
to move the country forward, not ransack.

109.
"Remember sixties' scarcities?" he, mad,
said, "stockpile cabbage every winter 'fore
the frost, and eat it boiled? Every comrade
did, choiceless in the sacrifice, uproar
curbed by policing neighbors. Ample food
was grown by the cooperatives, and 'sold' –
or so the branding went to best delude –
to distant fat officials, who controlled
rich stockpiles. We starved, they ate. Then we'd have
to melt our iron down in garden smelt,
give tithe in low-grade, useless steel. What gaffe!
And yet since 1990 we've all felt
such massive progress. Things have changed. It's not
our government today that hatches plots."

110.
He picked a piece of Kung Pao chicken out
of their shared dish upon the tabletop
and as he chewed more creases coursed throughout
his face, traumatic memories of sharecrop-
ping days removing liveliness. "Although
we've witnessed since things that should be outlawed,
corruption, graft and such, the top's outgrown
overt power grabs that launched mini jihads
to crush our country's culture. We've moved past
false Revolution and the Great Leap's wrongs."
Pre-hardship days, his faith in state had passed
as pleasing to her, patriot 'mong throngs
of lookers-on whose kowtow words were cheap.
"I worry now," she said, "you're blind, asleep."

111.
Zoom out from Fan and back in to Chengdu,
where Stel sought early bedtime. Morning thrill
had left a pleasant, woke-mind residue
of harmony with nature 'midst the mill
of city life. The scene had dreams precooked,
prepared for exploration when brainwaves
slowed down to better study overlooked
phenomena unconscious deigns to save.
Unbridled newness in her universe
exhausted, overpowered vague intrigue
of weekend exploration. Soon sleep's nurse
would put the healing salve on week's fatigue,
abet left cortisol's anxiety,
flush open mind to life's variety.

112.
Or so she wished. In next room minds burned bright,
both focused on the smashing of some rules
prescribed in books into brains' bits and bytes
as mandated in homework from the school.
Abu zoomed in on Chinese dinner fare,
first lesson in their textbook: hot and sour
soup. *That's inane,* he thought, *what savoir faire*
does book expect from us in supper hour?
Meals could be key... Rules mesmerizingly
constructed, he found growing appetite
for grammar. What book said were wise strings he
would copy dutifully, in hope it might
cement word-order rules inside his head.
His prof considered rote recall not dead.

113.
With focus more rehearsed, Ai sat right next
to Abu at the desk. She worked on math.
Though doing well by grade, its use perplexed
her. She perceived it part of trodden path
that China used to force-rank students, so
the need for high performance was quite clear.
She feared she might have already plateaued,
which shook the falsity that engineer
was her desired life track, a lie she kept
in recognition she'd need to support
her parents as they aged. That broad precept
the public swallowed easily. Purport
to go in risk's direction, and you play
a gamble with your kin's halcyon days.

114.
"Wǒ xiǎng hē yī wǎn suānlàtāng," Ab asked
that night at dinner, poorly. Eyebrows raised.
They passed the spiced soup as requested, grasped
his rudeness as of language learning phase.
"Dāngrán," said Long, then "hǎohǎor xuéxí,"
encouraging his guest to study hard.
He pleasured in host's purvey – serving tea –
but on each pour against full cup would guard.
In switch to English, Stella asked, "I saw
you fill each cup just two-thirds full then pause."
He twinkled, "Our tradition says it's flawed
to top it up." "But why?" Stel asked. "Because
it tells your guest that you'd like them to leave."
That logic, Stella thought, *was misconceived.*

115.
They sipped and supped. Ai's cup soon nearly ran
completely dry. She left one dime-sized drop
in base of porcelain. Like serviceman
her father poured from pot refill near top.
Ai's index and her middle finger tapped
the table absentmindedly. "I'm used
to *chai* with breakfast," Stella then recapped,
"with milk and spice and sugar." Long, bemused,
said, "Sounds like something England left behind."
Imperials had quite traumatically
scarred both their states, in different time and kind.
Ab irked naïvely and dramatically
his hosts by broaching smold'ring theme that blows
the even-tempered into furies' throes:

116.
"Did China have a conqueror?" he posed,
eyes innocently scanning 'round the room.
Wide pupils glimpsed looked down. He sensed he'd nosed
into a topic better left entombed.
Ai's mom jumped in, "Our history's complex,
with dynasties, invasions, wars, and clans.
It's hard to say that we have been annexed,
but there were many overlapping hands."
Then Long spoke up, "The China of today
is unified and stable. We can thank
the Party for creating that walkway
from chaos." (Ai bobbed head.) "Each file and rank
is focused on development within.
It's jobs and growth that help new China win."

117.
The mother riffed on hist'ry, "Stel you know,
tombed author who you mentioned, that Xue Tao,
was known for more than that portfolio.
Her curiosity and tech knowhow
helped her invent new paper-making means.
Her papers had these finely detailed lines
and rosy tinge that no other machines
in her time could create. She's now enshrined
less as inventor, more as poet. But
do not forget her whole life she combined
mixed interests that to others were somewhat
confusing." "We, too, haven't been confined
to boxes others had for what we ought
to do," Abu replied. "Is that what's taught

118.
in Tanzania?" mother asked, surprised,
with hint of curling lip upon her face.
"Not really," he explained, "you'll be chastised
for choosing things that aren't so commonplace."
He paused, and thought, continued, "If it's grades
you stand out with, you're fine. You'll get ahead,
see university. That mercy fades
if how you live your life is odd instead."
Her lip unbent, resumed its steady state,
compression lines of smiling smoothing out,
said, "I think you'll be able to relate,
then, to the ways that expectations route
our kids' directions." "Nonsense," stiffly snapped
Jiang Long to wife, "you still need to adapt

119.
to modern times and what's required! Right now
our country needs more educated youth.
Those scientists and engineers allow
our state to shed its infancy, to tooth!
We're masters now of making nature ours,
we reroute rivers, seed the rains, we plow
straight through the earth, control when floods
   discharge.
We'll use the stores with which we were endowed
to exit poverty, selves redefine.
We know the way: technology and math,
construction, planning, that's what moves mankind.
Lĭŋpó, don't see me as a sociopath,
we've talked through this before—what's culture when
our lives are doomed by famines yet again?"

120.
"My husband," she said slowly to the guests,
"fits squarely in the Party. His view's that
our future's all about where we invest."
"You liked that once," he added. "Technocrats
are necessary, Jiang, agreed. But what
I liked was that your vision was so big,
and you had eye for nuance Party's shut."
The dragon's souring face gulped down a swig
of tea to squelch belch fire and left the meal.
Without discomfort's pause, the mother turned
to Stella, saying, "I hope you freewheel
for yet some time, it does some good. Concern
for how to get ahead pollutes kids' minds.
Young years are not for competition's grind."

121.
Throughout these interactions, Ai sat mum,
eyes following each speaker's volleyed points.
Stel felt it wasn't first time that she'd swum
these choppy waters. "China disappoints
me, how it's turned our kids into machines
that memorize instead of think. That's why
we send Ai to your school. It contravenes
the expectation Party's unified
with common people; that's a risk we took."
To hear divergent views on Chinese life,
society, and politics had shook
Ai's view compliance was prime role of wife.
Too many fragment thoughts to keep the thread
of conversation, Abu asked instead,

122.
"I haven't asked how you learned English. Your
pronunciation's near American."
"Born there. My family moved twelve years postwar
to San Francisco. The hysterics when
the Communists prevailed had scared my dad.
He had an uncle living there who'd split
through Taiwan midway through the war. He had
a little business, said he could commit
some small sum to my father if he came.
So I grew up in schools that weren't like this.
To me that's sugar. Ours are aspartame."
She seemed to like the chance to reminisce.
"Of course, I had to work a lot, and go
to Chinese school on weekends. That helped sow

123.
the seeds for an eventual return."
She paused, her head a-tilt. She said, "Wait here,"
to indicate they hadn't yet adjourned.
Abu looked bright. She left, then reappeared
with what she called a 'souvenir', a slight
and aging book named *Brocade River Verse.*
"What left my family constantly contrite
was how the Gang of Four somehow coerced
the country to destroy its artifacts
and culture, starting 1963
when I was born. They torched text and land tracts,
erasing history. Back then, 'bourgeoisie'
was label put on anyone who tried
preserving them or not falling in line.

124.
In California mom read that to me
as bridge to homeland's hist'ry they'd destroyed.
Till eight when we moved back, this imagery
laced dreams, as bedtime stories filling void."
She tossed the book on table 'tween the two
rapt guests. "Although there's no heroes inside,
each page now read reminds this *ingénue*
rebellion's free—my mind's not occupied."
She coursed out, taking dishes to the sink.
Stel tightly gripped the poem book resting there.
Abu sought desk again to start to ink
calligraphy as homework. Stel, ensnared
by words on title page, found author's name
'Xue Tao' was who she'd seen in park's tombed fame.

125.
But each one perches on its own branch, Stel
recalled from note she'd found aground. She paged
through poems, and saw the right had English, spelled
out clearly, annotated. Left had aged,
distinguished Chinese script in running style,
like Middle English to the learnéd eye.
Ten thousand common characters compiled
their modern speech, Lao Yan had clarified.
But literary scholars needed more,
the foreword claimed, to understand the shades
of nuance in linguistics' old decor.
Light lines of ink formed fern-tipped promenades
of thousand years ago, when feudal lords
commensally lived 'longside nature's hoards.

126.
BLING interrupted reverie with bark
at Huhu, who mistook him as more food.
Stel asked Ai if she wanted to embark
on dog walk to help BLING be more subdued.
She nodded. "Back in Tanzania, I
could leave BLING out to roam the fields. We'd find
enough ways to have fun. We loved to lie
down in acacias' shade." "Dad did not mind
you outside play?" Ai asked, incredulous
no supervision freed kids to do stuff
past what classrooms required. "He's dead. To us,"
Stel pointed head toward BLING, "us is enough."
That no one knew that BLING existed kept
Stel from adverse attention's intercept.

127.
Ai walked as if competing, not in stroll.
"Ai, why are you in such a hurry? It's
a Saturday." Ai paused, "I have two whole
math homeworks." Stella felt at edge of wits.
"Come on! Ease up. You heard your mom explain
she doesn't need you at the top in grades."
"Choice is not mom's, choice is not mine," complained
Ai, "country make the choice." "No, there are shades
between. You have some say." "No, life is race.
Mom someday old. And Dad too. I can take
much care for them if studying can place
me in 𝓫ℯ𝒾𝒹𝒶…" (the college that can make
a plutocrat of anyone) "and we,
the kids, soon be China's economy."

128.
Stel didn't know herself how parents shaped
their children's views on virtue, duty, need.
In empathy she let off footfall's brakes
and moved at pace that Ai strove to proceed.
Once home, Ai hastily retired to books
of calculus. Loud English radio
was playing on the stereo. *It looks,*
Stel thought, *like Sichuan airwaves play the show*
I listened to at home. By that she meant
the VOA, Voice of America.
Quick channel flip showed local complement
called Xīnhuá. Latter seemed generic, the
aired stories sounded fluffy. She heard not
a single disagreement driving plot.

129.
On Monday Shi Laoshi conducted drills,
expecting weekend mostly spent at work.
Abu and Stel sat facing her. She grilled
them each in turn. It's not like Stella shirked
assignments, she'd just spent one day on them
and that was half of what Abu had done.
She hadn't thought a teacher's RPM
could question at that rapid of a run.
"Wǒ hěn xǐhuān mǐfàn," Stel tried. "Wǒ hěn
xǐhuān chī," teacher said, "mǐfàn gèng hǎo."
In here, Stel realized, no credit's won
for nearly-perfect answers. Just allowed
were sentences as memorized, err-free,
or "dàjiā dōu bù huì míngbái nǐ.

130.
Right post-interrogation marathon –
two hours with but a five-min bio break –
kids tottered arm-in-arm as pair to lawn
instead of cafeteria. Heads ached.
They'd learned that hunger's best reserved for facts
about Chinese, and stomach's needs could stay
in second place. "Prepare for more attacks,"
Abu nudged Stel on seeing boy make way
toward them. "He's rude one from last week's affront."
"His walk's not quite as stiff as last time." He
looked like he'd borne an equally sore brunt
from scolding as had they. Accordingly,
they didn't scamper off when he collapsed
on seat, with slumping shoulders, sulk unwrapped.

131.
Ignoring him, they waxed about the days
when expectations had been minimal,
no adult sentinels to disobey.
To use time as they'd then seemed criminal,
the constant looking back on times that flew.
Be born, be served, age into servant caste
as obligations endlessly accrue...
The idiom piqued interest of outcast,
whose eyes had welled but had not convalesced.
Boy sniffled, straightened, breathed, tried to remold
good outward face, cleared throat, and voiced request
with interruption, asking, "You enrolled?"
Stel was offended momentarily:
first bully, then forget so verily?

132.
She checked herself. "Yes, I'm enrolled," then closed
her mouth since she knew not where he would try
to go. "You English so good. How?" he posed.
"Where I grew up tongues were diversified.
Swahili, English, tribal language all
had uses." "Try bull language?" "*Kimasai,
Kichaga*, dialects of place." A wall
of understanding stood tall. She'd just try
the same idea, simplified: "I learned
in school." He got it then. Reducing thought
complexity left details undiscerned
unsatisfyingly, but won jackpot
of conversation partner hanging on.
Reward was worth the cost of slang things gone.

133.
"I think like Sìchuānhuà and Hànyǔ," he
said, catching meanings 'place' and 'school' intend.
"I speak Chinese, Han language. Maybe we
can talk? You teach, I teach." *Why'd he befriend
me all the sudden?* Stella thought, then gazed
again at his appearance, armor chinked
since being teasing bad guy. He was fazed.
She'd seen that he to cooler kids was linked,
thought maybe she'd dodge teasing with assent.
Before agreeing, Ai walked up, scowled. She
standoffishly spoke with him. They'd relent
peroxide level of acidity
in minutes. "I ask why he mean. He said
he not know you could English friend instead."

134.
"He's sorry? What has changed?" Stel then inquired.
Ai translated, boy nodded, then shook head.
He seemed unwilling to share what transpired:
to share a shame was not that shame to shed.
Ai guessed instead, "He so low in our class
he must want helps." She then recalled, "I heard
the mother angry he test bad, not pass."
"I'm angry all he wants is English words,"
Stel turned to him, "But fine. We'll buddy up.
You help me with Chinese, and I'll help you
with English. Here. Tomorrow. Follow up."
"Hěn hǎo! Zài zhèlǐ míngtiān jiàn nǐ," bluc-
no-longer boy replied, form raised with hope,
as if he'd slain an inner misanthrope.

Chapter 9

135.
Fluorescent lamps lit hidden conference room,
their bleaching light eliminating time.
The men within debated if lagoon
would soon be made of Fan's green valley. "Prime
geology for generation is
so scarce these days: this site's our only shot,"
reported Land and Resources, "my whiz-
bang scientists have plotted every spot."
"Our rivers' flows are growing volatile,
the age-old patterns offer no more use
predicting where the floods hit. Most fertile
producing regions lack the depth of sluice
required to drain the torrents that arrive.
Crops die. If lucky, families still survive."

136.
The Chairman looked across the room to see
if PhDs in Sci-Tech Ministry
agreed with bleak assessment nominee
from Land just gave. "Yes, Chair, we too foresee
more difficulty in predicting floods."
"And let us not forget that cities lay
right in the path of water, silt, and mud
and thus must fund walls keeping them at bay,"
old Housing added in, stress lines around
his worn eyes boring deeply into face.
Then Finance nodded his assent, "We're bound
to grow our infrastructure spend apace
with that uncertainty. Our budget share's
increasing year on year." Foreign Affairs

137.

sunk lower in his chair, "We'll face a storm
in all the Western press if we move now.
'Another million people's lives deformed,
so urban wealthy can face fewer brown-
outs', it would read. Three Gorges Dam was hard,
and we built that 'fore foreign coverage peaked."
"With due respect, we'd all best disregard
what other nations think. We're oft critiqued
by people on the sidelines who can't know
the trade-offs that we face within this room.
You've shown them that we'll interfere with no
internal matters elsewhere. Let's assume
they'll give us the same courtesy. Our trade
alone's enough to calm their stump tirades."

138.
Retort was worded deftly, with respect.
Still, disagreement slowed replying tongues.
"I'd like to know," filled Chair in, "what effects
on brownout rates will be." They knew he swung
with what the numbers said, true engineer.
"Our baseline's at completion eight years out:
four days per month of rationing is feared."
"Thirteen-point-three percent or thereabout
of lost productive time," worked out the Chair.
"With this in operation, we'll reduce
that down to half day monthly." "Everywhere?"
"For Sichuan," said man made to look obtuse
for failing to include that in report.
"Now tell me what the plan is to transport

139.
the million farmers on the valley floor."
"We want to make a pension fund for all
and give them roughly what they made before,
and also build some housing so the sprawl
in nearby towns and cities is controlled.
They'll move in waves as flats are built and bought.
Town commerce we expect to boost twofold
with all those pensions spent in single spot."
"They'll need it," countered Agriculture, "since
the prices of most staple goods will rise.
So in addition to the dissidents
you'll have townsfolk complaining 'bout supplies.
To wipe out such a huge productive tract
has sizable statewide food price impact."

140.
"You need not worry, Chairman, of protests.
I'll have the force to keep the peace, and plan
well in advance to verify no jests
that castigate the state can breach our ban."
Security, to none's surprise, looked smug.
Unlike the other Ministries, it could
dispatch whatever kind of state-backed thugs
it needed to enforce what it thought good.
"The media concerns me not a bit,
you've mostly proven that you're able to
deal with disquiet in electorate.
We've covered power and floods and food, but you,
Environmental colleague, you've said not
a word's dissent." (All feared that he'd been bought).

141.
Like rain accumulates, a silence grew
into a separate entity in room,
exerting power. He had till now eschewed
the chance to take the microphone. "A bloom
will always sprout once fire has passed. This case
is hardly diffcrent. Yes, we're sad to lose
such land. But there are plans to interlace
the crafted shoreline with some docks to cruise,
to rent a kayak or canoe, to tour
around and savor nature as we've shaped
it. Less is this about a loss endured,
and more about envisioned new landscape."
A dozen bobble nods turned men to mimes,
so Chair adjourned discussions for the time.

Chapter 10

142.
At dinner, huíguōròu caused pleasant wave
among the Tanzanian houseguests. They
back home for meat of any kind oft craved,
its treat had price reserved for holiday.
The mother asked quite perfunctorily
if Stel enjoyed the dishes that she'd made,
while serving her, like one chunk more will be
noshed proof assent was not a masquerade.
They gobbled it delightedly, with rice.
The father watched, his eating slow. "You're fast
already," satisfied that his advice
on chopstick use was used. "You're overcast
tonight," Stel boldly noted, having seen
him shirk from holding court at meal. His queen

143.
stole glance at him. He caught his swiveled head,
and reined in plain reaction of surprise.
Asserting so directly was unbred
from Chinese culture long ago. "The wise,"
he counseled, "surely never aim so straight,
but rather tack across the wind until
they've circumspectly sailed tact's twisted strait
toward port that has the goal they want fulfilled."
He paused for full effect, then shoulders slumped
and second sigh suggested he'd forgive
the trespass of a foreigner. "I'm stumped.
I've one decision likely to outlive
me, be my legacy. Yet I'm not sure
how much I trust that what they're selling's pure."

144.
That mildest mental smarting stunned Stel's need
to ask another question. Abu'd caught
a favorite term of his, and took the lead:
"They're crucial, legacies. Or get forgot."
"Hmm. Nevermind," the now-flush man replied,
a forearm sweep dislodging napkins from
the table. Fallen trash 'round every side
of dining table was eyesore Stel numbed
herself to, cryptic luxury of waste.
Why tidy sundry rubbish minuscule
on table? Best to batch it in one place.
Ab thought about excusing self for school.
With drops of fast-slurped soup still on her lip,
Stel also then retired to sistership.

145.
Recipient of reprimanding, Stel
felt shamed, self-righteous in two equal parts.
Back in the room with Ai, she failed to quell
disgruntlement frustrating tired-out heart.
"I'm understanding nothing! What's allowed,
what's not, why kids are so competitive..."
She liked her walks and dinners, which were how
she learned about the place she'd come to live.
With this, each one was ruined, one by Ai
and one by Jiang, and neither felt Stel's fault.
Recalling no days past disqualified
by cultural transgressions, her default
was to cast blame on present cast. (It's tough
to see one's own outsiderness in stuff.)

146.
Ai kept her head in textbook as Stel spun,
integral integrals were left to do
now that derived derivatives were done
and Ai was on page twelve of forty-two.
Stel watched her roommate's focus, flashbacks struck
to Tanzanian times she'd planned escape,
*To work so hard to get here, then get stuck
in hamster wheel?* she thought. *Best to have scraped
by back at home.* "Ai, you've reflex routine
from home to school to home, where homework's long
enough to make you drink tea for caffeine!
You're thirteen! Hasn't something gone quite wrong
to turn your childhood freedom into trance?
It's like you've never given play a chance."

147.
"I think I also nothing understand,"
said Ai, her right hand shutting textbook. "You
four weeks before said in your old homeland
that people have no monies. Here we do."
She swung her chair to face. "My father say
that is because we study hard for math
and science from first school, and that free play
is for the toddlers. Not for kids." That path
Stel'd seen well-treaded during supper talk.
Stel steamed. She partly blamed herself in that
she couldn't tell which tale was poppycock:
that juvenescence in the state's format
would drive the engines churning out more jobs,
or simply crinkle humans down to cogs.

148.
"I get it, Ai. Each person's part of 'we'.
That comes through clearly in the way you speak.
Where I come from it's also family
that makes decisions for you. Trying to eke
past poverty with powd'ry soil is tough.
You have to come together, take good care
of elders, cousin-brothers. Not enough
community means if your crops are bare,
you'll starve that season. What was different for
my childhood's that I lacked that base support,
no parents or relations to restore
stability when crisis hit. When short,
I did without. I'm lucky that I'm here.
I know that. Still, here's differently severe.

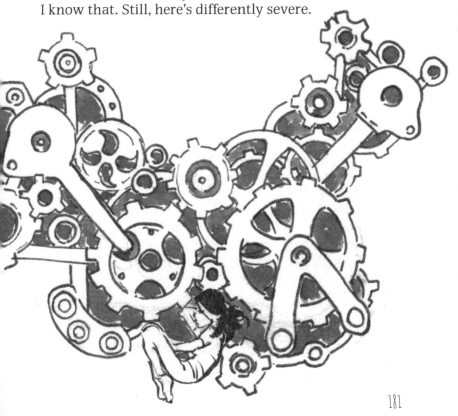

149.
At home I found a thing I wanted lots.
It filled the time between the daily chores."
She reached down, petted BLING. "We found these spots
nearby to go and climb, explore outdoors.
Acacia trees, savannas, forest on
the outskirts of our local peaks were game.
It meant that half our homework was foregone,
success was body's learning. We became
upgraded per own plans by time we slept,
my dusk self more like me than when dawn broke.
But here it feels like everything except
our dinner time is yet another yoke.
Here, every day is last one's copycat.
I want to be a person, not a stat."

150.
She'd worked herself into a tizzy, paused,
then gained momentum in the fall back down.
Continuing, Stel said, "We really caused
some things to happen; tried to help our town!
Our teacher'd lost a golden ring. Those climbs
we took on so to train ourselves to solve
what we had thought was actually a crime,
a theft. Then it turned out to not involve
a criminal at all! Well, not that part,
at least. Her husband poacher stole some eggs
from some rare bird, a big one, each like art.
It injured him, and yet he still bootlegged
them through the middlemen in town. Jerks pay
a lot to own what nature free displays."

151.
Her monologue brought forth a tangled knot
of memories, joys, regrets from how she chose
that night to give back Gumi's gold jackpot
despite misogyny owner disclosed.
Here Stel sat with another woman who
faced different pressures, though to still conform,
and bent her sense of self toward others' view
of how she should behave, and others' norms.
Ai lacked the same gift sitting in her hand,
an artifact to launch her on own way.
Stel wondered, had she kept it as spite planned,
if she'd be freer. Youth's naïveté
chose 'right'. Now vocalizing Gumi's wrongs
made Stel wish ring in hand where it belongs.

152.
Ai's stare made Stel unsure if words shared sank
in; language gaps oft caused chats to seesaw.
"It seem impossible," Ai said, the swank
of Stella's story struck her. "What you saw
is like the Journey West, one of our four
great novels." She looked over at the wall,
at grassland poster on the closet door,
and said, "Your story is like that, a 'tall
tale' is, I think, right word. They happen in
the places far away of city. Not
a can-imagine thing. Small kids here win
school competitions, tests. It is what got
Chinese to growth and jobs." "The Chinese, sure.
But where's the *Ai* in that? It's premature

153.
to say your life is bound to turn out just
the way society expects it to.
Competing at this rate means you'll combust
before you ever find what to pursue."
"I know what to pursue. It is the good
of home place, build it up more," Ai explained,
"first, engineer. If very good, I could
enroll in Tsinghua." "What if unconstrained?
How do you know that engineering's where
you'll find your love?" "Choice not existing, Stel.
I get good money, then can maybe care
for parents, have my family." "No, rebel
a little! I had nothing till I found
my independent self," Stel stroked her hound

154.
to calm again. "You're right," Ai said, "than me,
you had much less. No parent and no friend."
"You have no friends now," Stel said flaccidly.
"Ha! Here you miss so much," Ai did contend,
"we talk, QQ, like SMS. We each
to other offering support. You look
for what you know. You think that it has reach
here. Maybe you can't see." Had Stel mistook
reality through blue-tinged glasses? Sure,
the students that she knew back home obsessed
sometimes about their grades too. But they were
less categorically so plagued, so stressed.
Or were they? Did she really comprehend
what built belonging 'pon which folks depend?

155.
She'd soured at stench of conflict in the air,
and stormed a bit when Ai'd claimed she was wrong
about her observation. She compared
this country's ways with what she'd known lifelong,
experience and eyes and mind were all
the tools she had to craft perspectives from.
A want for peace caused her to reach for small
anthology beside her bed. Succumb
to swirling thoughts of nature, pleasant swoon
to poems that freed *esprit* from city's pull.
Its spirit leans like a thin hook, read "Moon",
or opens round likc Han-loom fans, eyefuls
were dreamed. *Whose slender shadow's nature is
to be full*—Abu popped to mind. It's his

156.
approach to life this poem described. How strange,
that classic China threaded long ago
the link between the moon's endless phase change
and how human ambition's to outgrow
our born-form size. Its closing line was: *seen*
from everywhere in human world. She saw
Abu as moon, directing figurines,
conducting constellations. Image gnawed
at her, this conjured hidden power it claimed.
Of course she wanted him to reach his dreams.
But something felt still empty in this fame.
As Ai said, who was she to claim esteem's
obtained in one same way for everyone?
Was knowing selves quite ever fully done?

157.
An only-partly satisfying sleep
expectedly brought forth another day.
Stel stayed composed, avoiding slip toward weep,
but raggedness pervaded vertebrae.
Per yesterday's agreement, she arrived
back at the courtyard tree to meet the boy
who sought an English partner, a contrived
transactional camaraderie. BLING toyed
with sticks on ground, and snapped his jaws at bugs,
on constant prowl around the premises,
preferred to being kept as housebound slug.
The boy walked up. "Hello!" (The genesis
of language partnership.) "Um... how are you?"
he asked, as textbooks all instructed to.

158.
"I'm fine, and you?" Stel said, suppressing laugh
at awkwardness rote language forced them toward.
"I'm fine," he said, "my name is Qin," his half
of scripted conversation she abhorred.
"And what is your?" "It's 'what is *yours*?' And mine
is Stella." "I from China. Where is yours?"
Stel guessed that he learned quickly from the line,
despite its incorrectness. Reassured
this might be useful use of time, she eased.
"I come from Tanzania." "Where is that?"
"In Africa. What is it in Chinese?"
"Fēizhōu. Nǐ shìgè Fēizhōu rén," voice flat
on neighbor syllables in high first tone.
Reminded how hard tones are, Stella groaned.

159.
"Yes, I'm an African," she switched, "Nà nǐ
de lǎojiā zài nǎr?" Stella slowly read
from workbook on her lap, asking where he
was from ancestrally. Qin looked ahead
and failed to register she'd asked a thing.
Repeating it, she pointed at her text.
Her tones, she feared, were quite embarrassing,
and in this case left native speaker vexed.
"Zài Sìchuān, zhèlǐ. Wǒ de jiārén dōu
shuō Sìchuānhuà, a 'dialect'. You, read
this sentence," touching text. She did. "No, slow."
She did again. He spoke and remedied
pronunciation errors: "Mouth more wide."
That helped, she thought. *Could friend be better guide*

160.
than teacher? Being understood enthused
her. "Wǒ zài túshūguǎn xǐhuān dúshū."
At hearing this, Qin suddenly effused,
spoke words she didn't get, although she knew
from body language it was praise. Progress
felt good. The lesson carried on, a mix
of English and Chinese. They both obsessed
on other's grammar, pausing oft to fix
it. Thoughts of speaking error-free relieved
the worries keeping them from all attempt.
A half-hour's back-and-forth for both achieved
some cleaning of what started as unkempt
enunciation. "Wǒmen míngtiān zài
zhèyàng liànxí shuō mǎ?" Stel tried. "Yes! Bye!"

161.
She hadn't thought before they met that she'd
want to repeat the conversation with
this boy. Yet, speech when topic's refereed
felt comfortable, and closer to the pith
behind adventuring she'd known back home:
the thrills she'd found in nature were about
the serendipitous surprise biome
provides. In words, fortuity reroutes.
The barriers of understanding shroud
each person in a shifting set of veils,
attempted meanings in words said aloud
not meeting expectations of details.
It felt intrepid, using mind and lung
to make herself known in another tongue.

162.
BEEP BEEP!, BEEP BEEP!, BEEP BEEP! alarm
  clock screamed
one Thursday morning, after having snoozed
three times. It unstitched dreamed world seam by seam,
left real one. Cortisol in Abu oozed.
He'd nearly broken morning's long routine
of rising early, walking route to school,
and camping with his books in kids' canteen.
This daily practice had become his fuel
for memorizing characters, required
for every day of class. In fact, he'd made
such rapid progress Teacher Shi desired
he switch into a higher class. Upgrade
augmented pressure to perform, so BEEP!
lit up adrenal glands, dispelling sleep.

163.
Once clothed, he rendezvoused right at the front
door where their shoes were all deposited.
With us today? thought Stel. The stress' brunt
was worn upon his face, not closeted.
Outside, the warmth of summer'd fallen. Steam
still poured from tiny shops, backlit by sun.
It blew toward them, as if they were downstream
of aromatic brook of breakfast buns.
A man in padded comrade jacket stood
beside repurposed oil drum that, near-capped,
pumped fumes like only makeshift smokestack could.
His puffy hands crushed dough, balled up, and slapped
it down in crescents into crucible,
bare-handed as if skin weren't fusible.

164.
"Oh! Lǎo Li hǎo," Stel said, familiar with
the aproned man with concrete hands, his pastes
arranged in glass jars on the shelf. "The fifth
looks good today, I need a sweeter taste.
Dì wǔ gè. Wǒ yào chī tián," she explained.
"Tián de, Xiǎo Xīng, qǐng nǐ bié wàngjì!"
corrected he (when adjectives remained
without possessive "de" aberrantly
they oft weren't understood). Her daily bite
of pastry came with tutelage. "How did
you get so comfortable nigh overnight
with speaking?" "Wasn't overnight. That kid
that I've been chatting with has helped me drill
some real-life phrases. Turns out that until

165.
I found some mystery in trying to learn
I didn't want to spend the time. When all
I had was a dull textbook and a stern
instructor, I'd just focus on the small
details in grammar that she pushed us to.
I missed the fact this class is meant to be
the stuff we need to know to go pursue
our Pioneer adventures here." The fee
for egg-filled salty, spicy, sweet, or plain
jiānbing was 'round a couple yuan. Abu
then realized that since he'd been enchained
to classroom text, excelling through and through,
he hadn't found the way to move from writ
to spoken word, omitting half the kit

166.
of language in the first place. Stella'd been
at work at conversation for some weeks:
"I think I'm finding ways now to begin
enjoying these attempts to take a peek
into the lives of people." "When we met
we mostly found our classmates boring," he
recalled, "what's different here?" "They can offset
the loneliness of being here. I'm me
when I can share some of myself." "I don't
have any need for sharing. Will it boost
my study speed?" "Dunno. You're stressed. It won't
hurt," Stel shared, hoped idea had seduced
her brainy friend. Ab pondered friends as tools
for lexical expansion past books schooled.

167.
When history concluded, ten past twelve,
he lettered little sign in block-script, which
invited other kids who sought to delve
into the ways exchange could both enrich
their grades. He borrowed name from Pioneers,
'The Afroasiatic Cultural
Exchange' it read, with characters that neared
that meaning. Though kids swirled like vultures, pull
of sign and Abu weren't enough to bring
a population to the table. So
he sat alone, passed up. He tried to ping
their housemate Ai, who'd come to say hello.
Conceivably with friends, too! No reply
arrived to SMS. What went awry?

168.
Stel said demand was high for English chat,
so why were folks avoiding offer? This
was wasted textbook time if it fell flat.
He wished again for help from homestay sis.
He spotted her and Stel step into hall,
and beckoned them to join to seed the group.
Ai did, looked smug, and said, "I hear you call
for help first time now," then sat down and scooped
the sign up, got a pen, and edited
the words so it read 'English Corner Here'.
Known phrase like that was more accredited,
and standard in this case would friends endear.
A partner's presence others would attract
to catalyze exchanges, table packed.

169.
But, not so quickly. Ab still had his books
arrayed out on the table, looked as if
he'd built his own library study nook
of Babel tower spires, from bricks of glyph.
Kids walked right past with cafeteria
trays loaded with foods—words he'd memorized.
Could food talk test his budding theory the
meal time in China's sacred? Passed corps sized
his study fortress up and steered selves clear.
Ai pitied, took the hardbacks, pads, and sheets
down carefully and stored them with his gear.
Stel sat down, eased in, surveyed Ab's defeats,
breathed deep and put a warm smile on, looked 'round.
Thereafter came success: a first friend found.

170.
It was the boy that teased her some weeks back,
now friendly from their one-on-one exchange.
Behavior's change turned Ab amnesiac,
forgetting past transgressions had estranged
them. Now a peer connected to lots more
found value in his interactions with
young Ab and Stel. *Become what they adore,*
by being foreign coveted wordsmith,
Ab thought, bemused by popularity
arisen from such mundane daily skill:
he had but expat titularity,
knew English by default and not by will.
I'll have to find, he thought, *more gifts unsung*
I didn't know would help climb power's rungs.

CHAPTER 11

171.
The view through dusted window of the car
transitioned from gray urban bleak to green,
alive with farms. "They're fed by reservoir
some hundred miles away." Aquamarine
canals branched out like tentacles from run
of river, feeding pipes pumped up the hills
to plots. Jiang Long, the father, had begun
narrating nature's features. Overfilled,
they'd crammed into the family vehicle,
two parents front, kids in the middle, BLING
and Huhu sharing back. Through scenes fickle,
his color commentary's constant ring
was all that Stel could pay attention to.
It let him show a new dimension through

172.
which he was better understood: a guide
and champion of Sichuan Province who
was born there, felt that heritage as pride
and therefore strived to give an overview
to all guests, filled with admirations. "This
is China's breadbasket. We're at the crux
of where one billion eat." The cloudiness
that kept the sky mid-tone, reducing lux,
meant plants must thrive without the blaze of sun
that Stel enjoyed from Tanzania. Plants
popped out from mountain terraces, each one
jonesed jolt genetically that photon grants:
the ATP to broaden networked root
while stretching ever up toward solar food.

173.
They'd left their home vacationing, like rest
of China for Mid-Autumn Festival.
"Our duty is to help those who've senesced,
like Shushu, mother's uncle. Restive, he'll
be pleased to see us, no one else will come.
I used to write to him when I was small,"
the mother had explained. Now Stel succumbed
to mesmerizing visual, enthralled
with all the landscapes passing past her eyes.
They'd gone from sprawl to plains to foothills, wound
up mountain range tops, looming oversized
compared to skein of road upon the ground.
Stel hadn't seen sierras crossed by lanes,
kinks serpentine that level uphill gains.

174.
With traffic jams from holidays, it stretched
into the longest car ride of her life.
Geography this drastic felt far-fetched,
like heaven gouged out gorges with buck knife,
then set down snowmelt rivulets at base,
excusing hasty handiwork with gleam
of river rush distraction. Air encased
with icy vapor ambient sunbeams,
diluting color of hills furthest off
when spied at apex of a corner's curve.
A cobalt colored sky, peak down to trough
of gully's brook. This place had been preserved,
a jewel geology itself had wrought
compared to smog-skied urban mega-knot.

175.
The undulations mountain road carved kissed
recesses' recollections in Stel's mind.
She'd somehow seen the ways that these rocks twist
before, the angled schist, the ridge decline.
When eyes fell closed, impressions on her lids
felt navy blue and monochrome, as if
Poseidon's dolphin chariot left skids,
a watermark embedded hieroglyph.
These placid pools of thought inside her brain
were punctuated by a memory
that burbled up toward more conscious domains.
What is it? Stella thought, *this gem, or me?*
She hadn't pieced together if she'd seen
this canyon flood in once-dreamed scene marine.

176.
The reverie of countryside made way
for one of Ai's mom's seventies vignettes:
once moving back she'd become protégé
to Shushu. She'd become a suffragette
on seeing how the revolution changed
suspicions he'd held into faith in state.
She saw hypocrisy: state's work estranged
from goal that women's rights gain equal weight
as man's. Strict household that she grew up in
maintained that antiquated sense of role
she'd hoped the revolution would begin
to overturn instead of to ensoul.
Though none could vote, she'd tacitly explored
more ways to women's voices bring to fore.

177.
While details of inspiring past were shared,
Abu's head bowed in ignorance of tale,
clear focus on his textbook unimpaired
by mother's turn toward radical female
by witnessing the secular belief
of uncle she'd been shipped to live with. Stel
had no idea a wee farming fief
had shaped the mother too. To say farewell
to countryside of well-known plants and leave
for city took a boldness that she found
attractive. Woman had not been deceived
by strictures expectation used to bound.
I ought to figure out what father does,
Stel thought, *to better know how mother was*

178.
led off, away from radicalities.
Perhaps in lengthy hours the kids were schooled
she used her husband's rank *royale*, city's
slow bending to her will as woman who'll
discreetly advocate for women's rights
within society that kept them down
with rigid gender roles? Did she requite
the centuries of being but pronoun
and not protagonist, through quiet schemes
to shape society more squarely with
the voice of women? Stel liked these daydreams
that overlaid on factual the myths
of grander consequence that hist'ry books
pull out and weave in retrospective looks.

179.
Imagining the puppeteer behind
the puppeteers of that society
caused Stel to close her heavy lids. Reclined,
the ride passed fast in sleep. Anxiety
swept into dreams again, the same sad flood.
At last she woke when car pulled up to farm,
down lengthy rain-worn path half dirt, half mud.
Outside Ayi and Shushu kept alarm
off faces, saving face. Stel felt their eyes,
recalled conflict with Ab that sprung from when
at school same happened. She'd too been surprised
when she'd first seen Chinese, the workers in
her province came to build a road to mines.
And then, like now, the newness soon declined.

180.
The farmhouse organized itself around
a central doorway, richly oiled old wood
maintained to best degree. Its top was crowned
with lucky crimson paper wishing would
gold fortunes fall on those who pass beneath,
a message reinforced with diamonds of
red cardboard, nailed on like two welcome wreaths,
both faded pink beneath the sky's sunned love.
The characters upon them upside-down
in way that Stella'd seen in city meant
a higher chance prosperity'd come 'round
according to its homophone. Words bent
themselves to double meanings in Chinese,
tradition rich in wordplay hard to seize.

181.
Beyond the door the differences began
to individuate this rural house.
Its single floor reminded of floorplans
of homes in Tanzania. They would douse
the dust out front in summers to make sure
their discharged topsoil didn't fill the lung.
The hardpack clay in walls had too endured
what weathering had decades' seasons brung.
Where washed away from heavy storm and time
new rocks of colors mimicked in the hills
were stacked to fill the holes. A layer of grime
caked terracotta shingles, windowsills,
and cracks in grout, yet couldn't nearly blight
the cheer that Stella felt for rural site.

182.
The motorcycle here seemed so much more
at place than scooters zipping 'round Chengdu:
the less ground ground up as a basis for
paved roads, the more for plants to have sprung through.
Small farms, she knew, were never flush with cash
so every green square foot made likelier
by end of year you'd have built up a cache
of calories' insurance. Sightly were
the woods behind the home, set at hill's edge.
The land too steep to cultivate, it stayed
as nature had intended. Yard's short hedge
looked edible, like cabbage, and man-made.
Impression struck immediately that all
these pieces had their usefulness. The sprawl

183.
of city long behind them, Stella breathed.
The greenness of the draft was hefty, wild,
organically fulfilling. She had sheathed
her diaphragm in shallow draw of child
perforce to cope with urban smog. But here
the air seemed almost pushy in its urge
to permeate the pilgrims. Last frontier
where verdurous assault had thus converged
was in the massive wood where she, Abu
and BLING had found Miss Gumi's ring. "Nǐ hǎo,"
said Shushu, then "huānyíng." Ai's mother moved
toward both with grin and wide embrace. The plow
at rest against the farmhouse showed fresh wear,
a tool to harvest fest's vowed fresh feast fare.

184.
"Wǒ hěn gāoxìng," Stel made out from Ayi's
quick speech, excitement in the tone belied
stiff bodies. Ai traced their plot's boundaries
in back of house, and Stel joined her astride.
Abu came too, the first to ask their host
and sister what the giant, round brick stove
was used for—far too large to cook or roast
the common foods, resembling treasure trove
with smokestack. "Time ago, the Great Leap for
the Forward," Ai replied, "ask country all
to metal tool and pot melt, give up. War
to fast make industry. Did not work. Stalled."
"The rulers broke the country and you still
wed your fate to fulfilling their state will?

185.
Since independence, we have never had
regimes' directives forcefully policed
in households," Stel said, hinting at ironclad
power held by PSB's enforcement beast.
Ai understood more than she could express,
and pulled the essence out of what Stel spoke.
Ai'd hoped to fuller rationale profess,
for Stel's slight had conditioning evoked:
"Past problem, okay now. I know from Dad."
"Upheaval every decade recently
scarred people, my books mentioned," Ab did add.
"The Party line that old folks, seasoned, see
is that you must give up control to be
a part," said Stel, "of this society."

186.
"Not right," Ai's icy look showed that her pride
was under fire. "That past, where China been.
Today the problems harder. And inside
the government is better peoples. Men
try always building better China. We
must do best for one billion every day."
Ab pondered difference in immensity
compared to forty million in the fray
in Tanzania. Twenty-five countries
equivalent in single bundle tied
together by bureaucracy. Bluntly,
he saw how they had near-beatified
past leadership. Distracted from the scene
by nature, Stella turned from Ai's smoke screen.

187.
The kids strolled past Jurassic furnace. Light
was fading slightly, heatless sun sank, peeked
one streak through dip in hills of hematite,
whose long spine ridge made circular physique
of valley bowl. Skies clearer than Chengdu's,
where crisp, bright orb was bled diffuse by smog.
Its amber rays reflected down, clung to
diagonal small panel, metal log,
and box atop the roof. Stel pointed, asked
what the contraption was as subject change.
It gathered all the sun in which it basked,
she learned, and put it through some heat exchange,
and made hot water at a zero cost
to cook or bathe through harshest heat or frost.

188.
Ai used Stel's curiosity to pick
back up the reason government was good—
in gesture thoughtful, real, and politic
they'd subsidized these heaters over wood,
decreasing smoke, deforestation, and
allowing homes without access to grid
some benefit before the network spanned
so far to reach them. Farms lost out amid
the electricity demand that towns
and cities showed. Since farmers couldn't pay
as much, priority for them went down
and richer peers in cities took away
those scarce electrons. "How'd you know all this?"
asked Stella of impressive foster sis.

189.
"My dad work all it out. He tell me so."
This little bomb took Stella and Abu
off-guard: they realized they hadn't known
what their host parents every day did do
when they walked off to school. Small wonder Ai
held such a Party line, though young. Her mom
had counterbalanced stiff perspectives plied
by father. She sat right in eye of calm
in household storm of pro- and anti-state.
Amazement was then interrupted by
their auntie's call to dinner. Heading straight
back in, the scene seemed full of stimuli:
a mind refreshed with inquiry constructs
new truths, sheds what quotidian obstructs.

Chapter 12

190.
With gānbiān sìjì dòu and nánguā plates
for vegetables, plus rice, plus river snails,
each chosen thus to reinvigorate
the health and luck, as per tradition's tales,
the feast was hearty. Duck and dumplings too
graced table, and each setting had one cup
for tea and one for spirits. Shushu drew
a bottle from the back room, "Bottoms up!"
in rough translation drew some adult cheer.
To see the dish::rice ratio so big
still went against the wallet-strapped austere
upbringing Stella'd had. She thanked the pig
in quiet word for giving them its life,
as she was taught by Grandmum. Shushu's wife

191.
explained in local dialect each dish
had meaning in the feast, and Jiang Long turned
the tales to English. "It is Ayi's wish
to know what you both think," he said, "you've learned
so much about this country now. How does
it look and feel compared to yours?" "I can't
find where to start," Stel said, "I guess because
my mind keeps changing, as I learn. Tell Aunt
Ayi I like her place, and China too.
They're really different to the naked eye
from what I know from home. Here you've pursued
fast growth, fast change. I'm trying to figure why.
I see it even here: your farm's got lights,
a step above our kerosene at night."

192.
Translation gave her time to think. "I'll add,
I'm struck how peaceful, calm it feels out here.
The city by comparison is mad."
The aunt's reply near whisper, "What appears
so calm can hide so much you cannot see,
the controversies farmers always stew."
Translating this accommodatingly
was mother, stepping in. "Recall when you
read 'Wind' by Xue Tao at the end is line,
At night a path among the pines is des-
olate and sad. Out here you're not confined
by space, but by the view you're somewhat less
than people in the cities." Jiang's look pierced,
wife's eyes conspiratorially fierce.

193.
Manila ultimatum folder stared
back at the Secretary from his desk.
It asked a comprehensive view prepared
reporting on to what degree grotesque
environmental consequences would
result from building this new dam. To flood
such drastic tracts in every likelihood
would alter sediment deposits, mud
distributed in patterns not seen for
millennia. The Chair sought all details.
The Secretary's stakes on planned lakeshore
were not to be this easily derailed.
The trick would be to find the line where truth
could blur to all but master bloodhound sleuth.

194.
A blend just right, he thought, will make it sound
as if a couple species take a hit.
That hurts but shouldn't run into the ground
approvals. And I'll need some counterfeit
assessment of the anaerobic rot,
perhaps based on assumptions that we'll clear
organic residue from farmers' plots
before submerging them in water. Queer
accounting for the carbon wouldn't prove
incriminating. Hopefully none pose
the methane question, since he had removed
its mention in the press. The only foes
were Agriculture and Interior;
their chance of winning ever drearier.

195.
Quite long ago as child he'd been Red Guard,
the middle school patrols enforcing Mao.
His puissant silver tongue left him disbarred
by boss who'd felt his power was threatened. Vow
to someday rehabilitate his brand
had fueled resolve when he was forced to toil
as peasant in decrepit hinterland,
the punishment for all accused turmoil.
He'd seen the land denuded, clumped soil turned
from loam to dustbowl, powderized like souls
of those he worked with, sum of Party's spurned.
Though loving nature, overriding goal
became to rise past trauma and regain
his dignity before that false arraign.

196.
Back in the time before the Red Guard, he
like other boys delighted in the Earth,
watched firs and tallows sway absorbingly
in partridge-laden winds. His childhood mirth
was artless, effervescing through his play
with toys in dioramas nature made
ostensibly for his amusement. Sway
from early light naïveté to shade
occurred when vengeance overtook his mind:
to be deprived of rights put all else last.
No conifer outweighed his years maligned,
so nature'd take another blow if asked.
As Secretary, now that pile of gold
was his to take to heal the wounds of old.

197.
Across a labyrinthine set of halls
in bureaucratic fortress, sat the Chair,
with deputy of PSB on call
to snoop into his colleague's cloaked affairs.
"The Secretary, I've come to suspect,
has vested interests in this dam. I want
you to identify what indirect
investments he might hold. He oughtn't vaunt
this project quite as fervently if he
were holding true to what his Ministry
is tasked with. I suspect complicity
with someone. Be discreet. When finished, please
report to me directly. I'll be back
next week to bust this kleptomaniac."

198.
Jiang switched the subject swiftly. "What's the news?"
he asked of gracious hosts. The following
exchange occurred in flurry, words like 'lose'
and 'fear' and 'fair' flew 'round, with swallowing
of caustic accusations. Kids confused,
they waited patiently and ate their food.
The bickering increased as adults boozed,
yet seemed to not cause any souring mood.
Ten minutes in, the mother turned to kids
to share what Ayi'd laboringly told:
the province once decided to get rid
of half a million family farm households
because they lived in valley ringed in by
some overlapping mountain ranges high

199.
enough to make a floodplain quarter-mile
in depth. That height made electricity
from hydro economic and worthwhile.
Her cousin led a life simplicity
would envy, didn't know a trade besides
the age-old art of cultivation. When
forced into town, he soon began to slide:
unwittingly they'd fashioned mice from men
by robbing them of dignity of work.
No money in the pocketbook could quell
the scathing goblins that within him lurked.
Ripped off, away from purposed life in dell
it wasn't long before he chose to part
this world, fatigue at leeching in his heart.

200.
Details of Ayi's story further grim,
accentuated how it must have felt
to cede career on governmental whim.
The payment to offset where they had dwelt
came late, and less than promised. Wealth was used
as selling point persuading folks to leave,
then claims for those amounts were all refused
once families relocated. "These days, we've
chance of like crisis here. The rumor mill
round Fan says Party's putting plan in pen
to dam and flood this valley too. None will
confirm it, but one local councilman
whose opposition tendencies are clear
has hinted possibility is near."

201.
Abu looked sullen, dragged by bygone world.
This type of story seldom had effect
on him, Stel thought. His story she unfurled:
"From Syria to Turkey family trekked,
then Tanzania next to reinvent
themselves, for loyalty. They bought a farm
at uncle's urging. That was what kin meant.
They wanted to be close to him. The charm
of farming was corrupted as rains notched
a drought, and parents tilled the soil to dust.
Their midlife change of jobs, completely botched,
left hungry mouths. It takes time to adjust."
The dignity effects of daily work
seemed unconfined by any culture's quirk.

202.
Jiang Long had set down chopsticks and tuned in
to narrative that Stel shared. Too engrossed
by learning of the demons lodged within
that boy from past detailed, he played poor host
and failed to translate back for in-laws. Toasts
decelerated, teacups took their place.
To turn productive elderly to ghosts
in culture that cast work as sign of grace
brought worry to his mind. The old endured
so much upheaval, many decades missed.
To hear from son who saw dad thus unmoored
was hauntingly a future, reminisced.
His heart would break to himself be denied
his livelihood and watch it impact Ai.

203.
"Good Uncle, pray tell me which councilman
you heard in opposition," said Jiang Long,
"you know discussion's classified. Till Fan
and others in this farmland basin prong
hear Party proclamation on what's best,
that rumormonger'd best to still his tongue.
The last thing China needs is false distress
to spring from mouth upon whose station's strung
authority of our officialdom.
Maintaining order means maintaining minds
in tranquil form of beneficial mum
until the spokesman shares what Party finds
is best for those affected. Proffer trust
to cadres duty-bound to do what's just."

204.
"So tell me, Secretary, just how much
displacement you're envisioning." "Well, sir,
we forecast that the water's set to touch
the land of near a million." "I'd prefer
to know the demographics. Are they young
and able to relocate? Capital
from relocation payment could be flung
productively in ways compatible
with training them and integration. But
if they're all old, our challenge changes in
its very definition. Old folks cut
off from support are left estranged. It's grim."
"Since youth have moved to cities, sir, the share
of elderly's two-thirds of those left there."

205.
Back at the dinner, chopsticks' plastic ticks
and jostling arms for reach made background noise
layered in a dissonant yet rhythmic mix,
with punctuating lines in filtered voice,
mouths full. The guttural provided bass
and click of polymers on melamines
like maladjusted metronome whose pace
had self-doubt, like a tango Argentine.
The sonic texture mimicked what they'd heard
in restaurants: the pandemonium
of eating they had culturally concurred
was diamond loud; when soft, zirconium.
Why mumly masticate and feel contrite
when body's sounds express the tongue's delight?

206.
Above the munching, crunching overheard
and Lazy Susan click-spin 'round and 'round,
Abu let fly a question he'd deferred
about the bountied grub that did surround:
"This pork that's red—it's sauce, not blood, that's right?"
Not tasting pork back home caused innocent
yet pointed questioning to follow tight
behind each unfamiliar dish. Slow went
his progress picking up the words for foods.
"Dāngrán, said Ai, ('of course' in mother tongue)
"it called the hóngshāo ròu." "The name alludes
to redness, hóng from sauce cooked one hour long,"
threw in her mother, educating through
these unassuming tidbits. "Is bamboo

207.
pigs' food, then?" Abu asked, for having seen
so many stiff stalks marking lines outside.
"Not much. They actually have the best cuisine
by eating food detritus meals provide.
They scarf down things we haven't room to eat –
and let me say, to watch them eat's a sight –
and turn it into table-ready meat."
Stel added in, "We're similar, despite
the different species. We use goats for that."
They talked how livestock's rural life's linchpin,
before the question of what habitat
can best serve China's pig production. "When
I know that answer I'll get back to you,"
said Jiang, who worried he already knew.

208.
"Esteemed colleagues in Agriculture, please
re-share your estimates of price impacts
on common foods if we should choose to seize
these lands now farmed as quite productive tracts."
The Chairman showed no disapproval, nor
excitement—no reaction better served
his arbitration mission, guarantor
that interests of the nation be preserved.
"The farmers on this land hold mostly small
and fractured plots, passed down from fathers for
some generations. Few have wherewithal
or credit to invest in or explore
the benefits of mechanizing. Their
production's therefore small, they often share

209.
their labor in return for others' aid
at planting and at harvest times. They grow
rice, rapeseed, wheat, soy, corn, tea, peanuts. Weighed
against production China-wide, they're low
enough to barely change the price if stopped.
We estimate at most a one percent
increase within the region." "What's been dropped?"
replied the Chairman, timbre malcontent,
"a million farmers growing food each year
do almost naught to change the price? I get
hands' inefficiency compared to gears
but have to think there's more to story yet.
You know a dinner isn't ready till
there's pork, beef, chicken, duck, or gutted gills."

210.
"We looked at meat as well, sir, and we found
that pork production plummeted elsewhere.
About a third of pigs the nation 'round
come now from Sichuan. That has swelled. The share
was only ten percent two decades back.
This basin that we'd flood accounts for 'bout
a third of that, suggesting on this track
the price would rise a tenth." "That's all throughout
the country?" "Yes." "And what about nearby,
what price change hits the local market stalls?"
"Accounting thoroughly for trade's supply
between the provinces," speech slowed to crawl,
"stochastic estimates have prices rise
about a quarter." "That would be despised."

211.
When all had eaten up to point of burst
to trudge through long-lost time the mother posed
a walk. Elders uninterested dispersed
and tidied up or prematurely dozed.
Abu, Ai, Stella, mum, Ayi, and BLING
went sauntering around the property.
The night was still, with lightest chilly sting
preluding winter. Past downed crops were trees,
mute sentries lined up in between the plots.
They cut the winds that ripped the topsoil at
a greater strength each year, gusts forty knots
when storms rolled down from mountaintops to flats.
Decreased predictability impaired
poor farmers' chance to reap what they prepared.

212.
Deep space provided backdrop to the field
of cypress, pine, and oaks. "That mountain there's
too steep to farm, but makes a nice windshield
for common folk like us to farm downstairs."
Stel'd missed displays of trees that punctuate
horizon less predictably than squares
of rooftops, urban concrete chunks whose straight
lines' trigonometry all eyes ensnare.
The unpredictability of stars
to untrained eyes was as a splotch of paint,
a glowing mass whose sparseness vastly jars
with density imposed by land's constraint.
Stel recognized some forms she knew, recalled
she'd seen no constellations from the sprawl.

213.
Once walk concluded, Ai took Stel by hand
and guided her to grandest bedroom. They
as guests would share what luxury farmland
could muster: past the etched-wood entryway
stood four-post bed that through the darkness shined
a muted red, as if dawn redwood knew
its namesake, and with sunlight intertwined
so as to slightly beam. Carved curlicue
on bedpost showed that artisan's intent
was to create an object that would bless
its passengers' nocturnal Nod descent,
symbolically those sleepers dispossess
of worldly stress. Confucian duty bound
free will stay hid by day, in dream be found.

214.
"It's not that hard to fall asleep when I'm
at your place in the city," Stella spoke
to Ai, and thought about the anodyne
sensation urban buildings all evoked.
"There's something raw when nature's in your face,
when stars are mixed up in the hemisphere,
that feels like you're at once where commonplace
and foreign meet. The air lacks phlegm out here,
lacks dust and anxious buzz of city air.
It has this humid freshness that I want—
one whiff tricks senses, makes me feel elsewhere,
adrift on thoughts of home." The doleful taunt
would linger in the breeze as blanket fold
compressed her soft and slow till dreams took hold.

215.
In dream she woke to sunlight, ventured out
to see the road trip canyon. Bounded rise
of mountain arc 'round basin awed, the route
escaping farmland valley hid from eyes.
From stance on bound'ry crest she watched the flood
turn tawny cut-straw plains to inland sea.
Her feet gave way as nude cliff made from mud
eroded, void of roots' fast guarantee
that ground stay grounded. Foot-thick currents swept
her quick from shore. At sea, her panic swelled.
She'd grown up thinking water's to be schlepped,
not massive 'nough to buoy bodies. Held
by crushing, clashing currents, flailing for
her life, she sank beneath the rapids' roar.

216.
She woke in sweat with gasp as if her lungs
had stilled themselves throughout aquatic dream.
She bit her teeth upon her outstretched tongue
to stop their chattering. Her breath was steam
that populated air with haunted shapes.
Her stirring stirred up Ai, who whispered, "Stel,
what wrong?" in tone as if with mouth agape.
"It's just a nightmare," she replied, "I fell
into a flood and drowned, I lost control."
Ai took that in. "You study so much, you
have stress, no break," she said, tried to console
with logic's explanation. Stel withdrew,
feared fact that visions left her mind unmade,
as stitching holding selves together frayed.

217.
"I think you see you most in charge," Ai said,
"like do the things correctly then can make
the things you want to happen more, instead
of other things." Stel heard through word mistakes
a reticence from Ai toward self-made ways,
a doubt that hustle's real. Stel breathed and paused
to think of energy used every day
to mold her world, how much of it she'd caused
to go her way. It worked. It also crushed.
The high stakes testing Ai lamented too
hung heavy on Stel's neck, yet clearly mushed
she and Abu to China. Misspent youth
is well-spent youth to some: rejecting friends
for facts accelerates the adults' ends.

218.
At dawn a songbird covey made alarm,
reminding world to start afresh, a new
chance to exert control on earth, to farm,
turn produce from fields otherwise bamboo.
Ai's words hung low in Stella's waking mind,
who wondered if past bent too toward nerd's deed,
directing so toward triumph she'd defined
herself. (She'd muse for years.) Meanwhile, birdseed
that Ayi'd scattered 'round the grounds brought brood
of wingéd friends from morning call to sills.
At breakfast, three small creatures came and cooed
from Marley's *Exodus*, their rounded trills
reminding those familiar everything
would be all right. Stel's reverie did spring

219.
upon the recollection of those words,
since reggae held a special place back home.
The *bongo flava* music she once heard
was hip-hop born from Rasta beat and tone.
Between two bites of saturated rice,
a porridge made from last night's residue
that's dense in calories to quite suffice
for day's work in the fields, a lone cuckoo
descended when were absent other fowl.
The mother was delighted, turned to tell
the story of this cunning bird whose foul
adaptive parasitic habits well
ensured survival of her species. "She,"
began the lesson, "undeservedly

220.
lacks stamina to raise her hatchlings, but
must somehow keep her species live. So what
has she devised to get out of this rut?
A strategy thought uncompassionate
exploiting all her less quick-witted peers.
She waits until a mother bird flies free
then zooms down, finds one egg, and slides it clear
beyond the nest edge, drops her own, then flees
and hides again. When mother bird comes back
she'll nurture equally this foreign egg,
not noticing it's different from the pack.
And so the cuckoo gets what by own leg
she couldn't have provided for her own,
except by using others' stepping stones."

221.
Jiang muttered in Chinese to hosts, to share
the conversation with them. They, of course,
knew how the cuckoo handled birth unfair
by finding ways to channel others' force.
"A man who holds power differs just a bit,"
he said in English, comment meant for Stel,
"for he won't need to sneak around to get
the thing he wants. Authority compels,
eliminates the need to wait." "Yes, but
to have another knowingly commit
to things against their interests means that what
they do for you is but proportionate
to how you whip them," wife said, "getting done
the goals you've set means sharing them with none."

222.
Abu sat wide-eyed, listening as sponge
to two philosophies that clashed on how
to change the world: one military lunge,
the other more guerrilla. Jiang allowed
his wife her point with deferential nod,
appropriate for family audience.
"Let's show our guests a sample patch of sod
where nobles once considered gaudy thence-
forth crafted wonders standing test of time:
a testament to leadership of wise,
enlightened leaders helping people climb
to heights that they'd not for themselves devise."
And so they planned a drive to see craftsmen
of engineering feats in Dujiangyan.

223.
Jiang proudly stood at lookout on the shore,
scanned outward through an unexpectedly-
clear sky, laid eyes on structure he adored
that tamed a river's wrath. Reflectively,
he started through its history. "Back when
this region was in Warring States, an age
around two-fifty BC, leaders then
saw nature as as nasty and enraged
as other kingdoms. Yangtze's curves left silt
amassing so that plains nearby were prone
to floods, and with them famines. So they built
a structure that could tame it. See that stone?"
He pointed, "That, they made with heat. Those rocks
weren't blasted, nor did they have tools to knock

224.
them free. Instead they set up massive fires
right at the base for warmth. Cliffs would expand
and crack with chill that followed dying pyre.
Eight years of bonfires set by hands of man
were needed to create that channel. Wood
was fashioned into tripods so to hold
those bamboo bundles of the levee. Could
you think of any project quite this bold
today, near-decade burrowing and four
years spent constructing what you wanted? Yes,
but only here. Millennia of lore
are testament to how we have finessed
the contours of the natural world just so
to fit our needs." His braggadocio

225.
struck Stel as overbearing. Though she knew
that Jiang Long's pride for China ran quite strong
she hadn't seen it as temporal glue
adhering past with present. Did he long
to play a part in China's narrative,
to build great things so he could point them out
as monuments each that would dare outlive
their architects and engineers? "A drought
is only harmful to the unprepared,
a flood the same," he said, "so we flipped from
the victim to the victor when we paired
control of flow with irrigation. Come,
and let me show you its museum." He gleamed
as if the water flow were his bloodstream.

226.
Surprise though it might be to readers who
grew up in places where museums exist,
it was the first time Stella'd seen a room
whose only purpose was to reminisce.
It housed a hundred artifacts or more
each from the era when the dam was built.
Their purpose was to sit, be seen and stored
away from light and air that might make wilt
those trinkets anchoring our histories.
She'd known of naught but herd and house and land
that passed down on the kinship list. Glories
were kept in word and story, not in hand,
back home. It felt peculiar someone paid
to build a place to show the old and grayed.

227.
She split from Jiang and strolled with Abu past
the cabinets of items labeled in
both English and Chinese, none colorfast,
each fading. "I'm afraid I'm feeling grim,"
lamented Stel, tad puzzled by the place.
"It's like I'm happy that they have these links
back to their heritage. Yet, all encased,
they don't feel real. I like things that can sink
into my hand, that have a weight and feel.
No thing can be authentic without touch."
"That's 'cause they're not your culture. They're surreal
to you, like folklore. Shared ID is clutch,"
Abu replied, "were this all Syrian
like Jiang I'd think this work Shakespearean."

228.
A knock on Chairman's door. "Come in," he said.
"I've that report on cultural impact,
prepared at your request." The overfed
young Secretary dropped it, quickly backed
toward door when stopped. "Thanks. Please come in,
sit down."
He nervously complied and eased his weight
into the cushions' grip. "You're known around
these offices as erudite. The late
Qin state and peers in ancient Sichuan were
the subject of your dissertation, no?"
"Yes, Chairman. Analyzing what's interred
beneath our feet to learn what there's to know
about ourselves has been my passion since
my childhood." Forte words and tone evinced

229.
his pride that Chairman knew enough of him
to ask this type of question. "Help me, then.
I see what you've prepared is far from slim—"
he motioned to the volumes staff had penned.
"I'd benefit from listening to you,
from hearing what a scholar stands to gain
or lose if we should flood these avenues
our ancestors did tread and their remains."
Forgetting of his station, young man launched
into his personal philosophies
on research inquiries that would be staunched
were artifacts 'tween hills be lost in seas:
"Of course you've heard, Chair, sir, of Sanxingdui,
who showed that China's cultures fanned, conveyed

230.
modernity through interaction. Back
before we found their artifacts we'd thought
we came from Yellow River stock who'd whacked
through wilderness to settle widening plots.
The jade and bronze from Sanxingdui revealed
our core beliefs 'bout where we came from wrong!
The archaeology left in those fields
could also shift where we think we've belonged:
it's recognized as having been a nest
of culture for four thousand years. To veil
it would leave permanently unassessed
what may be some material detail
about our lineage. With truth unknown,
respectfully I'd say you should postpone."

Chapter 13

231.
The rhythm of the term returned once break
wrapped up. To see the countryside as foil
and have a chance to circumnavigate
the province, touching tree and creek and soil
relieved some pressure Stel and Abu felt
that urban life was clipping wings they prized.
And so it was a blow to Stella dealt
when she walked in on Abu unadvised
and heard him speaking to himself, as if
gone proper mad! Yet further, it was in
Chinese! "My friend, you've fallen off the cliff,"
she said, her laughter startling him. She grinned.
"Oh *dada*, I'm just doing what they've asked
and memorizing paragraphs. The task

232.
was kinda dumb for both the first two hours
but then I guess it sank in more and more.
I've memorized new structures, each empowers
me little bits to speak." "You do abhor
to make mistakes," Stel offered. "That's just it!
I'm only open to a sentence when
I know the grammar's liable to fit.
I study rules, fail, do it all again
and still can't drill them in my head. So why
not follow Teacher Yan's example to
commit to them instead? Subconscious ties
inputs together smartly. He's accrued
a thousand perfect sentences without
immersion, all because his will's devout."

233.
"You're more than will!" Stel countered. "Just recall
those early days of marveling at bugs
and grasses, ferns, and fauna, or nightfall
that time we took you from your home then trudged
through forest's wolfish gauntlet. Your fireflies
collected in that jar brought us the light
to find a place of safety till sunrise.
Our fun was simply poking stuff. Despite
the fact that we're ahead now, freed from that,
I'm feeling something lost along the way."
"That fun was then," Abu said, face still flat,
"we're here because they want us everyday
to study like we'll be important soon."
"I'm out if soon's much past this afternoon."

234.
Stel didn't often quarrel verbally
and didn't know what made her turn that phrase,
perhaps chrysanthemums in herbal tea
intoxicated with relieved brain haze.
She hadn't realized her testiness
and so, oblivious, continued on:
"I'm out regardless! I'm depressed with this
repeat refrain of yours, one thin view drawn
from culture, parents, airwaves – I don't know –
that all you're meant to do is better than
the next guy, climbing, climbing toward the dough,
the recognition. That's what makes the man?
To care about what other people think
Lao Tzu said locks us up inside their clink."

235.
"I'm prisoner of something," Abu laughed,
"and probably of this room first, foremost."
"You've put ten hours in. Yes! You're overstaffed
on tasks that oughtn't leave you so engrossed.
You're memorizing paragraphs! Is there
a bigger academic waste of time?"
Fatigue had let his guard down: "Guess my lair
has grown a little stale." "Let's break," Stel chimed,
and so they put on shoes and collared BLING
to head on walk to Qingyang Palace, Green
Ram Temple, built in reign of old Zhou kings.
Millennia'd since passed, grounds overseen
by Taoists. Tourists went there now. Some monks
from Two Immortals Monastery slunk

236.
across the grounds to points unknown, their tasks
both steps and whole of following the Way.
Ascetic business there still clung to past,
traditions that the years could not decay.
Stel gazed up at the trees stretched overhead,
and thought of generations they'd lent shade,
of thousand birds for which they'd been homestead,
of million thoughts aired in their colonnade.
Abu gazed straight at pillars bearing roofs,
and thought of weight of history each bore,
of texts old monks beneath them mulled, aloof,
symbolic duties that they underscored.
BLING sniffed discarded sunflower husks for meat
forgotten for some morsels left to eat.

237.
They chose this place because it offered green
and peace in equal measure, even crowds
adopted tranquil ways inside. Gate's clean,
tall running-script calligraphy avowed
that balance lay therein, for all to find.
An acolyte was circulating 'round
the courtyard, gifting out to humankind
some quotes philosophy held as profound:
a set of teachings from Lao Tzu. His texts
were braids of truth and mystery, ripe for
ten reinterpretations. Look perplexed,
Abu reviewed the pamphlet. "Useful, or
another propaganda piece?" Stel asked.
"It's nothing if not full of deft contrast,"

238.
replied Abu, who scanned translations to
see if he could pick up more vocab. Stel
preferred to read the quotes for Teacher's clues
about how life works, so she then compelled
Abu to hand it over. "When content
to simply be yourself and don't compare,"
she read aloud while pacing down cement,
"then everyone will so respect you." "Fair,
but half the pamphlet's contradictory,"
Abu said, "He who conquers others strong,"
he quoted in *entendre* victory,
"yet he who conquers self is mighty." Gong
announced a ceremony past the walls
ringfencing tourists. "That's the thing that calls

239.
me, wanting to be strong and mighty both."
"I don't think that's what Lao Tzu's trying to say,"
said Stel. "Well, so the little paper quoth!"
retorted her companion. "Taoist Way
is found by choosing wisely. Read right here:
'to know another is intelligence,
to know yourself true wisdom'. Pamphleteer
wrote up two options, both with relevance,
so you could choose between the goals. It goes,
'to master others gains you strength', then gives
a better choice: 'to master self bestows
true power'." "No, it's through others we'll outlive
our body, bones, and brain. We rise above
our deaths through reputation, stories of

240.
the things we've done in life, both big and small.
I told you that my family's legacy –
before our move to Africa – enthralled.
And carried on our stories' legs, we'd be
regarded royally from place to place.
Red carpets rolled out just because some thought
my granddad's nod had the power to erase
a bad host's social standing! I was taught
that eminence was in itself the ends,
and that once having it you'd have the means
for anything and everything." *Naught rends
the heart,* thought Stel, *like best friend coming clean
that actually his purpose every day's
to climb so high that folks beneath obey.*

241.
"So that's why you've forgotten me," said she,
gaze cast toward feet, deflated, quietly,
"my social ladder rung's below your knee
now that you're climbing up." A sigh let free.
"Outside of Fan it's like you chose to meld
into your textbooks, that's your only fight.
You've shunned adventure's spirit. Now it's spelled
so clearly why, I see I lack the might
to help you get ahead. So why waste breath,
and dawdle on these silly walks with Stel,
or eat jiānbing with her? They won't cheat death,
won't generate the stories you can sell.
No. You've revised our friendship. I lack sway.
You search for gold, I've wrong friend dossier."

242.
Her eyes welled up. "So much for Pioneers...
At least I got the Afro-Asia right
and guess it took us past the biomes peers
will ever get to see." Aphasia's bite
stunned Stel. She'd trekked to Ab's first night on hunch
that doodled boat meant wished skedaddle loomed
in mind, the same desire to somehow crunch
the vast globe down to size they could consume
in single, zealous go, ditch status quo
of generation that was theirs. She'd been
expecting her adventure peer to grow,
myopically projecting him as twin.
Such hope for sameness was far too sublime:
compatibility can change with time.

243.
"It's like you think intention's good enough,"
Abu retorted. "It can get you far,
but up until you're in command of stuff
you're always at the whim of those who are."
He looked her in the eye. "I'm here to make
a fortune to unlock the future you've
been pining for in daydreams. Well, awake
and see it takes some grit if you're to move
from lowest social rung. They love to kick
you back and watch you fall. You know as much.
That Xue Tao poem you like, 'Moon', shares the trick:
be but a slender shadow now, till such
times come so as to be seen everywhere
in fullness you've long known, then oh, they'll stare!"

244.
"Well if you're going to bastardize the poem
at least pay it the honor of some thought:
you're arrogantly thinking—" "Let's go home—"
"Hold on! I'm not done yet. If you're moon, ought
you drift somewhere away from Earth? To be
out showing off your fullness you'd be left
detached from all these folks you want as plebes,
you'd win the game by stretching widest cleft
you could from fellow humans." "Shut up, Stel!"
exclaimed Abu, "I just was trying to use
a thing you knew so that you'd get it. Hell,
I wasn't trying to start another goose
chase quarrel 'bout approach. Just let me be
the self that brought me here to China. Please."

245.
With turnabout they turned around, to walk
back through the cultured grounds to Way-ward gate,
where single step's departure brought the hawks
whose hawked wares grounded mind in life postdate
simplicity of monks' upkeep. The goods
were manifold in shape and color, size,
each held a tiny bit of livelihood
for shopkeep, poverty left undisguised.
The tchotchkes thrust at them for 'best friend price'
revolted for their uselessness, but too
enticed as way to give back, as device
to spin cash carousel with revenue
and keep our feral economic ride
at breakneck, safe from discontents' shanghai.

246.
Initial entry hawker gauntlet had
not struck Stel. Coming from Chengdu streets, it
was baseline commerce pace among comrades.
Once inside monastery, then peace fits.
But life repressurized at exit: Stel
saw beggars wanting alms, who followed close;
bold hawkers reached out, grabbed, and joshed, and
    yelled;
in gold each singlemindedly engrossed.
Yet who was she to judge them? She'd escaped
poor station of her childhood neighborhood,
had chance to quench own lucre thirst till slaked.
Revolting? Yes. But too, she understood:
had she wound back the clock to choose again
she would have pawned the ring to businessmen.

247.
Back home Abu retired to language tapes,
while Stella curled with BLING in bed and wept.
She had no other way to stage escape
than burrowing in plush fur while BLING slept.
Unsettling her were crossed paths toward power's grasp,
approaches unarticulated that
in momentary flashes she'd try clasp
without success. Soon Ai came for chitchat
and saw that things were wrong, so offered to
take Stel with dog to favorite river park.
Fear sourness would make her scoffer, few
strong words were shared by Stella. Ai remarked
on this-and-that occasion'ly to still
discomfort, trying to exude goodwill.

248.
"I talk with bàbā, māmā after trip,"
Ai said, "you make me think of questions that
I do not think before." The sidewalk slipped
from following the street toward river. Gnats
stirred up from water's surface swarmed their heads
and left both swatting clear their breathing air.
"Well, what about?" asked Stel, to pick up threads
of conversation not of own affairs.
"I think that maybe what my father say
about each person need to do good for
our China is for best, but other way
are also good." "What made you doubt before?"
asked Stel. "Dad say there's lots Chinese must do
and it's a duty that I born into."

249.
"It might be," Stella said, "but where we're born
is merely starting place for who we are,"
reflecting on her childhood in the corn,
abandonment, neglect, their psychic scars.
"You see my country differently," Ai claimed,
"you ask about the history, ask why."
She paused to fit words to her thoughts unnamed,
then went on. "Listen I to how you try
to know past China and my China now
remind me of some pride I have for what
ancestors made, their culture." "So fact Mao
destroyed so much must hit you in the gut.
That guide your duty? Make cash, keep mouths fed
so stomach's needs move north toward heart and head?"

250.
"My mom see more that is to do to make
a better life for women. This is not
the thing my dad can see. He think of lake
and road and infrastructure." "Megawatts
are needed to enable how you live.
Where I grew up, that electricity
was nowhere near," said Stel, contemplative,
aware of mild affirmed complicity
with mindset Jiang and Abu held. "I see
two needs, both good, I do not see before.
Help self-define, help too economy,"
Ai said, revealing neither'd be ignored
to build ideal societies. Ai'd freed
Confucian self from judging maverick breed.

251.
Like water on a desert hardpan sits,
Ai's revelation pooled on Stella's skull,
not percolating through to brainy bits
where normally sagacity was mulled.
Had Stella dozen years more under belt,
or alternately angels watched the scene,
they'd wisely worry that the cards life dealt
would in the future drive a wedge between
Ai she defined and sought to be and Ai
the pressures of society would mold—
for even best intentions' great supply,
augmented with both station and with gold,
can bend and fold and break beneath the weight
of expectations 'they' covertly state.

252.
But as it was, with youth in fullest bloom,
precocious and perceptive as she be,
Stel failed to recognize they weren't immune
to spice of life, to Fates' own potpourri.
She didn't know Ai's pedigree forbade
her heart-led superego shown just then
from overriding gendered, quite man-made
requirement Ai'd be bland as mannequin
were she to try to climb the Party ranks
and follow in her father's footsteps. There
weren't any ways for women to outflank
conforming orthodoxy till they'd share
more seats of power and so rewrite the rites.
Naïvely, Ai still glowed with self-delight.

253.
Ai's present views had been defined by past,
at least 'past' version she'd been told. Compared
to Stella's, they struck obvious contrast:
compliance over independence. There'd
be no more heavy topics for a while,
Ai having maxed her energy to share
and Stel still mulling Abu's mercantile
desire to climb to rank of billionaire.
Their walk proceeded back off nature's grounds,
the bound'ry punctuated by concrete.
They strolled back to the vertical compounds
of urban order's suite blocks on repeat.
Fast after supper, Stel excused for bed
to stop depressing day from further spread.

254.
Atop her bedside nightstand sat *Brocade*,
compendium of river poems she liked.
She hoped to sweetly seed her dreams, blockade
subconscious' flood nightmares that had psyched
her out, drowned her in sense she's trivial.
By keeping with the theme of water, but
recasting it in light convivial
she hoped to break from nighttime bad dream rut.
Stel opened to the page she'd left ajar:
Behind a ribbon of the evening mist,
distills chill sky, and melody of far
off waterfalls like ten silk strings; she kissed
the cover as she closed it, calm again.
She'd not have been had she read to the end.

255.
Bent also under Mother's influence,
that night in Fan, Ayi reached toward her tome
by light of kerosene so dim she'd squint,
the same sweet book of Xue Tao's river poems.
In Chinese rather than translation, she
turned too to "Spring In Autumn", very same
as verse that Stel read. Its calamity
had been cut short, ignoring couplet's aim:
...comes to my pillow, tugging feelings and
thus keeping me awake in sorrow past
this midnight. Waterfalls where meadowlands
she'd farmed this life would turn from grassed to glassed:
this feared reality brought tears, boiled blood
each time she thought of life beyond the flood.

256.
Fluorescent flash too fast to follow flung
from ceiling slots inset above the seats,
aseptic light itself well-known among
officials seeking chairs 'neath its deceits.
Attendees filled the same ones as they had
the last time, with a single truancy:
"Forgive me colleagues, I've found one comrade
new place to sit so we can fluently
discuss the dam without conflicted views."
Chair motioned to the seat where earlier
had sat Environment. "We're overdue
for truth, yet his accounts seemed pearlier
than possible for flood of such a size.
His lakeside holdings left him compromised."

257.
Twelve well-disguised quick surveys of the room
showed twenty-four dilated pupils' fear
as brains behind each dreaded Chair'd exhume
his own portfolio as racketeer—
for though not all had holdings that would count
as patently corrupt, they knew the game
that let the higher-ups create accounts
to bring the lower-downs to public shame.
The Chair continued, "All your arguments
for needing electricity are strong:
there's finite places with bizarre blueprint
for hydro at this scale so those hour-long
and longer brownouts go away. We need
more raw power, this I know, so let's proceed."

258.
Two junior-most betrayed allegiance when
they cheered as if attending NBA
and watching Yao Ming slam dunk. Councilmen
with more experience held tongue and stayed.
Frivolity in public – let alone
in Party meeting dictating the fate
of million peasants – wasn't quite condoned
and here could thoroughly incriminate
offending parties. Men stilled once seeing
the equilibrium in room they'd spoiled.
The gracious Chair pretended there'd not been
a breach, continuing the speech: "We've toiled
to craft a better life for folks in town,
distributing the social costs around.

259.
In normal times for normal problems, this
apportioning's the best way to proceed.
With bigger questions, our shortsightedness
can interfere if unaccompanied
by patient, pregnant, perspicacious pause
to ask ourselves if act for action's sake
fulfills our obligations – every clause! –
to serve our boss and brethren. Each mistake
at infrastructure's scale can't be withdrawn,
they're irreversible. So any 'yes'
creates one future, leaving ten foregone.
Responsibilities aren't dispossessed.
So in right company (he gestured at
the empty chair) let's be good technocrats

260.
and comb through all the details of the choice."
He ordered shuffled papers at his hands,
arranging into little stacks by voice
he'd seek for counsel. "Ministry of Lands,
you stated earlier the perils floods
continue posing to our cities, and
suggested dam could best distribute mud
and silt to suit a settlement build plan.
In parallel, math shows that dredging out
that silt accumulating on dam's wall
incurs recurring costs. Are those about
the same as what we'd budget out to haul
the sandbags called for in emergencies
when floods are coming?" "Cash divergence these

261.
two options have is minimal. Of course,
to take a mitigation mindset curbs
prevention in the long term, since resource
then follows crisis places it perturbs.
Respectfully, I'd recommend a view
toward longer-term prevention, with the dam,
acknowledging the choice is up to you
and subject to competing hard demands."
The Chairman nodded, shifted topmost stack
of papers lower down and looked at next.
"Security, we know you're crackerjack
at making sure decisions that have vexed
the masses don't cause revolutions. Mum,
preserving public equilibrium,

262.
you ease decision-making in this room,
for which we thank you. Order's paramount."
Whenever PSB came up, a gloom
descended on some faces. Their account
of that department was not unlike hens
suspiciously regarding costumed wolf
that paces just beyond securing pens,
disguising noxious hunger 'neath lamb's wools.
Another stack of papers shifted down,
and Chairman turned to Sci-Tech to explain
assessment asked for, detailing what drowned
grassed hectarage would do to air and rain.
"Combustion in industrial process
creates airborne acidity, smokes stress

263.
ionic bindings hydrogen pursues—"
"No need to wade through technicalities."
"Of course, Chair, beg your pardon. Air infused
with this discharge won't cause fatalities."
Supporters 'round the room sighed with relief,
each knowing that approval'd likely stall
should scientists conclude with strong belief
that dam would cause more acid rain to fall.
"There is, of course, a second type of harm,"
overtly prompted Chair, "so please go on."
"Indeed. Perhaps the cause for more alarm
is way decomposition's undergone
aquatically in absence of—" "The gist!"
"Oh, yes. I'm sorry. Methane's what we missed."

264.
The Chair's Socratic style too challenged to
continue given time pressures, he said,
"Like many of you, comrades, I pursued
a PhD. I studied watersheds.
Decomposition anaerobically
of plant material will loose a gas
much worse than CO_2. Our probity
demands we calculate how much this mass
of methane impacts our ability
to honor Paris' Agreement signed
to law by President. Agility
is limited in governance. Confined
by that, state's aegis isn't infinite:
we're duty-bound to act within state's writ.

265.
Yet, independently of that, we've failed.
We've failed to zoom in past our macro views:
debates have been incredibly detailed
on large-scale consequence, from rains to coups.
I scheduled us this meeting after break
Mid-Autumn Festival would give us all
so I could see myself the place the lake
would flood if we move forward. What befalls
these people living in that basin? We've
the power now to displace our uncles who
themselves once shouldered revolution, heaved
outdated feudal China into new,
more modern times. They fought so we could live
these better lives. Is this what we then give

266.
as payment? This displacement? Honor past
and present, future with an equal weight
to build a China we'll be sure outlasts
the disagreements time will procreate."
He paused to let the silence emphasize
his point, and knew his words would make them think
of aunts and uncles, mothers, fathers, wives,
and husbands, cousins, friends, all social links
they and their families had to rougher times
when cataclysms crashed each decade's dreams.
"Recall our relatives who spent their primes
constructing China, building this regime
that's brought us order, growth, stability.
Have not they earned old age tranquility

267.
to live out days on farms they've tilled since we
officials in this room could barely crawl?
To take a million mostly elderly
and force them anywhere would cast a pall
of loss across the venture, turning folks
against us during times we're doing fine.
It takes a crisis nationwide to coax
the people to support an act maligned
against their ancestors. We're not there yet.
I won't approve the dam. I know we need
more electricity. For that, I'll set
Sci-Tech, Finance, and Industry to lead
the search for better power source that won't jilt
our forefathers. Dismissed!" And so was guilt.

268.
Decision echoed in his head. The room
cleared out at his command. In emptiness
a voice spoke up, though he knew not of whom.
His eyebags showed him under plenty stress,
enough, perhaps, to hear things. His face blanched.
"Chirr after chirr, as if in unison
though each one stands alone on its own branch,"
the words familiar as if used in one
close memory – oh, what could it be? – that tone
was muffled, feminine, and foreign. Wait!
Of course! It was in English. Wife had shown
their homestay daughter verse she would restate,
aloud through wall at night he'd hear her say
the poems aloud, recited like one prays.

269.

Satori shocked his senses, sparked surprise
as suddenly he thought back through debate
with comrades in the room, thought improvised.
But no... subconsciously threads did predate
this conversation and the tack he took.
And one by one those threads' loose ends frayed out
displaying selves in places overlooked:
pork price ask came from Stella's probing snout
bewildered by this meat she didn't know
back home; compassion's plea for elderly
was sown from story of Stel's friend's plateau
collapsing when they'd shifted shelter free
from Middle Eastern or'gin to a place
where foreignness reset earned social grace,

270.
and seeing parents' dignity so wane;
the probing questions on the Sanxingdui
arose when he found way to entertain
the kids on ride home, so he planned swing they
would make to a museum to see preserved
these artifacts displaying where they're from.
He'd never recognized these small things swerved
the ways that he'd then turn around to plumb
his colleagues, test their reasoning. Mere kid
approaching life with curiosity,
agendaless herself had put on skids
some trillion yuan at full velocity
toward terraforming turf. Child's words reversed
so deftly who would, wouldn't be, submersed.

Chapter 14

271.
That night Stel slept perturbed again by dream
in which the flood swept her to aqua brine.
This version was more nightmarish extreme,
as she adream lived as a Frankenstein:
imagined psyche lived in different shape
amalgamating what she thought Abu
looked like with her own body. The seascape
subsumed shared frame and sank them into blue.
They quarreled such that by time she awoke
who'd domicile there was never solved.
Of course, dreamed mix would not directly yoke
reality, so in sunlight dissolved.
Long days stretch longer when what intervenes
is not sleep's rest so much as replayed scenes.

272.
Perturbed Stel lived next day two ways, at once.
She lived it easily, as people do,
in thoughtless movements through irrelevance.
She also lived it watching self for clues,
in metacognitive self-critic mode,
the one employed when conscious of one's ways
and seeking further data. It bestowed
examples interactions overstay
their welcome, sponging up resulting mood.
Some whipsnap words from nettled teacher slipped
into her morning psyche; they'd preclude
participation when friends tried conscript
her into lunchtime games. Rigidity
of self-inspection blanched the day of glee.

273.
"Where do I land," Stel wondered, "on Ai's line
between intentions true to self and those
made by and for society?" Entwined
two selves still lingered from seen image dozed.
Her vulnerability to influence
of dream did disempow'r to nth degree.
She sought to snap out of continuous
autoptic scrutiny. "It's new to me—
and haunting. Let's dispel this mental haze
with Ab once and for all, since it's his feud
that got under my skin these past few days."
Come homework time she barged in, though 'twas rude.
From scholar's fortress he prepped to recite
books' memorized subsections through the night.

274.
"Abu, we've gotta talk. You've known me for
the longest time of anyone. You've seen
the me I was when littler." He pored
through book with fervor of *mujahideen*,
without regarding entrant guest's request
he disengage. In doorway statuesque,
Stel stood distressed with shock of heart abscessed.
Myopically, Abu kept eyes to desk
and shut them time to time as lips retraced
the sonic foils of incantations writ
in lifeless Chinese text, the savored taste
of memorizing, sweeter bit by bit,
of words that left his mouth addictively
cued dopamine feedback predictively.

275.
"Ab. Really. Over here." He snapped from plane
collapsing colorful dimensions of
the lived experience to dull, contained
pursuit of marks. To Ab, naught stood above.
"What's up?" "I'm still upset about our fight."
"Why? You have your way, I have mine. I asked
for space." "What if I want to reunite?"
"I'm not convinced you ever fully grasped
exactly what I'm doing here. If you
want social time, go get it. Millions wait
for English buddies." "No..." "But me, my tru-
est colors show at desk, on tests, on straight-
and-narrow climb up out of pit of birth."
Such path would sacrifice once-moving mirth.

276.
Since finding him in Gumi's class, he'd been
lead rider in race peloton toward fate:
she'd followed him when he sets sights to win
the scholarship above all their classmates.
Perhaps they'd better balance earlier
before their choices held much consequence,
when escapades and quests seemed pearlier,
and so much so that play was common sense.
Stel wondered how she'd get by if he weren't
in pole position for decisions faced,
blew her one way. She'd drafted close and learnt
she needed separation from the pace.
"Recall the dragonfly, Stel. You envied
its windward flight. So why not commend me?"

277.
Enough. Enough! She tried. She felt absolved,
if scared. In own room she distracted with
a ritual in which she laid, dissolved
into a cuddle puddle with BLING, smith
of her first maturation years ago.
She played fond film reels of the hijinks they
enjoyed together, frozen mind's tableaux
of time they'd since outgrown. Outgrown? Betrayed?
The night outside tried darkening each min
and lost against the powered city lights.
This urban nexus Stel found self within
itself was geared to strip and disunite
its residents from natures, Nature, Earth,
so threatening one's compass of self-worth.

278.
Ai came back in and Stella snapped from trance,
recalling their last walk in Wangjiang Park.
Ai needed only briefest fleeting glance
to see that Stel was feeling rather dark.
Ai couldn't help or handle, left the room,
itself an act that left Stel bleeding more
until a minute later she saw whom
Ai'd gone to fetch as wiser, old mentor:
her mother came in, sitting down beside
her and her BLING on floor, and put her hand
in tenderness on Stella's head. She spied
the telltale signs of loneliness there spanned.
No inquiry on how Stel'd been depressed,
the mom began to tell of how US

279.
had shaped her early views, had been her home.
"Dad shipped to San Francisco in an age
of rapid change, an era polychrome
in US history. There burned outrage
pre-Summer Love, in 1968.
Young folks had flooded west to occupy
the neighborhood where Ashbury and Haight
met; dad said seemed like everyone was high,
the place was looked down on as youth's excess.
I later learned it was prime time; chicks rose
together naturally so to progress
toward tiny slice of rights. How? They exposed
the world to inner, private selves they'd hid
and tried stuff parents wanted to forbid.

280.
I'll skip the gory details, but those terms
'sex, drugs and rock and roll', we'll say suffice.
By twelve I heard these artists who confirmed
that somehow we'd been hiding paradise
inside, our truth left unexpressed. Once I
heard Janis Joplin say, *after they see
me, when their mothers feed them all that lie
of cashmere sweaters, girdles, just maybe
they'll have a second thought, that they can be
themselves and win,* or something close to that.
Folks missed our Chinese 'home' relentlessly
but, born there, I felt me in habitat
that welcomed people simply 'cause they were
themselves, too, people. What was popular

281.
was being more yourself. It made sense in
my head and when I listened to those tracks,
but making real-life friends had really been
impossible because English syntax,
pronunciation, grammar, and accent
are hard—I only later pieced background
together 'bout what those zeitgeist cracks meant.
To live in multifamily home compounds
the challenges because you always speak
your native tongue. I learned so slowly. I
was living times of cultural mystique
as voiceless fringe observer on standby.
I was too timid, young. Where'd I fit? Gee,
nobody tells you how society

282.
should be approached as outsider. Myth you
will melt in melting pot's convenient crap.
No clear way in, I balked and I withdrew.
That's reason why we signed to host a chap
or lass, a foil for Ai from far away:
I grew from when life forced me to define
who I was separate from the noisy fray
and want to offer others so inclined
the chance when young to do the same. You're there.
You've fallen off the highs new places give,
you're questioning yourself, hyperaware
of all these differences in how you live
when thrown into the unfamiliar. Well,
don't compromise yourself, my little Stel,

283.
'cause Joplin says you're all you've got." She paused
her consolation, drew in lengthy breath,
and looked how Stel's face crinkled, pinched lines crossed
on eyes closed tight, as if to stay the death
of little voice that thought she'd stay a kid
somehow through thick and thin of drawn-out years.
Sad silent sensed sepulture slowly slid
child's spirit 'neath the earthen biosphere,
to grave where personality's rejects
accumulate in boneyard pile. Host loathed
to feel partition's pain from vivisect-
ing psyche, molting needed for her growth.
We shed to pyre defunct intangible,
in pain whose need cannot itself then dull.

284.
With dampened cheeks, one Stella's head raised just
enough to vocalize selected phrase
while staying low enough to hide her fussed
frown countenance rubbed salty with malaise.
"What changed?" she asked with softness, reaching for
the threads of hope that psyches tightly cling
to as their trusted future guarantor
that something better time shall this way bring.
"I found a couple people not unlike
me, those who liked what revolution meant
but never looked for center stage or mic,
that era's silent ninety-nine percent,
the ones who felt the cause as strongly but
lacked ways to join the larger syndicate.

285.
By day I went to school, then after hung
with friends before my uncle got home, talked
about freewheeling liberal yardsticks flung
at us by radio. By nightlight, gawked
at literature less racy, stuff to ground
rebellious days in commonality,
like that serenity when we astound
ourselves with nature in totality.
Duality, I think, kept me afloat:
I found enough community in folks
around me, then could crawl into remote
redoubt in mind where no one's voice could coax
me into thinking anything but what
I thought myself. My body had to shut

286.
them off each day for some amount of time.
That's when I started reading namesake, Xue—"
"Wait, namesake? Your name's Xue Tao too?" Stel chimed
in, interrupting. "Partly. Well, halfway:
they couldn't change my family name, but first
or given name was up for grabs, so 'Tao'.
So anyway, I found I was immersed
when reading what she wrote, and seeing how
she picked out tiny things and magnified
their relevance to larger life. Escape
is necessary. If the countryside
is too far in reality, then shape
it in your mind and spend time there at play."
Tao did not see if her story'd allayed

287.
the downness Stella felt. Words sometimes take
a time to percolate past hardships. That
duration's unpredictably opaque.
One hoped her redirection could get at
the quickest way to move on: alter aim.
The mother Tao delivered wisdom thus:
allow Abu his quest's default goal (fame),
but don't be dragged into his ego's fuss.
Five years in flux for Stel would pass before
she'd master it. But seeds were planted, so
sewn into soil for sprouting far offshore,
and years from then just north of Mexico
would germinate and grow. But let's not zoom
too far till Volume Three's tale is exhumed.

288.
The memories pockmarking young teenage stage
that anchored its significance to Stel
predominantly came before this page.
Remaining months unfolded parallel
in daily repeat action mirroring
the schedule that the schoolkids had to date.
In retrospect, first months were dearer thing
than staid routine that followed. Naught elates
quite like experiencing firsts of sense:
from touch, taste, timbre, tone, tradition, tongue
come neuron fireworks that light immense,
expansive mental caverns dark when young.
Caves luminesce as we senesce, but lose
flash-bangs originalities suffuse.

289.
Attentive readers might predict Abu
would further build his mental citadel
so to remediate chance will's askew
of his ambition's dictates. Grit'll quell
the staunchest mental dissonance, and he
had pride and culture backing up that pluck.
Indeed, that grit made glue constructively
to bond his cinder castle. He felt luck
had fatefully delivered chance to rise
beyond low berth of birth, and duty now
was to deny distracting worldly ties
to study till his technical know-how
would cobble ladder stretching over walls
that being born in poverty installs.

290.
In rounding out the cast, the least was known
about the way that Ai'd push China, or
the way that China'd pull her. Fates had blown
sweet-smelling change – or hint thereof – before,
at least to mother. Would Ai also lift
beyond the Party fence? Some things condemned
deserved retrial, not ongoing short shrift,
like equalizing women country'd penned
into subservience by custom. Where
would badass women fit in China's mold
of gender once the pathbreakers declare
the obsolescence of how males controlled?
These hints of thoughts were tiny seeds today
with mother's tending blossoming someday.

291.
The rapeseed, rice, and peanut fields of Fan
remained free of deluge, at least while Jiang
held seat as Party Chairman. Other plans
would be drawn up to keep production strong
across the province. Hydro's human cost
of yet another million displaced, old,
and blameless lifetime farmers would have crossed
the moral line. Perhaps, as deaths are tolled
and rural demographics shift, the math
could look much more attractive, decade hence.
At least for now, however, elders' path
to tenure would require no self-defense.
As Ai predicted, honoring the past
alongside present built a world to last.

Epilogue

I bypassed ping-pong, karaoke, phones,
smoked sceney cigarettes, and net cafés,
for no one arc could more than draw the bones
of frantic Chinese change then underway.
Ai strived like Tao to be gen's unicorn,
covert in power she'd play as untamed shrew.
Deep change included me, as I was torn:
be true self more as Stel, or as Abu?
We spent five years of walking tightrope line,
me showing him the world, him gripping fears
low grades would cause his scholarship's decline,
support withdrawn then sinking Pioneers.
The pressure waves gave him delirium;
I'd try restoring equilibrium.

Half decade chained to desk's lost time to live.
That's maybe hypocritical from me.
I learned from him the aid that structure gives,
from daily dedication to studies.
Abu was brilliant at conformity:
school offered ladders up, like Ai believed.
Mold self into whatever form need be
to climb them? Fine. Just work. Now more. Achieve!
Obeying sickened me as years amassed,
yet never seemed to shake his deep-held faith
grades righted status, led to fortunes vast.
He 'llowed himself be haunted by that wraith.
New tools, hard times showed novel path to power
as I'd find life in adulation's shower.

Volume Three

Prologue

I've written this, and feel I sit atop
a secret, an admission owed to you.
You ever feel your past is but a prop,
a cutout crafted to disown past rue?
Solidity of character at stake,
I feel compelled to clarify how I
myself discovered young Abu's namesake
so we can trust each other eye-to-eye.
Craved to be Superwoman, Mister Scrooge,
alive with power of strength or power of cash,
attuned to information subterfuge,
I twisted truths with hashtags, mished and mashed.
By end of tome, I hope that you see me
chalk-drop once blackboard's proof reads *QED*.

Stella

Chapter 15

1.
America, America the great!
The jewel! The shining cities on its hills!
Its ports where eager, huddled masses wait
to have their immigration dreams fulfilled
were elevated literarily
from Ellis Island out to Galveston,
these junctions where the traveled wearily
were processed toward their futures: gal, sis, son,
guy, bro, and daughter, generations tied
by universal freedom *sapien* hope.
But legacy of welcome nationwide
that day was overturned by misanthrope.
The entry lines for refugees stood still
by madd'ning stroke of Boy's base-blessing quill.

2.
The protests galvanized support across
a nation wide in differences. They spanned
full spectrum's ideology. The laws
allowing refugees from Muslim lands
were well-established by both precedent
and joint agreements in the Global North.
So unilateral stay's circumvent
caused indignation then to bubble forth.
Beyond the confines kept by TSA
these folks from every walk of life converged
with signs BUT SUDANESE ARE DOPE!; BLESS THEY
WHO'VE SUFFERED; FREEDOM'S NOT RELIGIOUS PURGE;
and hundred more expressing love for kin –
however distant – seeking their way in.

3.
Amid that clamor they touched down, naïve
to shock that hit the landed world mid-flight.
Youth taxied, shuffled out, and were received
by immigration battery. Nonwhites
were separated out to special line
without an explanation to the crowds
arriving, joyful refugees combined
with citizens and tourists. Rights allowed
them when they'd boarded plane half-day before
mercurially changed: resettlement
was cloud-high hope on boarding, once ashore
their glass-shard dreams were shattered. "Rebels sent
to harm us," propaganda presses pressed,
and so they turned guests' welcomes to arrests.

4.
The ban how it was written was quite clear:
rescinded visa if you came from X.
The country set was bluntly engineered
so sample from their populace reflects
a hundred het'rogeneous backgrounds,
a host of histories and dialects,
with single commonality pack's bounds:
each mostly Muslim, crossing every sect.
Stel's life was changed when Syria on list
of countries banned meant Abu'd be detained.
They'd spent since childhood nearly bound at wrist
yet she'd be free and he'd stay there enchained.
Pushed off to different lines for processing,
Ab was lost in Boy's pand'ring law messing.

5.
As citizen of elsewhere, Stel could pass
through entry gate that stopped Abu. His dual-
held citizenship meant he'd be harassed
despite its extra richness as a fuel
for culture's melting pots. Stel got her bags,
emerged to crowds of colors Benetton,
diversity she'd not seen outside mags.
Most all held protest signs, from tenets on
acceptance, love, and shit that Jesus said,
all tidal props that flooded her whole view
voiced neighborly respect to Muhammad.
Meanwhile concealed by crowds, suits countersued
and fought for rights on laptops, slinging suits
to stay the staying system at its roots.

6.
Not understanding those dynamics, I'd
not linger, jeopardize ability
to live here. Ab's been misidentified
by heritage, he'll get mobility
and join me in the homestay soon, Stel thought.
They'd faced much greater struggles times ago,
this was misunderstanding overwrought
like streaking satellite dubbed UFO.
She left the airport 'cause she'd confidence
they'd reunite in barely time at all,
with help from Hill or Pentagon. Hid prince
not that night, nor the many after, called.
From moment Stella stepped on US soil
it tore part self from hip, left seething boil.

7.
Frenetics of arrival overwhelmed,
Stel didn't grasp in full the consequence
of what was rotting into grosser realm
around her, as lies trumped mere common sense.
Events of import that historians
craft out of static flowing headline tales
don't offer victims solace. Boy's deed stunned
public to apoplectic. Life unveils
significance of tragedy with time
in textbooks generations later read
and ask survivors of. Though not a crime,
it traumatized and also pilloried
the 'other' for no reason. First act cruel
distracted (model used for future tools).

8.
Stel thought these things apologetically
and mostly to herself. Time's since healed parts
of sadness once so strong emetically
so to prevent her writing from the heart.
You'll read about events that happened since,
as there's still much to Stel beyond Abu.
But know that her cognition's dissidence
on that day had first rift and from there grew.
She'll tense at every border crossing now
not out of fear for self, but memory how
the vagaries of power can disendow
us humans of our kind. In trauma, vow
solidified alongside loneliness:
she'd find way to strike 'gainst Boy's phoniness.

Chapter 16

9.
Clad head to toe in loose-fit garments that
reminded lookers-on of Coolio,
bro Cadence opened stained-glass front door at
the house Tao's stories told of. Few trees poked
through nearby sidewalks. Shared-wall housing rows
were like Chengdu, but only third as tall.
It seemed that half the block some time ago
was crafted by same hand, from door to wall
to hue to trim to structure, each was same,
cut cookie individuality.
They had more decoration than could claim
Chengdu concrete grim grid brutality.
He knew that afternoon that Stella'd come
to live with them as homestay mother'd done.

10.
"I'm Cade," he said, extended Chinese hand
like Stel had seen a hundred times before.
She noticed, though, voice tone from different land
where skintone didn't make you foreigner.
Cade, eighteen, stood before her, looking just
as Chinese as a one could look, and yet
pronounced his English words *sans* slightest rust.
It was the first occasion that she'd met
a person whose façade explained old roots
without an indication of where they'd
grown up themselves. It begged her mind reboot
by challenging what nearly two decades'
experience had taught her: how you look
determines your insides like cover's book.

11.
It wasn't like she knew a thing about
this boy in fat man's clothes who welcomed her—
but rather that her ears and eyes did doubt
conclusions of the other. Seldom were
they quite so contradictory. "Hello,"
said Stel, "I'm Stella." "Sweet." A pause. A fist?
Cade held his fist in universal bro
position waiting for its bump. Stel missed
the signal, then with sigh he dropped it, stepped
back from the doorway so to let her in.
She hoisted suitcase with two hands and schlepped
her way up final stairs inside. Her skin
began to throb with regularity—
she realized that Cade's posterity

12.

were nowhere to be found: foot thumps she felt
were *sonic*. Now her ears and skin agreed
(suggesting in the ear-eye bout, ears dealt
the greater share of truth once refereed)
that bodily discomfort stemmed from sound
so booming so as not to emanate
from any one direction, but around.
Stel's startled face was noticed. "Featherweight!"
exclaimed her host exasperatedly
as if he'd seen the weak act thus before,
"You'll get it someday." Captivated, he
continued, "Stuff you can't hear's hidden. More
you crank the volume, more you stand to learn."
He grinned and clockwise gave vol knob a turn.

13.

...my single dog, she tuned in, *radio
needs this, they say you can rap* – lost the thread –
except for Jesus – something shady hos –
if I talk God my record winds up dead.
The words flowed fast and slow, legato blend
through presto, then andante, back again,
with simplest rhythmic kick at bottom end
and autotuned falsetto howled amen.
When *God show me the way because* came on,
Cade sang, *the Devil tryna break me down,
the only thing I pray,* all pretense gone
in mien *is that my feet don't fail me now.*
Atop the futon, arms Titanically
thrown open, he was vibing manically.

14.
The chanting undertone of militants
that backed up central vocals faded out,
turned home civilian from this billet gent
on futon tried to make into redoubt.
He turned the volume down, grinned widely, pleased
and clearly amped past equilibrium.
Stel hoped that her expression had appeased
her host. He queued a sequel bigly from
his phone, crouched slightly, folded arms, leaned, faced
her, asked *Who's hot, who not? Tell me who rock?*
then booming from the stereo came Mase
verbatim. *Who's Dolce down to tube sock?*
Cade knew each line, threw Rolie in the sky,
waved side to side, and shot Stel wolfish eyes.

15.
If whole scene hadn't been so shocking, Stel
may have had time to think, react, concern
herself with all its implications. Spell
of vibrantly impromptu show had turned
her inner critic off. As audience,
she'd freedom to enjoy absurdities
sans judgment. On the whole, was awed immense-
ly by the way that Cadence stirred, lit. "He's
a favorite, B.I.G.," he said, sound low.
He caught her staring at his chain, its swing
still slight from all his shaking. "That's my dough,
my scrilla, cheese, my hundees, all my bling."
With 'BLING' her instant snap-back to real life
cut legs from under her as if with knife.

16.
She woke half-step away, laid down on couch,
disoriented in both time and space.
She turned her head to survey room, saw slouched
an old man in a sweater who'd replaced
Cade. Stel guessed man was homestay host, who'd served
in same capacity to Tao long back.
He'd aged in ways that seemed to have conserved
a baby face beneath time's coats shellac.
She said hello and waited. Waited. Then
tried one more time in louder voice. No sign
of recognition was detected, when
descending from the steep staircase incline
came Cade, relieved and laughing slightly. "You
can try to talk to him. Don't overdo

17.
it though, it's kind of futile. He's quite deaf.
It's why – well, maybe half the reason why –
I play the stereo so loud. As chef
and general caretaker sort of guy
I figured I inherited the right
to also make myself the DJ." "Huh?"
"He doesn't hear a thing, so I delight
in setting my own soundtrack. Back when the
now long-gone family was around, I could
like, never do this. Well, if they're all out,
abandoning me in this house, I'll 'hood
it up. I'll rap. I'll swag. I'll vibe. I'll shout
alongside Homeboy Sandman, J5, Nas,
The Tribe, Madvillain. Biggie taught me floss

18.
and jig on Fortune, that's the way to be."
Stel looked across the room at calm old man
who'd scarcely moved from where he flaccidly
had melted, liquid man on gold divan.
Her lengthened time in consciousness birthed quip:
"I get it now. You're patent twins—the clothes,
the mannerisms, age, and choice of hip-
hop. Clearly all genetics." Juxtapose
a young adult's tsunami presence and
dried salt sea's liveliness of elderly
deprived of sense of senses' full command
to get a sense of helter-skelter she
perceived right then. "Fo sho'," he played along,
he pointed toward divan, "his bling game's strong."

19.
She laughed, then when it passed came back to clues
about what Tao had hinted went on here.
"So you're caretaking here, or I'm confused?"
"To outsiders I guess that's what appears,
but honestly the label don't mean shit."
She feared that she'd offended him, but how
she couldn't guess so backed down. "Did I hit
my head? I think I fainted when you wowed
me with your chains." Though cast with humor's hook,
the mention snagged in Stel's own mental flesh
as brain began to spiral on what took
place back at SFO, how crowds were threshed
as if humanity were wheat and chaff
determined by skin tone on photograph.

20.
"You might have, I dunno. You blacked out right
onto the couch. I guessed you just got slammed
by jet lag, stuff like that from flights."
He stopped to pop lock Brother Ali's jam
he'd put on in the background. "You don't stop?"
a foggy Stella asked from where she lay,
eye-level dance in foreground, with backdrop
of disconnected man with brain decay.
Cade winked, replied, "I can't, I won't. It's all
I got, this hustle. Gave up fighting long
ago." Stel didn't grasp his talk of brawl
but came back to the point before the songs
took over air with boomed compression wave
and asked where rest of family was. "Well, they've

21.
gone some time back, in search of other stuff.
It's me and Yeye rockin' out alone."
Voice quiver pitch suggested 'twas enough
of that discussion topic. Cade switched tone
and gleefully announced, "That's why I'm stoked
you're finally here to warm things up. I spoke
to Auntie Tao. She said that you evoked
thoughts of her younger self, when she got woke
by hanging here." "I do?" "Yep. High school's passed.
She hopes you'll open to life's multitudes."
Stel liked that Tao made rosier forecast
than how face felt: cracked porcelain, now glued.
Behind it lay pure loneliness, its grief
too fresh to salve with hip-hop creed relief.

22.
Perhaps jet lag, perhaps the trauma, or
perhaps the simple power of stuff that's strange
conspired to give her blackout rest, restore
her verve to see the US. Broad was range
of things so far: injustice off the plane
was followed by a so-so BART and bus,
then homestay bro with front like Gucci Mane,
and elder man who heard no thing discussed.
These weren't the things she'd thought she'd find the first
  – or even maybe last – day she'd be here.
Four years in Chinese high school long since nursed
her want to re-become a Pioneer.
Adopted in all ways but legal means
let her and her Ab grow to seventeen

23.
alongside Ai in Sichuan's breadbasket.
Perhaps more accurately, alongside
her crafty mother Tao, whose dynastic
ties stretched back to the sixties here stateside.
A couple years before she'd set her mind
to making sure adopted kids would get
a shot to see her Golden State affined.
No one had thought Abu would be beset
by icy ICE at first step onto land,
to purgatory rather than to goal.
But Stella knew not what to do, her hand
was powerless in land of Super Bowl.
She'd rather focus inward and breathe deep,
in focus plugging cracks through which fears seeped.

24.
Day stroll down gum-lined Page Street innocent,
Stel paused to see the trees for what they were,
abloom with buds and ringed by succulents
in pots fit as if from couturier.
These concrete-punctuating plants' points drooped
as if they owned the fact that they were there
as cardboard is to theater set, to dupe
quick-passing audience of nature's flair.
These spiny things betrayed that season'd changed
by shedding all their signs of chlorophyll,
so silhouette of tree was rearranged
to skeleton in floral store of will.
As optical relief from angles' rights
they softened street despite appearance blight.

25.
Stel's feet paced rhythms influenced by cracks
where pavement's slabs were visible in cast,
stride lengthening to platforms' comfort's max
so feet touched ground where concrete massed, set past
these artificial fault lines. Were she to
place toes upon these chasms, there was chance
by superstition that she'd then accrue
bad luck. She hadn't time for that. Askance,
a dreadlocked homeless tan Caucasian, tall,
looked through her with the eyes of living dead
she guessed had come from huffing gasohol
or maybe something higher-class instead.
He passed in peace, which Stel attributed
to luck avoiding cracks distributed.

26.
The street she strode stretched lazily between
the avenue that passer-by called home,
the Haight, (where years ago ten thousand teens
declared the summer 'Love' and freely roamed),
and Oak, fast-moving one-way past a park.
A corridor for residents, its mum
demeanor balanced selfies, hashtags, marks
from Facebook checking-ins that hit eardrums
when standing next to Ashbury. Stel liked
proximity to hubbub, but remove.
And so she chose that first time that she'd hike
this thoroughfare until she knew each groove
as DJs do their records, or as she'd
once known her Tanzanian backyard's weeds.

27.
Commitment to a place, however new
felt somewhat grounding, pardoning the pun.
Pretending long-intended rendezvous
with place she ended up maxed out the fun.
She'd first accepted self when finding out
authentic ways to interact with where
she lived, rejecting other kids' devout
regard for social hierarchy's compare.
This grounding exercise warmed limbo's chill,
by actively embracing place as gift.
No matter length of local window, she'll
make best of it through such a mindset shift.
In sight like from old *Annals*, eyes latched on
to shiver-leaving redwood lit by dawn.

28.
It stood before a house six feet offset
from pavement, unlike others huddled fore,
its bark deep brown, its spire like minaret
sky-shouting nature's prayer toward clouds' low floor.
For just three paces' time the rising sun
lit haloed *sempervirens* to become
the orienting axis on which spun
beliefs that all's divine of deism.
Stel snapped from accidental reverie
to see a lined-faced elder friendlier
than wand'rer passed. Ma'am held accessory
of garden shears in hand, intently her
attention hunting out improper stem,
bud, branch, blade, twig, or weed then trimming them.

29.
Stel stopped as neighbor, faced a butcher's scowl
appearing when she asked of redwood tree.
"Its root growth's been impossible! It's fouled
four water pipes in thirty years, the fee
ten grand each time. I want it dead and gone."
"But passers-by would lack the sense they'd left
for ancient California. Mastodons
back then were still dwarfed by these as they crept
amid the undergrowth to gobble ferns!
You've raised this natural statue linking to
the way this land will rapidly return
if we're to go extinct. Primordial stew's
short on ingredients. So, I guess, thanks
for keeping it." Her mansion showed she'd bank,

30.
so Stel said, "It's your duty to give back
by paying, cause you can. Sad, isn't it
when rich wrap selves in blankets of greenbacks?
To covet greed is self-imprisonment."
Stel turned her back and walked. The gardener
was left befuddled by backhanded words
and didn't know if she should pardon her
or take them as a compliment. Two birds
flew east to west above their heads, wings swift
and beating, bleating geese's honk broadcast.
The forceful sound felt prehistoric, gift
from unadulterated epochs past.
Encouragement to tend to nature's health
was worth the words to neighbors hoarding wealth.

31.
She saw that long ago someone had done
the same, once turning eyes toward end of street:
on intersection's far side there begun
a vast expanse of greenness, space replete
with cypress trees and pines from Monterey
alongside eucalyptus crescent leaves.
The monochrome light's drift left faraway
blue contours where horizon's line they cleaved.
Expansiveness of field and farm she'd known
back home in Tanzania seemed remote.
She sensed this ecotype had overgrown,
its upward stretch its zygotes' antidote
to man-made boundaries that left it caged,
exhibit zoolike. Maybe her teenaged

32.
rejection of all governance cast shade
upon her view. She wondered if she'd been
her stupid childhood self when seeing laid
so grand a park, would she have noticed yin
of nature tempered by the yang's control?
She sensed teen days' complexity compound
and knew not if the universe on whole
was faster toward full entropy inbound,
or rather if the changing force was how
she saw the things that 'round her'd always been
all present. She decided least for now
to shelve the thought till caffeine coursed within
her blood, the serum separating clear,
clean thought from swirls that morning'd not cohere.

Chapter 17

33.
The caffeine she'd accustom to was poured
from curvy spout by hand in four to six
establishments ten minutes' walk, no more,
from her front door. Devouts nigh Catholic
in dedication to these expert brews
existed, but Stel doubted made up most
the clientele. Instead, the crowdsourced ruse
was one that real estate best diagnosed:
the price of every room too high to bear
without a paying body in it meant
that sitting parlors, offices weren't there,
the space repurposed for a bed and rent.
So cottage industry of coffee shop
became the low-priced desk for laptops' lot.

34.
While living at Cade's residence she'd not
need to enlist in latte nomads' rank
since it had space the size of Camelot,
and cost that much, or so said Citibank.
The property a century ago
had had a stable, room for servants too.
The city then had yet to westward grow
from wharf. Homestead frontier's conservant few
had turned some nearby neighborhood of sand
into the park of Golden Gate with poo
of horse and straw and time, so meadowland
took root then soiled the way for worming yew
in Japanese-laid garden, bonsai, ponds
accenting taller eucalyptus fronds.

35.
Victorian beneficence in form,
the house attracted Tao's young uncle who'd
fled civil war. Its place was slum in norm
and price, its neighbors sought their solitude
for weed and ecstasy and LSD.
Before the Wars on Drugs and Poverty,
they said that life was poor but stressless, free
of three-strikes cop arrests. The polity
lived under radar of policing. Bands
like Grateful Dead, Sly Stone, and Jefferson
Airplane and Joplin grew from such badlands.
He wasn't part, became a chef. Person
he hoped to be, homeowner, soon he was,
where streets were endlessly alive, abuzz.

36.
He started out as line cook at Mel's Drive
-In, over on Van Ness, its melamine
and crooning jukebox spinning forty-fives.
He somehow got past city's average xen-
ophobic tendencies 'gainst immigrants,
and made enough to open up a shop.
Store hadn't any true discriminants
except that he worked sales nearly nonstop.
Compounding tiny growth in decades prior
to shifting of economy toward tech
meant tourist tchotchke land could be retired:
sell plot to startup, end days with fat check.
His silence in his older age made folks
suspicious he'd forgotten life, uncoaxed

37.
by pressures of the grind to stay aware
of goings-on. Withdrawn, he'd bought antique,
if run-down house, in neighborhood Foursquare
would rate well only after tech there peaked.
He spent days by the fireplace, where he'd think.
Of what? No live observer could explain.
Stel fancied something better shared with shrink
associations bypassing forebrain
in lengthy journey back through memories'
fragmented catacombs, the tunnels toward
the integrated sense of self. Roar, wheeze,
and crack and pop filled room, with untouched cords
awaiting immolation in the wings,
their sacrifice the entropy fire sings.

38.
In reminiscent chimneyed parlor, Cade
sat close enough to Yeye so to leap
if flames excitably had ricocheted
to light his socks, yet far enough so deep
and lengthy introspection could occur
untouched by expectation. So they sat,
with Stella furthest from the red fire's purr.
They listened to hearth's common tune, format
arrhythmic as the rains, their thoughts. Stel broke
the unagreed-to silence when two tears
fell out without intention. "It the smoke?"
asked Cade, who'd noticed. "No, it just appears
sometimes when sitting, thinking fondly 'bout..."
Abu. "The travel ban, I know." "Right. Doubt

39.
who'll make it through, return..." "And what they did
with those at SFO they turned away."
They'd earlier discussed how ban in mid-
flight used the bluntest form of dossier
to turn away real humans randomly,
how unjust to let papers leave folks flagged.
"How's single, mindless memorandum he
signed caused so much distress?" "You hear he gagged
the civil service too? It's like he can't
bear hearing anyone that disagrees
and so he fills his crib with sycophants."
They'd spoken angrily of appointees
that Boy had chosen, filling toady mold,
wall's Mirror Mirror lying choices gold.

40.
Though Cadence readily would jump right in
to bashing politics, Stel pulled far back
into herself. She sought control within
because, as alien, she had a lack
of vote to change this higher policy.
The company of people – even if
all new – made her feel tad less small. If she
took up Ab's case, she feared, she'd face sheriff
or equal law enforcement looking for
the smallest reason to call her a threat
they'd subsequently spin to crazed press corps
to turn her into someone who abets
this terrorism-theoretical
invented so marquis heretical

41.
face paints the headlines yellow, stokes the fears
of fact-rejecting base. It had deterred
more than enough to keep this Pioneer
in silence, though the law with her concurred.
Stel breathed and tried to center self as learned
in last few years in China, mindfully
in focus on how each breath in returned
control to conscious choice. "The grind'll be
a long one," Cade continued, trying to bait
Stel back to conversation, "four full years?
It's worse than that revenge war post-Kuwait!"
She didn't take it up, but volunteered
that melancholy wasn't normal mood,
from fear he'd think her past few days quite rude:

42.
"Hey, sorry I've been quiet, maybe sour.
I know that hardly makes for good houseguests.
It's weird, life's all new... yet again. The power
I'm used to's gone." "School?" "Partly, yeah, its tests."
"Tests! Those are all we've got from day to day.
You know *My Beautiful and Twisted Dark*
drops lines in 'So Appalled' from master Jay-
Z on how critics love you when your arc
is starting out, you're human, hustling
to make it, up on highs and down in lows
until you break through, that's when fuss'll bring
you back to gutter, fame leaves you exposed.
You've got your times you're underpaid and those
you're overrated. All those human woes

43.
you go through on the way are how you get
from place to place. I dunno anyone
who's crossed their bridge without a drop of sweat.
So don't go saying sorry when ain't nun'."
At that time Stella didn't really get
the ethos Cadence used to pick his fights
'mong all the questions laid in life's remit.
She'd later cultivate own copyrights
on personal opinions of the same—
and more than one she'd have to thank him for,
for in ensuing months she'd see his frame
intently balance duties he deplored
against belief whose strength was spidersilk
and oddly sung to him by rappers' ilk.

44.
"I'm feeling past my jet lag," Stel began,
"I think my head is finally clear enough
to hear how your arrangement with this man
evolved to where you are today." "It's tough
to tell it all," replied Cade, "maybe it's
for best if that one's kept on *d* and *l*."
Stel hesitated, couldn't call it quits,
and pushed a little. "What if you retell
that history, and in exchange I'll share
what happened to me when I was a kid?"
She hoped that give-and-take would feel more fair.
Perhaps the precip, or Stel's teary lids
together made the mood both damp and lit.
His stare turned human under mask, its grit

45.
appearing real first time in flick'ring light.
"You get the cut that's made for radio,"
Cade said, to limit Stella's appetite.
"I had my life, then I got played. Free? No.
Got that there skeleton I'm duty-bound
to keep for others. In exchange I eat
and get a bed to sleep in." Cade showed frown
then quickly squashed it. "You could say it's *suite*,"
he kept on, only so to laugh a bit
aloud. Some seconds passed. And then some more
and Stella understood that that was it.
Reciprocally she chose to staunch outpour
of what was in her heart that pushed out tears;
gave meager summary of Chinese years.

46.
She did admit she missed grades' ladders, as
she'd let slip earlier: Ab's hard routine
made fine companionship for her pizzazz,
and now without rungs' bar she felt unseen.
When done, she realized a certain thrill
associated with the keeping close
of secrets of identity. Distill
the truths into more palatable dose?
Not hard, she found. Instinctively she'd glossed
past all incriminating details that
if leaked could get her from this country tossed,
including fact she'd left home's broken slats
behind with permanence when China came,
a refugee in everything but name.

47.
Both seemed at limit of what they'd disclose,
so crackling fire again filled sonic space.
Some minutes passed in full group soft repose,
the youth like elderly in flames' embrace.
Without apparent trigger, Cadence pulled
his phone out, touched the screen, and walls revived.
He stretched out further under blanket's wool
with face of bliss like junkie once deprived
who'd found another hit. The stereo
lit up with hook of *Tanzania*, Stel
perked up to rhymes that artist buried. Flow
went: *Every day I gotta trust*, impelled
to *hustle hard, my grind is real... 'n dope,
I'm Gladiator like that Russell Crowe.*

48.
Inscrutable externally, Yeye
sat just as silhouetted as before
new beats came on. "You know what *flippin' yay*
is all about in this one?" Cade implored
her answer. "No," she absentmindedly
replied. "It's selling coke, his meaning's clear:
with hip-hop this bro di'nt decline, kid freed
himself by writing lyrics, all which mirr'red
his life. It's one by Lupe. Check it out."
This seemed to be the sole direction Cade
would take for further conversation's route,
track after track. Stel'd had enough. She bade
the silent shadow man and eager G
a peaceful rest and went upstairs to sleep.

49.
Of things worthwhile to pack for gap year, Stel
chose two specific volumes for suitcase.
The first was one that Tao herself compelled
a younger Stella read, and whose roots traced
to her own childhood: *Brocade River Verse.*
The second was tome partially forgot,
intent of which was letting her immerse
herself in youth's adventures. One sore spot
was that once touching down in Chengdu, it
was touched but once: Stel added tai chi trance
by riverside. Life made her sprint. She quit,
stopped finding *Annals*-worthy circumstance.
Upstairs, she set out Pioneers' old tome,
mused how to turn blank pages into home.

Chapter 18

50.
She *lala*'ed quite *salama* up until
alarm dukes unexpectedly clocked in:
with angering amounts of sheer goodwill
excited Cadence unleashed hellish din.
She heard him at the door, fists banged and banged
as if with urgency of life or death,
and in between each uzi round of whangs
he squeezed excited words from wheezing breath.
"Yo! Protest day! It's protest time! Let's go!
We got some place to be and Yeye's good.
The people's turnin' out! It's what we owe
democracy: to stand up when you should!"
Stel's sleepy mind obeyed, left brain still fogged,
put sweats on, then toward hoary morning slogged.

51.
For early on a windy Saturday
they weren't alone, the line of them, slow, pressed
toward protest goal beneath a flatter gray
than showed in week of wetness ENSO'd guessed.
Content in slowly coming up to speed,
Stel chose to not ask questions of her friend.
Her brethren pilgrims had large signs, like she'd
encountered in the airport. All were penned
in fonts of size to be seen from afar,
and had a range of messages, most on
how values once American were tarred
by sending off Hassans, Khans, and Gibrans.
They turned on Grove and there she saw the tall
bronze globe pierce sky of SF City Hall.

52.
They made their way into the throng, past news
vans ringing outer plaza, satellites
extended up to broadcast interviews
with soldiers in this values battle. Fights
were nowhere to be seen, the scene at peace
(to those without ability to hear).
To keep that order were dispatched police,
though Stella saw they didn't interfere.
Politely threading through the crowd, Cade led
to where most spirited of slogans were.
They parked, ensured no calls were for bloodshed
or brawling, then joined in cicada's *chirr*:
the independent voices synchronized
'gainst Boy's trumped-up campaign of flat-out lies.

53.
They navigated through the body of
the crowd, their shoulders pressed between the cells
comprising creature protesting that love
for those worst-off should truly trump all else.
These cells were groups of like and like who'd come
together, altogether swarm behaved
like group in any public setting from
the concert to the stadium: one slaved
to get from edge to center through the clumps.
They ended up amid a group who knew
each other, fists a-throb with accent pumps.
In Stella's last five years in packed Chengdu
she'd never seen a crush of folks this dense,
self-organized in common self-defense.

54.
They'd easily joined in to chorus chant
and with a growing sense of ease surveyed
the signs brought as a basis to incant,
surprised at breadth of arguments displayed.
THE PILGRIMS WERE UNDOCUMENTED said
one, other JESUS WAS A REFUGEE,
some claimed defeating ISIS would instead
be better waged and more effectually
in places it existed, per the facts.
Perhaps, though, Stella's favorite were two dogs
both labeled #ALTERNATIVECATS.
Each person seemed prepared for snapshots, vlogs
and blogs and Twitter bites and evening news,
if given channel to broadcast their views.

55.
They got that chance, it seemed, with smartphone fix.
A Valley full of techno-junkies held
palm-sized Tricorders high as sign-groups mixed,
appropriately mobile and, too, celled.
Stel saw a waiflike figure float through each,
albino pale with arctic eyes, no sign.
She chatted with whoever was in reach
and after thirty seconds turned to line
her selfie-stick with new group at her back.
She smiled and spoke into her blouse-clip mic
and so to HD video unpack
what being in the protest there was like.
She gathered, gathered, gathered, spoke, and spoke,
beamed stories up to YouTube to provoke.

56.
An amped-up Cade struck conversation with
the group they'd ended up amid, and soon
brought Stella into dialogue. "...each fifth?
Fo' sho', we're there," he said to opportune
recurrent invitation to cabal
relating to a thing Stel hadn't caught.
Emboldened by the friendliness she saw,
Stel asked girl wearing paisley-print culottes
a nutshell version of her story. She
detailed enthusiastically, with warmth,
then introduced herself as Tula, 'Tee'
to friends, insistent from that point thenceforth
Stel call her by the latter name. "My mom
reserves the long one for my firebombs."

57.
Tee winked, and Stella didn't know if to
believe oblique suggestion Molotov
lay on the table was a prescient clue
to where this might end up. A chapeau mauve
fell off a neighbor's head and into Stel,
as jacaranda blossoms did when wind
in youth balled zephyrs into season's swells
that left the trees of richest purples skinned.
She held it out for owner, who said, "Thanks,
I'm Mona," flashing eyes whose smiling lines
ran deep enough to put her in the ranks
of those whose nature's to be beacons, shined
for strangers in the darkness, all without
a conscious effort to draw others out.

58.
That aura lasted past when gaze moved on
and Mona turned to talk with friend whose sign
was on a glossy whiteboard, letters drawn
that said: "So many juvenile, maligned,
destabilizing policies have come
I had to buy a protest sign I could
reuse." Its holder pierced all near eardrums
with protest chants too loud to be withstood.
When Mona tapped friend to converse, she ceased
to give Stel full attention. Stella heard
the two comparing how they'd been policed
more civilly this time. Friend said, "What spurred
the Black Lives Matter crackdown was when fools
like anarchists came in and broke the rules.

59.
It's clear in modern hist'ry civil acts
of protest when sustained can lead to change.
Once peace is broken, po' overreacts
and threatened powers clamp down on broad campaigns.
It's key they still stay structured, on-point, to
maintain a culture in the protest group
attuned to this, and active—" "'Key' says you!"
jibed Mona, wink at Stel, as if this loop
of logic had been circulated lots
of times before and she sought soft reprieve.
The friend got hint but looked tied up in knots
at choking down the narrative she'd weaved.
She spotted Stella's stare and changed to whom
she spoke, continuing, "Each one's assumed

60.
to take responsibility if what
she sees is likely to bring violence.
This type of tactic's also shown to cut
street homicide—" "Beware, her sky opens
and rain just won't stop pouring," Mona laughed.
Throng's density made sardines of her friends:
she introduced girls pressed to fore and aft.
"Benita, this is Stella. Stella, Ben."
"Or Benny," Ben corrected. "Benny, now?"
Benita nodded gravely. "So it goes."
"It's nice to meet you Benny," Stel said, "How'd
you know this stuff? I didn't know that pros
of protesting existed, let alone
here in the States, where folks aren't really prone

61.
to any of this sort of thing..." her thought
had petered out, become uncomfortable
the further that she'd tried to wring the wrought.
She hoped the shouting scrum had squelched her dull
attempt at building bridges. Benny rose
to full height, shoulders back, and seemed rejoiced
an audience saw her for what she knows.
Her lowered sign she gave to Stel. "Here, hoist,"
she said. "It started back when Occupy
took root in Oakland long beyond when it
had died out elsewhere. Here we thought to vie
the battle past when other hypocrites
backed down from all the principles that spurred
them into action. Gone. Demands unheard.

62.
Before that was Zuccotti Park in New
York, on Manhattan, as a little camp,
a few folks whose persistence grew to coup
as message spread that modern world's big champs
were just the one percent. The ninety-nine
percent of us remaining wouldn't have
a chance to grow up in a world designed
with opportunities like theirs. You'd halve
and halve and halve and halve and halve again
and still need one more halving to equate
the pay of average CEO to men
they hired, still more than ladies. That debate
on inequality showed discontent
with how we'd let rich riches so augment."

63.
It wasn't that the story thusly told
moved Stella then to tears, as trauma had
a few times since arrival. But cold rolled
in cyclic gusts that wet all eyes unclad
in glasses for protection. "Holy nuts!"
said Mona, shivering and rummaging
through purse for warming shawl she dropped like klutz.
"This bag is getting more like luggage. Thing
fits three layers made for different weather you
encounter in an SF afternoon,
but wow, does it get heavy." She'd eschewed
the practicality of backpacks tuned
to lugging stuffs of daily life around,
without forethought replacements don't abound.

64.
Amid the cold, though, came a tiny hint
of tears from slate-gray sky, to bathe the crowd
lit up aflame about the tiny print
that turned their brethren into disallowed.
Though nice of clouds to empathize as such,
degrading Centigrade and rising breeze
would lava hearts cool igneous to touch
and turn a protest shout to protest wheeze.
The chanting dipped below its fever pitch
as most participants checked if they'd brought
sufficient rain gear so to make the switch
from clement to inclement. Most rethought
intended length of stay at gathering
imagining the thick rain slathering

65.
they knew was that which this way comes. Its drops
amassing from lone bowsprit cannonballs
into a broadside salvo of what sops,
the rain attacked the crowd. "Ah, god-sown schmaltz!"
laughed Tee, whose paisley'd started to soak through.
She hadn't moved to get umbrella and
protect herself, explaining this woke crew
would never be denied the chance firsthand
to spearhead the resistance. "Rain dries off.
You get wet, then time passes and you dry.
You only go when shivering," she coughed,
"enough to harm yourself." She glorified
the choice to stay with will and principle
and viewed the body as invincible.

66.
That streak of stubbornness that Stel'd enjoyed
(with some exceptions) in Abu was here.
The others felt it too like liked steroid,
deferring moves to Tee as puppeteer
in charge. The levity she kept despite
the chilly drops that came down almost warmed.
Five minutes in, two thirds had left the site,
for insulation homes provide from storm.
Stel hadn't staged a conference with Cade
to choose if they should stay or rather go.
She couldn't tell if this was masquerade
for sake of staying close to chat with Mo
or rather his release of long-confined
desire to hit the streets and feel the grind.

67.
So there they stood, unaltered sense that these
were principles to stand for nationwide.
They huddled like Gibraltar 'gainst the seas,
asserting ever-presence through what tides
the sky would try to replicate. Her fear
subsided as her conscious mind dissolved.
As church liturgy spellbinds hemispheres
of mind toward flow, so Stella'd too absolved.
They cycled through their chants methodically,
each binding their group tighter to the next,
respect augmenting for the oddities
who chose to stay through clouds' extended hex.
Awakening from trance compressed hours hence,
Stel saw Mo, Tee, and Benny pack, commence

68.
departure time. They shook like Shackleton's
Antarctic expedition, lips turned blue,
cheeks chalked. "Let's bust this tabernacle. One's
at risk of injury, check out the hue
of those there fingers. Periwinkle's match!"
joked Mona of Tee's color and her hat.
"You said the fifth," said Cade, "that's our rematch?"
They nodded yes, tooth chatter too checked chat
from going any longer. Trio left.
Stel felt Cade's arm wrap brotherly around
her shoulder, then they hobbled home. His heft
was more on her than him. For one homebound,
he'd had endurance bottled up. All gone,
he needed rest before he'd turn back on.

69.
No? Stel was wrong. Like Iron Man, he rose
with quick-found fusion Arc Reactor core
once home's front door swung open to the Bose
stack waiting for its chief emcee's encore.
Four buttons pushed on phone brought airwaves back.
"I ain't as great at sayin' stuff as Lu,
and didn't tell you why I think shit's wack
enough to freeze my ass off, risk the flu,
and get Yeye a sitter for a coup
by protest. Lupe can explain. Yeah, here—
*Reporting live from other side what you
hear's all a bunch of nonsense in my ear.
The rich man, poor man, all us gotta pay
'cause freedom ain't free, 'specially 'round my way.*"

70.
Post-hook it said *unnecessary-ness*
is protesting to get arrested. *That
goes right against my hustling ethics;* his
view that you can't make change 'hind jail cell slats.
Cade nodded head and mouthed the lyrics, rest
no longer needed with his songs' IV.
I go as left as a heart in the chest,
then answered in the worldly repartee,
'cause Horn of Africa's starvin' to death.
Attention to that line was dangerous,
and robbed her of her normal pace of breath
and sax riff looping back, all canorous
was now cantankerous: her mind snapped to
how Tanzanian farmers were trapped, screwed

71.
by how the knowledge passed to them's made false
by changing climate patterns. Rains would come
erratically, instead of timed like waltz
as they had been when they themselves were young.
The carbon fueling US fuel to buy
a trillion things from China, lifting their
economy was what also supplied
the greenhouse gas afflicting brethren's air.
Her heart went back to homeland, where 'improved',
more mechanistic farming hadn't spread.
Resiliency was thin. Grounds still hand-grooved
can only yield home calories if 'stead
gets hoeing, planting, raining all apace.
Asyncopation's risk is dying race.

72.
But what was *she* to do? She sat on couch,
with outer layers still sopping from the rain.
Her inner layers sponged up damp wilt. She slouched,
in feeling, 'spite day's thrill. Was it in vain,
this signage, chanting, congregation 'gainst
Boy's policies that lay outside their hands?
It felt more sceney in protest pretense
than likely to repeal the travel bans.
And further still from her sensed agency
lay Lu's bait 'bout the famines of homelands:
this climate change approach of 'wait and see'
meant farmers faced once-fertile loam turned sand.
As powerlessness consumed her, torpor swelled.
In contrast, she saw Cade as if in spell.

73.
His bodily appendages twitched, beats
of bass deciding where and when each thumped
to keep the time with rapper's rhyme caprice,
all while his body lower, lower slumped
toward couchbound nap. His mouth preoccupied
with acrobatic mouthing of this prayer,
unorthodox it be. He said Lu lied
lots less than Fox News pundit millionaires.
In viewpoint, Cade at protest found his kind.
Though few chose rhymes as proper worship form,
he liked new friends who acted unconfined
by Boy's nigh-evangelical reform.
As sky was falling, Cade's refuge was word
repeated so to self-sense undergird.

74.
That evening Stel lay on her bed, awake.
Like early Chengdu days made mind snowglobe
with newness hailing down and scarce a break,
her Bay experience now strobed the lobes
throughout her brain. Not only was high school
a thing past now, its substitute was nil:
once-rigid scheduled time now reeled unspooled,
and she could daily act with own free will.
From structured life to sudden liberty
left Stella feeling rudderless and, too,
quite bountiful (if lost). Such zip her freed-
up life would now enjoy! Yet, still she knew
without a way to capture fleeting nows
five more years would escape in lengthy drowse.

75.
New place, new time? New rituals, then, she
decided as the day's thoughts whirlpool drowned
the chance of evening calm. On bedstand the
tome sat that told when Gumi twirled fools 'round –
and namely Stel herself – its last half blank.
What better journal for the start of days,
she thought, *than symbol of when she broke rank*
with social expectations, dreamed causeways
to larger lives? The stories of childhood
spent too long lonely in that volume. Pen
in hand, she wondered if the protest stood
alongside other chapters of times when
she ventured out, took risks, oft failed, still grew.
Her ballpoint moved on, detailed just-met crew.

CHAPTER 19

76.
Crew hadn't lied: the fifth next month they showed
up right where promised: streets Laguna, Fell.
They packed old booths, dim tungsten golden glow
drop bulbs cast shadows sharply. "Tu – uh – tell,
me how you think that's truly something good
we ought to aim for," said topknotted man.
She smiled, "Well, first it's Tee, not Tu, so could
you do that courtesy? Thanks. Next, not 'can'
or 'could', but rather 'should'. Democracy
originates in power that labor keeps,
for what is labor? Us. Our paws, the 'we'
from mind to digit's pen on ballot sheets.
And in between election cycles, we've
responsibility to help aggrieved."

77.
Her explanation quieted the group,
with chastised man bunned quietest of all.
The moment's silence welcomed to the troop
approaching Stel and Cadence. Café small,
there wasn't too much room at built-in bench.
Tee, Benny, Mona, and few more sat there,
and bade them join on stools. "Joe here's entrenched,
and blind in his adherence doctrinaire,"
Tee said of man-bun. Stel'd seen most folks at
the rainy protest. Tee said, "He's read Rand
and seems to think Roark's staunch position that
we don't do jack collectively's good stand
on which to anchor politics," she rolled
her cigarette and eyes with equal cold.

78.
Now Stella at that time knew jack about
these persons Rand and Roark, how hero viewed
society as having blocked his route
to flourishing. But better not seem rude,
she thought, and nodded knowingly. "You weren't
all kidding 'bout your politics, were you?"
asked Cade, as Tee through windowframe lit, burnt,
and puffed her thoughts to smoke. "Assembled crew—
well, normal members," Tee began, and flashed
quick look toward Joe, "are dedicated to
the same shit we were chanting. Boy King's trashed
our rights? We'll fight! Self-medicate one, two?"
she motioned at the empty mugs, said, "Drake's,"
to show beer round as convo's ante stake.

79.
Though Stella'd few years back been forced to shoot
a dram of báijiǔ, she'd barely drank.
That first experience had made her boot
it right back up. She offered a, "No, thank—"
but Cade stopped her with hand on shoulder, stood,
produced a bill, and looked her square. She knew
the silently advised buy-round path could
ingratiate with Mo. And so ensued
her virgin night of drinking. Talk got big.
The booze smoothed Stella's nervousness to ask
the questions feared naïve: "But what's a Whig?"
"This rich teal guy's anarchic?" "Who are 'Basque'?"
She learned that he was white, and history
was truth mixed with tendentious sophistry.

80.
"The making of a revolution's..." Mo
slurred toward an answer many minutes hence,
"consolidizzing power in hands of—" Joe
jumped in midsentence, adding own two cents:
"Consolidating power now couldn't be
more clearly socially-acceptable
than in the form of money! Cash ain't free.
You get it when you've done perceptible
and paid-for service to society.
You've build a thing that people pay for, you've
improved—" Then Benny: "Insobriety
affects our guest, who's trying hard to prove
his matchstick tech empire can justify
his past work's soullessness as the bad guy."

81.
Again, Tee acted as the squadron lead
and cut retorting upstart off before
he launched on monologue about how greed
was optimal condition to explore.
What seemed quite clear was that objection's voice
would need its recognition from the chair,
with those attending making conscious choice
to echo and expand what had been aired.
It's not that there was no debate allowed,
but rather that the boundaries were set
so that opinions of the wider crowd
could not unwanted heresy beget.
Stel's night of tracing conversation's wend
told what she'd need to call each one a friend.

82.
Two rounds (or so) in, recollections blurred.
Benita glossed on technicalities
on who in DOJ risked job transfer
for surfacing some criminalities
the public waited eagerly to know
about the poopy-pants divisive Boy.
Cade paused his flirting with bench neighbor Mo
at Benny's scatalogicals: "Destroy
the name a homeboy holds, you've wrecked his life,
and every time joes think of him they'll hear
that echoed mocking word. You need your knife
of words, diminutives. Slice his veneer
so people see what's actually inside.
That's right about when they go run and hide."

83.
Mo thought that Cade's idea wasn't bad:
"I've pondered how, like, best to use the tools
that Boy used in his rise to power. Aired ads
had hardly swayed a person." "'Cause the rules
were changed from talking facts, reality
into attacks *ad hominem*," he said.
"And only Boy crossed lines. She fallibly
chose not to take that path to where it led,"
said Tee, to enter with a point on force.
Cade laughed, "The Coup (pronounced like 'coupe')
    once sang
somebody hits you, hit 'em back, of course,
pre-peace contract negotiation thang."
Though square at edges, knowledge of the street
made Tee like Cade enough to say, "Let's meet

84.
again next week, like, more than on the fifth."
"Fo' sho'," came quick reply, since he knew who'd
be coming back again, who to mack with.
The Momi Toby's Café crew'd include
all in attendance, 'cept that man-bun Joe.
Stel knows in retrospect she made it home,
expected Cade had kept her close in tow
preventing accidental Bacchic roam
through neighborhoods that had two lives:
in sun—boutiques and puppies, Ray Bans, teas.
In moon—an enterprise of who survives
the popo: tweaker, dealer weigh banned keys.
It's generally, among those who're concerned,
not quite the place one ought to traipse unlearned.

85.
Now, anyone begun teetotaling
who interrupted streak to great event
acknowledges the head's sheer total sting
that comes upon the morrow, skull's lament.
As powerful as Stella was in youth,
she wasn't one to buck that human trend,
and so by morning lingering vermouth
attempted four, five times to throat ascend.
Eleven in the morning brought the pound,
its strength convinced its source was cranial
but Stella knew Cade also lurked around
with cannon turret speakers. "Jay-Z'll
get you right back to good, Stel, don't you sweat,"
he cried, as she heard reference to the Nets.

86.
Cade asked, "You know of Jackie Robinson?"
I father, Brooklyn Dodger them, Jay rapped
the soundtrack, then, *I jack, I rob, I sin.*
Cade kept on, "He was first black to enrapt
white's baseball-watching nation, played in New
York City, Brooklyn borough, well, back then.
He crushed the competition, slew and slew.
If '47'd had ESPN
he'd have been highlight reel's clear MVP.
The airwaves and the TV did okay
at showin' he was ballin'. Them creepy
poor racist viewers may've tried to downplay
it for a while. But then they changed belief
when black man bested whites as baseball's chief."

87.
Less interested in lessons on stickball
than in anatomy's full-on revolt,
Stel sprinted to the bathroom, got sick all
contained in toilet where none could behold.
Some dignity recovered, face recleaned
she re-emerged, though woozily, and dressed
to act like she need not be quarantined
with weaker constitution than the rest.
Emboldened by her company, Cade said,
"They're great, aren't they? Last night was such a blast.
Well, 'cept that libertarian." "Oh, Ted?"
"No, Joc. There was no Ted. You really passed
out after that martini, no? Well, you're
up now. Let's take a walk. Sunshine's the cure."

88.
From up some thirty-six degrees off plane,
the yellow heat projected down on skin,
uninterrupted by the cellophane
of fog that strains its thicknesses to thin.
Responding to the manna fallen thus,
Stel's legs were still as redwood trunk at root,
concrete as dirt and body as the truss,
limbs fanning out so to reconstitute
with light, a human photosynthesis.
Once opened from their minutes of repose,
her eyes saw cardboard capsized, brim amiss
and contents strewn about—books, discs, free clothes.
"The Concrete Book Club," Cade behind her said,
"it keeps the homeless cognitively fed."

89.
The books were clearly used, and could have gone
to Goodwill down the block for tax write-offs.
"They'll leave this stuff outside from dusk to dawn
in hopes that someone picks it up." Rich toffs
were most of whom lived on the block by then,
with purchase prices topping million bucks.
That meant the watch-, repair-, and middlemen
were gone. In place were Teslas, tummy-tucks
and sidewalk book donations. "When I was
a child we'd celebrate new books at school
regardless of their subjects. Reading does
fill holes that some kids have, gives them the fuel
to carry on until their dreams mature,"
said Stel, recalling books as Abu's cure.

90.
Her face contorted minorly as she
said this and worked through memories that it stirred.
"It still makes little sense to little me
how something simple as the written word
that's trash inside a fat home's walls becomes
a treasure right beyond its well-locked door.
Near where I grew up is what you'd call slums,
where every object's cherished. Wallets poor
can't stretch to things of temporary use."
Uncurtained window cross the street showed space
that hoarding disposition had produced:
there, labyrinthine junky piles staircased
from floor to ceiling, each flight testament
to cheap stuff bought with incomes blessed, misspent.

91.
"You're upset seeing waste," Cade said, "and don't
look that much better with abundance." She
choked down the bile before it rose full-blown,
her body's reflex of acidity
agreeing with his piercing point. Sun's fire
occluded while they spoke, fog tempered heat.
Her skin again hoped pleasures minutes prior
would under clear-cast sun return, repeat:
somatically at equilibrium
when simply soaking in the good rays, till
her ego staged acts sequel, id succumbed.
Her classifying mind thieved body's will
to hedonistically with blinders tight
enjoy simplicity of warm sunlight.

92.
From bed's recover bay Stel's mind took leave,
so bored of its fixation on her pains.
No matter rehydration she achieved,
vasoconstriction's boa left migraines.
It rode that magic carpet freedom through
kelp forest thoughts whose fronds gripped at its pass.
None reached her with the traction to subdue
that flitting consciousness to own morass.
Enrapt in filmlike fever montage filled
with thousand unimportant points ago,
disoriented Stel lacked conscious will
and reeled through images of inner foes.
Pace slowed, and focused on the largest pox:
the inner critic voices she kept boxed.

93.
Some critic goblins lived in dark recess
of psyche somewhere too deep for smoke bombs
or gopher traps or any GPS.
They crept up periodically, spoke psalms
authoritatively to edge her toward
one action or another, often stuff
she didn't want to do herself. Their chords'
sharp melodies convincingly rebuffed.
She knew they lived for her, by her alone.
She thought their kind did haunt, taunt, tut and bilk
the minds of others too, cracked mental bones.
Hers wielded 'should's as smooth as buttermilk,
to point she almost sometimes thought them friends.
Nice means, however, need not make nice ends.

94.
As body's heartbeats bruised hungover world,
the mental space of faked escape was prized.
She figured in imagination's hurled
oasis, goblins would have been excised.
Perhaps they strengthened from fresh fuel around:
an unfamiliarity with how
to fit into Bay newness that surrounds
cued contradicting 'should's 'bout here and now.
School had been clearer. From what stemmed control
in dis-United States? Should aim be please
this crew, kowtow to Tee in title role,
or aim to such position slyly seize?
Should she involve herself as this crew vents
in public its dissent? Should dissidence

95.
move her here, now, today in different form
but like it had when she made worlds when young?
Should she accept this crew's thoughts of reform?
Should she make others up to still their tongues?
Should hanging out wreck body, as the gin
so clearly had to hers? Should she agree?
The goblins let her go from 'should' tailspin
and incoherence reigned again, carefree.
It surfaced bits of episode she thought
just must have happened on behalf of her,
though she lacked full-on proof of privilege bought
she doubted otherwise boon could occur.
As beneficiary in this next
stop's situation, Stella'd long felt hexed.

96.
Stage: Chengdu, China. Characters: Aunt Tao,
and uniformed official at a desk.
Props: one girl's passport photo, one highbrow
endorsing medal. Twist: Tao's strong request.
Backstory: two years networking through Jiang's
provincial seat of power up to the feds
in charge of choosing who among the throngs
of applicants will get a visa. Threads:
unspoken fear officialdom finds out,
and flawless terror middle manager
holds, headlit-caught and told to doc sign, flout
the rules. Result: surprise advantaged her,
so Tao left premises with hollowed threat
and Stella'd soon into the States be let.

Chapter 20

97.
Instead of Momi Toby's rendezvous
an even better plan sprung up to meet.
The nearly-exiled rich bunned you-know-who
was having a house party for the street.
He'd written something something in some 'code'
that made about one person every mil
click banner ads, and cleared a motherlode
when Facebook bought it. Overnight, a 'bill'
became a concept obsolete for him.
For life. For ever. Ever ever. So
he quickly bought a mansion on a whim
to copy Valley 'exit' path for bros.
Its bedrooms ten, Victorian in gild,
and bowling alley made for party thrilled.

98.
The theme was Halloween, and not a soul
was there in anything but full costume.
Stel'd styled herself an under-bridge type troll,
a Grendel clone like renter of the room
below the house where she, Cade, Yeye slept.
The laws preventing most evictions, good
for many for stability, here kept
psychotic hoarder living in the 'hood.
The nearest thing to specter that she'd known,
that renter made frock emulation cake.
Worn outstretched plaid, face made like bourguignon,
and arched walk stooped in Igor's hunch (with breaks):
voilà! The reference form humanity
dropped for the masquerade's urbanity.

99.
Not on such salty terms as Tee with Joe,
Stel sought him out at first when she arrived.
Soon Cade peeled off in lovelorn search for Mo,
and two rooms later she found him. "—survived!
Oh, dude, I can't tell you the stress that night,
just waiting for that VC cash to come.
Had it not cleared and payroll shorted, fights
for sure'd have broken out. We kept it mum—
morale, you know? You can't show armor's chinks.
Oh, Stella! Hi! Allow me introduce
you to my good friends, Jai and Lex. Need drinks?"
"Hi Stel. I'm serial." She'd been bro-duced
to folks who tally exits and retain
'entrepreneur' as title with their name.

100.
"Like Weetabix?" Stel asked. Jai looked confused,
"I haven't heard of them. Ex-Googler first,
then started cloud-based MongoDB fused
with better GUI for a—" such rehearsed
self-presentation with tech tidbits let
Stel tune him out. Did he seek to impress
with details of the fundraises that bet
piled fortunes of the rich on his success?
That was the only explanation. "Jai
is selling himself short, Stel," Lex burst in,
"we both bought oceanfront homes on Kauai."
It seemed to Stel both gentlemen nursed thin,
frail self-worth sense they hoped she'd validate.
She trolled with silence, left them pallid. *Fête*

101.
this size must have some normal people too,
she thought, and planned out how to extricate
herself from instant-rich who sought to woo
newcomers with these stories they'd gold-plate.
"Is that right? You must both be proud indeed,"
she baited, "I'm surprised, then, your costumes
right now are understated—is that... tweed?"
"We're both professors, see?" "Look 'round the room,
Lex. Dozens are outdoing you," she teased.
A fleeting panic flashed on faces. "No,"
said Jai, "ours will show better on IG."
He pulled his phone out, mansplained filters, showed
her how their thought-through getup was the best,
life optimized at smartphone screen's behest.

102.
A beachfront home. A virtual self on screen.
A thick cocoon of cash to warm the soul.
The contrast with the places Stella'd been
nigh walloped her: stressed life among the prole
had none of this. When riding to Dar's port
on *dala dala* she'd seen from the car
lives hoping for five cents to hunger thwart.
Here, jockeying was spending more like czar?
Injustice angered her, and outfit troll
was made complete as wrath made way to face.
Stel felt herself rejecting Lex's goal,
this cultish cash pursuit, this Valley's chase.
Stel's method-acted ogre right then peaked
and frightened guests with outrage-puffed physique.

103.
A hundred others at this posh soirée
would hopefully be less inclined to schmooze,
so Stella at that point turned, walked away
toward bookshelves in the corner, to peruse.
She'd rinse their smugness off with bookish spell.
Benita sidled up to newly-lone
Stel, giving her a hug. "You did so well!
Joe pawned me off to them. I truly groaned
when they talked how much equity they had.
I watched you ditch them even faster than—"
"You? Yeah, they learned from your snub they should add
their wealth in introductions. We began
with Lex's insecure self-worth of cash,
attractive as a raging scrotum rash."

104.
Srong Benny's blue short sleeves were rolled, her red
with polka dotted white scarf tied in bow
"Now that's the knot I'd wear atop the head,"
said Stel, derogatorily of Joe.
"Naomi Parker Fraley!" Benny said,
"a woman who became herself belief.
She's better known as Rosie," lips tight, red,
"the Riveter, true poster child, motif
that showed unconscious disbelievers chicks
could offer something of a greater worth
to that war crap made up by guys with dicks
deficient in their shape or length or girth
so to obsess them with power-seeking. Rose
helped mobilize support for GI Joes."

105.
Sure, Stella'd seen the famous posters. "She
was helpful how?" Stel asked. "She made them free.
Well, free to get a job in industry,
convenient, much-believed excuse to be
out working like the men had done before.
It took that change in folks' philosophy
to let a woman go and join the Corps,
the Waves, they called it, or fill bosses' plea
for labor, as supply had hit the floor.
That ammunition didn't make itself,
and millions of young men were off at war.
To normalize—" she trailed off, glared at shelf,
where sat four blue-bound books named *Zero To
One*, "working women." "What a hero!" "True."

106.
With Benny as Stel's Virgil through this hell
that equally was heaven to those who
had privilege 'nough to know the folks who dwelled
at that address, they searched through mansion, two
quite well-intentioned, social-minded souls
amid a sea of peers myopically
pursuing wealth-accruing techno-goals.
"The worst lack cause to think autoptically,"
said Benny as they searched for friends they knew,
"and plow ahead like AI's paperclips.
They've heedlessness. And consequences grew
augmented by tech's focus: pay per clicks.
Incentives all align to just do more,
with ignorance if more's what we abhor."

107.
"You're saying," Stella said, "all power is wrong?"
"Of course not," friend exasperatedly
replied in haste, "I say it's worse when prong
of *nouveau riche* defense is 'state left free
this market, so I found niche to exploit,
all's fair and legal'. Billions flow from new
unregulated sectors? 'Tech's adroit
at making markets', they'll say. 'Bugaboo
is government: it's too slow'. Crypto's fall
will happen, and will hurt the average Joe."
"But people," Stella countered, "buy it all.
That's how the sector generates the dough."
"You're furthering their argument, Stel." "Is
that bad?" Benita suddenly lost fizz.

108.
They wound up cherry staircase, banister
with carvings not unlike what Stella saw
long back in Fan, when stirrings sinister
sensed those corrupt would for themselves redraw
truth's boundaries to suit their fortunes best.
This made her recall that the reason she
improbably before the teeming rest
gained coveted American entry
was that she knew official couple who
had clout in China, family in the States,
and time enough to do what very few
were able to: take days, months to make mates
with frontline workers at the embassy.
Here, power was quick condemned; to Stel, it freed.

109.
In moody musing and their wand'ring search
they passed some objects making quite a scene:
the Oriental parlor, hushed as church,
held hundred seated devotees who'd been
(according to ad signage) hypnotized.
Stel figured Cadence totally approved
since B.I.G. was primo in his eyes:
and that so-titled single frankly grooved.
They entered sitting room, where pens for prayers
called guests to write on tiniest of sheets
they hung on wireframe tree. Each rocked as airs
were eddied in the wake of fleet elites.
That tree was one that Stella rather liked,
and so she wrote a wish she hung in flight.

110.
The quest concluded when they found their friends
in heavy conversation, likely buzzed,
out front door on the landing. "All the ends
will justify the means," Tee said, hand gloved
with opera-length hold for her cigarette,
itself handrolled, but otherwise the twin
of Audrey Hepburn's Tiffany's *vedette*,
while making clear no holds were barred to win.
Expounding ended right as girls came by—
or so Stel guessed, since conversation ceased.
She'd yet to learn to read from that dame's eye
when friendliness was true and when it fleeced.
They shivered on the porch and sipped from drinks,
mid-evening pause to prime the thinker's thinks.

111.
A conversation pause invitingly
let Stella pose a tiny question that
had lingered in her brain most bitingly
since understanding well-placed technocrat
was inside leverage that she'd had to use
to spring from China overseas to Bay.
"Is use of one's power always an abuse,
or is it fine so that you get your way?"
The question garnered looks, all malice-free,
as none expected such a query. Thoughts
exploded from the curiosity
as voices vied to vocalize life's 'ought's.
They fluctuated, thinking power was wrong
till challenged that they envied who was strong.

112.
Debate seemed stuck semantically until
Mo pointed out, "...men cited, looked up to,
all thought of blood: they planned and hoped none
    spilled.
It's not that power must equal violence. Glue
for them was reputation, image, brand.
Their oratory, organizing peeps
was power built up from plain old soapbox stand,
they gathered like a shepherd all their sheeps."
Tee said, "Once built up, it's how they deployed
that energy they'd activate, what cause.
That end's the point of judgment." This annoyed
kind Mona, who had nearly finished clause
toward same point, wrapping with tight logic's bow
before the interruption broke her flow.

113.
Deterrent interruption gathered steam:
"That's why I hold belief the Boy's a fiend,
a demagogue who's taken to extreme
this groundswell negativity convened.
Ignore a moment all the falsities
deployed to gain momentum in the chase,
forget that. In the present, fault is he's
continuing to mobilize the base
toward closing, judging, taxing, hating. Move
from faith in fact and science toward belief
and lose your basis to prove or disprove
if any action brings our lives relief.
Of course our gaslit lives feel under siege,
reduced to beg for some *noblesse oblige*."

114.
"I get you," added Cade, "that's just what Nas
was throwing down in 'Want To Talk To You':
addressing politicians as the boss
and asking each to step into his shoes.
Hey Mayor, 'magine this was your backyard.
Hey Governor, no jobs for nephew meant
his choice was selling crack or dying, starved.
And don't get started on Boy President...
Point is, those cats on top have gotta make
their choices like they lived with folks down low."
"That's actually the stance that John Rawls takes,
to maximize the good for worst-off schmo,"
said Benny, showing off her intellect.
"In Opposition, then, let's Boy reject."

115.
"An 'Opposition', as Tee names it, in
its very definition's anchored on
the shortfalls boyish Boy and toady kin
will bare to us from gilded pantheon.
You've anchored what you think in what you hear,
the same way knees' reflexes jerk when slight
and painless hammer pressure's put right here,
bypassing logic, reason, or insight.
The way you act's habituated, not
nuanced in any way or shape or form
that would discern what merits a boycott
and what is meant to merely misinform.
Of course, if Opposition's blanket warms,
then snuggle up and good luck through the storms.

116.
I fear your gear, however, cannot last
the lengthy tempest that he's out to brew.
Your blanket tatters 'fore the gales have passed,
your huddled, hail-hit bodies burned to blue.
An Opposition categorical
in all it says and does will end up spent,
exhausted by each tit tat roar, prick, pull
manipulation Boy that day has sent.
He's clever, pilfering your boldness by
recasting politics from single bouts
on issues to attrition, nullified
your verve by shelling you day in, day out.
To play his game, you stay in warfare's trench.
It's up to you to play, not warm the bench

117.
or even better yet, to change the game.
I can't become the 'Opposition'. When
that gets to be the dominating frame
you've given too much power up to his pen.
He knows that you'll say 'no' to everything
(an edge were he to have a strategy)
and thus controls your interests like a king."
Mo breathed. Tee countered: "So lay flat, as he
steamrolls our every interest every day?
That's hardly a position Che would take."
"Of course not, that *reductio per se*
is sloppy thinking. Still, you need to break
your habit of allowing someone to
dictate the things importantest to you."

118.
Stel listened to Tee's, Mona's back-and-forth,
surprised to hear Mo taking such a stand,
and finding in her words a truer north
than those of Tee to reject out of hand.
It wasn't wholly clear if others felt
the same in their unease for branding as
an entity whose primal purpose dealt
with saying 'no' to what another has
said publicly he'll do. Tee pressed, "Hashtag
big-O in Opposition's better brand
for social media." "Likes don't trash flags,
Confederate or otherwise. Grandstand-
ing is name's sole reward." On vote they'd be
'The Opposition' till none obeyed Tee.

119.
From cigarettes and hunger, booze and cold
came motivation soon to relocate
the conversation from porch tech bankrolled
to corner store to snack and eat. "Stoked, Cade,"
asked Mo, "they took the name? In that debate
they didn't hear my point; they're getting duped."
"I'm mixed," he said, "to stand against stuff's great,
like 'Ways to Kill a CEO' by Coup,
but that don't say a thing 'bout what to build
when revolution puts you up on top."
"Exactly it. We're not compelling; billed
as platform with no platform." Stel's eavesdrop
dropped as they paired off. Signs of Central Haight
bodega neared each step. Lit, open late,

120.
it greeted passers-by with mural of
Bob Marley backed by Rasta washes, quote
beside his head and Stel's, sat just above
eye height. White lettered, chosen anecdote
was: *Do not gain the world and lose your soul*,
which Stella felt germane to man-bun Joe,
wisdom is better than silver and gold.
Cade saw it, knew it: "Zion Train". He glowed
when music's lyrics intersected chat
and wove in similarities from past
to problems in the present. "Song's format,"
continued Cade, "makes painless the broadcast
of values held, folks listen and don't judge.
Our poppy narratives fix flaws begrudged."

121.
They entered as a pack: Cade, Mona, Tee,
and Stella, spirit of Abu beside,
with other randoms Opposition's creed
threw in their rabble, reasons each red-eyed.
Stel'd been to supermarkets, petrol stops,
convenience stores, and all the like before.
She'd never, though, been to them drunk. Hand propped
against the automatic sliding door,
she timidly extended heel inside,
eyes flitting for which safety handhold next
would brace her lest her wobbly knees both slide
directions that would leave her joints perplexed.
She found a faceless arm to brace her, stave
off spill, then saw the rainbow tidal wave.

122.
Beginning were the Gatorades, their hues
fluorescent and transparent, then came juice
cold-pressed and pulped, caloric greens' chartreuse
with wheatgrass, antioxidants infused.
They bordered bubbly bottles, fizzy brews
with saccharides of artificial make
once natural, like sarsaparilla, whose
plant tastes were copped from now-unknown namesakes.
Her fleeting count of flitting flavors slipped
into another thought once thirty notched.
Each product on its own was nondescript,
together they made Pantone color swatch.
"Too many," Stella drawled in escort's ear,
his mind by spectacle not commandeered.

123.
"These chips," her hand on dijon, barbecue,
then salt and pepper, vinegar, and shrimp,
"...but where potatoes sprout's so far... We grew
those back at home. What you have here's been pimped,
been whored to feel like something else. They've used
what's earthy, natural here to lure you. Can't
you see that they've bamboozled you? Peruse...
and find one thing your greatest – grandmum, aunt –
whoever's ghost ate when she was a kid!"
Her body slackened on the outstretched arm,
her roughshod speech forced Cade finally forbid
her from another sentence of alarm.
Her last resentful words: "You all are kings
with endless feasting, yet complain of things..."

124.
With world now spinning out, she tried the trick
perfected in her youth: deep breaths to cool
reactions. Liquor balked. She still felt sick.
This Bay, she seethed, *keeps breaking all the rules!*
Its homeowners abhor their lovely trees;
its workers now reside in coffee shops;
its wealthy want from feds tax liberties;
its youth protest the government and cops.
The Boy's distracting everyone, sucked air
from lungs that otherwise might get things done.
The 'Opposition' was their construct where-
by they'd solve any of this? Head still spun,
in own insolvency at unresolved
big questions, and as liquor guts dissolved.

125.
But Stella held on. Mentally, at least.
She needed time to process. Structure. Think...
She ought to talk to Cade... Yes? No! He ceased
to listen sometimes, readied lyrics' link
before time taken so to understand
the speaker's real position. He'd not do.
She needed medium, not guiding hand.
Who listened for Stel's story? Ink blots knew
what childhood put in *Annals* 'fore she stopped.
The pages listen, Stella thought, *it's me,*
my problem's me. Too gassed, I'd never opt
to speak to them. Gone now's exam blitz. Three-
ish hundred *Annals* pages yet lay white;
Stel now had stuff to write that might incite.

126.
In shop, crew parroted consensus in
Tee's 'Oppo' name (at least, those conscious still)
support, of course, both voiced and densest when
each member vied to climb hierarchy's hill.
They hadn't quite yet reached the age when such
attentiveness to social order ceased,
and so their own considered views were clutched
in fetal state to chest and unreleased.
Stel learned all this quite secondhand next day,
once Cade ensured her safely home in bed,
and she awoke with questions mind delayed
till times of sober clarity. He said,
"They didn't hear your rap against their food,"
explaining each toward leader Tee had cooed.

127.
Once water and caffeine began their course
to Stella's veins, enlivened, she replied,
"Thank goodness. No surprise that they'd endorse
the stuff she argued. Her charisma, pride,
and force of personality make crowds
of any type befriend her. That's a gift."
Stel's token guilt was having disavowed
new friends' consumerism, foregone thrift
that paired with lack of gratitude, eclipsed
by mem'ries of a world where infants starved.
The Cheetos, Lays, and Pringles, new teff chips,
and puffy lentils, gluten-free, flat, carved
in tasty little shapes gave greater choice
to stoner than world did to poor in voice.

128.
At this, Cade asked, above the speakers' hum,
"If you don't know what happened at the store,
the tonic, ice, and handle of Seagram's,
the chilling next to Buena Vista, or
the run away from that coyote howl,
then how were you awake till four a.m.?"
"Huh? I thought you slept." "I know you night owled."
"Ugh. Pass the water. Slowly. Sore day." REM
still strongly lingered after she had woke.
"I've got some scenes from each, I wasn't blacked
out. And what I do when I'm home's not spoke.
You ought to be ashamed your lack of tact
has let you tell a lady you keep track
of lights beneath her door." Cade took aback.

129.
"Ha. Hold your stones, check 50's 'Patiently
Awaiting' for the reference. Stel, you cranked
the stereo and kept it blamelessly
that high till you were done! You should have thanked
me – probably Yeye too – for passing out."
Though mental fog was lifting slowly, this
spurred recollection that she'd chose to flout
convention that nighttime should be mute bliss.
Cartoonists might have drawn the scene with 'WHOOPS!'
in bubble thought above embarrassed hunch,
as Stella's mind began to jump through hoops
to recall why she'd needed sonic plunge.
Excusing self, she traced back to her room
to see if she could find buds anger bloomed.

130.
In space's physicality, she found
no single artifact that could attest
to some nocturnal fanciful spellbound
mellifluous creation. Not outguessed,
she opened window wide to see if seat
on gently-angled rooftop had inspired
her overplayed fortissimo of beat
and yet again not single clue acquired.
In giving up the search, she sat on bed
and opened up her laptop. That was it!
The frontmost screen post-password loggerhead
was text arranged in structure, rhymed clause split
across two lines ten syllables apiece.
She'd penned a drunken sonnet as release:

131.
Imagine world as open, free as could
be grown with capital, consumers all
addicted to the message that they should
acquire from HSN and outlet malls.
In such society, the very wants
of populace await the marketer.
She knows psychology, design and fonts,
and shapes you to crave patriarchate's myrrh.
In its consumption, so you closen ties
in your life and in those you're talking to
with narrative big businesses' supplies
are happy ends themselves, no balking due.
The buyers thus detach from value they
ought on their own ascribe to goods. OBEY.

132.
The Shepard Fairey staple poster hung
above her desk had offered that last line.
It struck her that the artist had a tongue
so fierce as to make verses realign.
This message came from colors' boldened blot
and minimum detail in other parts.
The mind itself filled in the message, not
depicted, of how They control the heart.
In every man and child and woman who
tunes into Spotify or radio,
or dozen others, They'll seek to undo
the story *me alone can make me glow.*
It hung, reminding core assault was on
identity of we ourselves, long-conned.

133.
When Stella read what she had written drunk
a set of goosebumps stood upon her back.
It seemed to be expression of the funk
her conscious mind had yet to quite unpack.
Those thoughts that came to head in super-mart
were all too early to be well-expressed:
she felt like shopping friends were duped, in part
by normalcies unpicked by Cornel West.
The views that Stella brought, naïveté
of outsider were sharp enough to gash
and hot enough to boil, not seethe away
from balms commercials spread of sale-saved cash.
It felt like second, vast subconscious mind
had stolen typing fingers to opine.

134.
The paper's digital inscriptions were
as odd as graphite's glyphs at Wangjiang Park
that introduced the poet Xue Tao and her
millennia-encrusted wise remarks.
She checked her recent playlists, found that Rage
Against the (damn) Machine was in the queue
around the time she slept. LCD page
was left half-written, notes from days Chengdu
delighted and depressed as partial thoughts.
The marginalia was Rorschach test
whose indications were she was distraught
and feared that sleep of muse would dispossess.
'Twas old to Stel, from *Annals*: dissident's
nocturnal meditations left in print.

135.
Amusement beat out bashfulness. She cried,
"Hey Cade, come up! I figured out what I
was doing last night." She felt to confide
in him her sauced-mind's hobby fine. Gut shy,
he climbed the stairs and braced himself for sights.
He lightly laughed when realizing that
the thing was metered syllables. "She writes
when woozy? Fooled me!" Kneeled, with prize thing at
eye-level, he read Sonnet One and paused.
It took a sec to query body and
pinpoint its rigor mortis proper cause:
"Your verse is shiny. That's gold Talib's panned,
and Zion I, Sage Francis, Eminem,
Blue Scholars, Common Market, ten o' them

136.
on independent labels, Tonedeff shit.
You've rapped what happens when an alien
is dropped in as observant. Lone, left, split
from culture's cant sesquipedalian,
you weave interpretations of your own."
Now Stella hadn't known that Cade could drop
that GRE vocab like Cicero,
since canon till then referenced was hip-hop.
It rather pleasantly reminded: views
are only helpful insofar as they've
accounted for the full array of clues
available to show how folks behave.
Stel brightened, hearing hidden hobby held
in such regard by brethren who there dwelled.

137.
The cocktail socializing, alcohol,
elastic evening, and a laptop's light
precipitated high morale and scrawl,
inked crystalline memento of the night.
The chosen topic channeled Prodigy
in outrage at the system. Questioning
reach brainwash tentacles had clawed was plea
for an alternative progression. Zing
of message lay in challenge to the crowd:
examine how the narratives they hear
are crafted so the audience is wowed,
their authors corporate cogs, and not Shakespeare.
Mayhaps opposing Opposition meant
she'd pen eye-catching lines more self-ward bent.

Chapter 21

138.
The tungsten radiated tiny lux
from bulbs hung down to candles complement.
Another Tuesday night at Club Deluxe,
bar where the Opposition'd come frequent.
Cigar box pub partitioned from a den
where panoramic Californian views
were painted to horizons. Its bullpen
was leather bench seats circled into U's.
They sat a shoulder-length from perma-stage,
piano standup, PA system, seats,
and wicker tipping basket, worming wage
from first date couples feigning as elites.
Two bands a night, and seven nights a week,
it held a red, dark, neighborly mystique.

139.
It also held a standing group of youth
arriving after first band wrapped its set
to get their well gin shaken with vermouth
then raucously debate the internet.
They touched on social media, on rules
compared to norms, neutrality of bits,
philosophy applied not taught in schools
defining techno-worlds they'd grown up with.
No single conversation's end resolved,
they threaded into endless data stream,
recursive depths of which at times appalled
the late-come guests who tried to join the team.
Within, without, beyond the net, they strayed
toward human rifts Boy's politics had splayed.

140.
"Let's start with little Boy," Tee primed the group,
"Do you remember just how normal news
once looked? I mean, you'd get a weekly scoop
that merited a long-form look. Now who's
on every headline, making light of brawls?
And sometimes twice a day, the lunacy
redoubling to the point where Tylenol's
the only surefire route from loon I see."
"No joke," said Cade, "this stuff brings Sadville close.
Each time I see the news this dopey Boy
brings idiocracy. An Advil dose
won't do it justice, reach for opioids."
"Too soon," said Benny. "Heard his hush playdate
with some professional longtime playmate?"

141.
Joe asked, glossed over conflict. Cade said, "What
you gotta look at's fact he's lost his friends.
I mean, think of the other tykes now shut
out from his sandbox! Poutyface pretends
like he took over, told them all to go.
Well, maybe throwing sand in all their face
was signal that they oughtn't stay fo' sho'."
"Nah, not a chance," Mo said, "palms need more space
for those small hands to fling a thing." Folks laughed.
Tee barreled on, "They might have trusted him
had he shared list of all his toys." "That's daft—"
said Joe, "no rational observer thought
the Boy was there to make the playground nice.
We and they know his tempers, toys, and vice."

142.
"I'll tell you, Cade, the part perturbing me
does not pertain to Boy directly," said
a clear-voiced Benny, "disability
of learning should be managed by the Ed
instead of perpetrated from the top.
You saw that interview? Gold can't buy smarts."
"That's not the thing evoking my teardrops,"
said Mo, "we'll rebuild equity and arts.
I fear we've given godlike dynamite
to little tyke who lies to the adults
until they go away. He'd try to light
that shit so he could point to some results."
Nods 'round the table ended looking down,
apocalypse as topic earned ring's frowns.

143.
Restarting after down beat, Cadence hit
from different angle: "Flip-flops days apart
on bump stock ban revealed his feeble wits
reverse with two good naps and one good fart
to make more space for thinking in the brain."
Tee: "Hey, we're piling on. Let's figure out
the things to do this week to fight." "Complain?"
asked Mona dryly, wry smile doubling clout.
Tee dropped her gaze and almost cracked, her grin
in recognition of the bait. "That's first,"
Tee said, "and done, Olympically. To win
we'll maybe need to have done more than cursed."
"I'm tired of making phone calls to my rep
who's already decided his next step."

144.
The dearth of new ideas brought an end
to brainstorm 'round the time the band came in.
"Our lack of monies clearly will portend
demise of our attempts to brand-shame him."
Said Tee, "We're poor, Benita. That's why we
make friends with bartenders. We only get
one vote to change stuff each two years. Aye, fees
to steer democracy are known, steep bets
the likes of which our 'exit' brothers pay.
The rest of us got jack in pocketbook
and get outspent by crapbag NRA."
Stel: "Better to be Davy Crockett, hook
the masses with mythology aligned
to goals you have for wider humankind."

145.
"Of course that's better, being scion of
a demographic feeling unexpressed.
But that's unlikely when who's high above
is dominating discourse of the rest.
Cade posed a plan a month ago to slice
that fragile image that Boy holds so dear.
I still believe that would itself suffice."
And fit, Stel thought, *the ethos Pioneer.*
Cade said, "Ignore the way he prattles on,
he's clearly clad in emperor's new clothes.
The only kings are Presley and LeBron
and counterarguments are empty prose.
Poke holes in Boy's balloon while stoking rise
of other heroes, lead to his demise."

146.
House special greyhound lingering in glass,
Stel hadn't joined debate's more active parts.
It felt to her like psyches were harassed
by Boy's headline radioactive starts.
Of course a human being who believed
the world was out to get him would so act,
at every corner publicly perceived
as distanced from reality and fact.
"It makes no sense you're so incensed when there's
such bureaucratic insulation here.
When California flag arrives and bears
its grizzly, celebrate. Translation's clear:
economy's the king, and Cali's fine.
States rights ensure your lives won't be maligned."

147.
"That view's mature, I'm glad you shared it, Stel,"
said Tee, who looked sincere. "But, understand
you're not a citizen. You'll bear it well.
You've got your visa, paperwork in hand.
You go when pleasure strikes you. That remove
is not a thing that Nicaraguans have
or Salvadoreans, or many who've
risked life and limb and savings so to nav-
igate past Mexico, past border wall.
It's those lives that we're close to and protect
in trying to find a way to speed the fall
of Boy before at polls we reelect."
"To act for others is the mark of saints,"
said Stel, "but don't you think the better feint

148.
is rather, now, to focus on the things
that you control directly, right 'round here?"
"You underestimate the power phone rings
en masse to Washington's vote profiteers
can have. Calls can change legislation's word,
and legislation's words change what we do,"
said some green friend-of-friend. Stel: "That's absurd.
The logic fails. It's that myopic view
that forces you to Opposition. Tell
me ten reps' names in hundred who've campaigned
as centrists to the point where some new swell
of public feedback's done a smidge to rein
in partisan alignment with some bill.
You vote for bundles, not wise reps' shrewd will."

149.
Stel's knowledge of the goings-on and past
was aided by a ritual that she
adopted in late China days. She'd asked
Tao meanings of post-dinner news TV,
its telecasting always outpacing
the speed at which her brain could process thought.
Much like a mama bird, devout-faced, wing
extended for protection as it ought
to be for fledglings, Tao proceeded share
translations of the newests of the day,
from Yertle's stonewalls on Obamacare
to hints of some resurgent KKK.
Stel witnessed these events with full remove,
her brain sought only patterns in their moves.

150.
It wasn't common in the group back then
to force another person to the point
of naming names, specific facts or men
or dates, the backup bullets that PowerPoint
would have to prove a storyline. Therefore
it wasn't clear how rando'd handle Stel's
implicit gauntlet thrown to name there four
real people. Stel: "Reps' loyalty impels
adherence to the highest ranking force:
their party. In exchange, the day they need
that body to in turn their bills endorse
it does so willingly without hard plea.
Take last five years as data, tell me when
some phone bank blitz changed ways of councilmen."

151.
Debating misstep made of letting an
opponent off the hook by asking more,
Tee rescued him with answer. "That Grand Can-
yon state guy voting down on late-night floor
the health repeal. It stopped, debate expired."
"Dramatic, sure," said Stel, "but back one step.
He'd stated age would soon make him retired,
and freed from vote power-seeking. Plus, the prep
was hardly limited to one week's fuss:
the conversation raged for many months.
Folks lobbied 'gainst a greater blunderbuss
and won the keystone vote somehow, for once.
And then, of course, its gutting happened next
in unrelated tax bill Yertle flexed."

152.
Forgetting selves, the fireworklike debate
had Stella's voice both first, and clearly, heard.
The music rescued group's disputing state
by pouring melodies where further word
was absent. Jazz had ways of speaking to
the topic most at hand. One vicious sax
left Phrygian remorse lines streaking through
progression else devoid malicious tacks.
As even finest compositions played
depended on improvisations that
musicians conjured so to serenade,
so varied quality of their group's chats
as functions linearly optimized
by knowledge, logic, standing, plot, and guise.

153.
Rendition of the Monk tune "Round Midnight"
brought undulating somber moods enhanced
by lack of resolution Stel's bid might
erode belief in Tee. Crowd all entranced
by solos virtuosos each exchanged,
with nary any cue from one to next,
the new companion, Darla, soon estranged
the group with flash-on selfies meant for texts
with hashtag labels that the public knew.
Stel joined her friends in judging Dar for this
attention-seeking ritual in view
of real live people seeking sonic bliss.
Cade, next to her, said, "Yo, excuse me, ma'am,
but can you stop?" "Uh, what? It's Instagram."

154.
Cade's face looked like it lost its rhythm. "So?"
The single syllable did same to Dar.
Her pale face was blue screen of death: "Dunno
what's got your knickers twisted—it's a bar."
She clearly thought that selling alcohol
was in itself sufficient cause to pose
for photo stream, "Chill out, pal." She forestalled
feud by then typing in her phone. "New lows..."
said Cade. Stel: "Darla, you're here to be seen?"
"I wouldn't say it that way, but... uh, sure.
A million followers means every scene
is one more chance to show them my allure."
"Which is...?" "You don't know? Now I'm taste's own chef.
I'm sponsored, queen kingmaker in SF."

155.
Stel recognized Dar somewhat fuzzily
as roaming protest cute girl whose conceit
was smartphone self-absorption. Does ill she
was judged to bring exist at all? To meet
with leftward-leaning group and document
her presence to her followers gave cred
to Opposition's message. Cadence: "Spent
your life amassing followers?" "Instead,
how 'bout you think about it as pure fun?
I live my life. I share some bits. They flock.
I've got some bread. I scatter it for one
and pigeons come in quantities Hitchcock
would fear." She glanced from phone, "Delight enough,
remake your every act as public stuff."

156.
Cade's circuits fried, he gave up argument
and asked if Stel'd make like an Autobot
and roll out. "Walk or MUNI?" Bar crew'd spent
a long night all together, squatter's plot
arranged around a single table. Tips
solicited in basket weren't produced
since none of them had cash for more than sips.
Stel privately hoped as she'd been seduced
by music made, so someday she'd repay.
That pay-it-forward ethos quite skipped Cade,
with Kendrick's Pulitzer in mind replayed:
know what loyalty's to, use that crusade
encoded in your DNA, then shed
your skin, molt toward a single-cause purebred.

157.
They strode 'neath drooping yellow flowers with
arboreal aroma redolent
of rose like weeping willows' kin and kith,
an SF version of that red known scent.
They grew in tiny front yard plots, the wind
swept all their better parts into the air—
as face-down blooms, Stel might have had them binned
were they not nasally so debonair.
She liked to pass them by at night, and stop
to sniff, as proverbs so encourage us.
She did, and climbed with Cade up to the top
of slipworn marble steps to home. "Let's suss
out how we'll make Dar gone tomorrow, 'kay?"
Too gassed to argue, Stel gave ground: "Sure, Cade."

158.
"No, really, Stella, stuff like that ain't right.
We hang together as a group 'cause it's
a bitch to find new homies. Disinvite
the randos using membership for glitz."
"I didn't like her either, Cade. But what's
she guilty of? Some selfies in drum break?"
"It ain't frustration she mistimed the cuts,
it's disrespect to us. Her shots unmake
the reason that we came together." "Um...
you think that reason's what?" asked Stel. Cade said,
"To rise up, revolutionize, become
a righting force." "You think we've parlayed dread
toward anything? No, Cade, we've talked. You've macked
on Mona. Cade, there's no way to prove act

159.
of meeting up amounts to much when the
agenda's sit around, drink beer, and bitch,
to use your term." "Of course it won't, Stel, duh,"
he pedaled back, "but in that Dar enriched
herself on her affiliation with
the rest of us. We started this." "It's 'this'
that honestly I think is more a myth
than vehicle for righteous selflessness.
You do by doing. Pick a vision, then
go utilize the freedoms States protect
to get support of neighbor Chad, John, Chen,
Miguel, Vu, Thor, or Aikins, go connect
a dozen peoples' peoples with a cause.
That's what your hip-hop says." Take made Cade pause.

160.
"No, hip-hop raps about the artist's grind.
They drop own solo story and a beat."
"You've played me dis tracks. Those are well-designed
to piggyback on others, get retweets."
"You're missing fact that Darla's got no core.
It's hustle lived that differentiates."
"She's parasitic, sure. She used us for
mere background props." "Worse fissure's when she
    states
that what we're doing's hers." "Well, she was there."
"It's still appropriation." "Zoom back out:
you love hip-hop 'cause it describes warfare,
a struggle you feel's shared. Presume a route
from vid to better sense of self exists,
like does for music... then spare Dar the fist."

161.
Upstairs Stel found her room as it had been
when hours before she left it, nothing new.
So no excuse was there for glycogen,
adrenaline, or ATP to cue
a caffeinated buzz she felt, no fight
or flight, no strangeness physicality
had left as clue. So why on this one night
did she feel jazzed? The musicality
of that quartet? The liberality
of her progressive friends? Vitality
of conversation? Glib mentality
of vexing half-debate? *It shall pit Tee
against all things, all times,* Stel, saddened, thought.
She took up pen to said conclusion jot.

162.
Some stuff goes on, and you don't like it. So
you find some folks who think much like you do.
You gather them together and you go
to friendly spots with late or no curfew.
It's nice to see same faces week to week
and nicer hearing chorus of consent,
and thus you carry on. What makes you weak
is having deviation in convent.
Point one, your in-group's in if they agree.
Point two, your motto's chasing from behind.
You hear, refute, and protest. And point three:
you'll gather no converts of heart or mind
until you paint the pic of what could be.
Find unbelievers, dictate what 'good' means.

163.
"It's not the best," reflected Stella, eyes
reviewing poem in desktop draft. "But hey,
that's what I get from any improvised
attempt. The first draft's meant to just convey
the meaning. Only when the audience
is numerous and worthy does it make
sense to invest the time in gaudiness
to dress the message up." Then Timberlake
came on downstairs, and bassline racked the floor.
No, wait, Stel thought, *that's J Cole on JT,
and Elvis, Eminem, and Macklemore.*
He said blacks quibbled 'bout who's most shady,
and all the while there's one *gone snatch the crown,*
when they look up *white people snatched the sound.*

164.
Familiarity in course of days
had made it clearer when Cade cued up whom:
he played Talib, Cole, Roots, Jean Grae when fazed,
and Wu-Tang, Buddy, Monch to spark a room.
Embracing for a moment empathy
for how her housemate host felt following
their *tête-à-tête*, Stel breathed and then a fleet,
seditious thought came toward mind wallowing:
perhaps she had a real-life crown debate.
If what she heard from Darla had been true
and internet thought Dar's life somehow great,
then masses' tastes were open to the new
and, with some luck, Stel might just have the knack
to play a different game and tastes hijack.

165.
The smartphone form-fit in her hand, she pressed
the buttons bringing her to marketplace
where backend robots eagerly suggest
which apps to buy for her guessed target case.
A touch or two, some seconds, then *voilà:*
her Tricorder was now equipped like Dar's.
All folks from Pakistan to Panama
could follow now Stel's poetic memoirs.
She held her face up to her phone and screen,
iambic fourteen measured lines behind,
adjusted wrist and zoom for centering,
then clicked the pic for internet to find.
She nudged her friends to follow her with text,
hoped format wouldn't leave them too perplexed.

166.
Though inspiration's moment never would
come back to Stella, she guessed sonnets came
from want of structure. Fledgling adulthood
had freedoms more than younger years had claimed.
If Darla brought the internet delight
with live streams of her life, then there was hope
iambic oddity of Stella's might
find patrons for its word kaleidoscope.
She brushed her teeth and switched the lights and crept
beneath the silken comforter of bed
and wondered if, that night, while she there slept,
commemoration poem would stay unread.
The weight of covers ushered weight of lid,
till into hopeful slumber Stella slid.

CHAPTER 22

167.
With sun a honey lemon, chili cloud
drew contrast with the grape-in-season sky,
the evening periwinkle pooled to crowd
out other hues as darkness stretched beside.
As setting sun illuminated sand,
its angled tiny dunes like Tatooine,
the grains turned somewhat beautiful from bland,
alive in limelight looking tangerine.
The evening's fog avoided let sands play
a role in sunset scene at Ocean Beach,
Pacifica, or down in Monterey,
as equals to blue waves and humpbacks' breach.
When mist and murk diffracted direct light,
the lowly sand stayed unremarked as sight.

168.
The Opposition crew were in the crowd
invited for Joe's birthday, folks B-side
to back the headline bonfire pit. Smokes cloud-
ed minds in twilight. Man-bun poured the SKYY
with splash of tonic so to not be bland,
and dressed red cup with wedge of tangerine.
Guests drank, some polished figurines with sand-
ing paper, some did Henna tattooing.
Flat grill kept burgers cooking, Monterey
Jack bubbling atop, grease dropped through breach
'tween slats. The People Under the Stairs played,
preventing anxious Cade from feeling beached.
He hadn't sought to let Dar in his sight,
but Stella hoped he'd come to see the light.

169.
Stel walked with Cade and Mona down the shore,
a northward stroll to watch sun light the cliffs
not far. The oceanside brought stevedores
from coastal Dar (the city), fishers' skiffs,
and seafood barbecue aromas back.
Cade took his phone from pocket, waggled it,
raised eyebrows, looked at Stella: "Something wack?"
Stel shook her head. Mo, looking rattled: "Sit.
Sure? *Stuff goes on, and you don't like it, so
you find some folks who think much like you do.*"
"Is this an intervention?" Stel smiled. "No,
we don't think that you meant this as our cue,"
replied Mo. "Great. So whatcha think?" "You're nuts."
"Nah. But if so, I blame your rap." "The cuts

170.
aren't what I'm used to," Cade admitted. Mo
said, "We're just checking. It's the first time I
got late-night notes from you and – I dunno –
the stuff you sent all made me wonder, 'why?'"
"You, actually," said Stella. Mona smiled
as if she had suspected so, "The name?"
"Yep. Didn't think you'd guess. You came off mild
till taking Tee to task on Oppo's aim."
Cade looked at ladies quizzically, "Please clue
me in to cipher you appear to share."
"Sure, cutie. Think back to the night when you
kept Stel alive post-party, when I dared
to tell Tee she was wrong." "Ah," Cade said, terse,
and pieced together Stella's sonnet verse.

171.
"You saw my oratory didn't work.
No listener seemed keen enough to stand
for reason: 'Opposition's no framework
for change. Of course, it makes a heady brand.
It taps the verve they like in Tee, the fire."
"Which drove me crazy, Mo. That's why I wrote."
"It's fun to read, but really won't inspire
as her invective does. The antidote
is something else." No one spoke up. Cade looked
as if idea backed off tip of tongue.
Mo went on, "I think Tee's got crew well-hooked
on anger train, pushed out debate among
us. That said, we weren't on track to get clout
regardless, and we're friends. And friends hang out."

172.
They stood and brushed the sand from off their bums.
Stel looked toward party: "Creepy! I'm not fond
of scene back there. Looks wicked." "Those props? Dumb,
ignore them. They're a statement." Folks had donned
Guy Fawkes masks someone brought, all faces gone.
"What *are* they?" Stel persisted, spotting Dar
now 'midst the revelry. Cade: "Costumes spawned
from revolution. Benny'd know." "So noir,"
said Stel." Mo: "Here they're probably a farce,
they're photogenic. Crew's not murderous –
I think, at least! – enough to play the parts
for real." They neared. One people-herder fussed
with who should lean which way so selfie pic
showed acme of themselves and party tricks.

173.
"On second thought, let's let that run its course
before going back for burgers," Mona said,
"Stel, you still look a little bit divorced
from present. This was not some watershed,
big moment. Know we like what you wrote. And
we'll stay tuned for next episode." "Oh, that's
not worrying me, no. But thanks. Wet sand...
brings back a lot. These coastal habitats
were 'bout as real as outer space when I
was young." "You grew up far from water?" "Ponds,
lakes, creeks, we had the small stuff. Nothing wide
as ocean." Clouds arrayed now as dull fronds
to fan hid sun. "This much was dream where I
grew up, like Disney tales or lords' Versailles."

174.
Mo smiled, "It's funny, line between what's real
and what's imagined. Disney stretched my mind,
and it's pure make-believe; French feudal zeal
was fact, yet feels remote. I'd leave behind
the latter for the former." "I recall
a teacher's stump speech saying lands exist
I'd not heard of, but trusted. Guess that's all
you can do: trust." Cade: "Truths themselves subsist
on stories. They're one in the same. Believed
your teach who spoke of oceans? All folks err
toward trust. We think we'll know if we're deceived,
'spite fact that tales are honed before they're shared."
"You're saying I should distrust everything?"
"No. I say you should know you've puppet strings.

175.
Pull them yourself. I bridge my dreams and days
with hip-hop ethos, all about the grind.
I caretake for a grandpa who displays
behavior nearly Keller deaf and blind.
I wake up, wrap the story 'round me tight,
and turn to it to fuel the day. The church
identically pretends." "They think it's right."
"The process is the same. We keenly search
until our brains have facts to match our guts,
and suddenly decide we've hit the truth.
We stop predictably, mute what rebuts."
Cade looked back to the fire's pleased Fawkes-clad youth,
shrugged shoulders as if truer point could not
be made, debate concluded: truth's kill shot.

176.
Round bonfire motley masses huddled close,
as onshore gusts left heated scene quite cool.
Conversants ranged from kind to bellicose
depending on which drugs they'd used as fuel.
The people carving little men obsessed
with rasps perfecting human form in wood.
Mo asked and learned they partly were protest,
to burn small Boys in effigy, and stood
as well as Burning Man idolatry.
They saw no oddity in such an act.
One even said, "You know, my doll's a plea
to Powers That Be – if they exist – for tact.
Boy's 'fuck-it-all's a message I want heard,
and like, that's buried by his flipping birds."

177.
Admission brought the vodka birthday boy
into their conversation. "Evening, Joe.
And happy birthday," Cade said. "Do enjoy
the Lagunitas, Pliny, Veuve, Bordeaux
chilled over there, my tiny gift of thanks
as host to you for coming," Joe replied.
He put two other dried-out logs as planks
beneath the grill face. "Meat's all getting fried
from being too up-close and personal
to all that flame," he said, and moved toward Mo.
"Ugh, every time behavior's worse! Until
he has someone to use and lose, Lord knows..."
Joe: "Tula, what the pleasantest surprise!"
Tee: "Birthdays don't mean lechery's advised."

178.
"Affection, dear." "Nope, slime. I'll help police
your callowness. Say, take that champagne case
at spot where most folks guzzle Dos Equis
as blatant signal you won startup race.
Consider discount food and beverage." "First,
you're welcome, and it's good to have you here.
And next, you think me far too Randolph Hearst."
"Your bathrooms, Joe, have crystal chandeliers."
"That's taste," he said, "and better to have all
instead of solo one in *ensuite* bath.
You give no credit that I've shared." "The gall!
It's ostentatious, shoving in our path
repeated signs that you're rich and we're not."
"That's never my intent. The cash I've got

179.
is meant to let me have more fun with friends.
Stop, look around: tonight my grill convenes.
I'm glad you're here. Remember that's the ends
when thinking so unkindly of my means."
He turned to pose as self-styled Charlemagne
for portrait Dar requested by the fire,
a standing Citizen aware that Kane
regretted turning from his Rosebud flyer.
"I've got no beef when big men throw down seeds,"
Cade added, "I don't need to like them to
eat up their meals for reals. This belly feeds
just fine when I'm the small fry. Kings keep crews,
look after all their entourage. Just clowns
pretend that wealth is worn without the crown."

180.
"It's hard to talk to Joe without the thought
that he, right there, in front of you, could fix
your lifetime's worth of problems: house, car bought,
plus cash to live off, if he just handpicks
you as a case for charity," Tee said.
"I don't get what you're really trying to solve,"
said Mo, "you're caught somewhere in your own head,
in thinking his green stacks would all resolve
your conflict. At Deluxe you savaged wealth
in politics, now envy Joe's the same.
You're chasing what erodes your mental health."
Stel thought: *and ought to try a different game.*
"Hey Mo," nudged Cade, "let's chill. Don't work up sweat.
Come Stel. You wanna try a cigarette?"

181.
He pulled a pack of dark blue Spirits out
and Stella thought of many reasons not
to finally try. "They say to fear it. Doubt
that story heard, decide yourself. Upshot
is if you like it, then you're more alive."
"But Cade, they give you cancer. That's more dead."
"You get my point. And you, Stel, won't nosedive
down some long chainsmoke chimney." Mona led
them slightly from the group so zephyr blew
their pending plant exhaust the other way.
The crowd's clothes ranged from thrift store to J. Crew,
no single dominating dossier.
It pleased to see diversity (at face)
lit by camaraderie and pit fireplace.

182.
Forbidden fruit it wasn't: all Stel's life
she'd hacked upon encountering the smog
ejected by a cigarette, the knife
of acrid vapors jamming muscles' cogs,
unleashing breath control in coughing fits
made worse by sharpened inhalations of
the same putridity of death stick's hits,
recycled exhaled smoke dropped from above.
But those, Stel thought, *reactions were in youth.*
I'm in control now, I'm the one to choose
between experiences my own truth.
Kneejerk rejection's laziness in views.
So something in the way of offer'd made
decision come from where brain'd not forbade.

183.
Stel guessed Mo seethed at Tee: she wanted oil
to soak her canvas fist in fire and flip
a flaming phoenix at Tee's mind turmoil,
oblivious to its own authorship
of life. Tee drifted out like bleeding ink,
its point diluted, watery, and weak.
She was a victim of her doublethink:
you can't excoriate that which you seek.
In that, her course to individuate's
identical to every other's, so
her journey dumbly mimics. Did coup take
more than awareness she's her only foe?
Cade lit one up, held high the glow in fist,
then passed to Stella, quite the dramatist.

184.
A deep breath taken in, yet split in two
helped Stel avoid the coughing from the past:
a carcinomic breath when taken through
a filter, mixed with standard air, could last.
Immediately her left brain turned a-right
and noticed nuance in environment,
as if faint stars' cast temperature of light
increased a hundred Kelvin (three percent).
As nature came to focus, so did *chi*,
perception's center migrating from core
of every limb out to skin actively
exposed to air, like waves expand to shore.
It felt like life both calmed and stretched out thin,
translucent tickling film through which soothed sin.

185.
"Tobacco's powerful," shared Stel. She stood
a little wobbly in the wind, post-drag.
"It's bad, yeah, sure, but also kinda good,"
said Mona. "Makes me feel a ghostly swag."
"And right away." "Yeah, really hits you quick.
The catch is that it just as quickly fades;
it's daring you to light another stick.
That's how uncautiously you'll spend decades
hooked on the stuff. My mom and dad both were."
"Oh... sad. I'm sorry, Mo. And yet you still
go smoke yourself?" "Addiction's not preferred,
Stel. They put this on me. Someday I will
take time to kick it, but for now the hit's
an easy way to rise above the shit."

186.
Benita joined with vape pen. "Stel!" she said,
"I liked your Insta-verse. Weird poetry
refreshes in the midst of photo thread.
I thought its cadence nice, its flow. It reads
a little singsong, little hard. I'd poke
a little on your syntax – oddly spliced –
but... fun." "Thanks, Benny." Stel coughed, slightly
   choked.
"In honesty, I had to read it twice
before I understood it." "That's the rub.
It makes you slow and think, it makes you read.
We swallow so much everyday hubbub
that chewing something feels like it impedes."
"As counterpoint, it's powerful. I stopped.
But, why'd you end at fourteen lines? I'd opt

187.
to read some more." "That's not how sonnets work.
They're just that long, ten syllables in each,
and singsong beat you mentioned," Stella smirked,
"remains throughout and can't be skipped or breached."
"It's up, and down, and up, and down, and up?"
"Not quite. It's down then up, five times a line."
"Screw that. I'd stop at one. That's crazy." "Yup."
"So why's it all that forcibly designed?"
"Blame Shakespeare? I don't know. Italians had
a form from Petrarch. Far too many rhymes
for English. William used an end dyad
resolving what three quatrains jointly primed."
"They taught this stuff in China?" "No, adult
thought I might like it 'cause it's difficult."

188.
"Ha. Clearly they were right. So why'd you put
it on the web?" "Remember Club Deluxe?"
"Yeah, what about it?" Cigarettes kaput,
they stayed between two cold-breeze-blocking rucks.
"Our evening wrapped," she looked at Cade, "when Dar
whipped out the camera for her followers.
If someone *that* blah's now a superstar,
and if I'm interesting, less hollow, per
the standards of our crowd, then why not play?"
"You're taking aim at her adoring fans?"
"Or others, there are lots of fish in Bay."
"The sea, you mean. But, yeah. okay. With plans
for what?" "Stay tuned. For now it's simply proof
attention can be gathered if you hoof."

189.
Tall flames behind the quartet made them turn.
Stel witnessed one scene, taken in two ways.
The first was by and for those of the Burn:
a coroneted chief's chant *ohm*, a blaze
of handmade figurines thrown in the flame,
a vestige of druidic sacrament.
The second was much more mainstream, and tame:
grilled meat, tunes, beers; textbook kicked-back event.
It struck her 'cause Cade nailed it earlier:
they both were true at once, if and because
participants believed they were. Each *chirr*
on its own branch. Four walked past where Tee was
mid-clink with man-bun, toasting prosecco,
Occult high, friends low? Cade said, "Mo, let's go."

190.
They took N-Judah past Parnassus, got
off right as it was crossing Cole, before
the tunnel to Duboce. "Right there's a spot
called Ice Cream Bar, old timey, sweets galore.
Let's grab a sundae prior to going home,"
said Cadence, who was thrilled by company
(both shop and Mo). Aluminum and chrome
of soda fountains, cookie clumps in need
of sherbet custard bedding laid in wait
upon their entrance, begging to be noshed.
"Pistachio ought to resuscitate
my senses," Mo said. "Yeah, you're looking sloshed,"
said Cade. They ordered, sat, and ate. "So, Stel,
I don't know of your childhood. Do pray tell."

191.
As innocent a question as it was
from Mona, hoping to befriend her more,
the inquiry was hard, namely because
it wasn't stuff Stel ever mentioned, or,
in honesty, could think about. She'd blocked
titanic portions out and all the rest
were bricolage that hopeful minds concoct
when overwhelmed with more than can ingest.
"I guess, you know, there's nothing special there,"
she started, then satori hit her square.
"Except, of course, the rescued puppy, cared
for him for years. We made a knockout pair."
"A dog? How fun! I didn't know you'd grown
up in a busy house." "Oh no... no. Lone,"

192.
Stel countered, "fairly quiet place, our home.
Just me and dog. The dog. And me." "No mom?"
"No mom." "Or dad?" "Or dad. Just grandmum." Foam
on root beer float flowed over on her palm,
and gave her an excuse to wipe and think.
One dog. No parents. That was clean and clear,
a normalcy that wouldn't make you blink.
She dared to step out further, "Pioneers
are what we called ourselves, our duo." "Chic!"
exclaimed a stabilizing Mo, impressed.
"That's dope," said Cade, "I never got a peek
into your past." That came at Stel's behest.
They both seemed eager to learn more. Stel drew
electric breath at such a smooth debut.

193.
Stel flipped the script thereafter, asking more
of Mona, so to fill time till they'd part.
It worked. Back home, Stel's heart still little sore
from thinking of her past, she planned her art.
Instead of writing a riposte 'gainst ways
the Opposition acted, she'd not fret.
More power could come from ditching everyday
of young years, words erasing held regrets.
She opened Apple, flipped her screen to black,
turned out the other lights, and let prints drift,
imprints of mind, touchprints on keys, the plaque
of memories she'd repressed mixed up. She'd riffed
some basic facts that if restyled could
become the basis for a Stel childhood.

194.
From up to down to fortunate and hexed,
from gladdening to maddening, agree
adventuring you'll find in pages next
is true as memories made can be to me.
Unchained childhood began with what you'll read,
in many ways adulthood too was born
as self-reliance started supersede
conformist expectations feared outworn.
While chiseled by untempered nature's edge
I'd get to know my dog and friend like book.
We had but one another's binding pledge
to rise till social mores were overlooked.
This tale is mine alone, of nicer youth,
shared now so followers can trace own truth.

195.
If verse instead, she thought, *can focus on*
advice to pass to younger cherubs, I'm
then freed to use embellishment as con
to polish points so that they better shine.
She opened up her Insta feed and saw
last two days' waiting time was good for biz,
as friends online reacted with some awe,
housemate included. In the comments his
emojis ranged from cross to righteous fist,
the first for dropping references to nuns
and second as a sign he'd too resist
the insularity it argued shuns
transparent dialogue over opaque
so that we'd all together this world make.

196.
That 'friend' of whom she'd written fit the beat
but complicated later tales to come.
It felt much easier and, well, discreet
to craft a narrative of only one.
She climbed out on the roof and sat a bit,
her favorite spot to let her mind off-leash.
Great sagas looked up to did not omit
supporting characters. A good pastiche
would do as such. Perhaps she'd kill two birds
with one verse, if she stole first eyeballs then
minds from Tee's hangers-on with crafty words;
and also come to peace with self again?
Important would be pacing of the clues
such that no one suspected long-con ruse.

Chapter 23

197.
That week, the weather forecast warm and still,
they chose to move the meeting spot outdoors.
Stel didn't mind they'd picked the drugging thrill
of hookah bar near Geary. New routes, tours
among the city's many hangouts came
because they found that getting table at
Deluxe was harder every week. The fame
of Darla's selfie post weaved fable that
hot spot to be on weeknight was that bar.
Though bittersweet to leave a place they'd liked,
they recognized more business meant its star
musicians might get tips deserved, were psyched.
It also sanctioned group to range, explore
what manifold metropolis had stored.

198.
The night was late for weekday, early for
the other things that fueled the Tenderloin.
Across the street were chicken wings ('galore!');
at corner stood a group transgender. "Coin
to spare?" asked limping, nappy blanket-wrapped
man walking by. "No, sorry," Tee replied.
"GODDAMMIT! *Fucking* arrogance," he snapped.
Tee wasn't rattled, knew that he'd subside
and watched him stumble back to cloaking night.
"Well, that was awkward," Benny said. "Eh, it's
a part of SF. Can't be too uptight.
To him we're ATMs. It kinda fits:
he'll ask, sometimes he'll get, sometimes he won't."
"I'll give him something," Benny said. "Please don't."

199.
Joe: "Why? Aren't you some socialist?" "In part.
But it's a thing of practicality.
Made this mistake before. He's gonna start
harassing more. The act – er, gallantry –
will sink our evening. But if you're inclined
to give once we're all done and heading home
then go for it." Benita in a bind,
she nodded, backed down. Homelessness syndrome
presented symptoms similarly all
across the city: cussing, restlessness,
and stench and drugs, sometimes graffiti's scrawl.
Some voters wanted to invest less, kiss
them all goodbye by pulling services.
Tee: "I think what makes rich folks nervous is

200.
their inexperience, not knowing what
a homeless guy is going to do because
where they grew up was segregated, shut."
"Uh, Tee, you know long back those Jim Crow laws
were struck down, right?" But Benny in defense
piped up, "Wrong point, Joe. Technically they were.
Repeal's not full repair. Use common sense.
You know life's more complex than that." "But her
whole point's that we were separated." "Yes.
We were." "We weren't." "You've heard of redlining?
Some basic hist'ry shows that we've compressed
together racial groups, whites headlining
the flight to like communities with gates.
Then taxes otherwise that modulate

201.
school quality and opportunity
fly too. Think back to how you grew up, Joe.
Your peaceful neighborhood community,
SoCal McMansion tract grid tan château
was populated by professionals.
I bet it didn't have the working class.
You're not on hook for some confessional
of racism. Point's that no poor trespassed,
and so you lived in bubble, couldn't know
in any way about the other half,
caught in a personalized Truman Show
staged all by where your parents lived." He laughed,
dismissing Benny's point without reply,
a maddening reaction from the guy.

202.
"Across the street there, Nazareth Hotel,"
said Tee, of building run-down at first look.
"You think if you grew up there you'd excel?
You'd have a place to study, read your books?"
She paused to let it sink in. Man-bun heard.
The windows barred in iron, broken screens,
and doorstep feces spoke louder than word.
"The name aside, I don't see Nazarenes
too plentiful 'round here." Joe nodded, said,
"But kids don't grow up in hotels." "Oh no?
It must be hard to dream from featherbed,
but that right there's what's called an 'SRO'.
Think dorm room," she said, waving off his phone
procured to look it up. "With methadone."

203.
It then was Stella's turn to check the web
and figure out the reference. Heroin
addiction, Google said, was often ebbed
by methadone, drug fairly narrow in
its application. Café waiter came
to get their order, said the minimum
was pipe per sidewalk table. Joe asked, "Name
best-selling flavors sir, please." "Mint with some
small bit of bitter apple's pretty good."
"One mint, one bitter apple, then. We'll mix."
Man left. Tee said, "Geez... think what parenthood
would be like with your neighbors turning tricks."
Tee spoke with some authority, immersed
in humanizing stories as a nurse.

204.
Or rather, she was studying to be
one, and she clocked her hours of practicum
as aide at nearby clinic. "One, two, three..."
the waiter counted to exacting sum
as he set down each apple tea and wrapped
bright colored plastic mouthpiece, sanitized.
Next door in nook a lumpy figure napped
on cardboard fresh from Amazon, man-sized.
In absence of another subject, Tee
continued musing, "I don't get how both
the cities here, inhabiting same wee
landmass, but forty-nine square miles, are loath
to interact. It's like same footprint holds
creased heaven, hell, and purgatory folds."

205.
Stel thought about how life at study desk
contrasted with what Tee described went on
across the street, kids left in Kafkaesque
depressing halls to grow up, shared-floor johns.
Adults could try controlling where they went
and who they interacted with, but when
in such tight quarters couldn't circumvent
their thin shared wall with halfway-housing men.
Kept far from danger, close to textbooks moored,
Stel didn't have a basis to compare.
Both she and they had much they had endured.
Won't everyone have items to forswear
from any, every past? *To have regret
is simply to be human,* Stella bet.

206.
Hydraulic Cadillac from sixty-two
refurbished in a candy apple red
rolled by with JBLs on Changes, Tu-
pac's single wondering when he'd get dead.
The part about if cops cared cued car chant:
"Philando! Sterling! Garner! Clark! Brown! Rice!"
all murdered black men. Tee said, "Sucks I can't
do much to help in clinic. Doc's advice
was try to put up barriers, protect
ourselves from patients, so to better care
for them. I can't. That feels more like neglect.
There's lots of moms our age in doctor's chair."
The waiter brought both water pipes with hell's
own inner fire beneath coals gray ash shells.

207.
With hookah passed around and topic hard,
excuses went unspoken as to why
most Opposition quieted. Safeguard
for difficulty's often to be shy.
As silence played with minty apple fumes
their normal buzzing hive was dully fogged.
Their thoughts were skyjacked by the swirling plumes
that densely danced from bowl pipes waterlogged.
"Cade, you grew up 'round here, no?" "Not nearby,
Joe. More The Richmond, downhill from the park.
You know that slope Arguello has? Steered my
phat yellow black Big Wheel down in the dark,
completely wrecked it, broke a collarbone
and spent six weeks of kindergarten home."

208.
"Ha!" "Yeah. With no one home I had to go
down to the ER by myself. Dad worked."
"Good god." "Ain't that bad, everyone's got woes.
It's mostly funny," Cade said as he smirked,
"And if there's one thing rap has taught me, it's
that all of us should thank like whoa the fact
that we ain't living where we're blown to bits
by bump stocks, rockets, IEDs, or smacked
by cops, or dealers, bullies, all that stuff.
You wake up breathing? Treat it like a dance."
Except, Stel thought, *when waking calls the bluff
of dreams lost childhood might get second chance.*
She chose not to go down that rabbit hole,
and poked to turn the ash-entombed charcoal.

209.
That night they had the privilege yet again
of being graced by YouTube's homemade queen,
young Darla (less Hong Kong and more Shenzhen
in person, contrast to her life onscreen).
No one in Opposition would admit
to telling her where this week's meeting was
since Cade had made it clear she didn't fit
and didn't like how she did what she does.
"We're live from Nile Cafe," she said to cell,
"where apple-mint is on the menu, and
though you may want to show up as a belle
avoid high heels 'cause this is crack pipe land!"
The group aghast, her bright composure's wrath
smacked of the empathy of sociopath.

210.
Dar's camera angled so the group was cut
out, showing only her and neon sign.
"Dar, what you're doing's illegitimate."
"Cool off, I'm joking, Tee." "It's beyond line
that anyone of decency would draw.
You're making advertising money from
a joke about folks so fucked up they gnaw
their own teeth out to cope." "Well, they've succumbed
to drugs, their choice, they know what happens." "Dar,
you've never met an addict, never talked
to one, and never understood streets scar
with more abuse. You think if you were stalked
and lived out here the cops would give a shit?
Crack use begins 'cause folks have gotta quit

211.
all sleep at night, for safety. Nap? Get knifed.
Or rather, the alternative's a drug.
And so in fear she'll choose to save her life.
Then you show up stilettoed, looking smug
to smoke and joke and midnight toke. Get out."
With selfsame plaster smile protecting face
Dar stood to leave, no sign there'd been fallout,
dropped five bucks on the table, turned with grace
and strode away toward cocktail bars. "Hear, hear!"
said Cadence, toasting apple tea to Tee,
"for driving incubus who's insincere
away!" Mugs raised to hostess. "Tee, truth be
forever spoken so to power." "Her? Dar
was hardly power." "Her fans in numbers are."

212.
"Let's not go back to power talk, friends. We're here,
we're liberated from our parasite."
"Still here!" said man-bun Joe, grin ear to ear.
"She's worse, Joe. We see you in fairest light,
and even some day might give tiny think,"
Tee grinned to match, "to cutting you some slack.
But not tonight." She finished with a wink
on face-dark side not seen by most of pack.
"Well, I, for one, am suffocating," he
said to the group, "and I don't mean by smoke.
San Fran's too much sometimes. Airbnb
of interest soon? Drive north toward Cali oak
and cypress territory, Mendo coast?"
They'd text through deets if Joe would play the host.

CHAPTER 24

213.
A fact Mo mostly glossed over before
was long-held fondness for all Disney flicks.
Stel couldn't know if Mona heretofore
had loved them or if she'd played politics
on sly with Cade while dating. Anyway,
in evenings all too frequently they now
dropped princess films instead of Dr. Dre.
With stereo recovering, Cade vowed
to keep up Stella's education in
most useful life insights in canon rap.
In meantime, they'd watch Ariel and Gwyn
and Alice. Stella liked the more madcap
and, since she hadn't seen them as a kid
sat in to watch when not by Cade forbid.

214.
"You're kidding, Stel. You really never watched
a single one of these on VHS?"
"Not kidding, Mo." "That's nuts. By four I'd notched
through all of them. Loved every sorceress!"
Stel settled on the well-worn couch, the stuffed
green armchair held up Yeye too. They'd stopped
pretending he was present. When he huffed
it gave a little signal life still bopped
somewhere inside. It would be comforting
except for that it happened loudly, twice
a minute. Cade sat too. "My bum hurting
you here? No? Good." "Your hips, to be precise,"
said Mo. "Ain't no one here got hips except
you, babe." She rolled her eyes. "He's still inept."

215.
Arrayed on Roku's screen on long timeline
was every cinematic masterpiece
(and every dud) since 1939,
when Snow White first appeared. Soon rasters fleeced
the household through invented CRT,
aired color prime-time broadcast MGM
produced of *Wizard's Oz*. To see art be
alive in technicolor, gleaming gems
of emerald to poppy fields bewitched.
Home's glowing box made place to gather 'round,
a transfixed cell that advertisers pitched,
a group that coexisted *sans* own sound.
From 1950s hence, boob tube equipped
producers to keep mass opinions gripped.

216.
The trio's watch list that night sidestepped time,
not chronologically laid then to now.
Tonight they picked between Steven Sondheim's
Dick Tracy songs and Menken's score that wowed
from start to finish, snagged Academy
Award, and fueled *Aladdin* fandom far
into the future. "Don't look bad to me,"
said Cade, regarding green eyes of Jafar.
"I'll pass on a detective story, Mo,"
chimed Stella, hoping votes of two cult fans
would let her let them watch grouch Iago
connive with Grand Vizier against Sultan,
watch one-time urchin rising from the streets,
from magic carpet wishes to elites.

217.
Cold open introduced a story told
by merchant who himself had not been part,
of ordinary bronze lamp, dullish gold
whose magic changed the fate of one upstart.
*A young man who, like lamp, was more than seemed,
a diamond in the rough.* A scarab's flight
to start Saharan moonlit second scene
unmasked hid cavern treasure, entrance site
imposingly betoothed. To enter there
required a soul of rightest kind to spelunk,
zigzag down pitfall stairs to belly lair.
Within, to find among the priceless junk,
amid bejeweling gems that stole the eyes,
the object of true power required the wise.

218.
A chase right after that showed viewers who
protagonist would be, Aladdin. He,
denied a basic education, food,
or housing, had to pilfer what he'd eat.
When chased by guards, he took a hint and faced
the facts, that *you're my only friend, Abu!*
He tiptoed 'round the law, each step erased
that sign that he'd existed. *Nom de plume*
where needed was so used. The Golden Rule
in Agrabah was: *who has gold, makes rules.*
The royalty immunely ridicule
the urchins who had neither bread nor jewels.
Fantastic Genie helped illuminate
what might become were Al to ruminate...

219.
"Hey Stel, wake up." "Wake up, sis." "Sleepyhead!
You missed my fave important magic parts."
"Oh, sorry. *Oof.* I guess I'm needing bed,
I drifted off when Robin Williams starts
to act out swank false dreams Al'd realize,"
said Stella, rising up from off the couch.
"Oh yeah, once cave betrayed reseals." "Ugh. Guys,
I'm pooped. I gotta sleep." Cade's cushion slouch
suggested he and Mo would stay downstairs,
so Stella trudged up happily alone.
She liked to see them having good times. Pairs
in Stella's view turned life from steady drone
to melody complex as Brahms or Liszt.
Plus, she now knew how her duo'd exist.

220.
Abu, a bit like ghost, swayed to and fro
atop his lanky legs as if the wind
could flip him either way, as it does clothes,
considering while Stella, hopeful, grinned.
This boy could have been raised where cuneiform
was not an ancient, dead, forgotten script,
and yet his look at school was uniform,
normalcy's carbon copy: backpack zipped,
a woolen sweater frayed below his neck
its navy blue to contrast khaki shorts,
on which were several daubs of muddy fleck
from football falls. Stel thought she glimpsed a quartz
or milky pendant hung beneath his maw,
a necklace carved as crescent moon and claw.

221.
"*Another* post, Stel? You said you were tired,"
said Cade in morning coffee line down Haight,
at thin, long shop named Stanza. "I'm rewired
sometimes when night drags on and it gets late...
I'm sheets to wind in body, but my heart
can't seem to slow down, I've no hope of sleep."
"That's when you gotta pull Top 40s chart,
pop records on, lay back, and chill, and steep."
"We're different, Cade. I used to read in bed
to calm myself and seed some better dreams.
But being here is jarring. Routines fed
my past life. Writing here's a new regime
to clear my mind and conscience at day's end.
Plus hey, it's fun to play god with the pen."

222.
"Cortado, please." "And one quick brew for me."
"Are these all pastries from that Mission Beach
Café? Hot damn! I'll take croissants. Um... three?
You know, Stel, royal living's within reach
when shiz French bakers worked for centuries
perfecting's what's mere add-on at the till."
"Oh, wow. That's good. My mouth's adventuring
from here to Paris in that bite." Life's ill
was wholly remedied for seconds as
her inner epicurean took hold
and fixated on almond razzmatazz
that baker'd brewed with butter, sugars bold.
She'd once heard Chengdu jiānbǐng chef voice wish
to travel world. Too poor, he did in dish.

223.
They sat at coffee bar between those who
showed up with laptops to scroll Facebook feeds
(subconscious addict's act one falls into,
distracting from want to accomplish deeds).
The art on wall reminded Cade of this:
"It's all in Pressfield's book, *The War of Art*,
the ways we try take our aim, and miss,
self-undermining of creative starts."
"Hold on—you read?" asked Stel, who'd seen him just
use leisure time to study Busta Rhymes.
"Ha. Yes. We've all got many sides. We must,
to face the day, no? Single paradigms
make Jack the dullest boy. Well, 'cept Jack White."
Stel found it pleasant man so quite forthright

224.
could harbor alter ego life to boot.
He took a moment to wax lyrical
on how the book explains all acts are moot
except The Work. What's stratospherical
is only the result of clocking time,
of casting self as true professional
whose livelihood is squarely on the line
and therefore acts somewhat obsessional
to get The Work completed. Substitutes
do not exist but Working. Facebook and
email replies, and tweeting, phone, and news,
and cleaning, it's like never-never land
escaping mandate set for self. You choose
to actively engage, or else you lose.

225.
"So why'd you get drip coffee, black? They've got
baristas with the talent of Mos Def.
Espresso? Fine. A capp? Great. But brewed *pot...?*
If coffee used the term I'd call them chefs!"
"Brew's mostly for the moment I look down,
from charcoal surface back reflects my face.
In liquid mirror, everyone looks brown
regardless of their color, origin, race.
There's something grounding in that image, it
transports me back through places where I've gone.
It gets me thinking." "But it tastes like shit,
go Jay-Z cappuccino style!" "Ha. Wrong,"
said Stella, sipping, "mere acquired taste."
"You cray. That acquisition effort's waste."

226.
They drank their chosen beverages a bit,
attentive to the funny swirling steams
that rose up mathematically to knit
the solid, fleeting plush forms of daydreams.
"You know, if you were small enough, this mug,
this tiny cup of hotness, would create
your local weather patterns. Thermal slug
sheds heat to air and porcelain at rates
so different so to make a tiny wind
among the closest molecules." "You wack?"
asked Cade. "No, I'm just thinking. Disciplined
reflection can be better than Prozac."
"But you don't pop SSRIs." "No inked
prescription keeps my coffee black," Stel winked.

227.
"Whatevs. I haven't thought 'bout beverage norms
in rap. Bacardi, Hennessey, and shots
are standards. Cristal clearly outperforms
Courvoisier... what do folks drink on yachts?"
Stel smiled, and didn't know. Cade pivoted,
"Back on that thermal thing, the place that Joe
suggested's snuggle-cold. I'm riveted
to see if something sparks with Tee." "I know!"
"Those coasts in Mendocino he suggests
are likely covered up, inbound fogs stay
around there." "No fun. Think he'll take requests
to change it up?" "He might." "When's Groundhog Day?"
"Last month. Why, Stel?" "I heard there might be snow,
which I've not seen, if cold hangs in Tahoe."

228.
Stel pulled her cell phone out for blizzard of
her own devising, starting campaign to
pump up a Tahoe winter trip and shove
the coast aside. Highlighting plan's gains through
a quick-recorded Snapchat snap and chat
on group thread on WhatsApp, she waited for
her audience feedback. A thermostat
in screenshot weather forecast she'd sent bore
a 'forty-five but sunny' near the lake,
compared to 'fifty-one but rainy' in
Gualala, Jenner, and Fort Bragg. "Let's take
a chance of sunburn over raisin skin!"
she wrote as caption. Answers came back quick:
group trusted Stel that mountains made best pick.

Chapter 25

229.
At crack of dawn, assembled via Lyft,
the Opposition and its caravan
met near Patricia's Green to stow and shift
its baggage and its riders. Spared a van's
unnecessary rental by enough
new members interested and bringing cars,
they got a mole instead: Darla had bluffed
way in with pseudonym, and drove. "If ours
is first to get there, we'll leave front door cracked
for you, with key back in the lockbox, 'cause
the hot tub's where it's at, and that's a fact."
The thing Joe hinted is that grocery was
a run for someone else to do for brews.
He'd picked up house, so others split the booze.

230.
The drive bore Stel through California's heart,
north of the city m.A.A.d and suburbs Bay,
and skirted edge of vineyard-lord ramparts,
where royalty in Napa's DNA
fuels wino feudalism, workers picked
the grapes that Parker'd rate once barreled oak
turned taste just so, their wages capped quite strict:
their retail price Baroque, the workers broke.
That land passed quickly, bypassed to the east
with climb to delta region levees saved.
Like Dujiangyan, to tame aquatic beast
of local nature, infrastructure slaved.
Past Sac-town rose the foothills of the chain,
Sierras of Nevada mountain skein.

231.
The highway climbed toward something called 'the pass',
that sounded like a hassle if it snowed.
They got there uneventfully, Stel asked
what hubbub was, why place was so forebode.
"When storms whip through, they'll dump both snow
    and ice
right here, and cops will check you've put on chains
if you're not four-wheel drive. It's rolling dice
if so much falls they close it till it drains.
And even when it's fine there's vehicles
out in the shoulders messing with a tire:
they've not used slip-on chains. It's miracles
and puppy dogs today that none require
that extra grip. Look right, there's Donner Pass—"
Stel gazed at snowed-in cannibals' crevasse.

232.
The highway wound both up and down, they'd moved
from altitudes where oaks and buckeyes shined
then cedars, firs, and dogwoods. Pines had proved
superiority at timberline.
Then all the sudden, as with peaks, road fell
below the isoclines that oxygen
decided were too high to really fill—
in ways, the highway had outfoxed the hen,
allowing human passengers with ease
to cross a mountain pass that, times past, killed.
"It's this geography that guarantees
you'll lose the game," said Darla who'd distilled
decision points on Oregon's long Trail,
(the game) that always made her players fail.

233.
Descent from mountains' heights down toward the lake
for which 'Tahoe' was shorthand was a ride
that took good choice of gear for engine brake
and showed why California's countryside
inspired some enlightened greats like Muir
and Ansel Adams and Chouinard. When they
got through the valley corridor and steered
right to encircle lake, Stel could survey
sheer beauty stretched before her: everywhere
surrounding water body was some peak
in snowcap hat, alone and solitaire,
its guarding only due to its physique.
Volcano's buckling yielded sentry range,
a circumstance that none could prearrange.

234.
Stel wondered how long such a gorgeous source
of water'd pooled here for the ponderings
of wily engineers who'd quick endorse
a plan to make electrons, somber things
with hydropower. Here, capacity
would hardly be constraint, the snowpack melt
each year renewed supplies. Rapacity
was not her normal lens, and so she felt
a little guilty jumping to the thought.
Experience in China'd left a scar,
ex post blame for precluded gigawatts
made Stel police her voice, lest chance words mar.
She breathed, and witnessed lovely nature for
intrinsic value held, and poise restored.

235.

In dream she woke to sunlight, ventured out
to see the road trip canyon. Bounded rise
of mountain arc 'round basin awed, the route
escaping farmland valley hid from eyes.
From stance on bound'ry crest she watched the flood
turn tawny cut-straw plains to inland sea.
Her feet gave way as nude cliff made from mud
eroded, void of roots' fast guarantee
that ground stay grounded. Somehow currents swept
her quick from shore. At sea, her panic swelled:
She'd grown up thinking water's to be schlepped,
not massive 'nough to buoy bodies. Held
by crushing, clashing currents, flailing for
her life, she sank beneath the rapids' roar.

236.
The verse took partial shape in mind before
it curled to letters pencil lead could etch.
It started as an image that implored
its audience to savor grandeur's sketch.
With regal air of old daguerreotype,
the panorama seared on mind's eye screen.
True sunshine there had no compare on Skype
or Shutterstock-like versions of the scene.
Such things were seen by human eyes alone,
experiences photographs kept boxed.
Stel knew that digital had stolen throne,
through IG feeds as fake as views Xeroxed.
In person, optic treasures were hers, seen
indelibly as light prints mercury.

237.
That pencil, too, was still a few hours hence.
She'd reach for it in rented bedside drawer
in use of literature for self-defense
and *coup d'etat* both. Followers would store
her stories' words alongside own lived views.
Life outlook stems from miscellany kept.
And so to be creator of new news
neared Stella to a childhood refund meant
to soothe regretful soul she'd studied so.
The goblins on her shoulders, on her back
kept her at books until eyes bloodied. Throw
all youth toward cramming, spawn amnesiac.
Like canvas or a page, it left a space
imagined better lives could go replace.

238.
Between the riding and the writing, Stel
accompanied the troops to grocery store
where she avoided overwhelming tell
that she was overwhelmed. Coterie's chore
to think through food and beverage kind of fit
the fact that rich man in the hot tub soaked.
She so remarked to Cade. "He's blind to it?"
"Yeah, probably. When you're in bath suds cloaked
it's elementary to think of next
big business venture capitalists fund."
"No joke." It seemed apparent how wealth flexed
to multiply itself while system dunned
remaining have-nots, telling them they ought
to save more of the cash they'd never got.

239.
With Flying Dog, Rogue, Sudwerk, Twenty-First
Amendment in possession, they arrived.
In kitchen where they stored it, Fendi purse
lay there in place conspicuous, contrived.
Cade translated for Stel, "That bag right there
with taxes costs 'bout ten weeks minimum
wage if you're working full-time." "Tee is heir
apparent to Joe's fortunes?" "Winnin' some
already, far as I can tell." He placed
the precious object elsewhere, cracked a beer,
explained, "So it won't accidentally baste
in cocktail juice and lose its value here."
"Oh, hey Stel!" shouted voice from outside, "Be
a dear and mix me something for the heat!"

240.
"Mimosa or Paloma, Vieux Carré,
a Rob Roy, Aviation, Daiquiri,
Old Fashioned, Gimlet, Boulevardier
Negroni, Sazerac, or Dark Stormy,
Mint Julep, Margarita, Martini,
a Moscow Mule, Manhattan, Mojito,
a Bloody Mary, Gibson, G&T,
White Russian, Rusty Nail, or Sour Pisco?
Perhaps Hot Toddy, Vesper, Whiskey Smash,
a Clover Club or Scofflaw, Sidecar, Pimm's
Cup, Cosmopolitan, or shall I mash
them all together following my whims?"
Bar speech she'd hoped would tease was dry. Blandly
oblivious reply: "Long Island Tea!"

241.
Stel flipped to page in barman's book on shelf
describing how to balance sours and sweets
to so mixologize. "Whew! I myself
would never drink this." "Yeah, it overheats
the liver and the brain right proper quick,"
said Benny, putting beers up in the fridge,
"it's yoozh a well drink with a whopper kick,
like nectar to fraternity swarms' midge."
Stel followed recipe, resisted her
desire to strike back at the demanding
yet clueless benefactor. "It occur
to you as Oppo we should be ranting
about the supposition that we do
the chores, as poor folks?" "Yes, and clearly to

242.
you, too, Benita." "Yet, you make his drink."
"I won't blame him for rudeness he can't know."
"Can't know? You're joking." "Do you ever think
what his life's like, with toadies close in tow?
With everyone agreeing to what he's
proposed, some consciously and others not,
those not because they think that courtesy's
due to the *nouveau riche?*" "It's Camelot,
with knights and honor, deference, all that,"
said Cade, to add to Stella's side, "ingrained."
Benita took it in, defenses flat,
with curiosity they both maintained
positions counter to her read of things.
Stel noted theme for sonnet. "No one flings

243.
himself at us the way they do at Joe,"
said Stella. "Think you'd have the upper hands,
by being ladies, and attractive. Nope!
They go to where the Cash Rules and commands
the 'Everything Around theM'," Cade observed.
As Benny mulled it through, they let a pause
erupt into the kitchen. Undeserved
homage to someone solely, well, because
they made bajillion bucks seemed at once real
and quite ridiculous. Stel wondered if
she'd also been so supplicant, genteel.
It hurt a bit to think what made the diff
in getting her to US was the same:
proximity to man with true power's claim.

244.
"Hey slowpokes!" shouted voice from outside tub,
"I'm sweating water still, how'm I supposed
to drink my way to meeting Beelzebub
if I'm without an adult tea to toast?"
"Oh, always classy, that one," Benny said.
All smirked at smugness suffocating them,
and Stel walked out with beverage. "Shush, dickhead,
you're being served, be grateful!" Tee condemned
her doting suitor, also clad to swim
and sitting on tub edge, wet, steamy-blurred.
A locomotive's worth of vapor limned
her figure, nigh angelic. "Be our third!"
invited Joe, "and, mm-mm tasty, thanks!
There's room in here for all, amass the ranks."

245.
In reading situation, Stella hoped
again naïveté helped Joe choose words.
Insinuating 'third' suggested grope
was covert wish of this friend-cum-drunkard.
Though tiniest bit tempered by the ask
that she invite the masses, it repulsed.
Tee's patience with insouciance unmasked,
she said, "Joe dearest, words like that dredge gulfs
between you and the 'ranks'." "I'm welcoming!
What's criminal in that?" "You asked for sex."
"Of course I didn't." "Terms that seldom ring
to you as problematic or complex
resound more creepily to women. How'd
you'd feel if Grindr rando said aloud

246.
he'd rather like to take you in the butt?"
"That's different." "Oh?" "Cause Stella knows we're
  friends.
Cause I'm a pipsqueak. 'Cause no doors are shut.
Cause we're two and arithmetic, well, tends
to find that three's the integer beyond!
Now let's put that behind us, toast to joys,
and soak a bit? Such beauty *tout le monde*
would envy here, from trees to you." "Ugh. Boys."
said Tee to Stella, eyes rolled in defeat.
"I think I'd make more headway with a wall.
At least my words would echo back, concrete
proof they'd reached destination," unappalled
Tee carried on. She slid back in, submerged,
debate less complicated by heat's splurge.

247.
Stel went in, changed, came out, picked up new thread.
"So, Tee, I got to thinking as we drove
through Napa 'bout the wider watershed.
What happens to those trellised grapevine troves
when rains stop falling, in a drought?" "They'll pipe
some water from the mountain snowpack. Why?"
"I saw some roadside signs that seemed to gripe
about the irrigation. They're backed by
the workers there?" "Oh, no. They're too scared to
have any voice, 'cause some lack documents.
That census question hurt." "Blue states dared sue
about that, right?" "Yep, said it blocked true sense
of who lives here, repressing turnout. Gone
are days when district maps were fairly drawn."

248.
"But hypothetically," Stel posed, "if the
state had to make a trade-off choice to feed
that valley or the city, to stiff a
constituency, what would it do?" "Heed
first-come, first-served laws. Old farms drink most. Can't
break those entitlements. The state is bound
to honor them—or lawsuit time. Farms plant
their crops from them. Rescind and you'll have browned
and lifeless fields most everywhere." "Sure, I
get what you're saying, stuff of life and all.
But really, let's say water's gone, your, my,
and urban, rural lives all stand to fall
when taps run dry. What's California do?"
"I know that it's unpolitic taboo

249.
to talk like that if you're official. Press
on either side can blow that headline up."
"Then doesn't it leave you a bit depressed?
It's something you could act on, 'dread thine cup
shall runneth dry with climate change!'" "There's more
and pressing problems Opposition's picked,"
said Tee defensively. "A guarantor
of water's not important?" "It restricts
the things we'd work on." "Sure, but it would serve
this place you live. Plus, if that logic holds
you'd not be just opposing stuff," observed
Stel, boosting Mo's past point, "Your crew's power scolds,
but till it's channeled locally to build
a noticed change, it's bluster of strong-willed."

250.
Big bubbles burbled. Jets blew air. Tub hummed.
The lack of speech made operating sounds
jacuzzi belched the static bassline, numbed
the in-betweens of vocal battlegrounds.
"I like that thought-experiment you pose,"
filled sanguine Teflon Joe, "imagine that
a despot could control how water flows,
and had to balance MUNI and muscat,
the urban markets versus farmsteads. What
would well-intentioned functionary choose?"
"It's not an agronomic question." "But
of course it is!" "No, here you overuse
the theoretical, forgetting who
has options past farm gates." "Oh no, IQ

251.
is normally distributed. Bell curves
mean there's smart folks in agriculture, Tee."
"And speaking of, here: try some fresh *hors d'oeuvres*
from olive farms we got, plus local brie,"
said guest Stel didn't know who passed 'round plates.
"That doesn't mean," Tee snapped right back at Joe,
"that overnight a farmhand recreates
some new career from scratch. Raze Jericho
and get ten thousand refugees." "So pay
the displaced workers for the time displaced.
Remember, there's a despot?" "Fine. Defray
some social cost. But don't think you've erased
all negatives: when you got your degrees
did you get full-time offers? No. Trainees

252.
all have to climb the ladder, network, prove
themselves at base of totem pole for years
before they get the capital to move
up corporate ladders slowly, tiers by tears."
"Then pay them more. All time can be offset
by some amount of money." "No, it can't.
Imagine if you gambled, then lost bet,
had to go to Alaska and replant
yourself. You lose your friends, your kids do too,
and you know zilch about environment."
"Well clearly, I'd just go build an igloo
and solve it that way: quick retirement!
I'd fish and hunt some caribou." The flip
was armor coating him head to toe tip.

253.
Details of Ayi's story further grim,
accentuated how it must have felt
to cede career on governmental whim.
The payment to offset where they had dwelt
came late, and less than promised. Wealth was used
as selling point persuading folks to leave,
then claims for those amounts were all refused
once families relocated. "These days, we've
chance of like crisis here. The rumor mill
round Fan says Party's putting plan in pen
to dam and flood this valley too. None will
confirm it, but one local councilman
whose opposition tendencies are clear
has hinted possibility is near."

254.
With doubled verse that night inspired by day,
Stel sensed the outline of a tale emerge.
Its seeds sown long ago and far away
best fit divided self of life submerged.
Reintroducing structure lost to page,
she healed herself while seizing power long-schemed.
Eyes tuned in hoping themes that Stel'd encaged
matched unresolved ones that through their heads
   streamed.
The postings that began in politics
and stretched into critique and life advice
earned Stella trust and cred through scrawl to clicks.
She clutched to neckline stuffed dog who'd sufficed
to animate wild daydreams since her youth
and thanked him as the touchstone of untruth.

Chapter 26

255.
Next morning, all arose to lift up peak
in garb whose thermal insulation locked
their warmth quite tightly to their own physique.
Some wore rococo patterns that peacocked,
so indicating they were single and
with interest in companionship. Stel's coat
was mute and borrowed from Cade secondhand.
Cade's Forty Niners jacket antidote
to being thought a tourist, worn with pride,
they spent the morning hugging bunny slopes.
Stel liked the feeling when she'd start to glide,
bent knees in surfer style, before her hopes
were pummeled by a fall into a drift
of powder snow. Repeat the fall and lift

256.
enough times in a row, not standing down,
and golly gee, she'd found that balance! Loose
enough to waver, tight for slanting. Frown
wiped off her face for hours, she had deduced
the proper way of snowboarding. Cade had
grown up by sneaking out to kick and push
his skateboard, relic parents thought was bad.
That balance meant he seldom fell on tush
although it was his first time too. They broke
midday to get two Irish coffees, snacks,
and water. Reconvening, followed folk
to kindest blues the mountain had as tracks.
From off the lift on rim of cliff, they gazed.
It steeply dropped. "Well, shit," Cade paraphrased.

257.
The parallels to page were striking, eyes
cast down the mountain showed a folded sheet,
blank, birthed as such by nature as a prize
to she who'd first beat dawn to mountain meet.
From seated pose, straps closed on boots, Stel felt
pang of past fear of heights matched with recall
of dreamed appropriation of the veldt
as little girl who nature'd first enthralled.
Clad mightily, as swaddled by a god,
she sat immune to temperatures of ice,
intaking landscape whose pristine façade
she'd sully instant board she steered slipped, sliced,
and carved its own designs. Stel felt like fate
had crafted her broad contours, now ornate

258.
contrails were hers to kick up. Hot tub talk
now echoed. Water rights pre-Civil War
still bound the state? Revolt, then; break that lock!
Strange truths cascade from small things come before.
Chat had her viewing every tiny world
as microscopic diorama, sign
of macroscopic province tightly furled,
significance recumbent, fractal-spined.
She wasn't sure if she'd see everything
in everything there was to see, and hoped
alertness for the detail it did bring
would still remain once she was down the slope,
the beauty on the page her board would draw
in motifs followers alone each saw.

259.
Stel's eyeballs ranged unstopping 'round the soup
of life face planted in. She lacked right words
for how close-up inspection ever-duped.
A decade out she'd name them, overheard
in lyrics from Fiasco—he said that:
see big worlds have their little worlds that feed
on their velocity. *Stel saw how gnats*
gnawed carrion, in turn fed bigger breeds
from vaster canopies. The rap went on
said little worlds have lesser worlds and so
on to viscosity. *Those fractal spawn*
invisible to Stella's eye, earth's slow
yet macroscopic brilliance did enchant,
Vanilla Sky-*like memory bright implant.*

260.
The tip-top steepness menaced. Wide, the run
had room to safely fall. Cade said, "Avoid
that edge that looks Kinkade, the sides a ton
of trees start. Chutes between aren't to be toyed
with. They look hot, but if you get down close
you'll drop waist-deep and likely can't get out."
Stel looked, agreed that they were grandiose,
invitingly like fairytale quest route
into a dark and secret woods. "But Cade,
they're such a nice way out." Twin parallel
tracks showed they'd been traversed by ski brigade.
"That glint in eyes, Stel, drop it. Bears'll smell
you, wake and hunt you. *Rawr!*" Fake mitten paws
and beastly face flashed at her, Cade's plush claws.

261.
With pinprick firefly light as useless guide,
their travels through the undergrowth were not
entirely successful. They supplied
a modicum of safety, as they sought,
but moved them unawares yet further from
the banyan stand they'd set out first to find.
Abu's thick bag lacked bread: no trail of crumb
could guide once norths and souths were misaligned.
Then Stel burst out exasperatedly,
"Abu, can you please hurry up? We're lost."
"I'm gathering," he aspirated, "these,"
in tone deterring being further bossed.
He'd fished out oil-less lantern of clear glass
and with bugs' butts found means to light amass.

262.
They ratcheted their boots to stiffness ten,
Stel checked her straps and balled her fists. Cade's brief
suggested that, so when she fall again
she won't break fingers. "Use the falling leaf
if it's too steep to turn," he finished, stood,
and dropped into the well that gravity
with proper human intervention could
take him unharmed to base camp. Cavity
not looking any better with more wait,
Stel popped up and began descent on edge,
her goofy stance did reinvigorate
conviction she'd get down without a sledge.
She balanced till her vision ogled patch
of off-piste pine paths. Then a mogul batch

263.
snuck up – she wasn't looking, after all –
and sent her for a most unpleasant flight.
Airborne exhilaration met landfall,
where, due in part to dearth of Fahrenheit,
the iced ground was as concrete. Impact hurt.
Ameliorating temperature's shortfall
was fact she flew quite far, out to outskirt
of trail where deep-banked pillow snow forestalled
the shattering of limb on tree. A gulp
of air went down, Stel proved she breathed, relaxed.
Face up, she saw the spiral branches, hulk
of hundred years of effort, tall, unaxed,
commanding little scrutiny except
that of the pausing traveler plunge swept...

264.
The fear became reality as bark
stripped off the limb that levered Abu's feet,
his body dropped in unexpected arc.
With all his might he pushed, prior to the cleat
dislodging from its perch, toward where the bed
was sitting twenty feet below, its edge
five feet away. He wished he'd further spread
the pad of plants before he climbed, and pledged
that if, when hitting ground, he did survive
he'd never make the same mistake again.
The **THUD!** that struck as frame to ground arrived
brought water to Stel's eyes, which saw there, then,
unmoving body strewn across the brink
of ground and bed. She found her heart then sink...

265.
...into the pine's event horizon. *Mines,*
those moguls, Stella thought, *and laid, and breathed.*
This massive evergreen's but tiny tines,
a million needles soaking light so sheathed,
protected pinecones some day could drop down
to earth, be charred by fire, and sprout themselves.
With worlds enough and time, this dullest brown
compacted seed grenade makes stuff of elves
and ents and trolls and fantasies come real:
the forests of Red Riding Hood, the Shire,
or Narnia. In hindsight, tree revealed
the way that Stella'd move to reacquire
identity aligned with goals. "Hey, Stel!"
came distant wheezy shout. *Ha! Cade, too, fell,*

266.
she thought. Sound helped her right herself and scan
forbidden woodlands for some Day-Glo print
of gold and crimson. Far down slope a man
made an involuntary encampment
with flung possessions spread like glitterbomb
as if to mark the territory. Cade's
fall had been breathtaking, and bitter. Palm
to snow, Stel stood up, starting small cascades
of powder, weight of power. She steadied, swerved
her weight to right foot, leaned, and glided like
she hadn't moment past been tad unnerved.
Traversing slope akin to the Klondike,
she focused: body's aches took second slot
till she could get a closer-up snapshot

267.
of if he was okay. She neared and picked
left mitten jutting from the snow, still ten
yards from his body. "Stella, I predict
you'll find a hand-knit scarf there too," and then
she did, and held it up. "Okay. See chains?"
"What chains?" "My bling." "What color?" "Are you blind?
I wear gold everyday, bling brings the rains!"
Stel figured humor probably entwined
with health, so nothing's broken. Then they'd won!
A little excavation brought delight
when gold shined through the powdered water, sun
reflecting its own hue in chainlink. "Rite
of passage, acrobatics on the board."
"You spaced and tried a kickflip?" Quip ignored,

268.
Cade flailed his arms like mightiest T-Rex
and showed his dino strength: "I'm buried here,
ten years to life. Need bail." Indeed, prospects
for digging himself out looked fairly mere.
Stel gave him back his garments and his charm
and from her knees pushed loose the weight of snow.
It felt like wartime rescue of *gendarme*,
her soldier's duty *ex officio*.
Unburied after two short breaks, equipped
again with proper trappings for the cold,
they stood, and hoped the slope was nondescript
from there to base—or if not, then patrolled.
With granted wish, they carved down to the root
of profuse range without a parachute.

269.
"Whoa, Cade," said Stel, Keanu Reeves-intoned,
"that's gnarly gnar right there." She panted, breath
all visible. "Don't know who chaperoned
whom down the mountain this time. Cheating death
is special kind of thrill, you'd say?" Stel felt
like it was similar to cheating past,
but didn't want to talk about it. "Welts?"
"Not one," he said. They laid as angels, gassed
in snow. The clouds rolled by, the air was thick—
or, thicker than at peak, and difference sensed.
"If you could redo life, what would you pick?"
asked Stel of Cade, both prostrate, undefensed.
"Nobody's ever asked me that," in tone
of Genie came reply, "I wish I'd known

270.
that there's no race, no competition, zilch
defining us externally. It's us.
In ways, I feel like grades just serve to filch
all our attentions when we're young. The fuss
amounts to roughly nothing over years.
Some classmates graded highly ain't done jack,
some classmates dropping out have bank careers.
I didn't view myself as quarterback
until I started listening to rap.
Your hustle dominates your GPA.
If I ran course again, from that first lap,
I'd say, 'self, you a G' then go be a
right proper hustler, day one, no holds barred.
I walked too long down others' boulevards.

271.
And you?" he quickly asked. Attention shift
was noticed by them both. "My history.
No, my mythology," she said, then riffed
a short time more, then said, "It's blistering
and getting even colder. Let's go in."
In pine trunk skiing lodge pretending to
be paying guests, they scooped from cocoa tin
and brewed up balmy beverage blending two
parts milk to water, sugaring to taste,
which wasn't much when dominating thirst
was reason for the mug in the first place.
It also pleased their hands, and so they nursed.
The fireplace opened fires in places closed
a long time back, where kindling'd been exposed.

272.
"Mythology," reciprocated Cade,
"Before I close my eyes I fantasize
I'm livin' well," staccato serenade
came from him, *"when I wake and realize*
I'm just a prisoner in hell. That's Pac,
in 'Outlaw', first song that I memorized.
He rapped about the dissonance of Glock
with loyalty and love, with them-or-I's.
You'll learn a thing about mythology
by giving it a listen, '95,
on *Me Against The World.* It's gotta be
a classic on what we become, deprived
of all the civilizing things we claim
society and urban life became."

273.
The chocolate's richness fit the lodge decor.
It and the fire breathed life back in them both.
That life took form of words, and Cade said more
with distant look in eye. "And now I quoth:
What I say might save a life, what I speak
might save the street, ain't got no instruments,
(it's Killer Mike) *I got my hands and feet.*
I heard in 2012, and in some sense
it let me change what's *me*." "What do you mean?"
"Did Auntie Tao say much about me when
she fixed your visa?" "No, I knew she'd screen
whoever I'd be staying with, her ken
for people's always good. I trusted." "It's
not safety, it's that my whole life omits

274.
the need for any explanation. She
said nothing of her second-cousin Cade
because his dazzling personality
was two shades of a good accountant's: grayed,
and bland. I didn't know a thing beyond
the textbooks and the weekend classes dad
forced me to focus on. He had me conned
in hope I'd be tracked to Olympiad
in one of them. In honesty, I sucked.
I slogged because it's only thing I knew.
Nobody took one sec to deconstruct
that all I ever did was overdo—
and, being stretched, had expertise in none.
How's that for formula to wake your son?"

275.
He paused and sipped and stared into the fire.
"That song goes on, says that it's gospel, soul,
funk, jazz and even church, from pew to choir
at pulpit, players Pentecostal, goal
to preach the opposite of pop bullshit.
I liked it, liked that he put self square at
the target's center in a mouthful. It
was new to me, this way he pushed prayer that
the audience get woke in narrative.
Words put in wind come back like boomerang,
he said, with microphone, declarative.
He pointed it at crowd, they heard, they sang.
Just one song, Stel. I listened fifty times
and realized much more than nifty rhymes."

276.
"But that was 2012. You mean to say
the Cade I know's a reinvention?" "Sure.
Who isn't, Stella? Everybody's clay,
just some know that they've molding hands. Uncured,
we're pliable. There's boatloads of pop psych
attesting so. The problem's that folks fire
their clay in kiln because they rather like
themselves, get bored, get lazy, or get mired
in something, then they switch to stories of
their self as fixed, unchanging. I grew with
a story that was wrong, matured, then shoved
it back to history, replaced the myth
with something better suiting of the grind
that's more nutritional for hungry mind."

277.
The cocoa'd cooled to fancy chocolate milk,
depending how you saw it. Toes were dry.
Lodge rental desk continued plan to bilk
day-trippers of deposits on supplies.
No busy bodies busybodied two
who sat contemplatively near the heat.
They couldn't. Stories disembodied glued
them both together under each heartbeat.
"My legs are getting stiff, I guess it's time
to waddle back." "Think we're too late for spa?"
"Now knowing you, if so, I think you'll climb
into the bathtub, fill it up, and—" "Ha!
Baths ain't the same without the jets, sis. 'Ye
would never take a bath that's just halfway."

Chapter 27

278.
They walked through door an artisan had carved
to get back home to weekend rental where
full tree logs made the walls feel more enlarged,
as if the earth itself planned out the lair.
"A tundra Shire," Stel mused, and bounced to Cade.
"Yeah, less the rings and drama. And the orcs."
Though landlord had explicitly forbade
all parties, they prepared to pop some corks.
Their muscles in recuperative mode,
they quickly changed to swimsuits, brought fresh booze
and went to patio. Tub-goers glowed
appreciatively for the session brews.
Such gifts distributed, with words to greet,
they fell to chit-chat once they took their seat.

279.
"Oh, Stella! Saw those literary treats,"
bikini-clad, immersed-in-tub Dar said,
"you're such a modern William Butler Yeats
on Instagram! A repost to my thread
on Facebook got a hundred likes." "By whom?"
"I can't keep track of individuals
these days, folks skip creating to consume."
"On social?" "Yep. These posts and vids viewed fill
lost sense of self with betters: us." Stel asked
with no detected false camaraderie
how Dar'd become *so skilled* to have amassed
so many followers. Gam? Flock? Herd? Siege?
What could such groups of animals be called
when far too numerous to be recalled?

280.
Not needing 'nother nudge toward monologue,
Dar started in on juicy gossiping—
or so her tone inflected. Stel agog,
Dar leaned in, shared her secret sauce, tipping
her hand on every recipe she used.
She loved to be the expert. When her fans
in real life recognized her, and then schmoozed
she'd cancel what she had as other plans
to talk to them at length. To Stel's delight,
compatriots had tuned out and weighed the
case for, against, the MVP they'd knight
that season: Westbrook, Harden, or KD.
Stel figured watching NBA'd be fun,
but just for rest once *coup d'etat* was done.

281.
"You follow others?" Stel repeated back,
to memorize the early steps Dar said
paved way for some reciprocation, hacked
the altruism others claimed was dead
on world wide web. "Oh yes, and comment, too.
The more that you engage, the better your
small chance is that the web-linked content you
put in is read. Treat each as letter for
the person whose attention you're to catch."
Stel must admit that Darla had her flaws,
but also that she'd guilt not having patched
into this expertise. Conceit withdraws
the curiosities of audience:
Stel'd overdosed on Darla's gaudiness.

282.
"It's cold, it's snowing, and you lack a drink
to warm you up! I'll fetch another Spritz
for you," said Stella, gaining time to think
and write down all she'd learned in shorthand chits
on Post-It notes in kitchen drawer. She mixed
prosecco with some Aperol and ice,
took out a lemon, sliced it, and then fixed
it to flute rim. Feigned servitude was price
to get the shortlist of the things to do
to dominate all social media,
from Dar, the opposite of *ingénue*.
Stel'd choke it down to learn how speeding the
switch from Tee to her could go feasibly:
craft content taken nigh-believably.

283.
That 'nigh', that close-enough, gave benefit
of doubt in Darla's view. Her average fan
tuned in in wistfulness he'd turnabout
from bore to Bond somehow in mere short span
of YouTube clip. *Proximity to greats,*
Stel thought without so telling Dar, *was cause*
for every human striving since we'd apes
as parents. Broadcast how self wished-for was.
Produce the self on hero's arc, elude
the probing questions of the riffraff plebes:
your narrative itself would then intrude
their psyche, and then even if half leaves
they're left with the impression you're no peer
and grant subconscious halo you're premier.

284

"At home," Abu began, "I'm one of eight.
We once lived well in Syria, till war
broke out in Lebanon, and our estate
became a looters' target, laws ignored.
They ousted us from title to the land,
we fled to Turkey. Left in foreignness,
jobs, food, and shelter scarce, we'd not withstand
for long. So we came here. Now sore in this
is me, forgotten as my family copes
by squatting on some land and planting crops."
Stel felt familiarities evoked
in lamentation life's but farming ops.
"My parents told of past, but still remained
attached to story royalty's ingrained."

285.
The solid patio, a wooden deck
beneath the soles felt nearly stable as
the ground itself, an artificial tech
age-old to fool the feet with fable. *Has*
the moon scared off the clouds? Yes. Han-loom fan
I've looked to from all over Earth... Stel mused
toward end of night electric. It began
that way, at least, then somehow blew a fuse.
Some friends went off to privately do drugs,
some others had too much to drink, some more
expressed a need to get down, cut some rugs,
before their bodies told them they were sore.
And so like bulbs without electrons cool,
friends too turned off when left bereft of joules.

286.
That meant night's twin headlights were moon and Stel,
a treat worth savoring. She grabbed her pack
of cyan Spirits, snuck out for a spell,
and simply stood, appreciating black.
Black. Black of night. The black that eyelids keep.
The black of back of mind. The black of space.
The black unconscious passing-out of sleep.
The black of holes. The black of things erased.
Her lighter's spark ignited all that thought
flash paper-like, as retinas reset.
It's funny, how a tiny little dot
of fire reduces rest to silhouette:
near-literal case there of smoke and mirr'r
(less verse reflective so to witness steer).

287.
Door clicked. "You mind?" asked Joe with deference
that sounded genuine. She offered him
the pack in gesture of benevolence.
"Thank god it's not an EU pack. They've grim
full-color photos of what cancer does.
And, well, I'll say it works 'cause just one look
is all it took to kill my nicki buzz.
Cold turkey quit for two years, then retook
the nasty habit at my company.
I couldn't handle all the stress. The break
was time to think. Whoa! These have pungency."
Joe breathed unfiltered air to cope. Both faked
not being quite as cold as felt. "What brings
you outside for a pause?" "Oh, you know... things."

288.
Too dark to see if Joe had smiled or not,
Stel found she didn't really care to know.
In silence they traced through the inky blot,
searched stars for satellite or UFO.
He turned a moment taciturn, time passed
in space of simply silent being. Sky
had steady, pushing breeze that could outlast
the fragment clouds that tried to overfly.
Some time an interval in future, length
of cigarettes reduced to zero's ash,
Joe let his hair down, scrunchie's tethered strength
reduced to naught with no object to lash.
"Mm. Things," he said, "they're one of my faves, too."
"Just wondering in fact what we're slaves to."

289.
Stel onward waxed, found mental clarity
in possibility of vocalized –
thus shareable-with-others – verity.
Thick headbound stewing thought's too localized
to change an anything except own acts.
*"The 'hood'll oft embrace when you profound
with words,* Talib once said: your rep impacts
how strangers will receive you." "Sure, background
is helpful intro," Joe replied. "It's not
the background. That's Geppetto's trick, Joe: it's
the foreground, it's the puppet strings, it's got
you-by-the-balls reactively. No wits
insert themselves to intervene and say,
'Hey self, your bias makes you feel this way'."

290.
"Nah, I don't buy this bias stuff. I've read
half dozen articles on micro-whats-
it-called? Aggressions! I feel I can't tread
within a mile of that minefield." "The crux
is not that stuff. It's something bigger. Your
loquacious inner Joe at every turn
is analyzing data to restore
your sanity. With logic you discern
who's friendly, safe, and stuff like that. What sucks
is how irreparable snap judgments are,
'cause then that story's static, cannot flux
responsively to growing reservoir
of actual experience with that
one thing you judged. Perspective's stuck." Joe spat

291.
the taste out over rail without reply.
"Talib goes on, *I say shit they relate
to, and I keep it down to Earth.* See, I
don't think I'm down with what that last clause states."
Joe turned from strut to face her. "Let me guess,"
he said, "that's why you're gazing toward the stars."
Stel swallowed little laugh, "I must confess
your sleuthing and old Watson's are on par."
"I'm here to serve, milady," Joe took bow.
"But fine, you're sort of right. He's missing one
big piece. Because he's big, has listeners now,
he has the chance to change things. Twisting's done
by showing people could-be's, not what-are's."
"Whose insight's that?" "Ugh. Honestly? It's Dar's."

292.
"Yeah, people underestimate her. She's
put leg work into all those social posts."
"Sure, lots of high-slit leg shots." "No, not skeeze.
She's thinking through how medium best hosts
the aspirations of her audience.
She'll try stuff, test, refine, but never flaunt
that backstage work in public face." "Cements
a loyal membership, it seems." "Her want,
as best as I can tell, is but to be
a pretty normal person when off-cam."
"The trouble's that she ports with her TV
presenter's fake persona." "Trade-offs, ma'am.
Earn cash to live off from a shtick? Say yes."
"I'd choose a different path nevertheless."

293.
"That's fair. We've all a price." "When did you know
what yours was?" "Frankly, after Series B.
Up to that point 'twas fun and games to grow
our team, our sales, our traffic queries. Me?
I'd thought of it as just a thrill I liked.
With VCs breathing down our necks, the ramp
from ten to fifty million sales soon psyched
me out, I went from being our big champ
to feeling like I ran by being chased.
The motivation flipped, intrinsic to
extrinsic. Then I saw how cash replaced
my want to build for building's sake. Click through
to end of drama, after losing friends,
relationship, and nearly all weekends

294.
we won the startup game, and I retired."
"At thirty." "Temporarily. A break.
I'm answering to say that I was wired
to want to do one single thing, I ached
to do that one thing better than the rest.
It took me quite a ways. When that was drained
the market value set my price." "Divest
relationships, zoom in on options gained.
I get it, strangely." Joe was quite surprised,
expecting rebel's judgment as was oft
the case when conversations advertised
his fortunate post-economic loft.
"A long time back I made a choice like that,"
she added, saying no more 'bout the fact.

CHAPTER 28

295.
The blank page got its fill of pen that week,
or two, or twelve, who knew? Some form that time
can stand denomination in, oblique
to author who, herself, zoomed in to rhyme.
Reality compressed: expansively
as sky and heavens billions old reduced
to slim nocturnal peek, romance of the
space yet to fill kept Stella nightly juiced.
It's hard to know if motivation came
from endless pages' longing for marks black
or if instead it was the larger game
she played to prove to self she could hijack
the hearts and minds on web anonymous
and Opposition too, eponymous.

296.
Once sun went down, her curtains too drew closed
symbolically and factually. She offed
the lights, and let soundtrack superimpose
known world in headphones over-ear. The soft
progression from the mostly sensory
to wholly mental shed constraining shells.
For this, most others called dispensary
to chemically confuse their organelles.
Some rocket burn toward greatness jetted her
along in slipstream time, herself composed
composing poems she hoped embedded burr
that hitchhikes in the mind, sprouts, can depose
internal narratives that readers held,
best conquered parasitically, not shelled.

297.
Friends met up at the Ferry Building pier
to soak up morning sunshine, stock up on
some veggies, gloss political veneer,
and polish coffee off. A dock pylon
caught Tula's purse at pace and nearly yanked
her off her feet to plunge into the drink.
Stel wrote as if no things were sacrosanct
and posted poke: what if Tee were to sink?
They'd met up on Potrero Hill in park
that overlooks the shipping corridor
and watched the freighters dock, goods disembark,
to prompt again their group dysphoric chore
of asking if consumerism's worth
the price that it extracts from Mother Earth.

298.
On that, Stel'd written sonnet series, rant
in three full parts about hypocrisy.
She too was guilty, said that US can't
legitimately speak: its talk missed the
Accord in Paris, then got worse and worse.
Until she met a biking vegan who
forswore airplanes and lived off-grid *sans* purse
of coin, she wrote, she'd skewer those who drew
themselves to Green alignment. Actions set
the breadth and depth of carbon footprint. Words
are fun to bandy 'round in factions, yet
cannot help distance someone from the herds
as greener till accompanied with loss
of standard living. That's *Rime's* albatross.

299.
They'd spent a weekend day admiring dogs
in off-leash park at Bernal Heights, then biked
straight west, then south, to thickened banks of fogs
Fort Funston welcomed. Beachside cliffs they hiked
with Shiba Inu Labradoodles, curs,
kind mastiffs, toys of every sort, and Greg.
Amid the mostly drab caboodles were
two dogs of special merit. Stella pegged
them as the pinnacles of species known.
The first was Ruby, part-Chow rescue mix
maroon. Next, subtle as a sousaphone
with sweetheart's clunky maelstrom slobber licks,
retriever golden in most every way
was Greg. Named how? No owner near could say.

300.
Stel's recollection of that zoo had blurred
by late time that she'd sat to write, and so
took all Greg's loving spirit she'd inferred
and packed it into frame with room to grow.
She named the pet her BLING, and let it free
in catacombs of recollecting mind.
Friends took a class at place called Love Story
where yogis came to make selves more aligned.
Her writing there touched mysticality,
discovering the ways stretched bodies waltzed:
a 'practice' meant dualistic fallacy
of 'does' or 'does not' yoga's wholly false.
She commented and followed, won and lost,
and ever-slowly toward importance crossed.

301.
Each Opposition outing got its plaque
in fourteen lines iambic, rhyming too.
Her on-screen compositions she'd repack
into handwritten filigree to skew
the viewers' sense that each was artisan
and from the time when typewriters had reigned.
For future's internet liked partisan
renditions of times sepia prints had framed.
The periodic centering of font
in camera's eye gave Stella's days a pace
she only noticed 'tween her spells savant.
'Twas better marked by rest of human race
who slowly and with skepticism took
her story line and sinker. They were hooked.

302.
The days between must have existed, but
from gray they came, to gray they'd fade away.
As life unfolded, only what was cut
and pinned to paper lived another day.
Her followers liked piercing outside eye's
fresh take on life's mundanities – though not
with XKCD geekiness, but fly
enough to please – and thought them feyly wrought.
The comments back at times in meter came,
with subject-object-verb inversions aped
from her own lines as tribute. She shared fame
with those whose edits positively shaped.
Stel soon detected body politic
by tracing where those bodies thralled and quipped.

303.
First Fridays out in Oakland brought the house
from 'round the Bay, 'cept Joe and Tee, turned streets
to party block one wished for. Folks caroused
to live band beats and sweets and grill-smoked meats,
with temporary clouds from spliff-lit puffs.
From empanadas, funk, beer, crowd control,
and public-minded cops without handcuffs
arose emergent scene that could ensoul,
of how together to unite in gift
of waking up and breathing, having time
to human be, to humans try to lift,
to sunshine chill with stereo Sublime.
That melting pot befit the Oppo crew
who, as a posse, slowly strolled, perused.

304.
They chattered. "Took damn long to park, the roads
all seemed blocked off. Construction's everywhere."
"That's great news." "No it's not." "It is, it bodes
well for the housing prices. Millionaires
alone should not be who we let move in."
"Of course. Therefore I'm pissed that luxury
high-rises are high-rising." "But proof's pinned
supply, demand to price. The bugs you see
aren't bugs themselves, they're features: build more stock
regardless of restrictions, prices fall."
"Displacement, though, results. We've gotta block
developers, slow exodus to crawl."
"That's NIMBY-ism. Just resisting change?
That's bad as Boomers leaving us shortchanged

305.
on everything from pensions to healthcare.
Ignoring symptoms won't make causes cease."
"Of course they suck. We're yoked to their wealth's heirs,
but that's not issue here. You want to lease
the space of longtime residents to house
an influx of young people, who, for most
part spend each waking hour at jobs." "Espouse
prevention of displacement as guidepost,
and you can still build up, and densify.
Though do so carefully, relocate folk
in flights on-site. Building intensifies
the value of their property." "Great joke.
All Section 8 renewals leave place cleft."
"We've learned since then. Go check out HOPE SF."

306.
They came upon a sidestreet's local band
whose soul-funk left the Parliament, Cee Lo,
and vocalists (less-MJ) sound outmanned
and heavily outgunned. "We're Con Brio!"
they shouted to the clot of revelers
who'd stopped to bask in Freddy Mercury's
revival. Witnesses thought devils were
possessing frontman, such soul pure fury
could only be dark magicks' doing. At
set's end the hypnotized crowd then dispersed,
each person feeling like they'd seen unwrapped
entire human's being, best to worst.
"See? Push folks out, you lose great art like that."
"That's empty point, none know their habitat.

307.
Plus hey, it's better to have real debate
about the issues. Live-work spaces? Flats
so small they're called efficiencies? Lightweight
stacked manufactured units? Each combats
some downside in a different way. I don't
pretend to know the menu, but I know
that simple talking points both can't and won't
advance debate to where it needs to go."
They walked past local car show, every whip
tricked out with spinners, lights, hydraulics, sheen
coat fleck two-tone like Béla. Craftsmanship
perfected, anti-cool like Steve McQueen,
their engines roared, crank pistons dynamite.
And next to them rode custom low-ride bikes.

308.
A nearby speaker's Ozomatli beat
contrasted notes against Norteño band's
ranch polka ballad. "That's 'Cut Chemist Suite',"
said Cade, to meet his dutiful demands
on self to educate the masses on
the title, artist, zeitgeist, lyrics, themes,
and history of rap. Wheatgrass chiffon,
turmeric milk and other pyrrhic schemes
were sold at stalls in tiny cups. "A taste?"
they'd each get asked while strolling by. "No, thanks,"
they'd say, in dozen steps be offered paste
of cricket proteins marketed by cranks.
The walls were down, the town was out. Broiled, sun
spiced scene to cover up the snake oils spun.

309.
"Those bicycles remind me: we should think
about a way to pressure MTA
to get a realistic biking link
from Oakland to San Fran, across the Bay.
It's idiotic when the BART's so packed
and everyone's outdoorsy not to build
some architectural addendum tacked
onto the Bay Bridge sides." "Find me three skilled
artmakers from the *playa*, plasma tools,
and one expense account; I'll weld myself."
"Word. Wish I could. I hate these local rules
they say prevent it." "Why? A thick wire shelf
is basically what you'd need, not a road."
"Corruption's deep in earthquake building codes."

310.
"Especially appalling since research
has indicated happiness declines
with long commutes." "Design some Oppo merch
to fundraise? Kickstart that?" "Yeah, good luck." "Whine
enough on steps of city hall to nab
news coverage, parlay that into a—" "Nope.
You think that worked for one scared taxicab
medallion owner fearing he'd go broke
when Uber came? Nah. One voice is as good
as zero." "Even as a cohort they
lost out." "We're better for it." "Victimhood
is worst parley position to display."
"Yet here again we find while chat is free,
it yields us neither bridge nor strategy."

311.
"Reminds me of the times we phone banked. Do
reps even listen to constituents?"
"Sure, if they're fat-stacked part of the swank few
with millions up for grabs." "'Once rich, you've sense'
is bullcrap I've heard to self-justify
the politicians' begging rich man's view."
"With platform thus they further uglify
the tax code so their pass-through gains accrue."
Stel: "Guys, you did that thing you do, again."
"What?" "What?" "What?" "Spiraled out from what we
   want
into broad-based complaints." "Whoops, yep." "Amen."
"If what we need's a movement, Stel's savant.
Set all her followers against the boards
that regulate bridge, activate the hordes."

312.
"That's not a bad idea." "Stel, you ride
a bike yet?" "Nope." "Okay, let's get that did.
I'll take you to a parking lot, preside
Miyagi-like to your *Karate Kid*."
"I haven't seen the film." "That's fine, I'll be
your Chiun in *Remo Williams*." "Nope." "The Brain
that teaches Pinky?" "Just give up." "While we
are biking, we'll discuss." "Spare me the pain.
But cool, I'll go. Remind me why again?"
"Because you've gotta fall in love with bikes
so you can pitch to city councilmen
and generate ten, twenty thousand likes
so that they pay attention." "Got it." Now
they saw worth of Stel's sharpened sonnet plow.

313.
What's missing from the conversation was
fixation on the Boy's agenda for
the motivating zeal, the beehive's buzz.
They'd loosed their mental yoke from one deplored
and tethered it more locally. What once
were clear, binary judgments rendered at
the actions of a playground-burning dunce
took textures, grays when, rather, center sat
on their front stoop. The issues locally
were tougher virtue study cases to
agree on a solution. Vocally,
they whipsawed near as much, embraced a few
ideas that, with all compared, contrast
quite starkly with their spectrum of the past.

314.
The last event worth mentioning came when
a person in the crowd squealed, dropped his tea,
sent boba bouncing on the street. "Jen—Jen!"
he tugged at his companion's arm, and she
turned, saw, and chirped delightedly. They walked
away from splat, approaching Stella, and
asked if she wouldn't mind a selfie, cocked
the camera up, then snapped it. "We've been fans
since you dissected echo chambers of
the left, no high ground there." "No," Jen said, "since
adventure time with BLING. That part I love."
"We're on Vol Two. Does Ab become a prince?"
"You know," Stel said, "I think he does, but not
in quite the way you readers might have thought."

315.
"What do you mean?" "You're smart. You'll figure out.
And if you don't, then make it up." "Okay..."
they said, star-struck, confused but still devout,
"Your pivot toward the autobio plays
well with the masses," Cade said. "Pasts unlocked
attract strange trust. Embellishments were planned,"
said Stel. "For sharing so I bet you're stalked
by fans now? You've built quite the streetwise brand."
What Stella didn't say was 'No, no way.'
What Stella didn't say was 'No such thing.'
What Stella didn't say was 'Fluke today.'
What Stella didn't say was everything.
What Stella wrote and curated spoke more,
and let her – like those strangers – her adore.

316.
With no hint of defensiveness she said,
"Just here to keep it real, now that Tee's shied
away from us, found bank in Joe instead."
Some others thought that, rather, regicide
had long been plotted, as in Lion King's veldt.
They liked their new queen's style. Tee had coerced.
Stel left them space to air the things they felt,
which she'd pre-seeded with subversive verse.
From Jackie R. to Rosie Riveter,
with "R.A.P." and Cade's crusading choir,
she'd spun her stories so to pivot her
spectators' views that power's exclusive fief
was money. Overriding it? Belief.

Epilogue

Two sets of footsteps down the stairs next morn
betrayed the fact First Friday brought a fuck.
Still given to lightfootedness of dorm,
they'd been discreet about their bedroom luck.
Stel felt much more delight than real surprise,
from having witnessed careful flirt and dote.
Appropriate, like Disney would devise,
magnetic opposite attractions wrote.
To bedroom where Stel hibernated, hush
attempted whispers trickled up the stair.
She heard their evensong as Hardy's thrush,
its joy illimited to what was there.
She slipped on slippers, robe, then did descend
so to congratulate two happy friends.

She made three coffee cups in kitchen, brews
espresso strength from Aeropress, caffeine
enough to cut through multiple-hit snooze
and likely short-cut night of libertines.
Stel didn't know how long she'd need to chill
before the morning welcome for her friends,
so brought plush company with her, a twill
stuffed bat-eared fox, plus laptop. She could spend
half-day like this and barely feel she'd blinked,
as time is wont to dilate in the mind
when pasts imagined draw on, interlink
with presents of the zeitgeist of mankind.
Like flood, drunk stimulant washed clear her veins,
left fertile loam to feed inventive brain.

Before she made it into flow, they came,
two lovebirds hand-in-hand down staircase steps.
"Aww, thanks Stel," they said, not a hint of shame
in walk, and showing offbeat morning pep.
They sat. Cade asked, "How's newfound leadership,
dominion over where the Oppo goes?"
"Not bad," Stel said, "when pen's at speedy clip.
If late, then readers end up predisposed
to alternate perspectives." "Bother you?"
"Not really, things considered," Stel replied,
"I see my role as just to jog a few
new introspections loosing old bromides.
I hope they reexamine what they're taught
but can't expect to shepherd every thought."

"And who's this pal accompanying you?"
asked Mona, picking up the old stuffed thing.
"The friend my dreams spent long time clinging to,
reminder of adventure, my dog BLING,"
shared Stella. Cade looked proud, "Named after mine,"
he said, and pulled his chain out. "Stel's got some
that's similar," he added. "Silver shines
enough," said Stel, switched gears, "Your rule of thumb,
your north star, Lupe's 'Hip-Hop Saved My Life',
I get it now. *I write to make it right
don't like where I be,* talking 'bout the strife
around him, near fall back into the plight
of life on scraps. *I'd like to make it like
the sights on TV, nice and easy.* Mic

takes many forms." "I'm proud." "Poems satiate."
"Then never stop, write annals they'll exhume."
She smiled and nodded at such duty's weight,
felt equally on neck, where most presume
the medal that she wore plain jewelry.
From chain hung silver piece with Sichuan moon
and dragon wrapped she'd won from schoolery,
engraved with 'Stella', classic hero's boon.
One's given every year to the top-creamed
performer from the village, Stel's austere
and desk-bound, no-fun childhood was redeemed.
She'd always dreamed of being crowned emir.
No longer had she schooled like prison's cell.
She'd friend. And puppy. She'd rewritten Stel.

The Playlist

Listen here: www.bit.ly/rstella

Lupe Fiasco / *Dots & Lines*
PROFESSOR JAY / *Ndio Mzee*
Lei Qiang / *Crescent Moon Before Dawn*
Bob Marley & The Wailers / *Three Little Birds*
Janis Joplin, Big Brother & The Holding Company / *Women is Losers*
Coolio, L.V. / *Gangsta's Paradise*
Kanye West / *Jesus Walks*
The Notorious B.I.G., Mase, Diddy / *Mo Money Mo Problems*
Homeboy Sandman / *The Carpenter*
Jurassic 5 / *What's Golden*
Nas, Ms. Lauryn Hill / *If I Ruled the World (Imagine That)*
A Tribe Called Quest / *Can I Kick It?*
Madvillain / *All Caps*

Brother Ali / *Self Taught*
Gucci Mane / *Worst Enemy*
Grateful Dead / *Friend of the Devil*
Sly & The Family Stone / *Thank You (Falettinme Be Mice Elf Agin)*
Jefferson Airplane / *Embryonic Journey*
Janis Joplin, Big Brother & The Holding Company / *Piece of My Heart*
Kanye West, JAY Z, Pusha T, CyHi The Prynce, Swizz Beatz, RZA / *So Appalled*
Talib Kweli, Marsha Ambrosius / *It Only Gets Better*
Lupe Fiasco, Nikki Jean / *Hip-Hop Saved My Life*
Lupe Fiasco / *Around My Way (Freedom Ain't Free)*
The Coup / *Wear Clean Draws*
JAY Z, Santigold / *Brooklyn Go Hard*
The Notorious B.I.G. / *Hypnotize*
Nas / *I Want to Talk to You*
The Coup / *5 Million Ways to Kill A CEO*
Bob Marley & The Wailers / *Zion Train*
50 Cent, Eminem / *Patiently Waiting*
Rage Against the Machine / *Know Your Enemy*
Talib Kweli / *Get By*
Zion I, Locksmith / *Culture Freedom*
Sage Francis / *Civil Obedience*
Eminem / *The Way I Am*
Blue Scholars / *Joe Metro*
Common Market / *Every Last One*
Tonedeff / *Optimist*
The Prodigy / *Mindfields*
Elvis Presley / *(You're The) Devil in Disguise*
Thelonious Monk / *'Round Midnight*
Kendrick Lamar / *DNA.*
Justin Timberlake / *That Girl*
J. Cole / *Fire Squad*

Elvis Presley / *Jailhouse Rock*
Eminem, Nate Dogg / *'Till I Collapse*
Macklemore, Skylar Gray / *Glorious*
Talib Kweli, Styles P / *Poets & Gangstas*
J. Cole / *No Role Modelz*
John Legend, The Roots, Common, Melanie Fiona /
   Wake Up Everybody
Jean Grae, Natural Resources / *Negro Baseball League*
Wu-Tang Clan / *Bring Da Ruckus*
Buddy, A$AP Ferg / *Black*
Pharoahe Monch, Talib Kweli / *D.R.E.A.M.*
People Under The Stairs / *Acid Raindrops*
Lupe Fiasco / *Gotta Eat*
2Pac, Talent / *Changes*
Dr. Dre, Eminem / *Forgot About Dre*
Brad Kane / *One Jump Ahead*
Johannes Brahms / *Hungarian Dance No. 1 in G Minor*
Franz Liszt / *Die Forelle, S.564 (after Schubert, D.550)*
Busta Rhymes / *Break Ya Neck*
The White Stripes / *Seven Nation Army*
Mos Def / *Mathematics*
Kendrick Lamar, MC Eiht / *m.A.A.d. city*
Wu-Tang Clan / *C.R.E.A.M.*
Lupe Fiasco / *Kick, Push*
2Pac, Dramacydal / *Outlaw*
Killer Mike / *R.A.P. Music*
Kanye West, JAY Z, J. Ivy / *Never Let Me Down*
Logic / *Nikki*
Talib Kweli, 9th Wonder, Rapsody / *Every Ghetto*
Sublime / *Doin' Time*
Parliament / *P-Funk (Wants to Get Funked Up)*
CeeLo Green / *Bright Lights Bigger City*
The Prodigy / *Spitfire*
Con Brio / *Never Be the Same*

Queen / *Don't Stop Me Now*
Béla Fleck and the Flecktones / *New South Africa*
Neto Bernal / *¿Quién Se Cree Tu Recuerdo?*
Ozomatli / *Cut Chemist Suite*
Adventure Time, Pendleton Ward / *Adventure Time Main Title*
Lupe Fiasco, Nikki Jean / *Hip-Hop Saved My Life*

The Author

Dan prizes whimsy, abhors boredom, and has a middling relationship with focus. This combination led to Rewriting Stella. That, and a damn long drive to the Serengeti.

His sonnet obsession began as a gift-giving exercise. After a rather pleasant dinner one night he decided to write up the occasion in oddly formal poetry, offer shout-outs to each participant, and email it to them. None replied. Thrilled by market demand, he then made a habit of memorializing occasions in iambic pentameter. The power of the stories we tell ourselves and all that. Eventually Stella matured and those stories began to make sense.

At one point Dan could speak Spanish, Swahili, Chinese, Melanesian Pijin, and conversational English. At one point he could also do calculus. But what is life but a departure from points once thought important? If you ask Dan, he'll gladly tell you about that time helped prevent an outbreak of the bubonic plague in East Africa, how he used to be able to read a Chinese newspaper, and how he's mildly synesthetic. But only for a story in return.

The Illustrator

Paper, pencil and Zac have been inseparable since his youth. Zac grew up in the artists' community of Woodstock, NY where he began his endeavor of drawing from life. He attended LaGuardia High School of the Arts in NYC and pursued his focus on illustration at Parsons School of Design.

Says Zac: "On my commutes, I draw people who capture my eye. Polarities exist as an illustrator; the creative cartoonist, and the observational realist. I seek to find a balance between those polarities in my work and to be a creative realist or observational cartoonist. Every day is an opportunity to train my imagination to be a creative vacuum."

You can grab more eyefuls of Zac's work on his website (zactheartist.com) or Insta (@zacthemangaka).

red